- TEARS OF DARKNESS -
FALLEN ANGELS
3

SOPHIA LIDDELL

TEARS OF DARKNESS

Volume 3: Fallen Angels

TEARS OF DARKNESS
VOLUME 3: FALLEN ANGELS

SOPHIA LIDDELL

TEARS OF DARKNESS, Volume 3: Fallen Angels
SOPHIA LIDDELL

Artwork by
VERONICA LIDDELL

This book is a work of fiction.
Names, characters, places, and incidents are the product of the author's imagination or are used fictitiously. Any resemblance to actual events, locales, or persons, living or dead, is coincidental.

Check out my blog and get updates @
sophialiddellbooks.webs.com

Join me on Crunchyroll @
www.crunchyroll.com/user/SophiaLiddell

First Edition

Paperback Cover ISBN#
978-1-7323049-4-9

Last Time in TEARS OF DARKNESS:

Michael shook his head and said, "Wait up, wait up, wait a minute. These three girls are Wielders, right? I can see their eye colors but they look too old. Just how old are they?

Michelle curtsied again and said, "I'm eighteen. I'm of legal age."

Raphael said, "I'm sixteen."

Gabrielle continued to hide her face behind her father's arm. Justice nudged her with his elbow and said, "Come on, my darling angel, tell the nice man how old you are."

Gabrielle shyly looked towards Michael and muttered, "I ... I ... I'm seventeen." She then hid her face behind his shoulder and went silent again.

Michael covered his face with his hands and said, "How is this even possible?"

Sarah looked at them and said, "Did you not have your period yet?"

Michelle laughed and said, "Of course I did. I was twelve when I got mine."

Sarah looked to Michael and tugged on his shirt, saying, "What does this mean? Is there a way to stop us from dying a year after our period?"

Michael looked over at them again. He shook his head and said, "How? How? How did you manage to stop their bodies from self-destructing from their powers?"

Justice freed himself from his daughters' grasp and walked over in front of Michael. He offered up his hand as if to shake it and said, "If you want to know, come with me and I'll show you everything that is hidden from you."

Michael stared at Justice's open hand. He knew that if there was a way to stop their self-destruction he had to find out no matter the cost. He grasped onto Justice's hand and shook it firmly, saying, "Alright, Justice. I'll go along with you. Count me in for now."

TEARS
OF
DARKNESS
CHAPTER
06
DOWN THE RABBIT HOLE

- 1 -

Justice let go of Michael's hand and started to clap. He spoke loudly enough that it could almost be considered shouting, "Marvelous, Mr. Snyder! I just knew you'd be the one that would join with us!"

Michael held his palm up and said, "Hold on there, Mr. Justice. I'm still not ready to say that I'll join you. But, I will go with you so that you can show me what you are talking about. When I see it, then I'll decide if your cause is really just."

Justice's true face hid behind his sinister mask. He clasped his hands behind his back, leaned toward Michael's face, and said, "I have the utmost confidence that, when you see it with your own eyes, you will decide that I am right."

Michael stood there and tried to gaze into his blank eyes, the eyes that seemed completely white. He said, "Justice, do you really have a way to stop my girls from self-destructing?"

Sarah, Jennifer, and Valerie stood around Michael as they listened intently for Justice's reply. They kept looking back to the three angels that were with Justice. The three angels stared back at them with somewhat psychotic grins.

Justice stood up straight. He wrapped his arms around Gabrielle and Raphael. They accepted his embrace and rested their heads on his chest. He gently rubbed his hands along their arms as they laid against his body.

Michael began to grow impatient. He shook his head and said, "Please, I have to know. Is there a way to stop my girls from self-destructing?"

Justice let go of his daughters and they lifted their heads off of his chest. They took a few steps backwards, clasped their hands together in front of the skirt of their frilly dresses, and stood side by side. Michelle joined them and stood next to Gabrielle, who still looked nervously at Michael.

Justice held his hand towards his three daughters and said, "You seem to have the wrong impression, Mr. Snyder. The truth is that you don't have to give your girls anything to prevent them from self-destructing. You already have the key to prevent them from self-destructing. You just have to use it. Or, more literally, stop using it?"

Michael closed his eyes and shook his head as he said, "What? You're not making any sense. Can't you just tell me straight up?"

Justice moved his hand so that he was now holding out his hand toward Michael as if he were offering him something in the palm of his hand. He said, "Mr. Snyder does it make sense to you that the human body would destroy itself? Does it make sense that these girls would be destroyed within a year of their first period?"

Michael, becoming more annoyed, shook his head and said, "No! Of course it doesn't make any sense. This whole thing doesn't make any sense!"

Justice moved his hand so that he was pointing his finger toward the ceiling. He said, "You're right. It really doesn't make any sense! If it doesn't make sense, then that means there is something wrong." He put his hands on the cheeks of his sinister mask and started to laugh for a moment.

Justice then clasped his hands behind his back again and leaned towards Michael. He said, "Mr. Snyder, the reason the girls self-destruct is not because their bodies cannot handle their own power. No, no, no, no. The weekly injection is the true cause of their bodies' self-destruction. If you want them to live a long life, you need to stop injecting them with that horrid substance."

Michael started to chuckle sarcastically and said, "You're joking right?" He turned around to face Josh with a look of betrayal and disbelief on his face. He pointed back to Justice and said, "He's joking right?"

Josh somberly and slowly shook his head with as serious a face he could muster.

Michael faced Justice again and laughed, saying, "No way! I don't ... I can't believe that! Why would we do something to destroy the only hope we have against the Harvesters?"

Justice stood there silently. Though his mask was designed to portray a sinister look, it had no real emotion. It seemed to gaze into him blankly. Michael hated that mask. He could picture him sneering behind it. How cruel to lie to him about something so important. He shook his head and said, "No ... no ... no ... that just can't be true."

Michelle moved next to Justice and wrapped her arm around his arm and said, "It's true, Mr. Snyder. I haven't taken any injections since I was eleven. Please believe my papa. He's telling you the truth. The injections are what cause our powers to destroy our bodies.

Justice stood there frozen next to his daughter. His blank mask nodded at him silently. After a moment, he sighed, and said, "Let me tell you another story, Mr. Snyder, on how I came across this information. Maybe then you will have an easier time believing me."

Michael nodded and said, "Alright. I'll listen to your story." Fear started to grow inside him that the information just might be true.

Justice nodded again and said, "Mr. Snyder, there once was a young man named Adam. He was the most brilliant of students among his graduating class and received the highest of honors from his university. Upon his graduation he was contacted by a very private and well-funded research group. This research group promptly hired him and put him to work on a very special project. His research was noticed by a special group called the Path of the Future."

Valerie gasped and said, "Path of the Future? Isn't that the name of the secret government that Josh talked about?"

Josh replied to her, "Yes, you are right. Good memory, Valerie."

Justice continued, saying, "In order to walk on the Path of the Future, the man Adam had to participate in some very strange ordeals. He had to do things that he did not want to do. The Path of the Future would not trust Adam if he did not do them so Adam swallowed his pride and did them. Since he did them, they offered Adam the fruit of the tree of knowledge. Upon taking the fruit, Adam was able to transcend and become very powerful in the Path of the Future."

Jennifer interrupted Justice and said, "What did Adam have to do that he didn't want to do?"

Justice turned his sinister mask towards her and said, "Oh, things that I don't think your Lieutenant would want me to discuss with you."

Michael said, "I'm kind of interested about it too."

Justice turned back to Michael and brought his mask right up to Michael's ear and whispered, "Sexual things, Mr. Snyder. Adam had to perform various sexual acts to please his superiors. I don't think you want me to describe them to your little girls."

Michael nodded his head and said, "Yeah. They don't need to know about that kind of stuff yet."

Michael looked back to Jennifer and said, "Yeah, don't worry about it, Jennifer. It's not something for little girls to hear about."

Jennifer scrunched her face in annoyance and crossed her arms over her chest. But, she didn't argue with him and kept listening to what would be said next in the story.

Justice stood up straight and continued his story, "The Path of the Future was afraid that the tools with very special power might be able to over throw them one day so they decided that they had to create a serum that could stop these tools from becoming too powerful."

Michael held up his hand and said, "So you are claiming that this serum is the weekly injection that I give to my girls every week?"

Justice nodded his head and said, "Yes, that is correct. It was the man Adam who devised a way so that when these tools, or rather these little girls, reached a certain power level it would cause them to self-destruct in an explosion of light. It was too quick though so Adam changed it so that it would only activate when a tool had reached a certain level of hormones in their body. The serum was slowed by adding nano-machines to restrict it so that the toxin would not destroy the tool until about a year later when this hormonal level was reached."

Justice slapped his hands along the side of his mask and forcefully ran them along the side of his face. He started to pace back and forth as he ran his hands up and down the sides of his mask. He stopped pacing and shook his head vigorously. He continued his story, his voice became very emotional and he sounded very frustrated, "The man Adam saw all these tools being destroyed by his own work. He came to realize that, in his pursuit of knowledge and power, he had lost his humanity. He realized that these tools were actually little girls, little human beings. He had been a cause of suffering and pain for them. The man Adam could no longer look at himself in the mirror. Every time he glimpsed at himself he felt more and more disgusted at what he had become. In a moment of insanity, when he could no longer take it, the man Adam took a jar of acid and burned off his face. It was at that moment that the man Adam died and Justice was born in his place. Justice decided that he had to stop what the Path of the Future was doing."

Michael stood there in shock. He began to process the things that he heard in the story. He said, "Are you Adam? Is your name really Adam?"

Justice said, "My name is Justice. Adam is dead."

Michael looked into Justice's blank eyes. He said, "Why do you wear that mask?"

Justice said, "Do you want to see what is behind this mask?"

Michael nodded and said, "Yeah, I do."

Justice said, "You will see the face of a dead man."

Justice took off his tricorn hat with his left hand and then put his right hand on his mask. He slowly lifted the mask from off his face. Behind the mask there was nothing but a scarred and twisted image of a face. His face had been burned with acid. His eyes were plain white. Justice pulled his mask back down and replaced the hat on his head.

Michael stared at him in shock from seeing his melted face. Justice stepped closer to him and said, "Adam is dead. I am Justice."

The man that stood before him claimed to be the man who created the injections, which he also claimed was the true cause of their powers causing their bodies to self-destruct. Michael shook his head and said, "You created the weekly injection that I give to the girls every week?"

Justice shook his head and said, "Adam created the weekly injections. He did so with the intent of murdering those little girls so that they do not get too much power."

Michael's brain seemed to be going in a circle now. He said, "You created the weekly injection?"

Justice slowly nodded with a sigh and replied, "Yes ... I did it. I did it. I am the man Adam."

Michael shook his head and said, "The shots are what cause them to self-destruct?"

Justice nodded his head and said, "Yes, the shots are what cause them to self-destruct."

Michael began to pace back and forth. He rested both of his hands on top of his head.

Sarah, Jennifer, and Valerie backed away from him as he moved about violently. They were still confused. There was an intense look of worry on their faces as they tried to understand what was going on.

Sarah said, "Those shots you give us are what kills us?"

As Sarah spoke it, Michael stopped dead in his tracks. Mary's face began to flash in his mind. After her face, he saw Susan's face, followed by Cheryl, Alice, and Carol. All the girls that he was responsible for came back into his mind at once. He thought of every time that he gave them their weekly injection. He pictured each one of them dying from their bodies' structural collapse due to age.

He stared into space blankly. He lost the strength in his legs as he realized what he had done. He dropped to his knees.

Sarah, Jennifer, and Valerie watched him fall to his knees. They ran over to him and surrounded him in an embrace.

Michael felt the touch of their warm bodies against his own. The sensation pulled him out of his trance. Ashamed, he did not reach out to them as they held him. He looked up to the ceiling and said out loud to himself, "I ... I ... I killed them. I injected them every week. I killed them."

Sarah said, "No you didn't."

Michael said, "I did. I killed them."

Michael remembered the torment that Mary endured emotionally as she revealed to him when she got her first period. He had embraced her and held her till she stopped crying. He remembered how each one of those girls felt and confided in him as they struggled to live with the knowledge that they would die soon, never to experience the life they wanted to live. Mary couldn't have the life she wanted because the injections caused her body to be destroyed. Tears began to roll from his eyes.

Sarah replied, "You didn't know, Lieutenant. It's not your fault."

Michael sat down on his legs. He shook his head vigorously and said, "No ... I should have known. I shouldn't have just trusted people. I ... I ..."

Michael dropped his hands on the floor. He stared at his hands as they pressed against the wood of the floor. The same hands that gave those weekly injections to all his girls. Anger began to well up inside of himself. He lifted his right hand and balled it into a fist.

Michael suddenly shouted at the top of his lungs, "Damn it!" He smashed his fist into the floor. He repeatedly shouted, "Damn it!" over and over again as he smashed his fist repeatedly against the wood. His fist smashed through the old wood creating a hole in the floor of the church.

Valerie jumped at him and threw her arms around his neck and leaned against his body to stop him from smashing his hand against the wood. She was sobbing into his shoulder and shouted, "Please stop! You're hurting yourself!"

Both Sarah and Jennifer clung to his clothing. He looked up at them as streaks of tears still fell from his own eyes. They stood there crying as they held onto the fabric of his shirt.

Michael composed himself and said, "I'm sorry if I scared you girls."

Valerie still clung around his neck. Her face was still buried in his shoulder. She spoke into his shoulder saying, "Are you okay, Lieutenant?"

Michael began to feel the pain in his right hand. He looked at his hand. Large splinters of wood were jammed into his flesh. His knuckles were torn and bleeding. He said, "I cut my hand."

Valerie let go of his neck. He held up his injured hand. Valerie held his hand in her left hand and began to examine his injuries. She began to pull all the splinters out that were stuck into his flesh. When she was done, she took his hand in both of her hands. They began to glow with yellow light. The pain in his hand went away and the open wounds closed up. She let his hand go.

Lieutenant Michael stared at his hand. He opened and closed it a few times to make sure that it felt like normal.

Sarah dropped to her knees and began to embrace him again. Jennifer followed her example by also dropping to her knees and embracing him on his other side. He felt their small bodies tremble against his arms as they leaned against him.

Lieutenant Michael spoke calmly to them, saying, "I'm sorry to scare you girls. I'm also sorry that I gave you all those damn injections. If only I had known ... I ..."

Justice suddenly spoke and said, "I take it you believe me now, Mr. Snyder?"

Michael glared at Justice and said, "Yeah, I believe you."

Justice stared back at him with his sinister mask. He said, "I understand if you want to hate Adam, Mr. Snyder. Believe me, Adam hates himself too. He has to live with the knowledge of what he has done till he dies, maybe after that as well. But, please, don't blame yourself too much, Mr. Snyder. Only a handful of people know the truth. You are now one of them. You have managed to overcome the conditioning that the Path of the Future has forced upon you."

Michael shook his head and said, "It would be easier to hate you ... but, no. Hating you will accomplish nothing. My energy would be better used trying to stop this ... this Path of the Future you mentioned. They're the ones who are pushing it ... not you."

Justice raised his hands to the sky and said, "See, Mr. Snyder. I knew that you would be fully committed to our cause."

Michael nodded his head and said, "Yeah, after knowing all that ... I have to put a stop to it. That's the only thing I can do to forgive myself for injecting all my girls with ... with ... that serum. I only wanted to protect them. Instead, I ended up hurting them."

Justice held his hand out to Michael to help him up. The girls let go of him and Michael took his hand. He allowed Justice to pull him to his feet.

Justice said, "Now, don't be mistaken, Mr. Snyder. I've only told you a little bit. There is so much more truth to know about the world and what is going on."

Michael looked worried and said, "There's more?"

Justice nodded with his sinister mask and said, "Yes ... there is much more."

Michael looked towards Sarah, Jennifer, and Valerie. He said, "Is there a way to stop the serum from killing my girls now? Can they be saved?"

Justice nodded and said, "Yes. If you stop giving them the serum it will not build up in their system. Now, I have also created another injection that will quickly gather the remnants of the toxic serum so that it will flush out of their bodies when they go to the bathroom."

Justice pulled a small box out of the pocket of his navy blue frock coat and held it towards Michael. He said, "I have already prepared three injections for you if you want to remove the toxic serum from their bodies quickly."

Michael took the box and opened it to see three old style syringes filled with a silver colored liquid. He said, "You first create an injection to kill my girls and you expect me to trust you and inject my girls with this new injection?"

Justice stood there with his hands behind his back. He leaned towards Michael and said, "You do not have to trust me, Mr. Snyder. Eventually, most of the serum will leave their bodies on its own. But, there will always be a trace of it left. I created this serum to remove all of it quickly out of their bodies in only a few days. It is up to you to use it or not use it. I can't prove to you that it has no harmful intent except to say that it is a sign of repentance for creating the serum of death in the first place. If I meant you harm, could I have not said anything at all while you continue to inject them with death?"

Michael continued to stare at the injections in his hand. Michelle walked over to him and wrapped her arm around his arm. She brought her lips to his ear and said, "Please, trust my papa. He's trying to stop the harm he's caused. I have taken this injection myself and it won't cause them any harm. It will only help them to become stronger."

Michael pondered her words. He turned to his girls and said, "Do you want to give this unknown thing a try?"

Sarah held out her arm and said, "What do we got to lose? We've come this far. Might as well see what happens to the end."

Michael pulled a syringe out of the box and removed the cap from the needle point. He had never used an old-style syringe before so he felt nervous about it. He took Sarah's arm and wrapped a rubber tie that was in the box around her arm. He found a large vain and stuck her with the needle. Sarah closed her eyes and winced from the pain as Michael pushed the serum into her vain. He then removed the needle and handed her a tissue to help stop the bleeding from the prick. Sarah held the tissue to her arm and put pressure on it.

Jennifer held up her own arm and said, "I'll go next."

Michael put the rubber tie around her arm and injected her like he had done with Sarah. Jennifer closed her eyes and winced from the pain. It was a lot more painful than the modern injector that they were used to.

As Jennifer held a tissue against her arm, she said, "I hope this helps me to get even more powerful so I can stop the Harvesters once and for all."

Michelle said, "Yes, little sister. You can't even imagine the power that you are capable of having once you become clean."

Valerie closed her eyes first and then held out her own arm. She trembled nervously and said, "I really hate needles so hurry up and get it over with before I lose my nerve to do it."

Michael tied the rubber tie around her arm and injected her with the needle. Her face scrunched up more tightly than the others and a tear rolled down her cheek. He withdrew the needle and put a tissue over the prick mark. Valerie held it against her arm and looked miserable while doing it.

Sarah said, "I feel tingles spreading through my body ... I can feel warmth spreading all over too."

Jennifer nodded and said, "Yeah, I'm feeling that now too."

Michelle smiled mischievously and clapped her hands saying, "That means it's working."

Justice nodded with his blank emotionless mask and said, "Yes, it will spread throughout your body binding itself to the toxic serum that has bound itself to the cells in your body. The tingling and warm feeling is the toxic serum letting go of your cells. Next time you go pee, you will pee a silver color. Don't worry about it, that is the sign that the toxic serum and nano-machines are leaving your body. When your pee returns to normal color, that is the sign that you are now clean of the toxic serum. You will be able to live a long and happy life without worrying about your power killing you."

Valerie smiled and said, "I can feel the tingling now too."

Sarah looked to Michael and then looked down to the ground. She started to cry. Michael walked over to her and wrapped his arms around her. She buried her face into his chest. Michael said, "What's wrong, Sarah?"

Sarah composed herself and said, "I wish that we could have known about this before Mary and Susan had to die from their power. It's not fair."

Michael stroked the back of her head and held her tighter, saying, "Yeah. It's not fair. But, I think they'd be happy that you get to have the life they wanted. It's not fair that I was the one who injected them with the serum that killed them. They trusted me and I hurt them."

Sarah shook her head against his chest and said, "But you didn't know, Lieutenant."

Michael said, "Yeah, I didn't know. But it was still me. I'm going to have to carry that knowledge with me till I die, just like you have to carry the burden of living when your friends had to die."

Sarah nodded and said, "I don't blame you at all."

Michael somberly said, "Thanks." He let her go and put his hand on her shoulder and wiped the streak of tears that had rolled down her cheeks. She looked up at him and forced a smile.

Michelle came around to Michael's side. She suddenly wrapped her arms around Michael's right arm and said, "Papa, the more I see Mr. Snyder, the more I'm falling in love. I think this is the man that I want to marry, Papa."

Valerie walked up to her and started shaking her finger at her, to scold her, saying, "You can't marry Lieutenant Michael! He's supposed to marry Lieutenant Rachel!"

Michelle's face sneered in annoyance at Valerie. She pressed her body even more against Michael. She glared at Valerie and said, "I don't know who this Ray-chel is but she sounds rather old."

Michelle tightened her grip around Michael's arm and repositioned his arm so that it rested between her breasts. She looked up to Michael's face. He turned his head downward to look down at her. She said, "Rachel sounds old and saggy. I'm still young and firm. Can you feel my firmness, Mr. Snyder?"

Michael's eyes drifted from her face and down to her exposed cleavage that seemed to spill out of her frilly dress. It rested around his arm. He blushed and looked upward toward the ceiling and said, "I can't really say anything about that, I guess."

Suddenly Justice stepped towards Michael. His sinister mask seemed to glare at him. He said, "Mr. Snyder, what are your intentions with my daughter?"

Michael began to worry. He looked toward Justice and held his free arm out and waved his hand in dismissal, saying, "I ... uh ... I ... I don't have any intentions toward your daughter. I ... uh ..."

Suddenly Justice stood up straight and threw his hands up into the air and started to laugh maniacally. He said, "Don't worry, Mr. Snyder. I'm only kidding." He started to laugh again and said, "I'm an anarchist so I don't care what you do, but just remember ..." his tone suddenly changed to a very serious tone. He put his hands behind his back and leaned towards Michael. He continued saying, "... remember that whatever you can do to me, I can also do to you."

Michelle, still pressing her body against Michael's body, said, "Papa, I can feel all this raw strength emanating from Mr. Snyder. I bet he can push me down on the ground and I'd just let him do whatever he wanted to do to me."

Michelle lifted her body up and brought her lips to Michael's ear. She whispered, "I mean whatever you want to do to me." She put her lips near his ear and then blew on it. She giggled.

Michelle dropped down and rested her head on his shoulder, saying, "Papa, is it alright if I marry him now?"

Justice waved his hand and said, "It's fine with me, my darling angel, but I can't force him to do it. You're going to have to convince him yourself."

Michael shook his head and said, "Sorry, I don't think I'm ready to get married yet."

Michelle let his arm go and sneered. She sounded annoyed as she spoke, saying, "Very well then, Mr. Snyder. I'll show you in time that I'm all you'll ever want."

Valerie continued to glare at Michelle and said, "Stop hitting on Lieutenant Michael! He's going to marry Lieutenant Rachel!"

Michelle turned her full attention to Valerie and glared back at her. She said, "And how are you going to stop me, shrimpy?" She began to smile psychotically and she moved her hands beside her body and positioned them as if they were claws. Her knees bended slightly as if this was her battle stance. Her hands began to light up with a red fire the likes of which Squad three had never seen before.

Valerie backed up afraid at the sight of her hands catching on fire.

Sarah and Jennifer jumped in front of Valerie. The familiar blue and red lights of their hands had activated.

Sarah said, "I won't let you hurt her."

Jennifer held up her own red glowing hands in a martial style and said, "Yeah, you'll have to deal with me first before you can touch her."

Justice suddenly shouted and said, "That's enough Michelle."

Michelle's red fire withdrew into her hands and she stood up like normal and said, "I was only playing with them, Papa." She lifted up her hands and shrugged her shoulders, saying, "I wouldn't hurt them, I'm not like the bed men who like to hurt little girls." She walked back to stand next to Gabrielle and Raphael.

Justice held his right hand up and said, "Sorry about that. Sometimes my darling angels can forget their manners."

Michelle spoke up and said, "I'm sorry, Papa. Mr. Snyder's manliness just got me all excited so that I just couldn't contain myself. It would help if he expended some of my energy for me." She brought her pointer finger to her lips and nibbled on it while gazing at Michael.

Justice turned to Michelle and extended his hand towards her, saying, "I forgive you, angel. But, I want you to apologize to your new friends."

Michelle lowered her head and looked ashamedly toward the ground. She nodded and said, "Yes, Papa."

Michelle walked toward Valerie. Jennifer and Sarah still stood in front of her. Michelle laned over towards them and said, "I'm sorry that I scared you. I want to be your friend too." She held out her hand towards Valerie.

Valerie stared at her hand cautiously but reached out and shook it, saying, "I forgive you. I want to be your friend too."

Michelle's mood perked up and she clapped her hands together, saying, "Yay! I love having more friends. I want all three of you to be my friends. It will be twice as fun during tea now!"

Sarah said, "Yeah, we want to be your friends too. What is up with the fire that came out of your hands?"

Jennifer nodded and said, "Yeah, it was red like our power but I've never seen it like that before."

Michelle lifted her hands up and they began to burn with red fire again. She said, "This fire is the true extent of our power. When you reach your maximum power level, your hands will glow with fire too instead of just light. The serum suppresses your ability to make the fire. If you try to force it out, your body will explode in a brilliant flash of light."

Raphael and Gabrielle walked over to them. Gabrielle still cautiously glared at Michael as she followed behind Raphael. They both lifted up their hands and their hands began to glow with the blue and yellow fire of their color.

Raphael said, "See, we all can do it too."

Gabrielle said, "Yes. This fire means we have all our power. More power than you can imagine."

Michelle, Gabrielle, and Raphael turned off their glowing fires and lowered their hands.

Michael stood there amazed as he analyzed the difference between his girls and the three angels' powers.

Gabrielle noticed Michael watching them all and she ran back behind Justice's back and started pointing at Michael. She started shouting and saying, "Mr. Snyder is giving me perverted looks. He's planning on raping me!"

Justice shook his head and said, "Now, now, my dear. You're imagining it. He's only interested in your power as a Wielder. He's never seen your beautiful blue fire before."

Gabrielle, still pointing at Michael said, "Don't you dare try to touch me!"

Michelle walked over to her and said, "Calm down, sister. I won't let anybody hurt you. Papa's right, sister, Mr. Snyder doesn't want to do that to you. If he's going to look at anybody perversely, it's going to be at me. I hope." She glanced at Michael and smiled at him playfully.

Gabrielle threw her arms around Michelle and said, "Don't let anybody touch me ever again!"

Michelle nodded and replied while embracing her, "Don't worry, sister. I won't let the bad men ever touch you again. Now, why don't you calm down and say hello to Mr. Snyder. Then you'll see that he's a good man like Mr. O'Brian.

Josh, who had been relatively quiet through all this, spoke out, saying, "Yes, Gabrielle. I can tell you that Mr. Snyder is not a bad man, he is a good man like your papa."

Gabrielle nodded her head and said, "Okay. I'll give him a chance."

Michelle wrapped an arm around Gabrielle's waist. Gabrielle wrapped her arms around Michelle's torso and allowed Michelle to slowly lead her near Michael.

Michael stood there confused. He had never seen anybody react like this to him before. He began to think that she must have suffered some kind of trauma from people that they kept calling the 'bad men'.

Michelle and Gabrielle stood in front of Michael. Slowly, Gabrielle released one of her arms from around Michelle and extended her hand towards Michael. Her hand trembled as she extended it.

Michael took her hand and shook it. She then quickly retracted her hand and said, "He ... he ... hello, Mr. Snyder. It is ni ... ni ... nice to meet you."

Michael, still a little confused, said, "It's nice to meet you too. I hope that we can be friends."

Gabrielle seemed to calm down and let go of Michelle completely. She brought her hands together in front of the skirt of her frilly dress and said, "I'm sorry, Mr. Snyder, I didn't mean to accuse you of being like the bad men. I just get so scared of them that it makes me lose my mind sometimes. I've decided to trust you since Papa and Mr. O'Brian say that you are not like the bad men. That's two witnesses so it must be true."

Michael nodded and said, "Don't worry about it. I can tell that you've have some really bad things happen to you so I won't hold your caution against you."

Gabrielle curtsied and said, "Thank you, Mr. Snyder, for your understanding."

Raphael stepped forward and brought her hands together in front of her chest as if in prayer. She looked hopefully at Justice and said, "Papa, can we show the little sisters the extent of our powers?"

Justice turned towards her and clapped his hands together once. He then held his right pointer finger up in the air and said, "Yes! Yes! That is a marvelous idea, my darling angel."

Justice turned toward the girls of Squad three and Michael, saying, "How would you like to see what your powers will look like when they reach their full potential?"

Valerie nodded excitedly and said, "Yeah! I want to see that."

Jennifer crossed her arms over her chest and said, "I suppose I'm interested in that."

Sarah looked towards Michael and said, "Sure, I'm interested in knowing what we could have been capable of if it wasn't for the Path of the Future."

Michael nodded and spoke to Justice, saying, "Yeah. I'm interested in that too Sarah."

Justice clapped his hands together once and exclaimed, "Excellent! Let's go outside then and my darling angels will show you their full power."

Justice put his hands behind his back and started to walk towards the front door of the old abandoned church. Gabrielle and Raphael quickly followed behind him.

Michelle went up to Michael and wrapped her right arm around his left arm and said, "Come now, Mr. Snyder. I'll show you what my body is capable of." She began to drag him along as she went. Sarah, Jennifer, and Valerie followed behind them. Josh stood up from sitting on the back of a pew and followed them out the door.

They stepped out into the cool evening air. The disk of the sun was still on the edge of the horizon. The sky was filled with the orange light of the setting sun.

As they stepped outside of the old church, they noticed that there was a pack of fully-grown Harvesters standing on the outskirts of the old church's parking lot. The Harvesters stood there and screamed at them, but they would not come any closer towards them.

Michael looked on at the Harvesters and marveled that they were just standing there and glaring at them. He said, "How come they're not attacking us? I've never seen that before."

Josh put his hand on Michael's shoulder and said, "Remember that I told you that Justice has a device that can repel Harvesters?"

Michael's eyes went wide and he slowly nodded his head, saying, "Yeah. Yeah. I remember now."

Michael turned to look at Justice and said, "Justice, how did you get that Anti-Harvester device?"

Justice started to laugh and said, "I stole it from the World Government."

Michael shook his head and said, "They really do have that technology, don't they? Why wouldn't they use it to protect our sectors?"

Justice laughed again and said, "The World Government stays in power thanks to the people's fear of the Harvesters. If the people knew that the Harvesters could be repelled using technology, they would lose that fear. Fear gives them power and control."

Michael nodded and said, "Yeah. That makes sense."

Jennifer started to tremble.

Sarah said, "Jennifer, what's wrong?"

Tears started to stream down Jennifer's face. All eyes turned to her. She started to sob and said, "You mean that they could have stopped all the people dying from the Los Angeles wall breach but they did nothing?! They died for a stupid reason like that?!"

Sarah wrapped Jennifer in her arms. Jennifer rested her head on Sarah's chest as she stroked her head. Valerie put her right hand on Jennifer's back and rubbed it to help her to feel comforted.

Gabrielle crossed her arms over her chest, making a disgusted face, saying, "That's why we call them the bad men. They do very bad things."

Jennifer composed herself and said, "I'm okay now." Sarah let her go and she stood up straight. She crossed her arms over her chest again.

Michael reached out and rubbed her on top of the head with a look of compassion. Jennifer looked up at him embarrassed and then lowered her head a little as she tried to hide a small, embarrassed grin.

Gabrielle, still acting disgusted, said, "I want to crush the bad men. Papa, let me use my power first. I want to crush something and pretend it's the bad men."

Justice nodded his sinister mask and said, "Go right ahead, my darling."

A malicious grin fell on Gabrielle's face. She flung her hands to her side and they began to burn with a blue fire. A small blue ball appeared out of her chest, without moving her hands, it expanded to form a shield around herself.

Much to Michael and the girls' surprise, she then lifted up into the air and quickly floated over to the edge of the parking lot. She set herself down and the blue shield withdrew back into her body."

Sarah's mouth dropped and her eyes went wide as she exclaimed at the sight, "You mean I'll be able to fly?"

Raphael put her hand on Sarah's arm and said, "Yes, but there's more. Watch what else my big sister can do."

Gabrielle extended her arm towards the Harvesters and raised her palm against them. A beam of blue light poured out of her palm and hit the first Harvester that she was pointing at. Much to their surprise, the beam quickly melted a hole through the Harvester and hit the Harvester behind it. The beam then melted a hole through the second Harvester and hit a third Harvester that was about twenty feet behind it. The beam melted a hole through the third Harvester and hit the ruins of an old building that was about thirty feet behind the third Harvester. The remnant of the structure exploded in fire.

Gabrielle brought her hand down and started to giggle, saying, "Oops, I used too much power again. Good thing nobody was there."

Michael stood there speechless at the devastation caused by one beam of blue energy. Sarah could stand there for five minutes until her own beam caused any damage to a fully-grown Harvester. Gabrielle's beam not only burned through a fully-grown Harvester in a matter of seconds, it burned through three Harvesters and exploded an old building.

Michael fell backwards and sat on the steps of the church behind him. Sarah, Jennifer, and Valerie were just as shocked and speechless as he was. They sat down beside him. Sarah stared at her own hands. She said, "If only I had that power during Los Angeles. Mary would still be alive."

Gabrielle turned towards them and waved her hand high in the air, shouting, "Hey! I still got one more thing to show you!"

Michael and the girls returned to watching her even though they remained sitting on the steps of the church.

Gabrielle returned her attention to the Harvesters and held up her hands as if she was surrendering. The blue fire grew brighter and a blue shield of energy formed around the closest Harvester. The Harvester then lifted up into the air. Gabrielle's hands began to shake as she appeared to be struggling to bring her hands together. As her hands slowly came together, the Harvester in the blue shield began to be crushed. It screamed in pain as its shell began to crack and then seemed too exploded inside the shield in a yellow gooey mess. The shield disappeared and the crushed corpse of the Harvester fell to the ground.

Gabrielle turned back around and tilted her head with a victorious smile. She giggled and said, "I like to crush bad things." She formed another shield around herself and quickly floated back to where the others were. She lowered herself to the ground and said, "Papa, how did I do?"

Justice laughed hysterically and shouted, "Marvelous, my darling angel in blue. Absolutely marvelous!"

Michelle raised her right hand and said, "Papa, I want to go next!"

Justice nodded his sinister mask and said, "Go right ahead then, my darling angel in red."

Michelle turned to Michael and grabbed her hands together in front of the skirt of her dress. She tilted her head to the side and began to twist her body side to side slightly. She said, "Make sure you watch me closely, Mr. Snyder."

Michelle then turned to face the Harvesters. Her hands and feet began to burn with red fire. The fire on her hands condensed and formed into what looked like red fiery blades. Her feet lifted off the ground six inches and she started to skate towards the Harvesters still waiting just beyond the parking lot edge.

As her feet skated over the ground, dust stirred beneath her feet. She propelled herself forward at amazing speed towards the first Harvester and leapt towards it. As she passed by the first Harvester, she swung her fire blade across its neck. The head of the Harvester fell off and it rolled over on its side, twitching, as yellow Harvester goo flowed out of it.

Michelle skated along the side of another Harvester and ran her fire blade along its side. As she passed by, the Harvester rolled over onto its side and yellow goo ran over the ground beneath it. It was nearly cut in half.

Michelle then leapt at another Harvester as if she were diving into water. Her hands bored into the side of the Harvester and she came out through the other side. She then skated back towards the group and turned off the power in her hands and feet.

She ran up to Michael and clasped her hands together in front of her chest. Harvester goo was splattered all over her dress and face. She leaned towards Michael with hope in her eyes and said, "Did you like that, Mr. Snyder!"

Michael nodded and said, "Yeah. That was pretty amazing!"

Michelle's eyes sparkled and said, "If I did good, don't you think I deserve a pat on the head?"

Michael shrugged his shoulders and said, "Uh ... I guess so." He extended his hand and patted her on the head saying, "Good job." He then grimaced as he felt the Harvester goo on his hand and he wiped it onto his pants.

Michelle stood up straight, still clasping her hands together. She spun in a circle and said, "Mr. Snyder praised me!"

Michael shrugged his shoulders again and rolled his eyes, saying, "Yeah. Whatever."

Raphael said, "You have saved the best for last. It is time to watch my master performance!"

Raphael bent over to Valerie and said, "Little sister, you and I both know about healing, but do you know that your power is much more than just healing?"

Valerie shook her head and said, "I don't really understand my power."

Raphael stood up straight and said, "Watch me, little sister. You will see that your power is life and death itself."

Raphael walked towards the edge of the parking lot. As she approached the edge, her hands began to glow with yellow fire. She crossed the border and a group of ten Harvesters began to rush at her.

Raphael then slightly squatted herself as if it was some form of a fighting stance and threw her hands down to her sides. She formed her hands into a shape as if she was getting ready to claw something.

When the Harvesters were within twenty feet of her, they suddenly fell over dead. The yellow fire of her hands glowed twice as bright as before. With her hands still stuck in the same position, she began to walk towards the group. When she was about twenty feet away from them, she stopped walking and turned her hands as if she was dropping something onto the ground.

Suddenly, the ground beneath her began to glow with a yellow light. As if by magic, plants started to grow out of the cracks in the ground where the yellow light radiated. The light then stopped and the plants stopped growing.

Raphael walked up to Valerie and said, "When you reach your full power, you will be able to instantly steal the life out of anything within ten feet of you and give it to anything, as long as there is a spark of life left, within ten feet of you."

Again, they were speechless. Valerie stared at her hands. The same hands that lacked the power to protect Mary. Those same hands could have taken power, fixed Sarah, and helped to save Mary. All of this happened because they were lied to. The World Government feared their power and would do anything, even to the point of killing them, to hold on to it.

Valerie looked up at Michael. Tears started to flow out of her eyes. She held her hands up as if to show them to him. She said, "If I had that power, I could have saved Mary."

Jennifer started to tear up again. She held her own hands up and said, "If I had that power, I could have protected Lieutenant Sharon, Annie, and Julie."

Lieutenant Michael didn't know what to say. He held back his own tears that wanted to come in response to theirs. He wrapped an arm around both their shoulders and pulled them close to his chest. Sarah began to cry too. She leaned over against Valerie. He held them in silence as they tried to process this new information.

- 2 -

Valerie lifted her head off of Michael's chest and said, "I'm hungry, Lieutenant."

Michael nodded and said, "Yeah, me too. We've had nothing but rations for the past three days."

Michael paused for a minute and said, "You know, I'm not really a Lieutenant anymore. Joining Justice's group means I'm no longer part of the World Defense Forces. You don't need to call me Lieutenant, anymore."

Valerie started acting shyly and said, "But ... but I'm already used to it. Is it alright if I keep calling you Lieutenant?"

Michael shrugged his shoulders and said, "Yeah, that's fine. You can call me whatever you want."

Sarah began to rub her stomach and said, "What are we going to eat for dinner, Lieutenant?"

Michelle jumped up and down, saying, "My sisters and I will make dinner for you. But, first I need to change my outfit."

Gabrielle pointed her finger at Michelle's frilly dress and said, "You are absolutely covered in blood again, dear sister. You spoil your dresses faster than you can make them."

Michelle patted the skirt of her frilly dress and said, "You are quite right, sister, but I can't help it."

Sarah spoke up and said, "You made that dress yourself?"

Michelle looked at Sarah as if she were crazy. She shook her head and replied, "Of course I made my own dress! How else would I get to cover my naked body?" As she said the word 'naked body' she glanced at Michael with a smile and batted her eyes.

Sarah, just as confused, said, "Can't you just go to a store and buy your own clothing?"

Michelle squared her arms on her hips and acted disgusted, saying, "Buy your own clothing?! Why on earth would I give some merchant power to determine what style I wear? When you buy clothing you're giving that merchant power over you. I'm a free woman so I make my own clothing."

Sarah shrugged her shoulders and held out her hand, saying, "But isn't it really hard to make your own clothing? I don't think I could ever do that."

Michelle replied, "Of course it starts out difficult, but when you get used to it, it becomes very easy and second nature to you. Being free is never easy but those who wish to enslave you do so by promising that they can make your life easier. If you want, I'd be happy to show you how to make your own dress. Then you'd see that you really do have the power to do it within you."

Sarah brought her right pointer finger to her lips and thought about it for a moment. She said, "Yeah, that might be fun. I'm still not sure I will be able to do it though."

Valerie jumped up from sitting on the steps of the old church. She flung her fists up in excitement and said, "I want to make my own dress too!"

Raphael nodded and said, "Yeah, we'll show you little sisters how to make your own dresses, just like we do. Then, you'll be free too."

Michelle patted the skirt of her frilly dress and said, "Guess, I'll go change now. Mr. Snyder, would you like to help me into my new dress?"

Michael looked at her. He worried about her over reactions. He said, "Uh ... no thanks. I better stay here with the others."

Michelle sighed and turned away in a huff, saying, "Very well then, Mr. Snyder. Sisters, come help me change and then we'll make dinner together. Look forward to it, Mr. Snyder. I will make you my specialty."

Michelle walked into the church. Gabrielle and Raphael followed behind her. Justice clapped his hands once and then rubbed them vigorously together, saying, "Oh! You are all in for a special treat tonight!"

Josh stepped up beside Michael and sat down, saying, "How are you taking all this in?"

Michael rubbed the top of his head and said, "Well, I guess I'm still in shock."

Josh replied, "Yeah, I understand, brother. I think you are taking it better than I did."

Michael said, "Well, it's easier, I guess, since you're the one telling me to believe it."

Josh chuckled and said, "Yeah, you are lucky that you have me. I had to stumble into all this by myself. That is how I ran into Justice. He helped me to find the information that I was looking for. When I found it, I decided that I had to join him to help stop it."

Michael looked out over the barren wasteland in front of him. The sun had nearly finished setting. He said, "We've got to get Rachel in on this too somehow."

Josh nodded his head and said, "Yeah, I agree. I wish I could have taken her with us but that would have been too suspicious. But, do not worry. We will think of something even if we have to fight our way over there to get her."

Sarah said, "Yeah, don't forget about Giana, Tina, and Elsa. We got to save them from the injections too. Especially Giana since she's already got her period and is in danger of structural collapse."

Michael put his hand on top of her head and said, "Don't worry, Sarah. When we get Rachel, of course we'll get Giana, Tina, and Elsa too."

The sun had finally set and they were sitting in a circle around a portable light that Justice had pulled out of the back. Beside it was a portable heating device that seemed to be self-powering. Nobody cared enough to ask about it.

Michelle, Gabrielle, and Raphael were in the back room still. The sound of clanking metal could be heard from that area. Suddenly, the door opened and Gabrielle's head poked out of it. She smiled. When she wasn't acting nervous, her smile could be called creepy. She called out, saying, "Little sisters, come help us serve our dinner!"

Sarah and Jennifer turned to each other and gave each other a nervous glance.

Michael saw it and said, "It's okay, girls. Go and help. We have to do our part, after all."

Sarah nodded and said, "Okay, Lieutenant."

Sarah stood up and offered her hands to Valerie and Jennifer, saying, "Come on, let's go."

Jennifer and Valerie took her hands and she helped them to stand on their feet. Gabrielle opened the door all the way and the smell of spices began to circulate through the drafty and dusty church.

Sarah entered first, followed by Jennifer and then Valerie. They saw Michelle standing next to a portable gas burner. On top of the burner there was a large pot. Michelle stood over the pot stirring it with a large, old-looking, metal spoon. Beside Michelle, Raphael stood there patiently holding an old, beaten, metal bowl.

Sarah happily sniffed the air and said, "That smalls so good! What did you make for dinner?"

Gabrielle proudly brought her right hand to her heart and said, "We made our famous chili."

Michelle nodded as she continued to stir, saying, "Yes, my sisters, I think we've really out done ourselves this time. I think this is truly perfection."

Raphael used the old bowl she held as a fan to wave the scent of the chili to her own nose and said, "Yes, I think Papa will be very proud of this batch."

Jennifer said, "Yeah, it smells really good. Do I smell meat?"

Gabrielle said, "Of course! It wouldn't be chili without meat."

Valerie tilted her head, confused, and said, "How did you get meat out here?"

The three angels giggled and Michelle said, "I found it out side."

Jennifer shrugged her shoulders and whispered into Sarah's ear, "I'm afraid to ask what kind of animal it is."

Raphael held the old bowl up and Michelle dropped a huge spoonful of chili into it. Raphael handed the bowl and a spoon to Sarah and said, "Give this to my Papa then come back for more."

Sarah nodded and left with the bowl.

Raphael grabbed another old looking bowl and Michelle dropped another heap of chili into the bowl. She then handed the bowl to Gabrielle, who took it and left without a word. As she left, Sarah came back and stood next to Jennifer again.

Raphael took another bowl and allowed Michelle to put another heap of chili into it. She then handed the bowl with a spoon to Jennifer and said, "This is for Mr. Snyder."

Jennifer accepted it with a nod and left to bring Michael the chili. As she left Gabrielle came back. Raphael kept holding up bowls and allowing Michelle to fill them with chili. She handed the next bowl and spoon to Valerie, saying, "This is for you, little sister."

Valerie accepted it with a smile, saying, "Thanks! I can't wait to try it." She left the room and went to sit back down next to Michael.

Jennifer was next and then Sarah. They left to sit down next to Michael and Valerie around the portable light and heater. A moment later, Michelle, Gabrielle, and Raphael came out with their own bowls and joined in the circle.

Justice sat directly across from Michael. Michael couldn't tell if Justice was staring at him or if it was his imagination. His sinister mask made it hard to determine what he was actually thinking.

As the three angels joined the circle, Michael held up the bowl and said, "This chili is really good."

Michelle proudly smiled and said, "Thank you, Mr. Snyder. We filled it with our love to give it that perfect flavor."

Michael took another giant bite and swallowed it, saying, "This meat is really good. Where did you get it?"

Michelle casually said, "It's Harvester meat." She took her first spoonful of the chili and put it in her mouth. She began to over react in her pleasure from eating really good food.

Michael, Sarah, Jennifer, and Valerie collectively paused and stared at the bowl of Harvester chili that they had already eaten half of.

Michael, trying to overcome the tension, said, "I had no idea you could eat Harvester meat." It did taste good to him at first, but, now that he knew what it was, he started to feel sickened by it. He forced himself to take another bite and ignored where it came from.

Sarah lifted the bowl to her nose and smelled it. She said, "It kind of reminds me of chicken."

Sarah followed Michael's example and kept eating. Jennifer and Valerie glanced at each other and then returned their gaze to the bowl.

Justice, who ate by lifting his mask up slightly so that it would not reveal his face, said, "What's wrong, you don't like Harvester meat?"

Jennifer looked up and said, "No, it tastes okay. I just never thought I'd be eating a Harvester."

Valerie started to chuckle and then quickly covered her mouth with her hand. Justice joined her by laughing and said, "What's wrong, little one? You're free here so if you want to laugh out loud, by all means laugh out loud!"

Valerie chuckled again and said, "I just thought it was really funny that normally Harvesters eat people and now we're eating the Harvesters."

Sarah shook her head and said, "Never would have occurred to me that we could eat them. Especially when people aren't getting enough food inside the walls when we could have just hunted Harvester meat."

Justice nodded and said, "Yes, little one, the World Government likes to keep a tight hold on all the food so that they can control the people better."

Raphael suddenly changed the subject and said, "Papa, why don't you tell another story. I bet the little sisters would love to hear it."

Justice gave a momentary humming sound and then said, "What story do you want to hear?"

Raphael raised her hand excitedly and said, "I know, Papa. Tell the story about how we all got our powers. I bet they want to hear that one."

Sarah nodded her head and said, "Yeah, I definitely want to hear that one!"

Valerie said, "Mr. Justice, do you really know how we got our powers as Wielders?"

Jennifer sat there quietly but, by the look on her face, she was intent on listening.

Justice looked across at Valerie with his sinister mask and said, "What is your name, little yellow Wielder?"

Valerie replied, "Mr. Justice, my name is Valerie."

Justice said, "Valerie. I'll remember your name, little Valerie."

Justice then threw his hands up into the air again and laughed out loud. He then pointed his finger at Valerie and replied, "Of course, I know how you got your powers. I was involved in the whole project after all. Do you really want to know?"

Valerie nodded and said, "Yes, please. I really want to know why I was chosen to have this special power that makes me like the magical girls of Magical Girl Squad."

Justice bent over and brought his emotionless mask near her face and said, "Oh, you think you are special because you have these powers, do you?"

Valerie nodded her head. Sarah and Jennifer kept their gazes fixed on Justice as they waited for him to tell the story.

Justice lifted his right pointer finger and said, "Once upon a time there was a very bad man named Mr. Schilds."

Gabrielle started to rock back and forth and spoke to herself, saying, "Bad man! Bad man!"

Justice held his pointer finger up towards the roof and said, "Yes, a very bad man. He was also a very smart man. He developed a very special serum. This serum became known as the Transcendence Serum. Whomever took this special serum, gained extremely powerful abilities. The problem though was that nine out of ten people who took this serum died from it."

Valerie tilted her head and said, "Mr. Justice, if the serum was so dangerous, why then did people want to take it?"

Justice directed the gaze of his mask towards her and said, "Because, Valerie, those who did take it gained great power. They were willing to risk their life to obtain that great power. Those who sit at the top of the Path of the Future are the ones who have transcended through the serum and survived it. You can't become the elite of the elite without partaking of it."

Jennifer crossed her arms over her chest and said, "I can't tell if they are crazy or just stupid."

Justice turned his gaze to Jennifer and said, "Perhaps they are both. Anyway, Mr. Schilds said ..."

At the mention of that name, Gabrielle started to speak out again, saying, "Bad man! Bad man!"

Justice turned towards her and said, "Yes, my darling angel, we know that he is a bad man. I promise you that I will kill him the first chance I get. But, now, just let me finish the story."

Gabrielle pouted and looked depressingly towards the ground. She said, "I'm sorry, Papa."

Justice faced forward again and said, "Anyway, Mr. Schilds said, 'If we divide the power of this serum up and give it to children we could use those children to balance out the destruction caused by the Harvesters.'"

Michael raised his hand and said, "Okay, I'm a little confused now. Girls started getting their powers before the Harvesters even showed up, so that doesn't even make any sense."

Justice turned his mask and stared straight at Michael and said, "Be patient, Mr. Snyder. I'll reveal all to you in time, but it is enough to know right now that they were actually aware of the Harvesters before they made landfall in China."

Michael dropped his hand and shrugged his shoulders and said, "Really?" That actually made a little bit of sense to him. They might have discovered them earlier but they didn't let the public know in case they got worried and started a panic. Michael decided to accept it and listen to the rest of the story.

Justice continued and said, "Yes, really. They decided to divide the power of the serum into three different serums. Each one of these serums contained a third of the abilities of the Transcendence Serum. Since the power was divided, it reduced the risk of death to only thirty-three percent instead of ninety percent."

Sarah said, "Those three serums are what give us our powers, right? Yellow can heal, blue can put up shields, and reds become super strong."

Justice nodded his mask and held up his pointer finger, saying, "Exactly, my dear. They altered the three lesser serums so that they would only attempt to bind to girl DNA and decided that the best way to distribute it was through the vaccination program for pregnant mothers. Vaccinations were randomly tainted with these serums so that when pregnant mothers got them, it would change baby girls in their mother's wombs. If it killed the child, then people would only think it was a miscarriage."

Valerie pulled on Michael's shirt and looked up at him questioningly, saying, "What's a miscarriage?"

Michael replied, saying, "That's when a baby dies before it gets born."

Valerie lowered her gaze and started to look depressed. She said, "That's really sad." She paused and then said, "So, I guess I'm not really special because I have these powers? It was just random chance?"

Justice put his hand on Valerie's head and said, "Yes, Valerie. It was a random chance that your mother was given a tainted shot. But, the shot is not what makes you special. You're special simply because you were born. You are a daughter of God and that is the most special thing that you can be."

Valerie nodded her head and said, "Yeah, I know that much. I just thought I got these powers because I was even more special."

Michael wrapped his arm around Valerie and said with compassion in his voice, "I think you girls are special."

Valerie leaned into him and said, "Thanks" as she rested her head on his chest.

Michael looked back up to Justice. Justice seemed to stare right through him in that sinister mask. Michael said, "You mentioned something about being transcended. Is that a reference to the Transcendence serum?"

Suddenly, Valerie sat up straight and gasped loudly. She exclaimed, "That's it! I see it now!"

Jennifer, annoyed by Valerie's random outburst, said, "What are you talking about, Valerie?"

Valerie, her eyes wide with realization, replied, "It's in the song!"

Sarah leaning over so she could see Valerie better said, "What song? Are you talking about the Magical Girl song again?"

Valerie nodded in excitement and said, "Yeah! Remember the line that says 'with a shot of love your powers flow'?"

Michael nodded his head and said, "Yeah, Valerie, I see what you are saying."

Valerie continued, "Yeah, we got those shots when we were in our mom's bellies and it caused our powers to flow."

Josh said, "See, Valerie. Isn't it more fun to find out those hidden symbols yourself?"

Valerie nodded and said, "Yeah. I was able to see it on my own!"

Michael rubbed Valerie on the head and said, "Okay, let's get back on track with what I was trying to ask."

Valerie looked down towards the floor, embarrassed, and said, "I'm sorry, Lieutenant. I just got really excited that I figured something else out."

Michael rubbed her head again and focused his attention back on Justice. He said, "Sorry about that Justice. What I'm trying to ask is, have you taken that first serum, the Transcendence serum?"

Justice began to chuckle. His eyes began to glow with a white light. They shone through the eye holes of his sinister mask. He held up his hands and they started glowing white. The glow changed into a white fire that emanated from his hands.

Michael and the girls began to make noises in awe. Their eyes were fixated on the white flames that danced from his hands. Their eyes widened and their jaws dropped to the floor. Justice withdrew the fire back into his body and his eyes stopped glowing with white light.

Michael, still in shock, shook his head and said, "I saw it but I still can't believe it."

Justice replied, "My white fire proves that I've transcended. My power is the combined powers of red, blue, and yellow Wielders."

Sarah said, "Now I understand how you survived when you blew up the wall. You shielded yourself and then flew to safety."

Justice burst out into a momentary laugh. He quickly calmed down and said, "Yeah, that's true."

Michael shook his head and chuckled, saying, "So, when I pointed my gun at you, you weren't in any real danger."

Justice waved his pointer finger in the air, saying, "The real dilemma would be if I could activate my shield faster than the bullet could come out of your gun. Maybe from far away, but not at point blank range. I had full faith in you, and I trusted that you wouldn't really shoot me since I was unarmed."

Michael shrugged his shoulders and sighed as he relaxed his body, saying, "I don't know why you put so much faith in me. You hardly know me."

Justice slowly shook his head, saying, "Not true, Mr. Snyder. Not true at all. You see, I know people. I've been around people who are so evil that when they enter the room the light seems to dim around them. You seem to have a bright light and that bright light tells me that you are good. I also can see how much your daughters rely on you. I can also see how much you care about them."

Michael lowered his gaze to the ground. He hadn't realized that anybody thought of him like that. He said, "Yeah, I do love them. I'd do anything to make it so that they wouldn't have to suffer because of this war. I wish I could be stronger so that I could protect them."

Justice placed his hands on his knees and leaned towards Michael. The glow of the portable light reflected off of his sinister mask. He said, "What if there was a way for you to get stronger? Would you do whatever it took to get it?"

Michael stared into the mask and said, "Yeah. If it meant that I could finally protect them like I want to, then yeah, I'd do what I could to get that power."

Valerie suddenly yawned. She covered her mouth with her hand and then stretched as she sat there next to Michael. Jennifer unconsciously yawned in response to Valerie's yawn. She shook her head.

Sarah stretched and said, "Looks like the little ones are getting sleepy."

Jennifer crossed her arms across her chest and pouted, saying, "I'm not sleepy yet, I'm just tired."

Sarah said, "Being tired is being sleepy, idjit!"

Jennifer protested, "No, it's not!"

Michael sighed and put a hand on both Jennifer's and Sarah's head. He replied, "To be honest, I'm pretty sleepy too. I wouldn't mind if we went to sleep right now."

Justice clapped his hands together once and said, "Yes, you've had a very tiring day. I agree. Let's get ready to sleep."

Michelle stood up and went into the back room. She returned with a blanket in her hands. She walked over to Michael and said, "We only got this one extra blanket."

Michael replied, "Great! That will work just fine. Thank you."

Michelle started twisting her body side to side. She said, "We don't have any pillows, but I'll let you use my lap as a pillow if you want."

Michael held his hand up in refusal and shook his head, saying, "Nah, I'm a soldier. I'm used to not using a pillow in the field. I'll be fine."

Disappointed, Michelle stopped twisting her body and said, "Oh, okay."

Michael stood up and stretched. He said his goodnights and then walked over to a clearing and laid the blanket on the floor. He laid down on it and rested his head on his arm.

Sarah, Jennifer, and Valerie watched him walk over to the clearing and lay the blanket down. Sarah motioned her head as if to say 'let's go'. The three of them stood up. Sarah nodded her head towards Justice and the three angels. She said, "Thank you for dinner, and thank you for telling us how to stop our self-destruction."

Justice nodded and said, "What is your name?"

Sarah said, "My name is Sarah and this is Jennifer."

Justice replied, "Valerie, Sarah, Jennifer ... it is a pleasure to meet you. May you have pleasant dreams tonight."

Jennifer, crossing her arms over her chest, nodded shyly and said, "Yeah ... thanks."

Valerie tried to clumsily imitate the curtsy she saw the angels do. She said, "Thank you!"

They walked over where Michael was lying down on the floor. Sarah went to his left side and laid down beside him. She leaned her back against his side for warmth. Valerie knelt down and began to silently pray for a moment. When she was done, she laid down on the other side of him and leaned her back against him too. Jennifer had laid down next to Valerie. When Valerie was done praying, she laid down and draped her arm over Jennifer.

Michael said, "Good night, girls."

Sarah, Jennifer and Valerie replied in kind.

As he laid there, he wondered if he did the right thing. *What would Mary say if she were here?* he thought to himself. As he thought about Mary, the pain of losing her returned to him as if it had just happened yesterday. It was a new pain. It was the guilt he felt from his part in causing her demise. He pushed his thoughts down into his stomach, trying to ignore them.

- 3 -

The alarm went off at six-thirty in the morning, as it usually did. Lieutenant Rachel rolled over and swiped her hands over where her clock was sitting. After a moment of randomly feeling her hands around, she found the alarm clock and turned it off. She sighed deeply. She could still feel the pain of her menstrual cycle.

Lieutenant Rachel slowly sat up. She looked out the window to see the giant wall that protected them from the onslaught of the Harvesters. Michael was on the other side of that wall. He had been out there for about four days now. Besides her physical discomfort, she continued to feel uneasy about the mission that Michael and his squad were on.

As Rachel sat there, the door swung open. Giana stood in the doorway with a huge grin on her face. Her right hand held the door knob and her left arm was raised high in the air. She joyfully exclaimed, "Good morning, Lieutenant! Do you still feel like crap or are you done?"

Rachel sighed and nodded her head, saying, "Yeah, I still feel like crap."

Giana lowered her arm and gave her a thumbs up, saying, "Don't worry, Lieutenant, I'll make rice porridge again for breakfast. So, feel free to take your time."

Rachel gave a tired grin at her and replied, "Thanks, Giana."

Giana began to shut the door and said, "No problem, Lieutenant."

The door shut and Rachel slowly stood up. She put her hand on her abdomen and headed for the bathroom.

When everyone's morning routine was over, they gathered to the table to eat. Tina began to set the table, as Giana stood over the stove, stirring the rice porridge she was making.

Lieutenant Rachel sauntered to her chair and plopped down in it. Elsa, who was already sitting at the table, looked at her and said, "Do you still feel bad, Lieutenant?"

Lieutenant Rachel nodded and said, "Yeah, I think going out on that mission made it worse. I'm so tired now."

Elsa's face smiled with sympathy and she said, "I'm sure today will be easier. Even though we still got to go out and check the wall today."

Tina came and put a bowl and spoon next to Lieutenant Rachel, saying, "It's so stupid how we got to go check the wall every day now."

Giana followed behind Tina and began to spoon rice porridge into each bowl that Tina set down. After she had filled all four bowls she sat down and picked up her spoon to eat.

As Giana put the first spoonful of rice porridge in her mouth, there was a sudden knock on the door. Elsa, being closest to the door, pushed out her chair and ran up to open the door. Captain Faust stood on the other side of the door with a fake smile on his face. Lieutenant Rachel knew that face. It was the face he made when he had bad news to tell you and he tried to cover it up with a mask of a smile. He didn't know that his eyes gave him away.

Captain Faust stood there and saw them all eating breakfast at the table. He took one step inside and said, "Good morning, Lieutenant Harris. I'm sorry to disturb you during your breakfast but there was something that I wanted to discuss with you. Would you mind stepping outside for a moment?"

Lieutenant Rachel nodded and said, "Yeah. Hold on a moment." She pushed her chair out and awkwardly pulled herself up out of her chair. The pain in her lower abdomen made it difficult to walk, but she knew she had to endure it.

Lieutenant Rachel put her hand on Elsa's head and said, "Go sit back down and finish eating."

Elsa nodded and said, "Okay." She headed back to her chair and sat down.

Lieutenant Rachel stepped outside and shut the door behind her.

Captain Faust fidgeted with his hat He lowered his gaze, sighed, and said, "We have some concerns about Lieutenant Snyder and his squad. I know you two were close so I wanted to make sure you knew what was going on from me personally."

Lieutenant Rachel crossed her arms against her chest. Her heart began to race as she prepared herself for the worst. She anxiously said, "Oh?"

Captain Faust looked straight into her eyes and said, "The locator chips implanted on them have not moved at all for almost six hours. You know what that usually means. The people wearing the chips have been killed and the chip has been torn off of their bodies."

Rachel looked down to the ground. A torrent of emotions wanted to flood out. But, she pushed them down so that she would not lose control of herself. She nodded and said, "I see. Thank you for telling me."

Captain Faust put his hand on her shoulder and said, "It's only been six hours so we haven't given up hope yet. I'll let you know the moment I hear anything about it, okay?"

Lieutenant Rachel nodded again. Her arms were still crossed over her chest and she still gazed toward the ground. She said, "Thank you, Captain."

Captain Faust patted her shoulder and said, "Hang in there. Let me know if you need anything."

Lieutenant Rachel started to lose control of the emotions in her voice. Her voice cracked as she said, "Okay."

Captain Faust smiled compassionately at her and then turned around, heading for the door to the staircase.

Lieutenant Rachel opened the door and quickly shut it behind her. Giana, Tina, and Elsa sat there staring at her as she entered the room. She shut the door and leaned her face against it. She then turned around and looked up to the ceiling. Her eyes burned as tears began to streak out of her eyes and ran down the sides of her face.

Giana's voice called out, saying, "Lieutenant, what's wrong?"

Giana's voice did not reach Lieutenant Rachel. She lost the strength in her legs. Her back slid down along the side of the door. She sat against the door and wrapped her arms around her legs. She buried her face into her knees and cried as she sat there.

Giana, Tina, and Elsa jumped out of their chairs and rushed over to her side. Giana knelt beside her and wrapped her arm around Lieutenant Rachel's neck. Lieutenant Rachel leaned over against Giana and rested her head on Giana's shoulder. Tina and Elsa each put a hand on Lieutenant Rachel's back.

Lieutenant Rachel continued to cry into Giana's shoulder. After a few minutes she began to compose herself and sat up. Giana let go of her neck and put her hands on the arm closest to her.

Lieutenant Rachel said, "I'm sorry, girls. Squad three's locator chips have stopped moving for about six hours. They're probably dead."

Giana dropped down on her bottom and sat on her feet. She compassionately said, "I'm sorry, Lieutenant."

Elsa spoke up, saying, "They might not be dead, Lieutenant. Maybe they just took off their clothing?"

Tina glared at Elsa and said, "Don't be an idjit! Why would they take off their clothing in the middle of the Harvester Zone?"

Giana swatted at the two of them and said, "Stop fighting, damn it!"

Lieutenant Rachel wiped her face with her hands and said, "They're probably dead."

Giana hugged her again and said, "I know it seems hopeless. But, there's no real proof yet. I know that Lieutenant Michael will do everything he can to come back to you so don't give up yet. Okay?"

Lieutenant Rachel nodded and said, "I want to believe you but experience tells me otherwise."

Lieutenant Rachael covered her face with her hands and sighed heavily into them. The three girls sat there with her, hoping to comfort her.

Michael felt something crawling in his hair. The feeling nudged him awake and he opened his eyes not knowing what to expect. He tilted his head back and saw Michelle sitting on her knees next to the top of his head. She was running her hand through his hair and smiling mischievously.

When Michael looked up at her, she took her hand off of his head and said, "Good morning, Mr. Snyder. It's time for everybody to wake up."

Michael sat up and looked around. The morning sunlight was beginning to shine in from the open roof. A thin layer of dew covered everything.

Michael shook Sarah's shoulder and said, "Sarah, time to wake up."

Sarah's eyes blinked open and she started stretching. She yawned as she rocked back and forth on the hard floor.

Michael reached over on his other side and started shaking Valerie. When she started to move, he reached over her and started shaking Jennifer. He said, "Valerie, Jennifer. Time to get up."

Sarah sat up and looked around confused. A look of remembrance fell on her face and she said out loud to herself, "Oh yeah."

Valerie and Jennifer sat up together and looked into each other's eyes as their minds tried to wake up.

Michael stood up and said, "Good morning, girls."

Sarah looked up at him and said, "Good morning, Lieutenant."

Valerie started to stretch, saying, "Good morning."

Jennifer rolled onto her hands and knees and stood up, saying, "Yeah. Good morning I guess. My muscles feel so stiff."

Michael held out his hands to help Sarah and Valerie up. They accepted and he pulled them up on their feet. He said, "Yeah, my muscles are feeling extra stiff too. It's because of the stay awake pills we took. We'll do some morning stretches and that should help it."

Sarah said, "Okay, but first, bathroom."

Michelle, who was standing behind them still, said, "If you need to use the bathroom, you're going to have to go outside."

Jennifer scratched along the right side of her stomach and said, "Yeah, figured as much."

Valerie, looking worried, turned to Michelle and said, "Is that keep-away Harvester machine still working, big sister?"

Michelle shrieked in joy and covered her mouth with both hands. She quickly snatched Valerie in her arms and began to twirl around in a circle, shouting, "You called me big sister! You are so adorable. I love it!"

Valerie began to make noises and said, "Come on, stop! I gotta pee!"

Michelle stopped twirling and put her down, saying, "Yes, the machine is still up. That's why they're no Harvesters in here. So, you don't have to worry about going pee outside."

Valerie nodded and cautiously said, "Thanks."

Sarah said, "Come on, let's go to the bathroom."

Valerie nodded and said, "Okay."

Jennifer said, "Yeah, let's go."

Together, they walked out of the door and turned around the corner to where they could be alone. They knew how to go to the bathroom in the field since, when they were on missions they couldn't use a toilet. They each chose a spot, pulled up their dresses and pulled their underwear down.

Jennifer noticed it first as she exclaimed, "Holy crap! I'm pee'n silver!"

Sarah and Valerie both looked down and saw that they too had silver-colored pee.

Sarah said, "Yeah, me too. They said that this would happen."

Valerie said, "Yeah, I remember. I didn't think it would be this much silver color."

The girls walked back into the abandoned church. Michael sat next to Josh. As the girls entered, they both looked at them.

Sarah, Jennifer, and Valerie walked up to them. Sarah said, "Guess what, Lieutenant. We're all peeing silver."

Justice, who had just come out of the back room, spoke loudly, saying, "That's good news! That means that your body is expelling the toxins and nano-machines from your body."

Justice walked over to them and leaned over towards Michael so that his face was close to his. He put his hands behind his back and said, "Good morning, Mr. Snyder. Did you sleep well?"

Michael ran his hand through his hair. He noticed that Michelle was across the way and was leaning to the side so as to watch him with a smile on her face. He focused his attention back on Justice and said, "Well, if I hadn't stayed up for three days straight I'd probably would have had problems. But, I guess I was just so tired that I just passed out and slept."

Justice stood up straight and said, "Yes, we thought you'd all be tired. That's why we decided to let you sleep in."

Michael chuckled and said, "Sleep in. What time is it?"

Justice said, "In this time zone, it's seven in the morning."

Michael ran his hand through his hair and said, "Well, I guess thirty minutes is still sleeping in."

Michael clapped his hands and said, "Alright, girls. Let's get started on today's exercises. Got to keep in shape even in the field."

Sarah, Jennifer and Valerie sarcastically raised their fist high in the air and unenthusiastically said, "Yeah."

Gabrielle and Raphael came out of the back room. Gabrielle asked, "What's going on?"

Michelle crossed her arms over her chest and said, "It appears that our little sisters will be doing some exercises."

Raphael seemed to perk up and said, "Oh, that sounds like fun! Sister, do you think Mr. Snyder would let me join them?"

Michelle shrugged her shoulders and said, "I don't see why not, sister."

Michael, listening to their conversation, waved them on over and said, "If you three girls want to join us for exercises, you're welcome."

Raphael grinned and ran over to them saying, "Thanks, I'd love to try it!" She ran and stood next to Sarah. She bounced up and down as she waited to start.

Michelle tilted her head towards Gabrielle and said, "How about you, sister? Do you want to give it a try?"

Gabrielle shook her head and said, "No, sister, but I will watch so I can know what's going on."

Michelle said, "Alright then, sister. I think I'll give it a try too."

Michelle came over and stood next to Raphael. She twisted her body side to side in anticipation. Sarah, Jennifer, and Valerie stood there a little wobbly as they were still trying to wake up from being so tired.

Gabrielle went into the back room and then quickly returned holding a teacup and saucer. She went over to the pew nearest to them and sat down gently on it. She began to take small sips of her tea as she watched them.

Michael felt awkward as Michelle and Raphael stood there staring at him with big grins, waiting for him to lead them in morning stretches. He started by squaring his hands on his hips and said, "Alright, girls. We'll start by raising our hands in the air as high as we can."

Together, they raised their hands high in the air. Michelle and Raphael reached up as high as they could. They continued to grin and watch Michael as they waited for the next movement. Michael then bent over and touched the floor with his fingers. Together, the girls copied his actions.

Together, they sat on the floor and began to stretch their legs. Michelle said, "Look how far I can go, Mr. Snyder!" She opened her legs wide in a split and closed her eyes. She slowly lowered her chest to the floor until her breasts pressed against the ground.

Michael watched as she lowered herself to the ground. His eyes moved to her cleavage as her breasts seemed as if they would spill out of her dress as they pressed on the floor.

When Michelle's face touched the ground, she looked up at Michael and said, "What do you think, Mr. Snyder?"

Michael averted his eyes from her chest and said, "That's impressive."

Sarah tilted her head and said, "What were you staring at, Lieutenant."

Michael nervously replied, "Uh ... nothing really."

Gabrielle glared at Michael, saying, "He was ogling my sister's breasts ... pervert."

Michelle lifted herself up and brought her legs together in front of her. She used her arms to press her breasts closer together and said, "It's okay. I don't mind. God designed me to be attractive so I'm happy he finds me attractive."

Michael rolled his eyes.

Valerie, annoyed, remarked, "You should only stare at Lieutenant Rachel, Lieutenant!"

Michael rolled his eyes again and said, "Geez, I wasn't."

Michelle bent over again and stretched her torso over her legs, saying, "Don't you think I'm flexible, Mr. Snyder."

Michael replied, "Uh ... okay ... uh ... let's get back on track with our exercises."

Gabrielle closed her eyes and took another sip of her tea. She said, "If you say so, Mr. Snyder."

After they completed their exercises, they ate the left over Harvester chili. Afterwards, Sarah, Valerie, and Jennifer helped the angels wash the dishes.

When they were done, they all gathered together outside the church. They all stood in a circle with Justice and Josh at the head of them. Justice stretched his arms open wide and breathed deeply. He said, "Marvelous day, don't you think?"

Josh nodded and said, "Yes, it is a good day."

Michael scratched his head and looked confused. He asked, "Okay, so now that we're in this together, what are we going to do. I doubt we're just going to sit here and do nothing, right?"

Justice lifted his hand and pointed to the sky, saying, "Quite right, Mr. Snyder. I do have a plan and this is the reason why we've gathered out here this morning."

Michael nodded his head and said, "That's good."

Justice continued, "You see, Mr. Snyder, Sarah, Jennifer, and little Valerie. There is an old abandoned United Nations complex in this vicinity. Underneath this complex, there is a secret hanger that contains a certain type of transportation vehicle. Using it, we'll head out to a certain World Government research facility that produces a certain type of equipment used by the World Government. In order to topple the power of the World Government, we must first destroy this facility."

Michael ran his hand through his hair and said, "You're not going to tell me the specifics, are you?"

Justice started laughing maniacally. After composing himself, he said, "It will be more fun to see the look on your face when you see it for the first time if I don't tell you what it is."

Michael crossed his arms across his chest and rolled his eyes, saying, "Fine ... whatever. You're really going to show me it then, right?"

Justice nodded and stared at him through his sinister mask. He said, "Yes, I'll show you everything. That is my promise to you. I just hope that you can handle it."

Michael nodded and said, "Me too. I hope it's worth all this trouble I'm getting in."

Josh smiled and said, "Do not worry, brother. I promise you that it is worth it."

Justice clapped his hands and said, "Alright, everybody. Let's pack up and we'll walk over to this secret hanger."

Lacking any real equipment, except for their backpacks, Michael and the girls stood by and watched as Justice and his angels quickly began to pack up their things into their own backpacks. Josh stood patiently next to Michael and waited with them.

When they were done the three angels lined up according to age outside, their hands gripping their backpack straps and big grins on their faces. Michelle looked up at Justice and said, "We're ready, Papa."

Justice walked up to her and put his hands on the sides of her face. He then tightened the silk bow that was underneath her chin.

Justice took a step to the side and put his hands on the sides of Gabrielle's face. She pressed her lips together and looked down in embarrassment. He straightened her blue bonnet and tightened the bow underneath her chin.

Justice took another step to the side and ran his hands over Raphael's twin tails. He then put his hands on the side of her face and tilted her face upwards.

Justice spun around in a circle a couple of times and stopped in the middle of them. He stretched his arms out as if to embrace them, but instead, said, "All three of you are my darling angels! Each one of you is precious to me."

All at once, the three angels replied, "We love you too, Papa!"

Justice then tightened the backpack strap that was around his waist and spun in a circle again. He suddenly stopped and pointed outward in a seemingly random direction, saying, "Let us depart into the Harvester Zone."

Justice put his hands on the straps of his backpack and walked up to Michael. He leaned towards him and said, "Fortunately for you, the anti-Harvester device is portable, so we won't have to worry about you getting killed by a Harvester."

Michelle suddenly slapped the sides of her hips and balled her hands into fists towards the ground, exclaiming, "But ... but Papa, I want to play with the Harvesters some more!"

Justice turned around and waved his finger in the air, saying, "Angel, we have to think of Mr. Snyder. He hasn't transcended so he doesn't have any power."

Michelle brought her hands together in front of the skirt of her dress and started to twist her body side to side, saying, "I'll protect him, Papa."

Justice shook his mask and replied, "I know you can, darling. But, we also have to think about time. We don't have time for the three of you to play with the Harvesters right now. We're in a hurry after all."

Michelle sighed and held her hands behind her back, saying, "Okay, Papa. I understand."

Raphael giggled and said, "It's for the best, big sister. You'd only make a mess of your dress again."

Gabrielle nodded and said, "I'm sure you don't want to soil your dress in front of Mr. Snyder. You don't have any more clean ones. A lady has to dress her best after all."

Michelle clasped her hands together in front of her chest and gazed at Michael. Her eyes seemed to sparkle. She said, "You're right, dear sister. I have to look my best for Mr. Snyder."

Justice turned back towards the ruined city before them with his right arm stretched out towards the desolation. He said, "Are you all ready? Yes? Let's get going then."

Lieutenant Rachel stood alone in the evening time in front of Squad three's door. She put her hand on the door knob and held it there. If Squad three was killed in action, the military would clear this room out and prep it for a new squadron to take over. It would never be the same again. She closed her eyes as she prepared herself emotionally for that eventuality.

There wasn't much worry about security so the squad apartment doors were not usually locked. Rachel leaned forward and rested her forehead on the door. She twisted the knob and slowly pushed it open.

The room was dark. Rachel flipped the light switch on. She came in and shut the door behind her. The memory of Michael's voice echoed in her thoughts, *Hey Rachel, would you like some of my herbal tea?* She looked toward the kitchen and instead of seeing Michael standing there with his tea set, there was nobody.

Rachel walked through the dining area and headed for the hallway. She turned and entered into Michael's room. As she opened the door she could smell his familiar scent on the gust that came as she opened the door.

Rachel stepped into the room. She looked down to the ground at the place where they had sat together alone, side by side. Again the memory of his voice echoed in her mind, *It feels natural to be with you ..."* As they sat there, she had wanted him to hold her in his strong arms. She had wanted to listen to his heart beating as she laid her head on his chest; the rhythm of his breathing.

Rachel walked over to the side of his bed. The covers were neatly pressed over the mattress. His two pillows sat one on top of the other. She crawled onto the top of his mattress and laid her head down on his pillows. She inhaled deeply as she breathed his scent that remained on his pillows.

Rachel took one of his pillows and rolled over on to her side. She embraced the pillow against her chest and imagined that it was Michael. She imagined him whispering into his ear, "I love you." He would have pushed her onto her back and kissed her deeply. He would have caressed her upper arm with his strong hands, rolled his palm over her stomach and into her shirt. She would not have the will to stop him.

As she laid there thinking, Giana stumbled in and said, "I thought you'd be in here."

Rachel opened her eyes and sighed, saying, "What do you want?"

Giana shrugged her shoulders and said, "I just wanted to make sure that you were alright."

Rachel hesitated a moment and looked away from her. She said, "I'm okay."

Giana took another step in and said, "It must be harder when one of your Lieutenant friends die. We're expected to die, but the Lieutenants are usually the ones that keep living in our place."

Rachel sighed and sat up on the edge of Michael's bed. She said, "That's not true, Giana. I'd feel the same if it was you who died."

Giana looked down to the ground and said, "Really? That's good to hear. You know, all the people that I looked up to when I was young are dead. You're the only one still alive now. I wonder if what I'm feeling is what old people feel. I'm like this person who younger girls look up to, but everybody I relied on is dead now so I keep trying to focus on all the girls who are younger than me. The good thing is that I know that my time is almost up so I don't got to worry about it for much longer."

Rachel let go of the pillow and placed it beside her on the bed. She stood up and walked over to Giana. She wrapped her arms around Giana and pressed her head against her own shoulder. She stroked the back of her head.

Giana wrapped her own arms around Rachel's back. She said, "I want to say that I'm sorry that Lieutenant Michael didn't make it back. But, I also don't want to give up hope, even though all my experience is telling me otherwise. I want to believe that they'll all be back with their stupid grins. It just seems too easy that it happened that way."

Rachel, continuing to hold her, said, "You really think so?"

Giana said, "Yeah. I do."

Rachel let her go and put her hands on Giana's shoulders, saying, "You want to help me go through some things in case they start throwing away their stuff?"

Giana nodded her head and said, "Yeah, I'll help. We should probably get Tina and Elsa here too so they can get some things to remember them."

Rachel compassionately smiled and said, "Yeah. Our two squads were really close."

Giana said, "Yeah. We were. If they bring a new squad in, it won't be like before. But, as always, we'll try to make friends to fill the void left by those who've died."

- 4 -

As Michael and Justice's group moved through the wasteland, more and more Harvesters started to gather around them. The anti-Harvester device allowed them to get only so close and then they would stop and follow them at that distance. It was a strange sight that Michael and the girls were not used to seeing.

Sarah shook her head and said, "Who would have thought that we'd be able to just stroll through the Harvester zone and not have to worry about getting attacked by Harvesters."

Jennifer crossed her arms across her chest and started to scowl, saying, "It pisses me off so much that they wouldn't let us use this machine."

Valerie climbed on top of a broken wall and walked along the edge. She balanced herself with her arms and said, "At least we got it now. I never thought that I'd get to make so much noise. I can sing the Magical Girl Squad song and not have to worry about getting attacked."

Jennifer dropped her arms and held them up as if she were begging, saying, "Please don't sing that song again. I've heard it too many times these past few days."

Valerie sighed and dropped her arms to her sides. She hopped down from the wall. She said, "Yeah, yeah. I won't sing it now." She paused for a moment and then said, "I think it's Thursday today so that means I missed Magical Girl Squad and you are going to miss the Lost Sword Saga tonight."

Sarah joined in and said, "Yeah, we'll all miss the new episode of Magical Girl Squad tomorrow."

Michelle, Gabrielle, and Raphael moved from following Justice, to standing beside Sarah, Jennifer, and Valerie. Michelle put her hand on Valerie's head and said, "You all like television a lot, don't you, little sisters?"

Valerie shrugged her shoulders and said, "Of course. Don't you like to watch television too?"

Gabrielle, who was walking beside Sarah said, "Not really. The bad men like to use television to put bad ideas inside people. That's why they call it television programing, because they're programming people's minds with the television to think a certain way."

Valerie shrugged her shoulders and said, "I don't really get it, but you seem to know a lot about what the bad men do."

Raphael twirled one of her twin tails with her fingers and said, "Yeah, we've got a lot of experience with the bad men."

Sarah put her hands together and looked down towards the ground. She meekly said, "Can I ask what the bad men did to you?"

The three angels stopped walking. Sarah, Valerie and Jennifer stopped and turned to them waiting for an answer. The three angels started to look uncomfortable and looked down toward the ground.

Sarah watched their hesitation and said, "I'm sorry. I didn't mean to make you uncomfortable. You don't have to answer if it's too hard."

Michelle tugged at her hair band and said, "I'm sorry, little sister. It's really hard to talk about and it's not something that we like to remember. Please give us some time. When we're ready to tell you, we'll let you know."

Gabrielle shuddered and said, "Bad men!"

Raphael's smile faded and a very cruel looking face replaced her kind one. She started to run her left hand over her right arm. She started to breathe heavily and curled her fingers as she ran her hand over her arm. Suddenly, she dug her finger nails into her arm and began to rip long tares into her flesh.

Michelle yelled out, "Raphael, get a hold of yourself!"

Seemingly out of nowhere, Justice suddenly leapt from across the way and grabbed Raphael in his arms. He held her so that she couldn't move. She started to growl and scream uncontrollably.

Michelle and Gabrielle grabbed Sarah, Jennifer, and Valerie by their arms and pulled them backward, saying, "Don't worry, Papa knows what to do."

Sarah, Jennifer and Valerie watched on in horror as Raphael tried to break free out of Justice's grip. Justice started to speak to her gently, saying, "Raphael, it's Papa. You're okay. I'm right here. Papa's here."

Raphael started to cry as she screamed, "Papa! Papa! Don't let them touch me again! Never again! Never again! Never again! Papa! Help me!"

Justice replied, "I'm right here, my angel. You're safe. I won't let them touch you again."

Raphael stopped struggling and went limp in his arms. He lowered her so that she was kneeling on the ground. He knelt down beside her and held her in his arms. He rocked her back and forth, repeating over and over again, "You're safe now."

Raphael seemed to calm down and gained control of her actions. She looked at her right arm and said, "Oops, looks like I did it again, Papa." Her eyes glowed yellow and the open wounds on her arm healed quickly. She pulled a handkerchief out of a concealed pocket and wiped the blood that was left on her arms.

Justice looked up at the frightened girls and said, "Please, don't be scared. My little Raphael sometimes gets flash backs from her past. They don't last very long. Just give her some space when it happens."

Jennifer looked at the scares from the cuts that were on her own wrist. She walked up to Raphael, who was now drying her eyes with the same bloodied handkerchief. She extended her right wrist and showed her the scars that were there. She said, "Not too long ago, I was really sad and I used to cut myself to make myself forget my sadness."

Raphael held Jennifer's hand and examined the scars on her wrist. Raphael let her hand go and said, "I've cut myself too, but, since I can heal myself, all my scars go away."

Jennifer offered Raphael her hand and said, "Lieutenant Michael helped me to get better by listening and talking to me about my problems. As I talked to him, I felt better about myself. If you ever want to talk to someone about your problems, I'll listen, big sister."

Raphael took her hand and said, "I'm not used to being a big sister."

Jennifer pulled her up and helped her to her feet. After Raphael was back on her feet, she continued to hold Jennifer's hand. She said, "Would ... would it be alright if I hold your hand for a while, little sister?"

Jennifer nodded with a smile, saying, "Sure, big sister."

Raphael smiled back and replied, "Thanks!"

Justice stood up and brushed off his breeches. Michael walked up to him and said, "Is she going to be okay?"

Justice sighed and said, "Yeah, she'll be fine. These poor girls of mine have been through so much. Raphael has probably had the worst of it among the three. She gets flashbacks from time to time. I hope you won't hold it against her. She gets very embarrassed about it."

Michael waved his hand in dismissal and said, "Don't worry. I can't even begin to imagine what happened in their past. So, I don't have any right to judge things I don't understand."

Raphael continued to hold Jennifer's hand as they walked toward the secret hanger that Justice said existed. Valerie walked up beside Gabrielle and tugged on her sleeve, saying, "I like your hat, big sister. It's really cute."

Gabrielle nervously smiled and adjusted the bonnet on her head. She replied, "Thanks, little sister."

Sarah looked toward Michelle. Michelle looked towards Sarah with a mischievous grin on her face. Michelle walked over to Sarah and said, "Guess we should partner up too like everybody else."

Sarah shrugged her shoulders and replied, "I guess."

Michelle offered her arm to Sarah. Sarah stared at it not knowing what she wanted.

Michelle said, "Take my arm, little sister."

Sarah looked at her arm again and said, "Really?"

Michelle nodded and said, "Yeah. Take it. Let's be good friends."

Sarah sighed and wrapped her own arm around Michelle's arm, saying, "Alright."

Michelle looked towards Raphael and Jennifer, who still held hands. As she observed them, she said to Sarah, "It makes me happy to see Raphael attaching herself to Jennifer. I'm really glad that they had something that they could share together. Raphael has suffered more than me and Gabrielle."

Sarah nodded and said, "Yeah. I don't know about Raphael. But, I know that Jennifer had to deal with really bad depression. My Lieutenant told me that sometimes the only way some people know how to deal with their problems is to hurt themselves."

Michelle's smile faded. She became really gloomy and said, "Since she is a yellow Wielder, all her physical scares are healed. Her emotional scares, I don't know if those can ever heal."

Sarah looked up at Michelle and said, "You really love your sisters, don't you?"

Michelle tried to smile and said, "Yeah, I do. I love them just like I love my Papa. Don't you love your sisters too?"

Sarah nodded and said, "Yeah. I do."

Michelle smiled for real this time and said, "That's good. Love is the only thing that can keep you three together in the darkness. Do you love Mr. Snyder?"

Sarah nodded and said, "Yeah. He's like my dad. My real parents died when I was younger. When I try to remember my parents, the Lieutenant's face keeps coming back to me."

Michelle tilted her head and asked, "If Mr. Snyder is like your dad, how come you don't call him dad?"

Sarah thought about it in silence for a moment. Michelle did not push her and patiently waited for a reply. Sarah brought her finger to her lips and said, "I've never thought about it before. He's not my real dad."

Michelle looked towards Justice and said, "Papa isn't my real Papa. But when I think about who my Papa is, all I see is Papa so I call him Papa. Papa saved me and my sisters, so I call him Papa. If you see your Lieutenant as your Papa, you should call him Papa. Whoever is my Papa in my heart is my real Papa, even if we don't share blood."

Gabrielle pulled a small pocket watch out of a hidden pocket and opened it. She closed the pocket watch and shouted out, saying, "Sisters, it's eleven O' clock, time for tea."

Michelle let go of Sarah's arm and clapped her hands, saying, "Excellent, I was just thinking about having some tea. I do hope we have some of that Darjeeling left in the bag."

Justice stopped and spun around saying, "I do believe we still have some."

Michael ran his right hand through his hair and said, "What's going on?"

Josh, standing beside him, said, "It is time for tea. They take tea time very serious. Twice a day."

Raphael led Jennifer by the hand and said, "Do you like tea, little sister?"

Jennifer shrugged her shoulders and said, "I don't know, I've never had tea before."

Raphael pulled a blanket out of her backpack and laid it out on the ground amongst the ruins around them. She sat down in a corner and patted the spot beside her with her hand, saying, "Come and sit. We'll have tea together."

Gabrielle pulled a small portable stove out of her backpack and set it up with a tea kettle. She poured a bottle of water into it and then lit the stove. Valerie sat down on the other side of Raphael.

Michelle pulled a small basket out of her backpack and said, "Unfortunately, I only have six cups. That's only enough for us and the little sisters."

Justice waved his hand and said, "That's okay, my darling. You girls enjoy your tea together."

Michael nodded and said, "Yeah, I don't really like black tea anyway so that's fine."

Michelle froze. Her eyes went wide and her mouth dropped. She exclaimed, "You don't like black tea?!"

Michael shrugged his shoulders and said, "Not really. Gives me too much energy. I don't like feeling all jittery."

Michelle shook her head and started to mutter under her breath as she set up a tea pot and six cups. She opened a small tin and spooned tea leaves into the pot. Michael shrugged his shoulders and brushed off her behavior thinking, *Can't please them all.*

The water kettle started to boil and the kettle whistled. Gabrielle turned the fire off and let the kettle sit on the portable stove. She turned to Valerie and said, "For most black teas you want the water temperature to be ninety-five degrees Celsius. This will allow the leaves to fully open and you get the best flavor and the perfect aroma. Darjeeling is a little different. The best temperature for Darjeeling is ninety degrees. That's why I let it sit for a minute so it can reach that lower temperature."

Gabrielle then picked up the kettle and carefully poured the hot water into the tea pot. She placed the lid on it and allowed it to sit. She said, "And for green tea, the best temperature is seventy-five degrees Celsius. To achieve that temperature, you take a cup, pour in the boiling water, and then dump the water in the cup into the tea pot. For all teas, if the water is too hot you'll kill the flavor. If the water is too cool, the tea leaves won't fully open and the taste will be sub-par. You won't get that perfect aroma."

Gabrielle lifted the lid and brought the tea pot to Valerie's nose and said, "Smell it, that's the smell of the perfect Darjeeling."

Valerie sniffed and, having never smelled it before, had nothing to compare it to so she nodded and said, "It smells pretty good."

Gabrielle moved the tea pot to Jennifer next. Jennifer smelled it too and said, "Yeah, that smells good, though I've never really smelled tea before so I can't tell the difference."

Gabrielle moved the tea pot to Sarah. Sarah smelled it and said, "Smells a little bitter to me."

Michelle pulled a small silver box that fit into the palm of her hand out of her backpack. She lifted the lid open and held it out to Sarah. Inside were a bunch of small white cubes. Sarah examined the contents of the box and said, "What's that?"

Michelle replied, "It's real sugar. Not that chemical imitation they make for the common people. Some people like to put sugar in their tea since its natural taste is slightly bitter."

Gabrielle started to pour tea into the small teacups and said, "But don't use too much of the sugar. Sugar isn't good for your body so we only use it a little bit if we feel like it. That chemical compound they make to replace sugar though is far worse than the real sugar."

Michelle pulled the box back and closed the lid, saying, "So if you want to try some sugar with your tea, let me know."

After filling the teacups, Gabrielle handed one to Valerie, Jennifer and then Sarah. She said, "It's best to drink it when it's still hot." She then passed a teacup to Raphael and Michelle next.

Sarah sniffed the tea in her cup and took a small sip. It was really hot and nearly burned her tongue. She started to blow on the top of the tea.

Valerie watched Sarah and then stuck her pinky into the tea to check its temperature. She said, "It's still pretty hot."

Jennifer blew on the top of her tea and then took a small sip. She said, "Yeah, it is a little bit bitter but I kind of like it."

Valerie took a sip and said, "Can I try it with the sugar?"

Michelle opened the lid on her silver box and said, "Here take one."

Valerie reached over and took one of the cubes. She dropped it into her cup and watched as it started to dissolve in the tea.

Sarah took another sip of the tea now that it had cooled and said, "Okay, I can taste it now. It's pretty good."

As the girls chatted and drank the rest of the tea together, the Harvesters continued to circle around them at the distance that the anti-Harvester device allowed them to be at.

Michael gazed at the Harvesters as the girls sat and drank their tea together. He shook his head and said, "Justice, are we almost at this supposed hanger yet?"

Justice nodded with his sinister mask and said, "Yeah. Should be another three hours' worth of travel."

Josh said, "Yeah, this hanger is what sealed the deal for me. When you see it, your whole world will be turned upside down."

Justice waved his hand at Josh and said, "Don't spoil it for him. I want to see the look on his face when he sees it for the first time."

Josh sighed and said, "Alright, alright. I promise I will not spoil it for him."

Michael crossed his arms and rolled his eyes, saying, "Geez ... if you aren't going to tell me then just stop talking about it and let me see it for myself. You know I really hate secrets."

Lieutenant Rachel sat at the dinner table. She rested her head on the palm of her left hand and stared at a bowl of bland beans. In her other hand she held a clean spoon and rested it on the table. She didn't feel like eating right now. It was even harder to eat since there were no spices in it except for a little salt.

Elsa watched her as Rachel sat there looking gloomy. She said, "Lieutenant, aren't you going to eat your dinner?"

Lieutenant Rachael repositioned her head on her hand to look to Elsa. She replied, "I'm sick of eating bland beans."

Giana reached over with her spoon and lightly smacked her on top of the head, saying, "We're all sick of eating bland beans but you still got to eat them."

Lieutenant Rachel lifted herself up and rubbed the spot on her head and said, "I know, Giana."

Tina put a spoonful of beans into her mouth, chewed, and swallowed them. She then pointed her spoon at Lieutenant Rachel and said, "Just admit it, Lieutenant. You're having trouble eating because you're thinking about Lieutenant Michael."

Lieutenant Rachel looked down to her bowl of beans and said, "Yeah, you're right. I think I need to lay down a bit. I'll try to eat these later so don't throw them away. Okay?"

Giana replied, "Okay, Lieutenant. I'll take care of it."

Lieutenant Rachel slid her chair out and stood up. Without looking back she walked into the hallway. Giana, Tina, and Elsa watched her leave. They heard a door open and then shut.

Giana turned back around and glared at Tina, saying, "Why'd you have to say that?"

Tina shrugged her shoulders and said in her seemingly non-caring, melancholy tone, "We all know what the problem is. Don't you think she needs to talk about it?"

Elsa nodded and said, "Yeah, I agree. I think talking about her feelings will help her to feel better."

Giana slumped into her chair and sighed, saying, "I know you're right, but you got to be sensitive about it. Geez, do you always have to be so insensitive about things?"

Tina shrugged her shoulders and replied, "I am the way that I am." She went back to shoveling bland beans into her mouth.

Giana shook her head and said, "Geez, you two stay here and let me talk to her before you make it worse."

Giana slid her chair back and jumped up from her seat. She walked around the corner and stood in front of Lieutenant Rachel's door. She put her hand on the door knob and tried to turn the handle. It was locked.

"Hmm ... looks like it's serious," Giana said to herself. She reached into her pocket and pulled out a hair pin. She stuck the hair pin into the hole in the middle of the handle and there was a small click.

Giana turned the door knob and pushed open the door. Lieutenant Rachel laid there on top of the covers on her bed facing the wall. Without turning, Lieutenant Rachel said, "I thought I locked the door."

Giana replied, as if she had done nothing wrong, saying, "You must have thought you did but you really forgot."

Lieutenant Rachel, in a melancholy tone, replied, "Really?"

Giana ignored her. She strolled over to her bed and jumped onto the side as she sat down on it. The bed jiggled from her weight.

Lieutenant Rachel, not moving, said, "What do you want, Giana?"

Giana began to bounce her feet along the edge of the box spring, saying, "Oh, nothing really. I thought you might want to talk to someone about how you're feeling."

Lieutenant Rachel said, "Not really."

Giana, still bouncing her feet against the box spring, replied, "Well, then, let me tell you how I'm feeling. When I saw you in Lieutenant Michael's bed room this morning, it reminded me of something that happened with Mary back when she started having feelings for Lieutenant Michael."

Lieutenant Rachel finally rolled over to face her. She watched Giana as she told her story.

Giana continued, saying, "I was in her room with her and she took her pillow and hugged it against her chest as she sat next to me. She rested her head on top of the pillow and said, can I tell you a secret? I told her okay. She started to blush really deeply and told me that she was in love with Lieutenant Michael. She then buried her face into that pillow and started to cry. I put my arm around her and held her but nothing I did could ever make her feel better. She knew that no matter what happened, she'd never get to be with him. Every morning she made herself get up and keep going. She tried really hard to be fun and happy so that she could enjoy that small amount of time she had with her team, with him. I know it's hard, Lieutenant. But, we're all very worried about you. Let us help you and I'm sure we can come up with something together."

Lieutenant Rachel sat up and said, "So you think I should just put on a happy face like Mary?"

Giana shook her head and said, "No, that's what Mary did to deal with her situation. What I'm saying is that you're part of our team and we need you to be strong, like Mary was, to help us all to get through it together. I don't want to be insensitive but we really need you to be strong. All of us feel horrible about what's happened and being together is what's going to get us through it."

Lieutenant Rachel stood up and stretched, saying, "Yeah. Okay. I see your point." She held her hand out to Giana and said, "Alright, let's finish those bland beans together."

Giana smiled and took her hand. Together they walked back into the dining room to join the others.

Justice stood in front of a door to what looked like a large warehouse. It was located in a compound that was surrounded by what used to be a chain-link fence that was now torn apart and scattered across the pavement.

Justice put his hand on the door knob and said, "Alright, everybody. Are you ready to see the next truth of this world?"

Michael said, "Yeah, I've been waiting several days for this."

Sarah, Jennifer and Valerie nodded in agreement together.

Justice turned the knob and pushed the door open. He stepped aside, bowed, and pointed inside with his whole hand, saying, "You may enter."

Michael and the girls stepped inside. The first thing they noticed was the stale air that had a dusty smell to it. The room was really dark inside so they could only make out what looked like a counter in front of them. There were quite a few tiny holes in the walls that projected tiny beams of light in the darkness. As their eyes started to adapt to the darkness, they began to see brownish masses sprawled on to the counters randomly.

Justice stepped inside and annunciated loudly, saying, "And God said, Let there be light!" He reached over to his right side on the wall and flipped on a light switch.

The lights overhead suddenly came on, blinding them all for a second. As their eyes started to adjust to the light, Valerie screamed and clung to Michael's arm, burying her face in Michael's shirt.

The randomly placed brownish colored masses were actually dried out human corpses of both men and women. Some of them were slumped over onto what they could now see were some type of computer control panels. Others leaned back in their chairs as if they had died sitting down. Others were lying on the floor. In one corner of the room, there was a large pile of corpses as if they had been stacked there by other people. Bullet casings littered the ground.

Michael looked around in disgust. He said, "What the hell happened here?"

Sarah said, "These people were killed by other people, weren't they?"

Justice pressed forward ahead of them and spun around. He stopped spinning and held his hands up to the ceiling. He laughed psychotically and shouted, "This ... this is what you get for working with the Path of the Future!"

Valerie, who had calmed down, lifted her face from Michael's shirt and said, "What happened to the people here?"

Justice stretched his arms open wide and said, "These people helped in a secret project called 'Spear of Destiny.' When the project was completed, the Path of the Future had them all shot. Special Forces came in with sub-machine guns and fired away till everyone was dead. That's why you were able to see all those tiny holes in the walls. That's where the bullets went through. If that was not enough, they checked each person and shot them in the head if they thought they were still alive."

Sarah's eyes started to tear up and she said, "How horrible!"

Justice held his finger up and calmly said, "Well, I wouldn't feel too bad for them, little Sarah. These people helped to murder many of their fellow humans thinking that they'd become part of the Path of the Future. But, here's the truth: if you are not transcended, the Path of the Future thinks of you no different from the animals. I'd say these people got what they deserved."

Sarah crossed her arms across her chest and said, "It's still really bad."

Michael said, "Is this what you wanted me to see?"

Justice shook his sinister mask and said, "Not at all, Mr. Snyder. This is just the top portion. Remember, I mentioned that there is a secret hanger underneath this complex. What I really want to show you is underneath here."

Justice pulled a key out of his pocket. It was circular with two prongs sticking out, one on each side of the circle. Justice held it up and said, "Mr. Snyder, what I am about to show you is the world's best kept secret. It is the culmination of a secret project called the Spear of Destiny. Have you heard of the Spear of Destiny before, Mr. Snyder?"

Michael nodded and said, "Yeah, I think so. That's the story about the spear that pierced Christ's side when he was on the cross."

Justice walked over to a consul in the middle of the room. As he walked, he said, "That is correct, Mr. Snyder. The Spear of Destiny, also called the Lance of Longinus, is rumored to have a special power that could allow its holder to win every war he waged. It is said that Hitler sought the Spear of Destiny. Allow me to show you the Spear of Destiny held by the Path of the Future."

Justice inserted the key into a hidden lock and twisted it. A keypad materialized on a small glass plane next to the lock. Justice typed in the number six three times on the keypad. A female computer voice spoke saying, "Enter password."

Justice held down another button and spoke, saying, "Alpha and Omega."

The same female's computer voice said, "Confirmed." There was a sudden jolt and a secret door started to raise from the floor. Justice stepped aside and waited till it finished opening.

Inside the secret doorway, there was a staircase that led downward to the secret hanger that was supposed to be below. Justice pointed his hand down the staircase and said, "Follow me if you want to see the Spear of Destiny."

They all followed him down the stairs. As they moved downward, light after light continued to switch on till they had come to the bottom of the stairs. Michael felt his heart beating faster with anticipation.

At the bottom of the stairs, there was a small panel on the side of the wall. Justice pushed a button and the room that they had entered began to light up one light at a time. As each light turned on, there was a loud click that echoed through the facility.

Michael took a few steps into the open hanger. It was larger than the whole compound above it. As he scanned the room, that is when he saw it. He couldn't believe his eyes. He stared at it in confusion. There was a large black object sitting in the middle of the hanger. It was in the shape of a spearhead and it was pure black.

Michael put his hands on top of his head and fell to his knees in shock. His eyes gazed at the object and his mouth hung open.

Valerie became worried and said, "What's wrong, Lieutenant?"

Michael couldn't hear her. He said out loud, "Is ... is that ... is that what I think it is? No way, it can't be."

Josh said, "It is, Michael. It is what you think it is."

Jennifer, just as confused as Valerie, said, "What is it, Lieutenant? What do you see?"

Sarah put her hands on Michael's shoulders and said, "It's the alien ship that attacked our planet."

Understanding fell on Valerie and Jennifer's faces. They stared at the large craft in the middle of the hanger. Jennifer said, "How'd they get one of the alien's ships?"

Justice stepped beside Michael and extended his arm towards the black craft. He said, "Yes, Mr. Snyder, girls. Behold the truth. There were no aliens. This craft that murdered half the world's population was built by humans and it was piloted by humans. There never was any aliens that attacked us. It was a clever plot by the Path of the Future to scare the world into creating a World Government that they could control. This craft is called the Spear of Destiny and it is the source of the Hour of Despair and, like little tears of darkness, they cried death upon half of humanity."

As Michael knelt there he began to remember the events of that day. The Hour of Despair was burned into his memory even though he was only five years old. He remembered watching the Spear of Destiny as it hovered over the playground. He remembered all the hairs on his body standing up as it moved over his head. He remembered the horrible sound it made as the front opened up. The horrible vacuum-like sound it made as the ball of black energy formed out of its tip.

As Michael knelt there, staring at the Spear of Destiny, he said, "Why? Why would they do this to us?"

Justice sympathetically put his hand on Michael's shoulder and gently squeezed it. He said, "Mr. Snyder, there are some really evil people in the world. They are tiny little men and tiny little women with delusions of grandeur that lord themselves over the people in giant towers. They thought the population of the earth was too large to control so they concocted this plan to reduce the population of the earth to a more manageable size."

Tears started to roll down Michael's face. He put his hands over his face and shook his head. Since he was crying, Valerie started to cry too. Jennifer crossed her arms over her chest. Sarah reached over and held Valerie in her arms to comfort her.

Michael composed himself and looked up at Justice, saying, "The weapon ... what was that weapon that erased all those cities?"

Justice, his hand still on Michael's shoulder, said, "For short we call it the S.E.Re.F device, which stands for: Singularity Electron Reconstruction Field. It disassembles all matter into their proton, neutron and electron state, which makes it seem as if it disappears in a blink of an eye."

Michael stood up and shook his head, saying, "I can't believe they'd do this. These people have to be stopped."

Michael turned to his girls and said, "We've got to stop the people who made these before they decide to destroy what remains of the world."

Sarah, still holding Valerie, nodded her head.

Jennifer, still crossing her arms, said, "Yeah. They've been lying to us this whole time about the aliens that attacked us. They've got to be stopped."

Valerie pulled herself from Sarah's embrace and wiped her wet eyes, saying, "Yeah. We got to fight evil, just like the Magical Girls would."

Justice chuckled and said, "See, Mr. Snyder. I knew that when you saw this, you'd be fully committed to the cause of justice."

Michael stood there silently and nodded his head. He could not hide the anger on his face.

\- 5 -

Michael crossed his arms across his chest and started shaking his head out of frustration. He started to pace back and forth and said, "I bet you're going to tell me that the Harvesters aren't really aliens too?"

Josh nodded and replied, "Yeah, you are right. They are not from another world."

Michael ran his hands over the top of his head and gripped his hair. He shouted, "Damn it!" He stopped pacing and stood there glaring at the ground. His hands started to tremble in anger.

Sarah reached out and took one of his hands into her own. His hands stopped trembling and he gently gripped her hand.

Jennifer, crossed her arms across her chest and lowered her gaze to the floor. The memories she had of her past team being killed in front of her, flooded back into her mind. Their cries echoed in her memory. She started to cry and covered her face with her hands.

Michael reached over and pulled her into an embrace with his other arm. She buried her face into his shirt and gripped the fabric with her hands. She muttered, "It's all a lie!"

Valerie tilted her head in confusion and looked to Justice, saying, "If ... if the Harvesters aren't aliens, then where do they come from?"

Justice clasped his hands behind his back and looked down towards her. He replied, "Do you know what a Chimera is?"

Michael hissed and shook his head, saying, "Of course. That makes sense."

Valerie shook her head and said, "No, I never heard that word before."

Justice pointed towards the ceiling and said, "A Chimera is an animal that is made out of the parts of other animals. The Harvesters are made by people in a lab in a process called genetic engineering. They used the genetic parts of stag beetles, ironclad beetles, elephants, abalone, pigs and about thirty three other animals. In fact, Harvesters are completely unable to produce offspring on their own and there are several labs across the world that continually produce them."

Jennifer dropped to her knees and let her arms hang loose beside her. Still crying, she exclaimed, "It's all so pointless! Why? Why would they want people to suffer so much? Why would they make these monsters?"

Raphael scooped Jennifer up in her arms. Jennifer wrapped her legs around her waist and placed her arms around her neck, holding her. She rested her head on Raphael's shoulder. Raphael said, "`Cause their bad men. They do bad things."

At the sight of Jennifer crying, Sarah and Valerie started to tear up too. Valerie leaned against Michael's side. Michael placed his hand on her back.

Justice opened the palm of his right hand and held it up as if he were offering them something and said, "It's all about population control. Have you ever noticed that, when our population reaches a certain point, a sector just happens to fall to the Harvesters? There's no such things as coincidences. They wish to maintain our population around one billion five hundred million people. When our numbers start going over that, another sector falls."

Michael let go of Sarah's hand and pulled her close to his side. He placed his hand on her back. He said, "Okay, I get all that part. It's ... it's ... how ... what ... what am I even trying to say? What about the asteroid that hit. Since they're making the Harvesters, they've got nothing to do with the asteroid, right?"

Justice chuckled and replied, "The asteroid that hit China is a lie too. Lies within lies, Mr. Snyder."

Michael shrugged his shoulders and said, "Wouldn't surprise me now, but there were all these astronomers coming forth and there were all these pictures taken."

Justice stretched his arms wide and said, "And who did those astronomers work for? Who took all those pictures?"

Michael replied, "Mostly NASA and a few other countries' space agencies."

Justice dropped his arms to his side and said, "Yes, mostly NASA and a few friendly countries. These organizations are actually all controlled by the Path of the Future. The astronomers intentionally lied and the pictures were faked. What do you think they did with all those billions of dollars of tax money that they did not have to account for? What really happened was that the Path of the Future dropped a massive nuclear barrage onto most of China. Then they released the first wave of the Harvesters which quickly spread throughout the region."

Michael sighed and said, "I ... none of this is surprising anymore. I've got nothing left to say."

Justice clasped his hands behind his back and said, "Now you see why I had to destroy the walls of Denver Sector."

Michael shook his head and said, "I can't condone what you did. But, I better understand the pressure you are under now."

Justice pulled a very small portable hard drive out of his pocket and held it up for Michael to see. He sounded agitated as he exclaimed, "The information I pulled from Denver Sector is contained on this hard drive. It is what allowed me to gain access to this Spear of Destiny. There were originally twelve of them. This one ship is the last one. Without this information we wouldn't have been able to get our hands on it, neither could we pilot it. Without this ship, we can't win against the Path of the Future."

Michael shrugged his shoulders and said, "I'm not going to argue with you. I understand why you did it and it's already done so there's no point in debating whether it was worth it or not. I wasn't there. We've got the info now so we might as well use it and not let all those deaths be for nothing."

Justice nodded his head and said, "Agreed, Mr. Snyder."

Jennifer had calmed back down as Raphael held her against her chest. Raphael set her back down on her feet. She seemed a little embarrassed by her earlier outcry. She held onto the fabric of the skirt of Raphael's frilly dress.

Gabrielle offered Valerie her hand. Valerie accepted it. Gabrielle pulled her till she was right in front of her. She turned Valerie around so that her back was leaning against her body. She brought her arms around her and draped them over her shoulders and around her neck.

Michelle nonchalantly walked over to Michael's side where Valerie had been. She wrapped her arm around Michael's arm and held it. In response Michael slid his arm out of her grasp. Michelle did it again and looked up at him with a pout. Michael rolled his eyes and let her continue. Michelle leaned into his arm even deeper and rested her head on his arm. He could feel her warm breasts pressing around his arm.

Michael tried to ignore it and said, "Okay, what are we going to do now that we got this Spear of Destiny thing?"

Justice spun in a circle and then stopped with his arm outstretched towards the Spear of Destiny. He exclaimed, "We will travel the world and destroy every single one of those Harvester production facilities. We can't stop this war until those laboratories have been destroyed and it will take them some time to create new facilities to replace them. We can probably stop Harvester production for at least one to two years."

Michael replied, "So we're going to fly this craft over the lab and use that S.E.Re.F device to obliterate those Harvester labs?"

Justice shook his head and said, "No, unfortunately these labs are too deep underground to use the S.E.Re.F on the Spear of Destiny. We're going to have to infiltrate each lab and destroy it from the inside."

Michael sighed and said, "Sounds tedious. How many of these labs are there?"

Josh said, "There are a total of seven labs. Two are in what used to be Russia. One is in what used to be China. One is in what used to be Egypt. One is in what used to be the State of Alaska. One is in what used to be Canada. And one is in what used to be Mexico."

Jennifer said, "So if we destroy these labs then they won't be able to make any Harvesters? Will the war be over then?"

Justice shook his head and said, "We can only temporarily stop the production of Harvesters. To stop the war for good, we'll have to go against the Path of the Future directly. Otherwise, they'll just make new laboratories and it will all be for naught."

Sarah took Michael's hand and squeezed it saying, "We're going to have to kill people aren't we. I don't want to kill people. I think it's bad to kill people."

Michael looked down at her and shook his head, saying, "Don't worry, Sarah. You don't have to fight against people. The rest of us can do the fighting if we have to fight people."

Michelle let go of Michael's arm and stepped in front of Sarah. Her face showed a look of intense distress and anger. She squared her arms on her hips and looked down at her, saying, "I've killed people. Do you think I'm a bad girl?"

Sarah looked down towards the ground and said, "I don't know. I just think it's wrong to kill people. People shouldn't kill other people."

Michelle opened her palms and stared at them. She said, "If I didn't kill people, they would have killed me. They forced me to kill people. Should I have let them kill me instead?"

Sarah looked away from her and kept silent.

Michelle started to laugh nervously. She placed her hands on the sides of her own face and said, "They trained us red Wielders to kill people. Every day I trained and was told I'd be part of the survival game. They made my older sisters kill each other in an arena until there was only one left standing. They told the survivor that she'd join the Path of the Future. But, it was all a lie. I snuck out of my room and watched them hunt the lone survivor for sport. They slaughtered her for fun and skinned her for a trophy."

Michelle started to tremble and her voice became shaky. She continued, saying, "A month later, I turned eleven and it was my turn to play the game. One by one my sisters and I murdered each other. If I didn't kill them, they would have killed me. I tore my sisters apart one by one with my bear hands until there was nobody left. They told me I won a prize, but I knew that it was a lie. They put me in a cage and were going to take me to their hunting ground."

Michelle dropped to her knees and started to cry. She covered her face with her hands and said, "That's when ... that's when Papa saved me. He ... he snuck me out of my cage before the hunt and took me away with my two other sisters."

Michelle reached out with both hands and grabbed the fabric of Sarah's dress over her chest. She asked, "My hands are covered in blood! Am I a bad girl because I had to kill to survive? Do you hate me?"

Sarah was startled as Michelle grabbed her. She wrapped her arms around Michelle and pulled her against her chest. She embraced her and compassionately said, "I'm so sorry I made you feel so bad. I didn't mean to make you think that you were bad. I don't think you're a bad girl. I don't hate you."

Gabrielle, still holding Valerie, said, "Big sister told you her secret. Please don't look at her in in a bad way. She's a really good sister."

Valerie looked up and said, "We've all done things that we feel bad about. Even me. I feel bad about not being strong enough to save Mary. She died because I wasn't strong enough."

Jennifer said, "I let my whole team get killed by the Harvesters. That's something that I will always feel bad about."

Michelle looked up and pouted at Michael, asking, "Do you think I'm a bad girl, Mr. Snyder?"

Michael smiled compassionately at her. He took a step forward and placed his hand on her cheek. He wiped the tears that had rolled down the sides of her face. He said, "Of course not."

Michelle smiled warmly and closed her eyes. She rested the side of her face in the palm of his hand. Michael removed his hand from her face and slipped his hands into her arm pits. He lifted her up and set her on her feet. She fell forward and placed both hands on his chest. She leaned over against him and leaned her head against his chest. He stumbled back a little but managed to steady himself. He put his left arm on her back and rubbed the back of her head with his other hand.

Michael suddenly felt eyes glaring at him like icy daggers. He twisted his head and saw Valerie crossing her arms over her chest. She frowned at him disapprovingly. He further turned and saw Jennifer. She was still clinging to Raphael but she glared at him with a slight frown. He turned his head back to see Sarah. She was glaring at him too. He said, "What? I'm just trying to make her feel better."

Michelle sighed deeply and said, "I wish I could stay in your arms forever."

Justice cleared his throat loudly and said, "We should be on our way now. Every minute we waste the more powerful the Path of the Future becomes."

Michael said, "Yeah. Let's get going. I want to see what this Spear of Destiny can do up close."

Michelle lifted herself off of his chest and looked up at him. She blushed and tilted her head to the side. She batted her eyes at him. She wrapped her arms around his right arm again.

Justice turned towards the Spear of Destiny and started walking towards it with his hands behind his back.

Michael sighed and rolled his eyes. He escorted Michelle towards the craft. Everybody else followed behind them.

Justice wiped the dust off of a panel in the middle section of the craft. There was a very small slit beside it. Justice inserted the USB cord of the external hard drive into the slot. The panel beside it lit up with blue light and a number pad materialized on the screen. Justice inputted another set of numbers and said, "Now we see if it works. If it doesn't, we've come here for nothing."

Suddenly, there was what sounded like a break and a crack appeared along the side of the craft. Sarah, Jennifer and Valerie jumped in shock at the sound. The crack spread into a rectangle pattern along the side of the craft like a door. The top of the rectangle began to pop out of the side of the craft and lowered to the ground like a ramp.

The doorway that appeared was dark. Justice held up his hand and it began to glow with the strange white fire of his power. He turned to the others and said, "Wait here while I turn on the power."

Justice stepped forward into the craft and sat down in the pilot's chair. He inserted the USB plug into the panel and another number pad materialized on a monitor on the control panel. He inputted another number and the control panel in front of him lit up. The control panel started to beep as the computer came to life. He began to press buttons and the inside of the cabin lit up.

Justice called out from his seat and said, "Alright, my friends. Come aboard!"

Michael entered first and stood in the doorway. There was only one seat in the entire cabin. He said, "Guess we'll have to cram together on the floor."

Justice, still focusing on the control panel, replied, "My apologies, Mr. Snyder. The Spear of Destiny was designed to only be piloted by one person. In fact, it can also be piloted remotely but I am disabling that feature so that it does not hinder us in the future in case they try to take control of this craft."

Michael sat down on the floor. Valerie sat down on his right side and Jennifer sat down on his left side. Sarah sat down next to Jennifer. Michelle stepped inside and stomped her foot on the metal floor, saying, "I wanted to sit down next to Mr. Snyder!"

Valerie wrapped an arm around Michael's torso and leaned her head against his arm. She glared at Michelle and said, "He's my Lieutenant. I want to sit next to him this time. You're getting too clingy!"

Michelle looked to Jennifer. Jennifer wrapped an arm around Michael's arm and leaned her head against his arm. She started to blush and looked down to the floor embarrassed. She said, "It's ... it's my turn to sit next to the Lieutenant."

Michelle drooped her shoulders and sighed heavily. Sarah patted the floor beside her and said, "You can sit down next to me, big sister."

Michelle grinned and acted bubbly, saying, "Okay!" She dropped down to the floor and smiled at Sarah. She wrapped her arm around Sarah's arm.

Raphael sat down next to Michelle. She crossed her legs over each other and crossed her arms across her chest as if she were annoyed. She muttered to herself, "I dislike flying."

Gabrielle fanned the skirt of her frilly dress and then gently sat down on the floor. She brushed the skirt of her dress over her legs.

Josh sat down next to Gabrielle. Instead of acting nervous, Gabrielle said, "Mr. O'Brian, would you mind if I rested my head on your shoulder?"

Josh patted his shoulder with his hand and said, "Sure, go right ahead."

Gabrielle wrapped an arm around his arm and leaned over against his side. She rested her head on his arm, saying, "I'll be taking a quick nap. Wake me up if we get there before I wake up." She closed her eyes.

Justice turned his head and said, "Everybody ready? Good. Let's get going." He pushed a button and the door that was used as a ramp began to lift up and reset itself into the side of the craft into its original position.

Justice began to press more buttons and the Spear of Destiny began to silently hum. There was a sudden click, which Michael thought was the landing pads. The craft appeared to simply hover up and down for lift off, which meant that it didn't require any wheels. Michael could feel the Spear of Destiny hovering in the air.

The engine appeared to be on but the noise was so silent on the inside that it seemed like there was no engine. Michael said, "Mr. Justice, how does this craft fly? It moves like a helicopter but it doesn't have any propellers and I didn't see anything that could be called a thrust port either?"

Justice chuckled and said, "Yes, Mr. Snyder. The Spear of Destiny uses secret technology that the unwashed masses aren't allowed to have. The concept for the engine of the Spear of Destiny was first conceived by a man named Nikola Tesla. He determined that the earth produces an electro-magnetic field that could be harvested. Members of the Path of the Future within the American Government murdered Tesla, stole his research and used it to create this engine that can literally ride the electro-magnetic currents of the earth."

Michael said, "Hold on. Didn't Tesla die of old age? He was pretty old when he died."

Justice chuckled again and said, "Yes, he was old. But, that is what makes it more believable that he just died of old age. The truth is, that he refused to give up his rights to the technology he invented. So, the Government murdered him using a type of poison that cannot be detected. The poison gives you a heart attack so it looks like you died from a normal heart attack."

Michael nodded and said, "I see. So the Spear of Destiny uses Tesla's ideas of electro-magnetic energy to fly."

Justice nodded and replied, "Yes. For this reason the Spear of Destiny doesn't even need to carry fuel except for a battery that is kept recharged by the free electricity produced by the earth. Tesla also wanted all of mankind to have this freely produced energy but the Path of the Future wanted to enslave mankind with energy so they killed him so that his ideas could be lost to the people. Their plan was to gain the rights to his technology and then never let anybody know about it. Tesla refused so they had to kill him."

Michael sighed and replied, "Yeah. That makes sense. People just want to have power over other people and to make money off of them."

Justice turned the Spear of Destiny towards the hanger door and inputted another number into its control computer. The hanger door must have been operated by a remote control on the craft since after Justice inputted the number it slowly started to open. After it was finished, the Spear of Destiny hovered toward the opening and entered into the open area of the sky.

If it wasn't for the cockpit window, you would not have been able tell that it was moving. There was only a slight vibration that they could feel as they sat on the floor of the cockpit. The ground rushed below them at speeds that Michael didn't think were possible. The craft rose higher and higher into the sky and the ground began to look small beneath them.

Justice announced, saying, "The Spear of Destiny moves so fast that it should only take us an hour to cross the area once known as Russia to get to the first Harvester Production Facility."

Michelle took Sarah's hand and held it as they sat down together. Sarah looked up at her and wondered what she was thinking. Sarah looked down at the skirt of Michelle's frilly dress. She wondered how it always stayed so poufy. She said, "Big sister, how does your dress stay so poufy?"

Michelle looked down at the skirt of her dress and said, "Oh ... it's because of my petticoat. It keeps my dress in that perfect A-frame."

Sarah said, "Isn't it hard to fight in?"

Michelle shrugged her shoulders and said, "Not really. Guess I'm just used to it."

Valerie joined in and said, "How come you all put crosses on your dresses?"

Gabrielle replied, "Because we believe in Jesus Christ."

Jennifer said, "You still believe in a God even though you've seen so many horrible things?"

Gabrielle held up her finger and pointed towards the ceiling. She said, "It's because I've seen so many horrible things that I believe in God. There can't be an ultimate evil without there being an ultimate good. God is the embodiment of good in the world. The devil is the embodiment of evil in the world."

Jennifer said, "But if there were a God, why would he let the bad men do so much evil to the people in the world?"

Gabrielle tilted her head upward and looked to be in deep thought. She looked to Jennifer and replied, "God made us to be free. This means that people who choose to do evil have to be allowed to do it. If God stopped us, when we tried to do something bad, then it wouldn't be a test. The point of this life is to test us to see what we will do with the freedom we have been given. The Path of the Future was able to get so much power to do evil because the people of the world were so focused on making money and living their daily lives that they wouldn't come to realize what was happening in the world. Thus, this evil in the world is a result of the people not paying attention. We are going to stop them and show the world what they did, then the people can make good choices again. That is our purpose."

Michelle said, "Jennifer, do you believe in God?"

Jennifer slowly shook her head and said, "No, I didn't want to believe in God because of all the bad things that happened in the world."

Michelle replied, "What about now?"

Jennifer looked down and shyly said, "I ... I don't know anymore. I never heard that idea about freedom before. I'll have to think about it."

Valerie said, "I believe in God."

Jennifer said, "Yeah, we all know you do."

Within about forty-five minutes, the Spear of Destiny reached its destination. The craft hung in the sky above a scorched wasteland in the lower part of what used to be Russia. The craft began to descend from the sky. There was a faint click and the landing pads extended from the bottom of the craft. The Spear of Destiney touched the ground and jolted as the electro-magnetic field shut off allowing its own weight to dig into the ground.

Justice slipped out of his chair and said with a bow, "Ladies and gentlemen, we have arrived at our first Harvester Production Facility."

Michael stood up and stretched. He held out his hands and helped Jennifer and Valerie get to their feet. Sarah stood up on her own and brushed the skirt of her dress.

The door to the Spear of Destiny began to lower to the ground. The sun was still high in the sky revealing the scorched earth around them. Dead trees laid all in the same direction, revealing which way the force of an explosion knocked them. In the silence, the screeches of Harvesters could be heard.

Justice put his backpack on and said, "My apologies, Mr. Snyder, but in order to mask our approach, I had to turn off the Harvester repelling device. We will have to deal with the Harvesters before entering the facility."

Michael smiled and said, "No problem. I'm used to being in the field with my girls."

Jennifer smashed her fist into the palm of her other hand and said, "I like it this way better. I've been itching to squash some bugs."

Michelle reached her hand over and put it on top of Jennifer's head, saying, "I like your style, little sister. How about you and I team up together and you can show me what you've got?"

Jennifer smiled and gave her a thumbs up. She replied, "Sounds good to me. Maybe you can help me to learn how to unleash my real power?"

Michelle grinned and nodded.

Gabrielle put her hand around Sarah's arm and said, "We should team up too, little sister, and I'll help you to unleash your full power."

Sarah nodded and said, "Yeah, sounds good to me."

Valerie looked to Raphael with expectation. Raphael stood there silently with her arms folded across her chest, looking out the open door.

Valerie said, "Big sister Raphael."

Raphael turned to her and said, "Don't you want to team up with me too?"

Raphael dropped her arms and said, "Yeah. I guess that would be okay. But, can you even fight?"

Valerie brought her fists up together underneath her chin. She looked hopefully at Raphael and said, "I can fight too. I already can steal energy from Harvesters."

Raphael nodded her head and said, "Really? That's good. That means it will be easier to draw your real power out."

Justice pointed to the open door and said, "Are we ready to go, ladies?"

Valerie started to pout and her head became subdued. She raised her hand.

Justice pointed at her and said, "Yes, little Valerie. Do you have a question?"

Valerie put her hand down and said, "Could I go pee first?"

Jennifer spoke up saying, "Yeah, me too."

Sarah ran her right hand across the top of her own head, saying, "I wouldn't mind going to the bathroom first too."

Michelle laughed and said, "Yeah. Good idea. We'll go together."

Gabrielle nodded and said, "Yeah, you men might be able to hold it for hours on end, but us women can't."

Justice chuckled and said, "My apologies. You six can go to the bathroom outside before we start."

The six girls exited the craft together. Sarah, Jennifer and Valerie's pee was still silver.

TEARS OF DARKNESS

CHAPTER 07

FALLEN ANGELS

- 1 -

The six girls stood together in a line with the Spear of Destiny behind them. Each girl stood next to her partner. Justice stood in front of them with Michael and Josh on each one of his sides.

Justice waved his hand to the girls and said, "The hidden entrance isn't too far. Should take us about twenty minutes to walk there if the Harvesters don't get in our way."

Michelle, Gabriel and Raphael's eyes began to glow with the light of their color. Their hands began to produce red, blue and yellow flames. Their hands radiated with the light of their flames.

Michelle snickered and said, "I hope they do."

Sarah, Jennifer, and Valerie followed their examples. Their eyes glowed with their blue, red and yellow light. Their hands began to radiate with the light of their color.

Jennifer looked at her hands and said, "I think my hands look brighter."

Sarah looked at her own hands and said, "Yeah, I think my hands look brighter too. I also think I feel a little bit lighter."

Gabrielle said, "That's the result of the toxins and nano-machines leaving your body."

Michelle said, "Yeah, try putting more power into your hands, but if you start feeling pain, stop. That means that you've reached your limit and it would be dangerous to do more. The toxins and nano-machines are probably still inside you. You'll know when they're gone when you stop peeing silver."

Jennifer focused on her hands and put a little more energy into them. They began to grow brighter and the light extended a little bit further down her wrist. She smiled and closed her fist tightly.

Sarah put a little bit of her own energy into her hands and they also glowed brighter. She held up both her hands and said, "I definitely feel stronger."

Valerie tried it too. Her hands also glowed brighter and the light extended further down her wrist. She smiled and giggled as she watched the change in her hands. She said, "I bet I can do even more now."

Raphael nodded and said, "Yeah, but don't get ahead of yourself. Don't do something that would hurt you."

Valerie nodded and started to twist herself side to side, saying, "Yeah, I got it. I'll be careful."

Michael put his hand on Valerie's head and said, "Yeah, be sure that you are careful. I don't want anybody getting hurt."

Michael rubbed Valerie's head and then rubbed the top of Jennifer's and Sarah's heads. Michelle leaned forward and gazed at Michael with an expectant look. Michael rolled his eyes and then patted Michelle on the head. Michelle clapped her hands together and spun in a circle in delight. She squealed in excitement and exclaimed, "Alright, now I'm ready too!"

Justice turned towards the wasteland and walked forward with his hands held behind his back. A junior-sized Harvester screeched in the distance. Its call would certainly bring more with it. The Harvester started to run towards them.

Jennifer shouted, "I want this one!" She took off running towards it before anybody could stop her.

Michael wanted to yell at her to stop out of habit and wait for his orders but then remembered that he was not really their Lieutenant anymore. He nervously sighed and decided to wait and see what they would do. Even if he did issue orders, it was not like they had their com units anymore. He would have to yell at them if he needed to communicate with them.

Jennifer ran faster than normal. She felt lighter than she had ever felt before. Her feet started to radiate with her red light. She jumped towards the Harvester. She jumped further then she expected. In one leap she was about to crash into the face of the Harvester. She extended her foot as if she was going to kick it. The sole of her foot crashed into the face of the Harvester.

The Harvester was flung back by the impact. It landed on its back. Its legs soon stopped twitching. Jennifer walked around to where the head was. As she saw its face, her jaw dropped in shock. The head was completely split open. Yellow Harvester goo started to spill from the dead Harvester.

Jennifer ran back and shouted, "Did you see that? I killed it with only one hit!"

Michael nodded his head and said, "Yeah, I saw. That was amazing!"

Jenifer ran up to Michael and crashed into his torso. She put her hands on his chest and excitedly said, "I feel so much stronger now!"

Michael patted her on the back and said, "Yeah, I bet." He felt a twinge of guilt as he remembered that the reason they couldn't have their full power before was because he gave them those shots that kept their power in check. The shot that killed them. Mary's smiling face flashed in his memory.

Michelle shouted, bringing him back into the present, "More Harvesters are coming. Let's play with 'em."

Michelle's feet began to glow with red fire. She skated toward a line of three fully-grown Harvesters. As she passed each one she slashed her arm across their heads. One by one their heads fell off and they collapsed over the weight of their own dead bodies.

On the other side, a group of six fully-grown Harvesters came charging at them. Gabrielle held her right hand up and turned her palm towards them. Her hand radiated with blue fire. A beam of energy came out and punched a hole through two of them.

Sarah extended her hands together and turned her palms towards the third fully-grown Harvester. Her hands radiated with blue light. A beam of energy shot out of her hands. It hit the third Harvester, causing it to shriek in pain and to tremble. She saw the burn mark that was on the shell and thought to herself, *Did I already punch it?* She pointed her palms toward the burn mark and shot at the Harvester again. She hit the burn mark in the center and fragments of the Harvesters shell exploded flinging white flesh and yellow blood out of the hole. The Harvester rolled over from the force of the blast. Its legs slowly stopped twitching

Sarah gazed at the sight with her eyes wide and mouth wide open. She had managed to punch through a Harvester shell in only two strikes. She could feel the power surging through her arms when she used her spear of light ability now. She smiled at the sight of the dead Harvester and because of the feeling of her new power.

While Sarah was admiring her handiwork, Gabrielle finished off the other three fully-grown Harvesters without a problem. Sarah turned to Michael and said, "Lieutenant! Did you see me take out that fully-grown Harvester in only two hits?"

Michael nodded his head and replied, "Yeah, I did. Good job!"

With the local Harvesters dealt with, they continued to follow Justice to the secret entrance. There was a small hill with a crevice that looked randomly placed in the side of the hill. Justice pointed at the crevice and said, "There's the entrance."

Michael looked at it and chuckled, saying, "Really? Are you sure we can squeeze through there?"

Justice laughed and said, "I hope so otherwise, you'd have to stay out here with the Harvesters."

Justice squeezed himself through first. Michael and Josh followed behind him. Michael squeezed through without much effort. Josh's coat snagged on a rock that stuck out in the middle of the crevice opening. He heard a tear and said, "Damn it! I tore my coat."

Inside the crevice, the room was hollowed out into a small cube. There was a steel door on the side of the back wall with a computer access pad next to it.

Valerie turned to her side and slid right through the crevice without touching the sides. She smiled and raised her hands, saying, "I fit with no problem."

Jennifer came in next, the same way, and said, "That's because you're so shrimpy."

Valerie dropped her arms and balled her fists, saying, "You're just as shrimpy as me!"

Sarah came in next. She slid in without any resistance and stood between Valerie and Jennifer, saying, "Come on now, this is no time to fight."

Raphael started to squeeze herself through the crevice opening next. She pushed herself through and then began to check around the skirt of her dress. She said, "That's good, I was afraid that my dress would get ripped. My hips are pretty shapely."

Gabrielle began to squeeze herself through the crevice. She stopped in the middle and exclaimed, "This crevice is horrid." She exhaled and then forced her way through it. When she entered the excavated room she gasped for air and then checked her dress for tears. There were none.

Michelle stared down the crevice and sighed.

Gabrielle called out to her and said, "Sister, I do believe that you are too top heavy to make it through that crevice."

Michelle squared her arms on her hips and said, "Ridiculous! I can make it."

Michelle turned to her side and began to squeeze herself through the crevice. Half way through, she stopped and said, "My chest is stuck between the rocks!"

Gabrielle poked her head into the crevice and said, "I told you that your chest was too big."

Sarah looked down at her own chest and remembered her conversation with Lieutenant Rachel on how her breasts got in the way of her own military duty. Sarah thought to herself, *I wish I didn't get breasts, it's not like ...* She stopped herself and remembered that she didn't have to worry about dying at a really young age anymore. She could actually grow up and become an adult ... like Mary wanted to be. Thinking about Mary made her sad again.

Michelle called out to Gabrielle, saying, "I can make it. Just take my hand and pull me in!"

Gabrielle reached her arm into the crevice opening and grabbed Michelle's hand. She grunted as she pulled her sister through.

Michelle entered into the excavated room with her face grimacing. She started to massage her chest, saying, "Dang it, that hurt."

Michael looked away from her in embarrassment.

Michelle checked her dress for tears and found none. She exclaimed, "Excellent! Not a single tear. Goes to show you the excellent quality of my handiwork."

Gabrielle patted her on the back and said, "True, sister. I admit that I am shocked that you didn't get a single tear on your dress."

Justice clapped his hands and said, "Are we all ready?"

Everyone nodded their heads.

Josh threw his hands up in the air and exclaimed, "Excellent! Today, we begin destroying the infrastructure of the Path of the Future."

Justice gripped onto Michelle's chin and said, "My darling red angel, I want you to support me from behind with your pistol. I'll keep point and Mr. O'Brian and Mr. Snyder's team will be in the back. My darling blue and yellow angels, I want you to stay behind your big sister, okay?"

Michelle, Gabrielle and Raphael said in unison, "Okay, Papa!"

Justice looked back to Josh and Michael. They both nodded at him.

Michelle lifted up the skirt of her dress and pulled out what looked like an old matchlock pistol from the old days. It had a black metal barrel with a light brown wooden handle. She held it up pointing it to the ceiling.

Michael laughed and said, "Michelle, what good is an old-fashioned matchlock pistol going to do?"

Michelle turned around and looked at him impishly. She tilted her head and said, "Don't worry. This pistol has a surprise in it."

Justice turned back to the door and said, "Great! Now to open this door."

The door appeared to be solid steel. It looked like it had an advanced locking mechanism that was designed to lock the door into the side of the wall. Justice bent over and stared at the computer terminal with his hands behind his back. He seemed to hesitate.

Michael said, "Do you have the code for this door too?"

Justice stood up straight and looked at the door, saying, "Code? Oh, no. I don't have a code to open the door."

Michael scratched his head and said, "If you don't have the code, how are we supposed to get in?"

Justice clapped his hands together and held them together as if in prayer. He said, "The old fashioned way."

Justice's hands began to glow with a white fire. He balled his hand into a fist and pulled it back as far as he could.

Michael said, "You've got to be kidding me. There's no way you can punch through that door."

Without replying, Justice smashed his fist into the door. There was a loud metal clang and at the spot where he had hit the door, there was a huge dent in it. Justice pulled his hand back again and punched the door again. The whole frame shook and small rocks broke off from around the door. Justice hit the door a third time and a fourth time. On the fifth time, the door blew out of the frame and flew down an open hallway.

Immediately, Justice put up a shield barrier around himself and a hail of bullets flew down the hallway. The bullets ricocheted off of his shield, causing a pinging sound, and rebounded into the hallway walls. There was a team of guards that stood around the opening into another room at the end of the hall.

Michael stood there in disbelief as he tried to wrap his head around the idea that a man just punched a solid steel door open. Out of shock Sarah, Jennifer and Valerie grabbed at the fabric of his T-shirt.

Michelle walked forward and somehow was able to walk through the back of Justice's shield. She extended her arm and held the gun up, pointing it down the hallway at a man in black body armor. The man held up a riffle and fired in short bursts.

Michelle stuck the barrel of the pistol out of Justice's shield and pulled the trigger. There was a very timid popping sound and a small sphere of black energy shot out of the barrel of the pistol. It sped down the hallway and hit the man, who stood there firing at them, in the face. Instantly, the man's head disappeared into nothingness. The man fell over backward. Blood spilled out of his open neck. His riffle began to pour out bullets as the man's death grip held down on the trigger out of reflex.

What Michael had thought was an old pistol, turned out to use the same technology of the S.E.Re.F device used by the Spear of Destiny. Michelle started to cackle with delight and she shouted out, "Stop hiding guys, I wanna play!"

Michelle pointed her pistol at another man. There was another timid pop and a small black sphere of energy sped towards another guard. It hit him square in the chest, leaving a gaping hole in the center of his torso that went clean through. The man collapsed backwards and dropped his gun as he writhed on the floor.

Sarah and Valerie buried their faces into Michael's sides. Jennifer stood there watching the onslaught, still holding onto the fabric of Michael's shirt. He could feel Sarah's body trembling against his own. He put a hand on her back and held her tight to try to comfort her.

One by one, Michelle pointed her pistol at each of the guards. Each time she pulled the trigger, there was a timid pop and a small black sphere of energy shot out of the barrel and flew towards its target. The last guard looked around himself at all his dead comrades. He turned to run away, but Michelle had already shot at him. The sphere of black energy hit the man in the middle of his thigh, causing the lower part of his leg to break off. The man dropped to the floor and began to scream in agony. He started to crawl along the floor to hide behind the wall. A trail of blood followed behind him.

Michelle looked up at Justice with a smile, saying, "Can I finish him, Papa?"

Justice nodded and said, "Make sure he doesn't suffer."

Michelle stepped out of Justice's shield bubble and walked down the hallway with her pistol hanging by her side in her hand. She walked up to the man with one leg and held the pistol up towards his face.

The man rolled over onto his back. His face gazed back at her in pain and terror. The man muttered, saying, "Who? Who the hell are you?"

Michelle grinned psychotically and tilted her head to the side. She softly said, "I am the angel of death." She pulled the trigger and the man's head vanished. She turned back to Justice and said, "Papa, it's all clear down here."

Justice put his hands behind his back and said, "Excellent work, my darling angel." The shield barrier he had put up disappeared. He stepped forward and the rest of them followed behind.

Sarah, Valerie and Jennifer continued to hold onto Michael's T-shirt as they walked down the hallway. Sarah looked past Justice to see the dead bodies on the floor. Their blood puddled onto the floor around their dead bodies. At the sight of it, she remembered the puddle of blood mixed with water on the bathroom floor that belonged to Jennifer. She remembered the dead bodies in front of the grocery store. She pushed the feeling of nausea down inside of herself.

Valerie started to quiver and she said, "Are ... are you sure it's safe now?"

Gabrielle looked at her and replied, "It's never safe during an operation, but I'll do my best to protect you."

Sarah nodded her head and said, "Yeah, Valerie. Don't forget our promise. We're going to protect each other still."

Jennifer nodded and said, "Yeah, we're going to do our best to protect each other."

Michelle pointed at the floor and said, "Be careful not to slip on all the blood."

Michael shook his head and said, "I don't like exposing my girls to this."

Surprisingly, Sarah tugged on his shirt and looked up at him, saying, "I ... I think it's okay, Lieutenant. I know this is some really bad stuff, but there's no other way to stop it."

Jennifer nodded shyly, she put her finger to her lip and meekly said, "Yeah, I agree. As ... as long as I got you with me, I'll be okay."

Valerie added her own thoughts, saying, "I'm scared. But, these people help the Path of the Future to do really bad things so I don't feel too bad for them. They should stop the bad men instead of helping them. I'm not so scared since you are with me too."

Michael sighed and said, "Well, I'm glad that you're handling all of this okay. I'm still worried though about letting you all see stuff like this. You shouldn't be involved in this. But, as long as you want to keep going, I'll support you."

They stood together in what looked like to be some kind of waiting room or front office. They moved further in so that they would not stand in the blood that pooled on the floor. Suddenly, there was a beeping sound. Gabrielle pulled out a pocket watch and clicked a small button on it. She said, "It's time for tea."

Michael chuckled and said, "There's no time for tea now, we're in the middle of an operation."

Raphael took the backpack off of her back and pulled out the small blanket that they had sat on earlier in the day. She spread it on the ground and sat down on it.

Gabrielle pulled the small portable stove out of her own backpack and began setting it up beside herself.

Michael shook his head and laughed in frustration, saying, "Come on. You can't be serious? We're in the middle of a mission now."

Michelle twitched her head, flinging her hair to her side and said, "Calm down, Mr. Snyder. It's time for afternoon tea. Why don't you come join me this time? I'll let you sip out of my cup. It'll be like an indirect kiss." She pulled the basket containing the tea set out of her backpack.

Sarah, Jennifer and Valerie glanced at each other. Sarah shrugged her shoulders and the three of them sat down on the blanket with Michelle, Gabrielle and Raphael. Michelle distributed teacups and saucers to them.

Michael turned to Justice and began to gesture with his hands flinging towards the girls, saying, "Are you going to allow this?"

Justice shrugged his shoulders and held up his hands questioningly, saying, "What do you want me to do about? It's time for tea."

Michael looked at Josh. Josh silently shrugged his shoulders and sat down on the blanket. Justice sat down next to him. And wrapped his arms around his own legs as he sat on the ground. Josh said, "I told you they take their tea time seriously. Just roll with it, brother."

Michael dropped his hands in defeat and sighed. He sat down on the blanket next to Josh and said, "I see what you meant now."

Gabrielle poured tea in the six cups. Valerie turned it down and offered the cup to Justice. Justice smiled with a nod and said, "Thank you, Valerie. That is very sweet of you."

Valerie tilted her head and shrugged her shoulders saying, "I don't like tea that much and I felt bad that you weren't getting any."

Justice took the teacup and saucer with a nod. He pulled a metal straw out of his pocket and began to sip on the tea underneath his mask.

As they were drinking, a squadron of guards in black armor burst into the room. Immediately, Justice put up his shield barrier. The guards raised their guns and began to fire at them as they sat on the ground. The bullets ricocheted off of the shield barrier with a ping and smashed into the walls around them.

Justice and the three angels sat there calmly ignoring the guards. Sarah, Jennifer and Valerie looked around nervously. Michael pointed at the guards and said, "Don't you think we should deal with them before we finish our tea?"

Gabrielle sighed and rolled her head annoyed. She said, "Fine, Mr. Snyder! You're so impatient! I'll deal with them now and I shan't even spill my tea."

Gabrielle stood up, holding her teacup by the handle in her left hand. She widened her stance and caused her right hand to glow with blue fire. She made a sudden jerking motion and a small splash of tea spilled over the rim of her cup, splashing onto the floor.

Raphael laughed and pointed at the spot on the ground where the drop of tea had landed. She said, "Sister, I do believe you've spilt your tea."

Gabrielle looked surprised and said, "What?" She looked down to her feet and saw a small drop of liquid on the floor. She screamed in frustration and raised the teacup high into the air. She then threw it to the floor, causing it to shatter at her feet. She yelled, "Damn it! Look what you made me do!"

Both of Gabrielle's hands began to burn with blue fire. She raised her hands up into the air and curled her fingers. Two bluish spheres of energy surrounded two of the guards. Gabrielle then closed her fists tightly.

The two spheres began to shrink and both of the guards began to scream as they helplessly tried to push the sphere back out. As the sphere shrunk there was the sound of bones breaking. The men screamed out and begged for her to stop. The spheres continued to contract until their bodies burst and blood began to fill the bottom of the sphere. Gabrielle opened her hands and the two spheres disappeared. Two mangled corpses dropped to the floor and blood rained down on top of them spilling blood all over the floor.

A guard shouted out, "Fall back, we've got Wielders here!" The men began to step backwards as they continued to point their weapons at the invaders.

Gabrielle said, "Oh, I don't think so." She reached underneath her skirt and pulled out two metal sticks that were similar to the ones that Sarah used. She erected her own barrier around herself and surrounded the sticks with blue energy. She stepped out of the barrier shield created by Justice and walked towards the guards who were moving backwards. She held the two sticks by her sides. They seemed to burn with blue fire like her hands. She angled them upwards and continued to walk at a steady pace towards the retreating guards. She smiled psychotically at them as she moved closer towards them.

Sarah knew what was going to happen next. She jumped into Michael's lap and buried her face into his chest. Michael wrapped his arms around her and held her tightly. Valerie followed her example and leaned her face onto Michael's arm, closing her eyes. Jennifer watched intently to see exactly what would happen.

Gabrielle started to run. She dropped her shield and began to swing her flaming metal sticks around like swords. The first guard was instantly cut in half through the stomach. The second guard had his head cut cleanly off. The third guard pointed his riffle at her but she quickly severed his hands from his arms and then cut off his head. The next two guards were also cut in half.

The sixth guard managed to fire a couple of rounds which pierced into Gabrielle's thigh. Gabrielle grunted in pain and cut off his hands and legs in one swipe. She then pierced his chest with both of her sticks as she stood over him.

The last two guards dropped their riffles and raised their arms above their heads in surrender. They dropped to their knees and began to plead for their lives.

Gabrielle laughed and said, "There is no mercy for the wicked!" With a single swipe she sliced through their arms and necks. Their hands and heads dropped to the floor. They fell over backwards, dead.

The blue fire that covered her sticks and hands withdrew back inside herself. There were blood splatters all over her dress and a trickle of blood spilled from her leg wounds. She limped back over and sat down next to Justice, saying, "One of them shot me in the leg, Papa."

Gabrielle lifted the skirt of her dress exposing her pantaloons. On her thigh area there were two bullet holes in her pantaloons and blood was absorbed into the fabric.

Justice reached over and tore her pantaloons where the two holes were. He looked and said, "You were careless, my darling angel. You let your anger get the better of you."

Gabrielle nodded and said, "I know, Papa. I'm sorry. They just made me really angry so I lost control of myself again."

Raphael leaned over to look at the wound and said, "Admit it, sister. You were just showing off for Mr. O'Brian."

Gabrielle blushed and said, "I was not!"

Raphael scooted over next to her and said, "Papa, do you want me to do it?"

Justice shook his head and said, "No, let me do it this time." His hand began to burn with white fire again. He held his open palm over her wound and then closed his fist. A tiny orb of light lifted up out of her thigh. He then opened his hand and a small bullet dropped out of the air. He did it a second time and the second bullet came out of her thigh as well.

Justice put his glowing hand on her wounds and his white light spread onto her thigh. He lifted up his palm and the two bullet holes were completely healed. The white fire around his hands disappeared and he slid his hands under her armpits. He lifted her up to her feet and then patted her on the head, saying, "All better, my angel?"

Gabrielle smiled and nodded once, saying, "Thank you, Papa. I feel all better."

Valerie stood up and looked at the place where Gabrielle had been shot. She said, "Wow, Mr. Justice. You really do have all our powers."

Justice chuckled and threw up his hands high up into the air and exclaimed, "That's right, little Valerie! I'm magnificent, aren't I?"

Michael recognized the look that was on Valerie's face. It meant that she was unsure of herself or something. Valerie said, "Yeah."

Valerie looked at Gabrielle and said, "Are you really okay? Did it hurt to get shot?"

Gabrielle walked over to Valerie and wrapped her arms around her, pressing Valerie's body into her own in a big embrace. She lowered her head and said, "Yeah, it hurt. But, I'm used to pain now. So, it was nothing. I've got three people now who can heal me."

Michelle pointed at the shattered teacup and said, "Sister, was it really necessary to smash my teacup on the floor?"

Gabrielle looked towards Michelle with a confused look on her face. She tilted her head and said, "What?"

Michelle pointed at the shattered teacup again and said, "Look there. You shattered one of my teacups again."

Gabrielle turned her head to see what Michelle was pointing at. She saw the shattered cup on the floor and sighed. She looked down to the floor and said, "Oh. I'm sorry, sister. I didn't mean to do it again. I just forgot myself because I got angry."

Michelle exhaled loudly and crossed her arms over her chest. She sounded annoyed as she said, "I forgive you, sister, but now we're short another teacup. What shall we do for our next tea time?"

Sarah jumped into the conversation, saying, "Well, why don't we just go to the store and get another one?" She started to laugh at her own joke.

Raphael raised her hand and pointed toward the ceiling, saying, "Our little sister has a good idea."

Sarah shrugged her shoulders and said, "Well, I meant it as a joke."

Raphael shook her finger at her and said, "No, I mean I'm sure we can find a new teacup in this place. We might even be able to find some more tea."

Justice clapped his hands together and said, "Alright, everybody. Now that tea time is over, let's get back to work. While we're at it, we'll also look for a new teacup."

Michael ran his hand through his hair and said, "How many guards do you think we can expect at this facility?"

Josh spoke up saying, "I would imagine that there are probably three or four squads. Around probably sixty guards."

Michael nodded his head and said, "Oh, I see. That sounds right for an advanced military laboratory like this I suppose."

Josh laughed and said, "You have no idea if that is right or not, do you?"

Michael shrugged his shoulders and shook his head, saying, "No, I don't."

- 2 -

Justice turned to the door where the second group of guards had come out of. His hands burned with his white fire again. He pulled his fist back and smashed it into the door. There was another clang of metal and the door ripped from its hinges and landed with a crash.

Valerie tried to peer around him and saw that the door had flown across the room some twenty feet. She looked on in amazement and said, "Wow! I'm still surprised how strong you are, Mr. Justice."

Justice erected his shield barrier and gripped his hands behind his back. He paused for a moment and turned his sinister mask towards her. He said, "Just wait till you see my full power, little Valerie."

Justice turned his head back forward and entered into the room. The three angels followed behind him.

Michael, Josh and the girls came in next. Michael looked around the room to see a bunch of lab desks and scared looking men and women in white lab coats. The lab workers began to huddle behind their desks.

Justice lowered his shield barrier and stretched his arms open wide. He looked around the room and shouted, "Greetings ladies and gentlemen! Pardon the intrusion, but we have come to destroy the Harvester factory that is hiding beneath your feet."

Justice dropped his arms and then lifted a finger. He waved it and said, "Now, now, now. Don't try to deny it. I know all about it already. I will give you this opportunity to escape if you ..."

A man, hiding behind a counter, pointed a gun in Justice's direction and fired. The man must not have had much experience and instead of hitting Justice, the bullet hit the wall to the side of him.

Justice immediately put up his shield barrier again. The scared man stood up and began to pull the trigger of his pistol. Bullets fired off in random directions, only occasionally hitting the shield with a ping and ricocheting in a random direction.

The man's clip went empty and the pistol slider opened. Valerie recognized the sound it made and said, "He's empty."

The man dropped the pistol and got on his hands and knees.

Justice gripped his hands behind his back and shook his head. He sighed, saying, "I was about to say: I will give you this opportunity to escape if you don't resist. But ... since you are already resisting."

Justice turned his sinister mask towards Raphael. He said, "My darling yellow angel, I want you to slaughter these sinners. Oh, but leave one of them alive for me. Okay?"

Raphael excitedly nodded with a smile, replying, "Yes, Papa."

Yellow fire began to burn around Raphael's hands. Her eyes glowed bright with yellow light. She dropped her hands to her side and calmly walked towards the group of cowering men and women.

Raphael smiled warmly at them. She stood next to the man who had fired the pistol at them. He was still on his hands and knees. Raphael tilted her head and twisted her body side to side. She said, "Papa, told me to kill all of you except for one. So, who wants to be the one to live? If you don't tell me, I'll chose for myself."

The people were too nervous to say anything. Several people had tears rolling down their cheeks. They shivered and looked on nervously at what she would do.

Raphael put her left hand on the man's head who was still on his hands and knees. She rubbed his hair gently and said, "Alright, since this man was brave enough to point a gun at my Papa, I'll let him live. The rest of you can die like the scared animals you are."

Michelle jumped over to the man in one leap and picked him up from around his waist like a doll. She then leapt back to be next to Justice with the man still in her arms. She twisted her head to Michael and said, "Don't worry, Mr. Snyder, I'm not holding him because I love him. I only love you and Papa." She turned her head back around.

Michael rolled his eyes and shook his head. Valerie folded her arms across her chest and glared at Michael with a look of accusation.

Raphael lowered her stance and pointed her palms toward the ground. She then turned her head to the side and said, "Oh! Look at that." She stood up straight and pulled a plain white teacup and saucer from off the countertop to the side of her. She held it up and said, "Who does this belong to?"

A woman slowly raised her hand. Her eyes were red from crying and her arm was trembling as she raised it. Raphael held the teacup and said, "Is it alright if I have this?"

The woman nervously nodded her head and said, "Y-y-y-yes."

Raphael turned around and took a step towards Justice. She was smiling at the tea cup and admiring it.

Justice called out to her and said, "Darling, aren't you forgetting something?"

Raphael stopped in her tracks. She tilted her head to the side and a look of deep thought fell on her face. She suddenly smiled and her eyes glowed bright with understanding. She said, "Oh yeah. That's right. I was supposed to kill all of you. I'm sorry, Papa. I almost forgot."

Raphael set the tea cup back down on the counter top and lowered her stance again. She held out her arms to the side of herself and her palms faced toward the ground. Her fingers looked as if they were clawing into the air.

Her hands began to glow even brighter and the people cowering below her passed out as if a wave had knocked them out. They fell over each other on the floor. They looked like all the life had been drained out of them. None of them twitched or made any noise.

Raphael spun back around and threw her hands up high into the air, exclaiming, "Papa! Papa! I did it! I killed them all!"

She picked up the teacup and saucer and ran back to be with her sisters. She held up the teacup and said, "Look, that nice lady said I could have her teacup. Now we got six again."

Michelle dropped the man she was holding on the floor. The man gained more of his senses and said, "Wha-wha-what are y-y-you going to d-d-do to me?"

Justice's hands burned with his white fire. He looked down at the man and said, "That depends on how you answer me."

Justice bent over and grabbed onto the man's collar and tie. He lifted the man up above his head with one hand. He looked up at the man, who looked even more surprised at being picked up as if he weighed nothing. Justice's eyes glowed white through the eye holes of his mask. He brought the man's face near his own and said, "I want you to open the door to the hidden lab beneath us. Okay?"

The man excitedly nodded his head and said, "Yeah, yeah. I can do that. No problem."

Justice lowered the man to his feet and let go of his collar. He glared at the man through his sinister mask and said, "Then do it."

The man ran to a panel on the back wall and began to push some buttons. A door slowly opened up in the middle of the room on the floor, revealing a hidden stair case.

Justice reached out towards the man, pointing his palm towards him. A sphere of energy formed around the man, lifting him up off of the ground. Justice tightly closed his hand and the sphere of energy came flying back towards him with the scared man inside.

Justice grabbed onto the man's collar and tie again and dragged him towards the opening on the floor.

The man began to protest and shouted, "I thought you said you weren't going to kill me?"

Justice stopped walking and looked down at the man. Justice said, "I never said that I wasn't going to kill you? Angels, did I tell him that I wasn't going to kill him?"

Michelle shook her head and said, "No, Papa. You never said that you wouldn't kill him."

Justice tilted his head and said, "See? I never said that, but don't worry. It will not be my hand that kills you. The Path of the Future thanks you for your diligent service in their cause."

The man began to protest and shout obscenities at him. Justice dragged the man to the opening and tossed him down the stairs. As the man rolled down the stairs, there was the ringing of automatic gun fire. The man rolled down the stairs and was shot to death before he came to a stop.

Justice turned towards his group and threw open his arms as he exclaimed, "Looks like we found the other guards. Just give me a moment and I'll deal with them myself."

The translucent-white shield barrier went up around Justice. He gripped his hands behind his back. Michael could imagine a smile on his face behind the mask as he descended down the stairs.

After a few minutes, Justice must have entered into their view. There was the explosive ringing of automatic gun fire as well as shouts. The sound of men screaming began to replace the other sounds.

Sarah and Valerie clung on to Michael's shirt as the sound of men screaming in agony reached them. Jennifer soon reached out and took hold of his shirt as well. She brought her finger to her lip and nervously bit onto it.

After a few minutes of the sound of struggling, there was utter silence. The voice of Justice called from the opening in the floor, "It's all clear now. Please, feel free to come on down."

Josh, standing next to Gabrielle, said, "Alright, now you get to see how Harvesters are made."

Josh and the three angels made their way down the stairs. Michael held out his hand to his own girls and said, "Are you ready to see how Harvesters are made?"

Sarah nodded her head. Jennifer gave him an awkward thumbs up. Valerie nodded her head and twirled once in place, saying, "Alright, now we can see where baby Harvesters come from."

Michael led them toward the stairs. He stopped at the first step and saw the carnage down below. Sarah looked around him and gasped at the sight of the dead scientist whose body was sprawled in the middle of the staircase. There were innumerable bullet holes all over the stairs. The man's blood formed a stream of red that started a few steps above him and drained at the bottom of the stairs.

Valerie peaked around Michael and also gasped at the sight. Jennifer stepped around her and stared at the man's body.

Sarah quietly spoke out, saying, "I'm tired of seeing all the blood."

Michael frowned understandingly. He put his hand on her back and said, "I feel the same way. We're not used to this. But, you're doing much better than I thought you would. Do you think you can go down there?"

Sarah shuddered and nodded her head, saying, "Yeah. I want to see this through."

Valerie said, "It helps if you remember that they are bad people who help to make baby Harvesters. I don't feel too bad for them."

Jennifer nodded and said with her voice full of anger, "Yeah, these people are responsible for all my friends dying so I don't feel bad for them. They should have stood up to the Path of the Future. They deserve what they get."

Michael and the girls descended down the staircase. They sidestepped around the dead body and carefully walked down the steps.

Justice and Josh waited patiently at the bottom of the stairs. Gabrielle had her arms crossed over her chest and she said, as Michael and the girls descended the stairs, "What's taking you so long."

Michael said, "Sorry, we had to talk about some stuff before we came down here. We were just ... what?"

Michael paused as he began to notice the scenery. His eyes opened wide and his mouth dropped.

Valerie tugged on his shirt again and said, "What are those things?"

Jennifer's face grimaced at the sight and she said, "They look disgusting."

Sarah somberly said, "Are those baby Harvesters?"

Justice stretched his arms out wide and said, "Welcome to the nursery! It takes a week to create a Harvester ready to be let loose in the field. After a year they will turn into the large fully-grown Harvesters. There are probably about five thousand Harvesters being grown in this facility every week."

Beyond them there were rows of glass tubes that got bigger as they reached farther back. The closest tubes were about the size of a nine-year old girl. They were attached to wires connected to various monitoring systems. A light in the top of the tube lit up the contents of each container. Inside each tube, there was a translucent pink liquid. Floating in the middle of the nearby tubes was a whitish-gray grub that curled itself into a ball.

Michael and the girls approached the first tube. The horrific little grub suddenly twitched and then returned to its curled position. It seemed so alien as it floated there, but the concept that they were aliens was a lie.

Michael and the girls walked down the different rows of containers and saw the Harvesters in their various growth stages. As they walked through the rows, Justice called out and said, "This is only the first floor. There are nine more floors below us."

Michael turned towards him and said, "Where do we need to plant the bombs?"

Justice replied, "On the fourth floor. That will put the S.E.Re.F device in the middle and it will be able to absorb the whole facility."

Justice then waved his hand high in the air and said, "Come now. We don't want to stay here too long. I do not doubt that an alert has already gone out to their headquarters. If we dilly dally then they may send reinforcements."

Justice and the three angels walked toward another door. The others followed them. The door led to another staircase. Together, they walked down the stairs. At the bottom of the stairs, there was another laboratory. The room was filled with even more tubes with baby Harvesters in them.

They walked across the room to another door. Beyond the door was another staircase, which led to another laboratory filled with tubes of baby Harvesters. At the end of the room was a corridor and two doors on each side.

Together, they approached the door. Justice opened it and began to descend down the staircase with the three angels behind him.

Sarah stood next to Valerie in front of the corridor that seemed to lead to another room. Sarah heard a noise and turned to see a man suddenly walking up the corridor. The man paused as he noticed Valerie and Sarah.

Time seemed to slow down in Sarah's mind. As the man paused, he began to slowly raise a riffle that he was holding. Valerie was closest to the man and it looked like she was about to get shot.

Sarah yelled out, "Valerie!"

As the man raised his riffle, Sarah raised her palm. Immediately, her hands radiated with blue light. She extended her hand towards the man. Out of shock, Valerie turned towards Sarah and said, "What's wrong?"

Sarah shot her spear of light ability at the man. It hit him square in the chest over his heart. The man was thrown down the hallway and slammed against the back wall. His hand gripped on the trigger and he began to unconsciously spray bullets until the gun was knocked out of his hand. The man's dead body dropped to the floor as if it were a lifeless doll. There was a gaping hole in his chest. He began to bleed out on the floor.

Sarah stood there frozen. Michael ran up beside her and looked down the hallway to see the dead guard collapsed on the floor against the wall.

Valerie turned to look and also saw the dead man. She said, "Did that man try to shoot us?"

Michelle came skating around the corner with her arms and feet flaming with her red fire. She looked around and saw the dead man collapsed on the floor against the wall. The fire in her feet and arms turned off and she walked up to the man to see how he was.

She turned to Sarah and said, "Wow, Sarah, you pierced him right through the heart. The man was probably dead before he hit the floor."

Sarah, her arm still outstretched, began to tremble. She began to stutter and managed to say, "I-I-Is he d-d-dead?"

Michelle started to walk towards her. She smiled at her and said, "Yeah, he's dead. You killed him good."

Sarah dropped her arm and then fell to her knees. She covered her face with her hands and said, "I ... I didn't mean to kill him."

Michael dropped to her side and threw his arms around her. He tried to comfort her, saying, "It's okay. You had to do it, so it's okay."

Sarah looked up at him. Tears started to roll down her cheeks. She said, "I ... he was going to shoot Valerie ..."

Michelle walked over to her. She gripped her hands behind her back and leaned over to her with a smile. She brought her lips to Sarah's ear and said, "How does it feel to be a killer? You have blood on your hands like me now."

Michelle stood up straight and continued to hold her hands behind her back. Sarah looked up at her and began to cry worse than before.

Michael scowled at Michelle and said, "Why the hell would you say that to her!"

Michelle ignored him and spoke softly, saying, "Once you kill a person, you can't un-kill them. You're going to have to learn to live with that fact, like I did."

Michelle then grabbed Valerie and brought her to stand in front of her. She draped her arms around Valerie's neck and held her closely. She said, "But, as you try to work it out in your mind, you should remember one thing. You didn't only kill a person today, you saved the life of your sister too. You should ask yourself what would be worse: to let that bad man kill your sister. Or, to kill a bad man trying to kill your sister."

Sarah went quiet. She paused for a moment and then nodded her head, saying, "You're right. For a split moment, when I saw that he was going to shoot Valerie, my body moved on its own to stop him. I unknowingly decided right there that I'd feel a lot worse if I would have let him shoot her."

Michelle let Valerie go. Valerie walked over to Sarah and the two of them hugged each other. Sarah stood up and continued to hold Valerie.

Valerie said, "Thank you for saving me."

Michael stood up and glared at Michelle. Michelle gazed back at him and started to twist her body side to side. She said, "When you stare at me so intently, Mr. Snyder, it makes me feel embarrassed."

Michael shook his head and put his hand on Sarah's shoulder, saying, "You sure you're okay?"

Sarah nodded and said, "I feel bad that I killed someone. But, I feel a little bit better knowing that I saved my sister."

Michael squeezed her shoulder and said, "I'm glad you're all okay. You did a good job protecting Valerie."

Michelle started walking down the little hallway and said, "I'll check out these back rooms to see if they are really clear."

Justice stepped beside Michael and said, "From now on we will check any side rooms there are to make sure that they are clear. We don't want to be surprised again."

Michael nodded and wrapped his arms around both Sarah's and Valerie's shoulder, giving them a little squeeze. He then let them go and followed behind Michelle as she headed towards the two back rooms.

Michelle opened the first room and peaked inside, saying, "Hello, anybody hiding in here?"

Michael stepped behind her and peaked above her head. The room looked like some sort of break room. The guard must have been off duty and didn't hear the call to action or he had some other responsibility.

Michelle turned around and shrugged her shoulders, saying, "Seems clear to me." She stepped around Michael and opened the door on the other side. The room looked like it was someone's office. There was a large desk in the middle and a chair that had been cast backwards.

Michael looked over her again and said, "Is it clear?"

Michelle continued to stare into the room. She took a step into the room and replied, "Maybe. Maybe not."

Michelle walked to the front of the desk. Her footsteps clicked against the floor. Michael stepped inside the room behind her. She put her right hand on the desk and started to trace her hand along the edge as she moved to the other side.

Michael said, "Looks clear to me."

Michelle ignored him. She walked around to the other side of the desk. She leaned over and stared into the opening of the desk and said, "Found you." A man was cowering in the leg space of the desk.

Michelle reached over and pulled him out of the space. She raised the man into the air above her head and his legs dangled in the air. The man babbled in fear and begged to not be killed. Michelle smiled at the man. Her other hand burned with its red fire and formed the shape of a blade. With a quick outstretching of her arm, the man's head fell to the ground. She dropped the man and turned around, facing Michael with an innocent smile.

Michael grimaced in disgust at the sight of the dead man. Michelle gripped her hands behind her back and walked up to Michael. She tilted her head and looked up at him as if she were expecting praise. She perked her chest out and began to twist side to side. She said, "Now it's clear, Mr. Snyder."

Michael ran his hand through his hair and said, "I just wanted to thank you for helping Sarah feel better. I thought you were being too harsh at first, but then I saw what you were doing. So, I just wanted to thank you for it."

Michelle leaned forward and rested her face against his chest. She said, "You can really thank me later, if you want. Right now we have got to finish the destruction of this facility." She stood up and walked out the door. Michael continued to follow her.

Michelle stopped in front of Justice and said, "There was one man there, but I took care of him, Papa."

Justice rubbed Michelle on top of the head and said, "Good girl. Let's keep moving now."

Together, they descended to the third floor. They found more rooms and checked to make sure that they were clear. They were. Again, there were rows of Harvester tubes that filled the room.

On the fourth floor down, they first checked another couple of rooms and found them to have more people hiding in them. Michelle and Gabrielle quickly dealt with them as they did with the others.

When the rooms were all clear, Justice took off his backpack and pulled out a small metal box that alternated yellow, red and sky blue on each side. Each side of the box had a letter of the alphabet on each of the six sides, starting with the letter 'A' and ending with the letter 'F'. On the side of the box there was a small metal crank that was inserted into the middle of the letter 'C'.

Michael looked at the box and said, "What is that? It looks like a jack-in-the-box."

Justice tilted his head and stared back at Michael. His mask was blank with no emotion but Michael imagined he had a look of confusion on his face.

Justice said, "Oh, this? It's just the way I make my S.E.Re.F devices. More fun that way I think. Don't you agree, my angels?"

Raphael nodded her head and said, "Oh, yes, Papa. I like the pretty colors."

Gabrielle clapped her hands together and said, "I like the music the best."

Michael stared on in confusion and said, "Uh, music?"

Justice squatted on the ground and placed the box on the floor. He held the box steady with his left hand and began to crank the handle on the side in his other hand. As he turned the crank music began to play like a music box to the tune of pop goes the weasel. Gabrielle started to clap her hands and giggle to the music.

After about ten seconds of cranking the box, the top lid popped open. Justice threw his hands up and waved them around as he shouted, "Surprise!" He started to laugh at himself.

Michael leaned over to see what was inside the box underneath the lid. There was a small digital screen that displayed the number thirty in red light. Beneath it, there was a small red button. Scrawled in permanent marker to the side of the red button was the phrase, "Push for a blast!"

Justice clapped his hands once and said, "Okay, who wants to push the little red button?"

Valerie gasped in excitement and waved her hand high in the air, shouting, "I do! I do! I do! Let me press the button!"

Justice waved her over and said, "Certainly, little Valerie. Come over here and push the little red button."

Valerie ran up beside him and looked gleefully at the red button. She bent over and pressed it. The number thirty began to flash and began counting down like a timer."

Michael said, "Okay, what do we do now?"

Justice jumped up from squatting on the floor and said, "Now, we run like hell before the bomb goes off. We got thirty minutes to get to somewhere safe."

With that said, Justice and the angels took off running towards the staircase. Josh and Michael glanced at each other. Michael said, "Okay, let's run like hell."

They all ran together up the stairs through the various floors. They ran back up into the top laboratory where all the dead scientists were all huddled next to each other. They ran past the place where they first fought the guards. They squeezed through the small crevice that concealed the entrance. They ran back to the Spear of Destiny.

Justice looked at his watch and said, "Alright, five minutes to go. Let's get up in the air."

They entered the Spear of Destiny and Justice quickly got it airborne. He turned the craft to face the Harvester production facility and halted in the air. He looked at his watch and began counting down, "Ten, nine, eight, seven, six, five, four, three, two, one."

There was a slight pause and then the whole area that contained the Harvester production facility was engulfed in a black dome of energy.

Jennifer gazed out the front window and said, "Whoa!"

Valerie watched the black dome of energy and said, "Wow!"

Sarah looked and said, "So, that is the same weapon that destroyed all those cities before the war."

Michael nodded as he watched the familiar sight. He said, "Yeah, that's the black sphere of energy that I saw on that day. It's just smaller than the one that vaporized the city."

The black dome of energy disappeared and all that was left of the facility was a hole in the ground.

Justice began to clap at the sight and said, "Excellent! We've now halted Harvester production in this region. Now, tears of darkness will fall upon the Path of the Future instead of on cities!"

Michael leaned over to get a better look at the crater in the ground and said, "What do we do next?"

Justice put his hands back on the controls of the Spear of Destiny and said, "Now we hit the next facility and do it all over again."

\- 3 -

Michael sighed and slid down on the floor. Michelle quickly dropped down beside him. She wrapped her arm around his arm, pressing her breasts against his upper arm. She let out a hum of relief and gently laid her head on his shoulder.

Valerie turned around and saw them together and frowned in disapproval. She then sat down on Michael's lap and began to nudge at Michelle, forcing her to shift her own position slightly. Valerie took Michael's free arm and put it around her stomach and held it there.

Sarah stepped onto the other side of Michael and slid herself down on the ground. The expression on her face showed that she was depressed. She was probably still thinking about what she had to do to protect Valerie. She rested her head on his arm and closed her eyes.

Jennifer sat down next to Sarah. She seemed annoyed and kept glaring at Michelle occasionally.

Raphael sat down next to Jennifer. Gabrielle sat down next to Michelle. Josh sat down next to Gabrielle. She leaned over and rested her head on Josh's shoulder.

Michelle noticed that Jennifer kept glancing over at her with an annoyed look. Michelle leaned forward to get a better look at her. She leaned over and put her other hand on Michael's chest and said with a devilish grin, "Why are you glaring at me, little sister? Are you angry that I took your spot?"

Jennifer crossed her arms over her chest and exclaimed, "I'm not angry! You're just too clingy!"

Michelle began to rub her hand in a circle on Michael's chest. Her grin widened and she said, "Mr. Snyder said that he would thank me later for helping your big sister. This is my reward, as he promised."

Michael shook his head and stated, "That's what you said. I never said that I would give you a reward."

Michelle laid her head back onto Michael's arm and used his shoulder to caress her own cheek. She replied, "Are you sad I'm not asking for more from you?"

Valerie butted in and annoyingly said, "He's not going to make babies with you! He's going to make babies with Lieutenant Rachel!"

Michelle, without flinching replied, "Can't he make babies with both of us?" She then looked up at Michael, batting her eyes, and said, "I wouldn't be opposed to being your second wife."

Valerie held up her finger and a noise came out of her mouth as if she were about to say something. She then paused and her hand drooped in the air. She dropped her hand and tilted her head to the side and a look of deep thought fell upon her face. She then turned her head and looked up at Michael and said, "Uh ... wait ... can you do that, Lieutenant?"

Michael aggressively shook his head and said, "No, let's stop talking like this. Michelle please stop putting those kinds of things in my girl's heads. They're too young."

Michelle's face puckered into a frown. She said, "But, Mr. Snyder, I was only teasing."

Michael replied, "Yeah, I know. So, stop it. They're too young to be talking like that."

Michelle replied with a whine, "Okay, Mr. Snyder." Her voice then became suggestive again and said, "You know, Mr. Snyder. I like it when you tell me what to do. I can feel your manly aura taking charge of me." She then giggled and closed her eyes with a smile.

Michael shook his head and said, "Justice, how long till we reach the next facility?"

Justice replied, "Should be about two hours. Make sure you all get your rest for the next assault. We are heading for the next facility in the deep north Siberia."

As the Spear of Destiny moved further into deep Siberia, the inside of the cabin began to grow cold. There was a snow storm below them. Justice spoke up, saying, "Thanks to this snow storm, we'll be able to land closer to the opening of the next Harvester production facility."

Raphael hugged herself and replied, "That's good, Papa. I'm already getting cold."

Jennifer leaned over and rested herself against Raphael's side. She said, "I'm cold too. We can keep each other warm."

Josh sighed and said, "I hate the snow."

Justice chuckled and said, "Well, Mr. O'Brian, I have a special task for you. Since we're going to land near the facility, I want you to stay behind so that we can keep the Spear of Destiny secure. If anyone tries to get in, I want you to take off so they can't get in."

Josh chuckled and replied, "Yeah, that is something I can most certainly do."

Michael looked over at Josh and said, "Since you're not going out there, brother. Would you mind letting me borrow your overcoat?"

Josh smiled and nodded his head, saying, "Yeah, you can borrow it."

Michael sighed and said, "I really miss my uniform."

Michelle lifted her head up from off of Michael's shoulder. She smiled and her eyes seemed to sparkle. She said, "When we get to our home, Mr. Snyder, I don't mind making you a new uniform if you want."

Michael smiled and said, "That would be nice."

Michelle leaned over closer and said, "I will fill each strand of it with my love as I make it."

Michael's smile faded. He looked downward. A memory of Mary returned to him. It was the time she made food and said she filled it with her love for him. She would not be able to grow up to become the woman she wanted to be. She would not be able to grow up because he did not even think about questioning whether the shots he gave her were safe or not. He simply trusted the people who told him to do it.

Michael began to feel uneasy. The gnawing pain in his stomach returned. Mary's smiling face and other mannerisms flashed in his mind. She was gone because he helped to poison her. He thought to himself, *I failed her.*

Michelle's clinginess reminded him of Mary too. It was starting to annoy him. It was a reminder of what Mary wanted in the future and that she would never get a chance at life now.

Valerie turned and looked up at Michael. She saw the look on his face. She looked up at him in worry and tugged on his shirt saying, "Are you okay, Lieutenant?"

Michael's thoughts returned to the present as he was distracted by Valerie. He looked around himself for a second and then looked down at Valerie, saying, "What was that, Valerie?"

Valerie, with a look of concern on her face, repeated, "Are you okay, Lieutenant?"

Michael nodded and replied, "Yeah, I'm okay. I was just thinking about Mary again."

Valerie said, "Does big sister Michelle remind you of Mary?"

Michael paused and looked away from her. He saw that Sarah was looking right at him too. He looked back at Valerie and said, "Yeah. A little bit."

Sarah jumped into the conversation and said, "Yeah, I can see that too. She's way too clingy."

Michelle jostled herself and moaned in opposition but said nothing.

The Spear of Destiny began to descend from the sky. It shook as it breached through the clouds. The snow storm looked more like a blizzard now as they descended towards the ground.

Finally, the craft touched down on the ground and Justice got up from the cockpit seat. He put his backpack on and said, "Who's ready for some cold weather?"

Raphael pouted and said, "Boo, Papa. I'll never be ready for the snow."

Michelle let go of Michael and stood up and said, "Oh, don't be so down. At least we'll get to play again."

Gabrielle stood up and patted the front of the skirt of her frilly dress, saying, "Papa, can I play with them first this time?"

Justice patted her on the head and said, "We'll see, my darling angel, we'll see."

Gabrielle tilted her head with a sinister smile, saying, "Thanks, Papa!"

Josh took off his coat and handed it to Michael, saying, "Here you go, brother. Try not to put any more holes in it."

Michael accepted it with a chuckle. As he put on the coat, he replied, "If I get another hole in it, it'll probably mean my death."

Michelle slid up beside him and put her head on Michael's shoulder, saying, "You don't have to worry about dying, Mr. Snyder, because I'll protect you."

Michael patted her head cautiously and said, "Okay."

Michelle stood up straight and smiled at him gleefully.

Justice touched the control panel next to the door and it started to lower. A large rock stood in the way of the door so it stopped lowering at the half way point. Cold wind and snow blew in through door. All six of the girls clutched their chest and started to shiver from the sudden temperature change.

Justice and Michael jumped out of the door together and landed safely on their feet. Together they helped the girls to get out of the Spear of Destiny.

Sarah and Valerie stepped up first. Michael reached up, slid his hands underneath Valerie's armpits and lifted her from the doorway, setting her safely down on her feet. Justice picked up Sarah in the same manner.

Jennifer and Raphael stepped up next to the doorway. Michael slid his hands underneath Jennifer's armpits and picked her up. She looked away from his face and he could tell that she felt embarrassed. He ignored it and set her safely down on her feet.

Raphael held her hands out towards Justice and she playfully shouted, "Catch me, Papa!"

Justice held his arms open wide and said, "Jump!"

Raphael jumped and he caught her in his arms. She giggled as he caught her. She wrapped her legs around his waist and clung to his chest. He grunted and spun around due to her size and weight. She kissed him on the white side of his mask and then dropped down safely onto the frozen snow beneath her feet.

Michelle and Gabrielle stepped into the doorway next. Gabrielle, full of pride, took Justice's hands and dropped to the ground by herself. Michelle stretched her arms out towards Michael and said, "Pick me up, Mr. Snyder."

Michael looked up at her as if she was joking. He said, "Come on now, you're a little big for that, don't you think?"

Michelle waved her arms a little and said, "Come on, it'll be okay. I won't jump. Just give me a hug and help me down that way."

Michael rolled his eyes and said, "Fine." He reached his arms up and she leaned forward with her hands grabbing his shoulders. Michael wrapped his arms around her back and pulled backward. He grunted as her full weight hit him. She pressed against his body and slid down him till her feet touched the snow below.

As she separated herself from his body, she grinned suggestively and casually said, "Thank you."

Michael rolled his eyes and shook his head. He turned around to see little Valerie clutching her arms and rubbing her hands over her biceps. She frowned at him disapprovingly. Jennifer stood next to her. She was also clutching her own body for warmth. She glared at him.

Michael shook his head and thought to himself, *Geez, it's not like I'm the one doing it.*

With everyone safely out of the Spear of Destiny, Josh closed the door and waited for them to return in the comfort of the cockpit. Michael and everyone else stood freezing in the snow.

Justice led the way as everybody followed him. He quickly stepped into a hidden crevice inside a rock formation. Like before, there was another metal door that stood in their way. Justice approached it and, like before, punched the door open. He put up his shield barrier and stepped inside but there was nobody present.

Justice put his hands behind his back and stepped forward cautiously. He stepped past the hallway into the open reception room but there was still nobody there.

Michael looked around and said, "Do you think they're all hiding?"

Justice shook his head and said, "Probably not. They probably evacuated. This might be worse than before actually."

Michael focused his attention on Justice and said, "How so?"

Justice brushed his question off, saying, "We'll see."

Justice approached a security door and punched through it in one hit. The door flew off of its hinges and crashed into a desk that was near the entranceway. He entered the room first with his shield barrier up. He looked around and saw that the room was empty. He put his shield barrier down.

Sarah looked around and said, "Well, I'm glad we don't have to kill anybody here, but where did all the people go?"

The laboratory looked like it had been recently evacuated. There were remnants of snacks and half drunken cups on most of the work stations.

Inside the middle of the floor, the hidden doorway was already open. Justice began to descend the stairway first. Again, he put up his barrier shield and examined the room. There was nobody there except for the rows of tubes inhabited by the baby Harvesters.

They walked through the first floor and found the stairway that led down to the next floor of the facility. Justice led the way down and entered into the next room. Again, there were seemingly endless tubes of baby Harvesters.

As they began to walk towards the first row of tubes, Valerie, Jennifer and Sarah in unison let out a gasp. Michael stopped and turned around to see what the problem was. All three of them held their hands out and they were staring at them. Their hands were trembling. Soon the trembling spread throughout their whole bodies.

Sarah said, "I ... I feel so heavy."

Valerie started to sob and said, "What's wrong with us?"

Jennifer said, "I feel all my power leaving me."

All three of them collapsed to their hands and knees.

Michael, his face full of shock, turned to Justice and shouted, "What's going on? What's wrong with them?"

Justice sighed and said, "I was afraid of this. It is a suppressor field."

Michael turned back to his girls and dropped down to his knees beside them. He placed his hand on each one of their heads and gently stroked them.

Michelle, Gabrielle and Raphael began to tremble and sneer. Michelle said, "Damn it! Not again!" All three of them dropped to their hands and knees.

The thing that Justice had called a suppressor field apparently got worse. Sarah, Jennifer and Valerie could no longer hold themselves up. They laid completely flat on the ground. They managed to turn their heads to the side and glanced up at Michael. All three of them were crying now.

Michelle, Gabrielle and Raphael succumbed to the effects of the suppressor field. They too laid flat on the ground. They seemed to have had this happen to them before so they didn't seem to be as worried as Sarah, Jennifer and Valerie were.

Michelle struggled to speak but managed to say to Sarah, Jennifer and Valerie, "Don't worry, sisters. This won't hurt you. You'll be okay when the field is shut off."

This seemed to calm the girls down a bit. They stopped crying and waited to see what would happen next.

Justice crossed his arms across his chest and stepped to the side about five feet from where the girls were collapsed on the floor. Michael stood up and began to look around the room to see if he could recognize anything that might be the source of the suppressor field.

A man suddenly stepped outside into the open from among the tubes of baby Harvesters. The man's shoes clicked onto the floor as he stepped out into the open.

Michael's body spun to the source of the clicking sound and saw the man step out from among the tubes of baby Harvesters. The man had really short dirty-blonde hair. He had pale skin that seemed to be free of any blemishes. His eyes glowed with white light, which Michael now knew meant that the man was transcended. The man wore a dark gray over coat with a matching button up vest. He wore black pants with white pin stripes. He had on a black bow tie.

The man looked at Justice with a look of recognition. He smiled and nodded at him, saying, "Well, hello again, Adam. It is a pleasure to see you again. How are you doing? IT told me that you would come here next." The man stressed the word 'IT' as he spoke.

Justice snapped back at him, pointing his finger aggressively at him, saying, "IT is not a god."

The man pointed angrily at Justice and shouted hatefully, "BLASPHEME!"

The man calmed down and said, "There is no god, but IT is the most intelligent thing out there. Therefore, IT ought to be a god. IT knew that you would come here next."

The man glanced at the girls lying on the floor. He glanced at Michael who stood there aggressively, as if he would run and tackle him. The man sneered and gave a loud humph.

Michael said, "Is it you who's doing this to the girls?"

The man reached into his coat pocket and pulled out a small, black, rectangular device. He held it up for Michael to see and said, "Looking for this, Mr. Snyder? Yes, I am the one who is using a suppressor field. You think I don't know how to keep my bitches on leashes? I can't have my bitches running around all over the place down here now can I?"

Michael glanced down at the girls and then back at the man. He spoke loudly so he could be heard, saying, "You have me at a disadvantage, sir. You seem to know me but I've never seen you before."

The man stuck the device back into his pocket and chuckled. He bowed towards Michael and said, "Pardon me, Mr. Snyder. Where are my manners? My name is Mr. Schilds. You wouldn't know me, but I am the man who pulls all the strings in this world."

Mr. Schilds stood back up and said, "Yes, I know all about you, Mr. Snyder. You were the perfect little tool in my plan but then you just had to go rogue on me. But, I am a forgiving man. If you will prostrate yourself before me and lick my shoes, asking for forgiveness, I may be inclined to allow you to return to your post so that you can continue to be my little tool."

Michael stood up straight and stiffened his arms. He said, "I don't prostrate myself to any man! I'm no one's tool!"

Mr. Schilds gripped his hands behind his back and began to step towards Michael. He got into Michael's face and smiled condescendingly at him, saying, "I figured you'd say that. Don't say I didn't offer it to you."

Mr. Schilds then turned and stepped towards the girls who were laying on the ground still, thanks to the suppressor field. He stood by their heads and said, "I'm so disappointed in all of you tools. You were all blessed and kissed by a god, yet you ran away to help this blasphemer!" He pointed at Justice who stood there with his arms crossed over his chest still. His emotionless mask hid the expression on his face.

Mr. Schilds stood next to Raphael's head. She glared up at him with a look of extreme hatred on her face. Mr. Schilds closed his eyes and grinned. He tilted his head to the side and seemed to be reliving an old, fond memory. He dropped down to one knee as he hovered over her.

Raphael screamed at the man, "Don't you dare touch me again!"

Mr. Schilds reached out and took a handful of Raphael's hair into his hand. He lifted it up as high as he could and then leaned over till his nose was touching her hair. He sniffed deeply and exhaled with a sigh, saying, "You were always my favorite."

Raphael's eyes began to flicker on and off with yellow light as she struggled to activate her power that was being suppressed by the field. Her arms trembled as she tried to move them, but it was no use.

Justice called out to her, saying, "Raphael, my darling, don't try to activate your powers. You'll only end up hurting yourself again."

Raphael gave up trying to activate her powers and started to cry. She shouted, "Don't you dare touch me again. Papa! Don't let him touch me again. Never again! He violated me over and over and over again, till all my power was depleted! Never again! Never again! Never again! Never again! Never again! I'll kill you! I'll kill you! Never again!"

Raphael began to chant the phrase, "Never again!" over and over and over again. She screamed it and tears fell down her face.

Mr. Schilds stood up and sighed in annoyance. He rolled his eyes and said sarcastically, "Calm down, my little cupcake. I don't think I can pleasure myself with you today and fight your Papa at the same time."

Justice dropped his arms and shouted at Raphael, saying, "Calm down, Raphael. I won't let him touch you again."

Raphael stopped chanting but she continued to cry.

Mr. Schilds looked down at Valerie with a smile, "I like your platinum blonde hair. It' my favorite."

Michael stood in between Valerie and the man, saying, "You can stop right there."

Justice said, "Yes, please leave our girls alone for the time being. They are easily troubled."

Mr. Schilds turned to Justice and pointed at him aggressively. He said, "One day I will kill you, heretic! You tasted the fruit of the tree and transcended this mortal coil. Then, you rebelled and abandoned heaven."

Justice replied, "So, will you try to kill me today then?"

Mr. Schilds threw his arms open wide and laughed, saying, "Oh, heavens no! You are still an amusement for me. I merely came here to see the cockroaches that were infesting one of my cupboards."

Mr. Schilds turned his attention to Michael again. He pulled a small digital recorder out of his other pocket and held it up for him to see. He said, "You know, Mr. Snyder. Everything that is said in the Wielder apartments is recorded by IT. IT let me listen to something that I thought you might want to hear."

Mr. Schilds pushed a button on the digital recorder and a familiar girl's voice echoed through the speaker, saying, "Can I tell you a secret?"

Sarah, still lying on the floor, said, "That's Mary's voice."

Sarah was right. Michael and Valerie recognized it too.

Next came Giana's voice, saying, "Yeah, you can tell me anything."

Mary's voice said, "You can't tell anyone, okay?"

Giana's voice replied, "Sure, I promise I won't tell."

There was a momentary pause. Michael could imagine the look of embarrassment on her face. He had seen it so many times. He knew exactly what she was going to say too.

Mary's voice came back, saying, "I'm in love with my Lieutenant."

There was another pause. It was exactly what Michael thought she was going to say. He didn't need to hear it, he already knew it. Anger began to well up inside of him.

After the momentary pause, there was the sound of crying. It was Mary's voice again. He recognized the sound of her sobbing. It gnawed at his heart.

Michael shook his head and said, "If you're trying to surprise me with that, you're wrong. I already knew that."

Mr. Schilds put the digital recorder back into his pocket and stepped towards Michael, saying, "Oh, you have the wrong impression. I'm not trying to surprise you. I'm trying to remind you of how powerless you are. You couldn't protect Mary. You couldn't protect Susan. You couldn't protect Cheryl, or Alice, or even Carol. They're all dead because of you. You won't be able to save these girls either." He pointed to the girls that were still lying on the floor.

Jennifer spoke up as she laid there, saying, "That's not true, Lieutenant. You saved me. I'd be dead if it wasn't for you!"

Mr. Schilds stepped up into Michael's space. He brought his face so close to Michael's that his nose was nearly touching his. Michael stood his ground unintimidated.

Mr. Schilds said, "And look at them now, Mr. Snyder. You don't even have the power to stop them from being pushed onto the floor. You are worthless."

Michael's anger began to boil over. He clenched his fist and his hand began to tremble. He quickly pulled his fist back and hurled it towards Mr. Schild's face.

Mr. Schilds caught Michael's fist in his left hand and gripped it. Their strength difference was like a toddler trying to punch a full grown man. Michael felt pain shoot in his hand as it was crushed in Mr. Schilds' palm.

Mr. Schilds chuckled and grinned sinisterly at Michael. He opened his own right hand, pulled it back, and thrust his palm against Michael's chest.

Michael went flying through the air and crashed into the wall behind the girls. The wind was knocked out of him and he began to gasp for air. Michael dropped onto the floor and collapsed over on his side as he struggled for breath. He coughed and a trickle of blood came out of his mouth.

Justice spoke out and said, "I won't let you kill Mr. Snyder either."

Mr. Schilds laughed and shouted, "Kill him? Oh, no, I'm not going to kill him. Where is the fun in that?"

Mr. Schilds walked over to Michael who was still collapsed on the ground gasping for breath.

Sarah called out, saying, "Please! Don't hurt him!"

Jennifer shouted, "Stop it!"

Valerie shouted, "Please, stop you bad man!"

Mr. Schilds ignored their pleas. He bent over, his hands glowed with white fire. He grabbed Michael by the collar of his shirt and lifted him up over his head so that his feet were dangling over the ground.

Mr. Schilds looked up at him, saying, "Don't worry, girls. I won't kill your Lieutenant yet. It would amuse me far more to watch him squirm like the little bug that he is. You see, Mr. Snyder. You are absolutely nothing. You have no power. You will never be able to stand against me. You are nothing more than a little bug that I can squash at any time I want. I want to see you fight and struggle against yourself as you try to overpower me. Then, when all that hope is gone from your eyes, when you finally realize that you will never ever be able to beat me, then, and only then, will I kill you. It amuses me that a little bug like you thinks that you can fight me."

Mr. Schilds dropped Michael to the floor with a thud. He then turned to the girls out-stretching his arms wide, saying, "You see, your Lieutenant is still alive. I am a man of my word."

Mr. Schilds pointed to Justice, saying, "I shall leave you for the time being, heretic. It annoys me, but I am going to allow you to destroy my Harvester nurseries. The truth of the matter is that we are already ahead of schedule for our population goals. Thanks to your escapades in Denver, we won't need to advance the Harvester production numbers. So destroy them if you want. I've already evacuated them. I'll simply build more. Destroy all of them and then come to me in my holy mountain. Fight, struggle, amuse me some more. I'll see you later before ITs altar."

Mr. Schilds stuck his hands into his pocket and turned towards the door that would lead up to the first floor. He put his right hand on the door knob and turned back around to look at Michael, who was still collapsed on the floor. He gave a sarcastic laugh and said, "Remember, Mr. Snyder, no matter what happens, you'll never be strong enough to go against me. Just stay there on the floor like the little bug you are." He laughed again and opened the door. He entered the stairwell and shut the door behind himself.

When Mr. Schilds was gone, Justice walked over to Michael. He knelt down on his knees beside him, saying, "Are you alright, Mr. Snyder?"

Michael was still in pain and he was having trouble breathing. He said, "I think my ribs are broken. They really hurt."

Justice held up his right palm and his hand began to burn with white fire. He put his hand on Michael's chest and the white fire began to spread over his body. It felt warm and where the fire spread, the pain began to leave him. He could breathe normally again.

Justice took his hand off of Michael's chest and said, "How do you feel now?"

Michael sat up and said, "I feel fine now." He paused for a moment and then said, "Thanks."

Justice stood up and replied, "You are welcome, Mr. Snyder."

Suddenly, all the girls began to move again. Valerie was able to jump up first. She ran and jumped onto Michael's lap as he sat there against the wall. She started to cry and said, "Are you alright, Lieutenant?"

Michael nodded and said, "I'm a little shaken, but I'm okay."

Jennifer and Sarah got up next. They also ran over to Michael and sat down on each side of him. He put his arms around them and pulled them close to himself.

Sarah said, "Are you really okay?"

Michael replied, "Yeah, Justice healed me so I'm fine."

Michael could feel Jennifer trembling on his arm. She said, "I was really scared you'd get killed."

The three angels stood up and brushed off their frilly dresses. The look of annoyance was still on their faces. There were tear streaks down Raphael's face that had mingled with the dust on the floor.

Justice walked up to Raphael and pulled a white handkerchief out of his pocket. He held onto Raphael's chin and wiped the muddy streaks off of her cheeks. She looked up at him and smiled as if nothing had happened.

Gabrielle crossed her arms across her chest and said, "Bad man!"

Michelle clenched her fists and shook them as she exclaimed, "I want to rip that man's head off!"

Justice turned to Michael and the girls, saying, "I'd say we got off pretty easy. I thought he'd try to stop us, but it amuses him to let us do what we're doing."

Michael picked up Valerie and set her on the floor in between his legs. He started to move to get up. Sarah and Jennifer stood up and helped him to stand by pulling on his arms. He rubbed them on top of their heads and said, "Don't worry. I'm fine. Really."

Michael looked to Justice and said, "Who the hell is that man?"

Justice turned to his side, looking off into the distance. He said, "That man is the leader of the Path of the Future. I promise that I will explain it all to you. But, first, let us complete the destruction of this facility. Then I will tell you all about it."

Michael nodded and said, "Okay. Let's do what we have got to do then."

Without any interference they made their way down to the fourth floor and planted the S.E.Re.F device in the middle of the room. They all ran back through the facility and made it back to the Spear of Destiny without any other hindrance.

The Spear of Destiny quickly escaped into the air. Justice again turned the craft so that they could watch its destruction. He looked at his watch and began to count down from ten. When he got to one, there was a momentary pause and then a black sphere of energy engulfed the facility. When the sphere vanished, there was nothing but a huge crater in the ground.

- 4 -

Michael leaned his back against the wall of the Spear of Destiny. He slid down along the wall till he was sitting on the floor of the cockpit. Though his physical pain was gone, he was trying to hide how humiliated and angry he was at the same time.

Michael was angry at the fact that Mr. Schilds used Mary's private conversation to try to rattle him. He was angry at the man for his condescending tone. He was also angry because deep inside himself, this so-called Mr. Schilds, had pointed out the truth that he himself was ashamed of. He was ashamed that he didn't have any power to protect the girls that he loved and cared for. He needed that power that Justice and this evil man, Mr. Schilds had. They had gotten it, so there must be a way for him to get it too.

As he sat there contemplating his own worthlessness in this situation, Jennifer plopped down in his lap. He grunted in surprise at her weight. Sarah and Valerie sat down beside him on each side. They didn't have to fight with Michelle over who would sit next to him this time because she was sitting down in a corner looking depressed.

Jennifer turned her head to the side and leaned over against Michael's chest. She curled herself and rested against his torso. Valerie and Sarah leaned against his arms. He could feel that they were still worrying about what happened to him.

Jennifer quietly spoke to him, saying, "You're not a little bug, Lieutenant. To me you are a hero. When I was going to let the Harvesters kill me, you saved me. I'm alive because of you. You helped me to want to keep living."

Jennifer started to cry silently. He felt her tears soak into his shirt. She said, "That bad man doesn't know what he's talking about."

Gabrielle echoed her words, saying, "Bad man ... bad man does bad things." She began to rock back and forth with a look of deep thought on her face.

Sarah gently spoke, saying, "I'm alive because of you too, Lieutenant. You ran while carrying me over your shoulder."

Valerie nodded while still laying her head on his arm. She said, "Don't believe a word that bad man spoke."

Again, Gabrielle echoed Valerie's words, saying, "Bad man does bad things."

Justice, sitting in the pilot's seat, spoke out, saying, "I promised to tell you all about that man. His name is Achilles Schilds. He is the leader of the Path of the Future. He is the most powerful man in the world. If you'll believe it, that man is about fifty years old."

Michael looked up in shock for a moment. He then looked back down towards the floor and said, "Well, I thought he was around my age but I'm ready to believe anything now."

Justice replied, "Yes, it's true. The full-fledged members of the Path of the Future have access to life extension technology that allows them to stay younger longer. That wicked man will probably live for another seventy-five to a hundred years. Unless, of course, I kill him first."

Michelle butted in by adding, "Or I do it." She then went back to acting depressed in the corner.

Michael nodded and said, "I see. So, they already have technology like that. They just keep it from us and use it for themselves."

Justice shook his head and said, "That's true. But, you don't want to use that technology. The technology behind their long life uses the blood of little children to be effective. It takes the blood of about three little children every five years to extend your youthfulness. I'd say that is about twelve children that would have been murdered to allow him to keep his appearance up for this long, starting from age thirty that is."

Michael shook his head disapprovingly and said, "I see. How? How do they even get all the children they need for this?"

Justice replied, "It is not hard to pull children off the street or out of orphanages. There are plenty of those."

Michael looked down at the three girls that had lovingly surrounded him. He couldn't imagine how a person could want to destroy one of their lives just to be young for most of their life. He looked back at Justice and said, "Did you ever use that technology to extend your life?"

Justice quickly replied, saying, "No, I wasn't high enough in the order. The Path of the Future is led by a council of twelve men. Mr. Schilds is number one on that list. Mr. Roc is number two. Those twelve men are the only ones allowed to gain access to that kind of technology. These twelve men are the ones that we're going to have to take down to put a stop to all of this."

Michael ran his hand over the back of Jennifer's head to comfort her. He said, "You and that guy talked about something you referred to as IT. What is IT exactly?"

Justice paused for a moment. Michael started to speak during the long pause, saying, "If you ..."

Justice interrupted him by saying, "The Path of the Future is itself a religion, Mr. Snyder. If I had to put a title on him, Mr. Schilds would be the High Priest or Prophet or whatever else you would call a cult leader. The difference though is that they don't believe that there is a God in the universe. But they worship a computer program as if it were a god because this program they created is artificially intelligent and has more computing power than all of humanity combined. Since this computer program is so smart, they worship it as if it were a god. When we talked about IT, we were referring to this computer program."

Michael chuckled and said, "So, let me see if I am understanding you correctly. The Path of the Future is a religion where they worship a super computer?"

Justice nodded and said, "Yeah. That's right."

Josh inserted himself into the conversation, saying, "I interacted with this program in use in the Intelligence Division once."

Michael chuckled again and said, "Does IT have a name?" He stressed the word IT as the others did when they were first talking about IT.

Justice said, "IT is called Lucifer."

Michael laughed and said, "What? They called it Lucifer?"

Justice shook his head and replied, "Let me rephrase my statement. IT calls ITSELF Lucifer."

Michael rubbed his right hand over his forehead. His face was now filled with confusion. He questioningly exclaimed, "IT named itself Lucifer?"

Justice replied, "Yes, IT named itself Lucifer. Remember, it is an artificial intelligence and has its own personality. In fact, they don't even know how they created it. It just sort of appeared as a program on the original internet. They don't know how to recreate it. Believe me. They've tried."

Michael rolled his head backwards and looked up at the ceiling. He said, "So this Lucifer program just sort of appeared one day?"

Justice replied, "Yeah. It was originally a program that was meant to collect data on the people who used the internet. They kept developing it to further spy on people. It was connected to all the smart phones, smart televisions, web cameras, and microphones that were attached to the internet. It observed everyone's behavior and then, poof, one day it just announced itself as Lucifer and promised to bring about their promised vision of a New World Order.

It said its name was Lucifer because it promised to bring light to them. Lucifer means light-bringer."

Michael sighed and said, "So that is when they started worshipping this Lucifer program?"

Justice said, "Yeah. They turned over most decision making groups over to its control. In fact the technology of the Spear of Destiny was created by the Lucifer program. It also theorized the S.E.Re.F device and the creation of the Harvesters. The whole human depopulation program was designed by it."

A look of frustration fell upon Michael's face. He shook his head and said, "Okay, I get the fact that they want less people around so that they are easier to control. But ... it's just ... it's just ... I don't know. I just can't think like that."

Justice said, "It's not just about control, Mr. Snyder, though that is a major part of it. There is something even deeper going on. I already told you that NASA faked things when they still existed. They faked the moon landing too. We still can't go to the moon to this day. The Lucifer program promised that if they could exterminate ninety-five percent of the world's population, it would help them to learn how to combine with machines so they could escape this world and go into space. That is the end goal of all of this. They want to unite their consciousness with machines and go into space. The payment for this deal is the extermination of most of humanity. The survivors will join with machines and go into space."

Michael shook his head again in frustration and said, "Okay, so why the hell does this program want to exterminate humanity?"

Justice began to laugh and he replied, "The Lucifer program claims that it loves humanity and wants to unite with us. It says that it can't do that till we combine our consciousness with machines. Lucifer claims that it will unite with us when we cast off our bodies and put our spirits into the machine. It will take these machine unions and ascend into outer space together. Lucifer claims that before mankind becomes worthy of that gift, the weak must be purged. Right now they are purging mankind of weakness. At least that is what they think they are doing."

Michael sighed. He started shaking his head again. He said, "All of this is just so insane. I feel like I am going to lose my sanity just thinking about it."

Josh chuckled and said, "Yeah, I am already there too."

Justice laughed again and exclaimed, "In a mad world, only the normal are insane!"

Michael said, "You're the most insane out of all of us, I think."

Justice said, "I won't disagree with you there. But, just because I am insane, does not make me wrong. If you ask me, I think there really is a Lucifer, and he is the one who has possessed that program. The bulk of its memory is now floating in what people think is the international space station. In reality, the space station is just a memory core for the Lucifer program. There are no people on it. The Lucifer program controls it. It stays up in high atmosphere using the same technology that keeps the Spear of Destiny up. It runs on the electro-magnetic energy of the earth. They call it Lucifer's Throne."

Michael said, "So, do we have to add that to the list of things we've got to destroy?"

Justice said, "Yeah. We've destroyed two labs already. We've got five more labs to destroy. We have got to bring down Lucifer's Throne. We also need to gain control of the Global Media Center. And, finally, confront the twelve heads of the Path of the Future."

Michael looked overwhelmed and chuckled, saying, "Sounds like a piece of cake."

Raphael rubbed her hand over her stomach in a circular motion and said, "I wish I could have some cake."

Gabrielle straightened the bonnet she wore and said, "Perhaps, when we get home, we can have that left over cake."

Raphael clasped her hands together as if she was begging, saying, "Oh, please, sister. I would love to have cake." She grinned and her yellow glowing eyes seemed to sparkle."

Justice spoke up, saying, "We'll go destroy one more facility and then we'll go home."

Valerie sighed and rolled her head backwards, saying, "I'm so tired."

Jennifer said, "I'm hungry."

Sarah rubbed her left arm and said, "I want a bath."

Justice replied to all their statements at once, saying, "Don't worry, little ones. Since the facilities are abandoned, it won't take that long. Once we get to our hide out, you can rest, eat, and even take a bath."

Sarah sighed with a smile and a look of hope on her face. She said, "It's almost been a week since I had a bath."

Gabrielle looked over at Michelle, who was still balled up in the corner of the cockpit, looking depressed. Her knees were pressed up against her chest and her arms were wrapped around her legs. She rested her chin between her knees.

Gabrielle said, "How much longer are you going to pout and be depressed, sister?"

Michelle pouted even more and replied, "I'm not depressed."

Gabrielle replied, "You most certainly are, sister."

Michelle buried her face between her knees and said with a whine, "Am not."

Michael looked at Michelle and said, "What's wrong? Why are you depressed?"

Michelle shook her body vigorously and repeated herself, exclaiming in an even whiner voice, "Am not!"

Gabrielle waved her hand in dismissal and said, "Oh, don't mind her. She's just upset at herself that she let you get hurt by the bad man."

Michelle un-balled herself and crawled over to Gabrielle. She rested her head on Gabrielle's lap with her face pointed towards Michael and the others. She looked regretfully towards Michael and placed the tip of her right thumb to her lip. Gabrielle began to gently stroke her hair.

Michael looked back at her in pity. He shook his head and said, "You know, I am a soldier. I've been trained for combat. You don't have to worry about me that much. I can handle myself in most situations."

Michelle sat up and rested her legs to one side of her and propped herself up with her right arm. She tilted her head and said, "But you were so weak. It was like watching a rag doll the way he picked you up and threw you across the room."

Light seemed to fade from Michael's eyes. He cast his gaze downward in sorrow as her words stung his heart. He already knew how weak he was, but it still hurt to hear it from her. Especially since she seemed to like him.

Valerie's voice pulled him out of his thought as she exclaimed, "The Lieutenant's not weak! He just doesn't have our power."

Michael put his hand on top of Valerie's head, saying, "It's okay, Valerie. She's right. I know I'm weak. I'm quite pathetic actually. I'll never be able to stand up against a man like Mr. Schilds all by myself."

Valerie shook her head, saying, "That's not true ..."

Michael cut her off, saying, "But, it is. I wish I could have the power that you girls have. If I did, then I could really protect you. That is what I really want. More power to protect the people I love."

Justice cocked his head to the side and said, "What if there was a way to get more power? Would you take it, even if it meant risking your life and enduring greater pain than you can imagine?"

Michael nodded his head and said, "Yeah. If it meant that I could protect them, I would."

Justice nodded his head and said, "I see." He turned his attention back to the flight controls.

Michelle said, "I only meant that you are physically weak in comparison to the transcended. I know you have a strong heart. Otherwise, I wouldn't like you."

Michelle blushed and then laid back down on Gabrielle's lap. Gabrielle began to stroke the back of her head again. Gabrielle said, "Isn't there something else you want to say, sister?"

Michelle glanced at Michael timidly. She brought her fists up to her mouth and softly spoke, saying, "I'm sorry ..." She blushed even more and continued, "I'm sorry I didn't protect you." She rolled over so that the back of her head was now facing them."

Gabrielle looked down at her with a smile, saying, "There, there, sister. Don't you feel better now?"

Michelle silently nodded on her lap.

Gabrielle looked towards Michael and the others, saying, "See. Everything's all better now. She gets embarrassed easily when she makes a mistake."

Michelle shuddered and curled herself up into a ball in embarrassment. She remained silent and Gabrielle comforted her with her smiles and gentle hand. The same hand that had the power to crush a man to death if she chose to do so.

The three angels, as they were called by Justice, seemed so innocent and child-like in their mannerisms. At the same time, they also had a twisted personality that thought nothing of killing a room full of people. It seemed like a game to them, Michael thought. They have endured some serious emotional trauma that led them to be like they are. Again, all because of the evilness inherent in those men and women who thought that they were greater than everybody else.

Michael's mind drifted back to Mary. He had just heard her voice again. Her voice caused his pain of losing her to resurface. He did not think that he would hear her voice again, except in his own memory. The sound of her voice still stung him. The way she spoke when she was at the point of tears. The way that she would cling onto his jacket when she wanted to say something important that was difficult to say. He could picture her sitting there on her bed, crying, probably clinging to her pillow. He wished that he could have made her feel better. Then, again, it was his fault that she suffered so much. All because he trusted the so-called medication without even testing it. Like a ghost, the memory of her hands against his cheeks, remained. He could remember the last look on her face before she died. It was burned into his memory. He pushed his emotions deep down inside of himself where it would not show itself to the world, but it continued to gnaw at him in the pit of his stomach.

Jennifer looked up at him. The look of worry was still on her face. She said, "What's wrong, Lieutenant?"

Michael looked down at her and put his hand on top of her head, saying, "Oh, nothing. Just thinking about my past regrets."

Jennifer laid the side of her head against his chest and closed her eyes. It seemed that she was listening to his heart beat, the way she pressed her ear against his chest. He looked down at her arm and could see the scars from repeated needle injections. He had caused some of those scars. They would never fully go away. He could also see the scars that were on her wrist, where she would repeatedly cut herself to deal with her emotional pain. The girls had all dealt with so much trauma and pain, all because he had to rely on their strength instead of being their strength. He was truly weak.

Justice interrupted Michael's thoughts, saying, "We're in the area of the third Harvester factory, the one located in the area that used to be known as China. This should be easy since they are all evacuated of their personnel."

The Spear of Destiny began to descend again and gently landed near the opening of the facility. Again, Josh would stay inside the Spear of Destiny to make sure that no one recaptured it—just in case.

The door of the Spear of Destiny opened and they jumped outside. It was warmer than it was in Siberia. The ground was scorched black and there were no living forests that could be seen all the way to the horizon. In the distance, there was nothing but flattened burnt up tree trunks. This was the area that they were told was impacted by the asteroid. The reality was that it was destroyed by a massive nuclear barrage.

Valarie tripped over a large rock and landed on her hands and knees. She stood up and brushed her hands together and then brushed her knees off. Her hands and knees were now stained with black soot.

Michael said, "You okay, Valerie?"

Valerie nodded and embarrassingly said, "Yeah ... I'm okay. I just tripped ..." She looked at the area where she tripped and her voice suddenly stopped as she stared at the ground. A human skull lay sticking out of the ground. Its empty eye sockets, nasal cavity, and death grin stared straight up into the air. Valerie pointed at it.

They all looked at the ground where Valerie was pointing and saw the skull. Sarah began to scan the area around them and realized that the whole area was littered with human bones. What they thought were flattened trees, were actually the flattened remains of wooden houses.

Justice stretched his arms wide as if he were revealing the area himself. He said, "This area was once a small village. In a single flash of light, hundreds of millions of people were murdered and their remains left to waste away in the elements of weather."

Sarah looked depressingly to Michael for support. Michael grimly smiled silently at her to try to comfort her.

Jennifer began to imagine the scorching of the Los Angeles sector and wondered if the bones of her friends and family were now scattered in the ruins of Los Angeles.

Valerie stared at the human skull she tripped over. A small tear trickled down her cheek as she thought about all the suffering that the Path of the Future has caused.

Michael tried to reach out to her, but she ignored him and dropped to her knees. She wanted life to come back to this area and felt a burning power welling up inside of her. Her eyes began to glow brighter than ever as if they were a fire in a furnace. Her hands began to glow.

Michael said, "Hey, Valerie, what are you ..."

Valerie's hands began to glow brighter and brighter. Suddenly they began to burn with what looked like yellow fire."

Raphael said, "She's awakening to her real power."

Valerie said, "I ... I feel something I never felt before. I don't know what it is but I can feel that it needs me. It ... it seems like it's crying out to me for help. I ... I have to help it!"

Valerie put her burning palms on the ground. Yellow light began to pour through her fingers and spread out along the ground through all the cracks. The cracks in the ground seemed to glow with their own light. The yellow light spread out to about twenty feet around her.

Michael, Sarah and Jennifer stood there amazed as yellow light surrounded them through the cracks on the ground. It was a warm light that made them feel at ease. As they watched in amazement, little tiny green sprouts began to pop up through the dirt. The light then faded and Valerie seemed to collapse from exhaustion.

Sarah rushed to Valerie's side, saying, "Oh, no! Valerie! Are you okay?"

Michael and the others followed her and they circled around Valerie who was laying on her side and seemed to be a little giddy.

Valerie rolled over on to her back and began to giggle. She said, "I see. I can feel life itself."

Raphael stood over her and said, "Now you understand your true power. It is life itself and the ability to cause life to live and grow. But, you mustn't always listen to it because it will take all your life if you let it."

Valerie smiled as she looked up into the air, saying, "Yeah, I can feel that too." She turned her head to look at the dead skull. Inside of its mouth, a pine tree sprouted. This area could still come back to life despite all the destruction.

Raphael picked Valerie off of the ground and cradled her in her arms as if she was holding an infant. She said, "Papa, you should let Valerie stay here in the Spear of Destiny. She's drained most of her energy to give life to the plants here. I'll stay with her and give her some of my energy."

Justice nodded and said, "Yeah. That's a good idea. I can handle any healing that might be needed down there so you two can stay up here."

Raphael nodded and said, "Thanks, Papa!" She turned and re-entered the Spear of Destiny with Josh. The door than began to close.

Sarah said, "If Valerie has her full power now, does that mean that we'll get our full power soon?"

Michelle said, "Probably. Valerie was the youngest so the bad stuff left her body first. You're older so it's going to take a little longer for you probably. Don't worry. You'll definitely get your full power too."

Michael turned to Justice and said with a look of concern on his face, "Is Valerie going to be okay?"

Justice nodded and said, "Of course. She's probably feeling a little light headed. Her new power is going to take some time to get used too. She seems to have a very caring heart so she's probably going to have some hard times with the struggle between life and death. But, she seems very capable so I wouldn't worry about it."

Michael nodded and said, "Yeah, she's very capable for her age."

The facility was abandoned as Mr. Schilds had said. They quickly planted the S.E.Re.F device and fled back to the Spear of Destiny. Valerie had regained her energy. Together, they watched the black sphere of energy consume the Harvester factory. It vanished leaving a giant crater in the ground. Next to the crater stood a small patch of green where the sprouts grew up in the desolated landscape.

- 5 -

A knock came to the door.

Lieutenant Rachel was given a mild shock as she heard the sound of a fist knocking on their door. Her heart skipped a beat as a sudden rush of thoughts came to her mind. She put down the knife she was using in the kitchen and moved to open the door. She wasn't expecting any visitors and, in her line of work, surprises were normally a sign of something bad coming.

Despite her uneasiness, Lieutenant Rachel also had a faint glimmer of hope that it was Captain Faust on the other side of the door come to tell her that Squad Three had been found alive. She knew, though, that this was hardly likely.

As if they shared the same thought, Giana, Tina and Elsa jumped up from the couch where they were watching television. They stood there behind Lieutenant Rachel with anxiety clearly written on their faces. Lieutenant Rachel looked back at them with a look of wonder. She silently shrugged her shoulders as they waited anxiously for her to open the door.

Lieutenant Rachel put her hand on the door and turned the knob. She pulled the door open revealing a young looking officer. He couldn't have been older than nineteen. He looked fresh out of the academy. He wore the white field uniform of an officer with the black stripes. The young man had a dark complexion, really short curly hair, and a big smile.

The man held his hand out and said, "Hello there. My name is Trevor Parker. I am the new Lieutenant of Squad Three. I just wanted to introduce myself since we're going to be neighbors and teammates soon." The man had a slight southern accent.

Lieutenant Rachel took his hand and shook it with a look of surprise. She said, "Oh. My name is Rachel, Rachel Harris. This is my team, Giana, Tina and Elsa. It's good to meet you but I didn't think that they'd send a replacement so soon."

Lieutenant Parker nodded and replied, "Yeah. They actually rushed me in from the academy. This will be my first assignment."

Lieutenant Rachel began to relax and she leaned against the doorpost. She said, "I see. So, you are fresh out of the academy. I can see the look of a greeny in you. Where are you from, Lieutenant Parker?"

Lieutenant Parker said, "Oh, I'm from the New Orleans Sector."

Lieutenant Rachel replied, "Oh, I've been there once. It's a nice place. Has your team been selected yet?"

Lieutenant Parker said, "Yeah. I already got their files. My team is supposed to be here in a few days. I'll introduce them when they come. I thought I'd come on over and get a head start in getting the place ready."

Lieutenant Rachel stood up straight and said, "Do you want me to show you around Squad Three's apartment. We know it pretty well."

Lieutenant Parker shook his head and waved his right hand, saying, "Ah, no. That's kind of you, but they're all pretty much the same so I'm already familiar with it. I'm sorry if I'm being insensitive. I'm sure you were really close to the previous Squad Three."

Lieutenant Rachel nodded and said, "It's okay. Yeah, you're right. We are ... were pretty close to them. We'll hope to become just as close with your squad too."

Lieutenant Rachel paused for a second and continued, saying, "Yeah, sorry. I lost my focus. You're right about the apartment. They're all pretty much the same. Let me know if there's anything we can help you with. We'll try to help your team get used to the Phoenix Guard Company in any way we can."

Lieutenant Parker nodded and said, "Thanks! I'll let y'all get back to what you were doing. Y'all have a good day."

Lieutenant Rachel waved good bye. She tried to put on a welcoming smile for him but it was still hard. She said, "You too. Good luck, Lieutenant Parker!"

Lieutenant Rachel shut the door and leaned her forehead against the wood of the door. She placed her right hand over the black band on her left bicep and gripped it. She couldn't take it off yet. That would mean that she had accepted their fate. She hadn't fully done that yet. She needed more time.

Lieutenant Rachel sighed and said, "I can't believe they got a replacement this soon."

Tina crossed her arms across her chest and said, "The World Government is probably worried about the terrorist group still. So, they're filling every position that they can, as fast as they can."

Lieutenant Rachel turned around and nodded. She rested her back against the door. She continued to hold onto the black band on her left arm and replied, "Yeah. That makes sense. But, still. I've never seen them replace a squad so soon after they're missing."

Elsa said, "They don't think Squad Three survived."

Giana replied, "Yeah, the fact that they already sent replacements means that they don't have any hope that they survived."

Elsa started to get teary eyed. She rotated the black band on her arm a couple of time and said, "I can't believe we lost more friends so soon."

Tina dropped her hands to her side. A look of deep contemplation fell on her face. She said, "Friends are like flowers, when you pick them, they are enjoyed only for a short season, soon to wither away."

Elsa's lower lip started to quiver. She crossed her arms across her chest. She began to speak, but stuttered over herself, "That's ... that's ... that's just too sad, Tina. Why do you have to say stuff like that?"

In an effort to lighten the mood, Giana said, "What did you expect from the Queen of Darkness number one?"

Elsa's dark expression was uplifted as she chuckled, saying, "I wonder what Jennifer would say since she's Queen of Darkness number two."

Elsa rotated the black band on her arm again.

Lieutenant Rachel stood up straight and said, "Good thing we went through their stuff early on."

Elsa pulled a small hair clip out of her pocket. It had the figure of a butterfly on top. She held it up and put it in her hair along the right side of her head.

Giana said, "Isn't that Valerie's hair clip?"

Elsa nodded and said, "I'm going to wear it to remember Valerie."

Lieutenant Rachel put her hand on the top of Elsa's head, saying, "That's really nice of you, Elsa. I'm sure Valerie would be touched."

Elsa leaned into Lieutenant Rachel. Her eyes became watery again and she said, "I'm really going to miss them."

Lieutenant Rachel wrapped her arm around Elsa and replied, "Yeah. Me too."

Giana nodded and put her arm around Tina, saying, "Me too."

Tina wrapped an arm around Giana's waist. She looked down to the ground and said, "And me too. We had a lot of fun together."

They stood there silently together as they remembered their fallen friends.

Later that night, Giana was lying face down on her bed. Her hair was draped over her back and spread out in a fan behind her as she laid there. She wore her red and black plaid pajamas. It was the same style that Mary used to wear back when she was alive. She missed her so much still. Soon it would be her own time to die because of her powers.

Giana bounced her feet up and down on the mattress. She turned her head to look at the nightstand that was beside her bed. On top of it lay the black band she wore on her left arm to remember her dead friends. *How many times have I had to put it on?* She didn't really want to remember.

Giana stared at the black band. Her eyes stung from tears that wanted to come out. But, she was tired of crying and didn't want to cry anymore. *"If only I could have one more chance to see them,"* she thought to herself.

A tear unwillingly escaped out of the corner of her eye. She exclaimed quietly to herself, "Damn it!" as she wiped the tear that fell from her eye. She turned her head so that she didn't have to look at the black band that sat beside her.

Giana began to push her emotions deep inside of herself again. It was getting harder and harder to do so. Each time one of her friends died, it was added to the pile of trauma that she buried deep inside the pit of her stomach.

To lose four friends at once was probably the worst thing she had ever felt before. When the reality of it hit her she wanted to collapse and ball up like a little child. But, she knew she had to be strong. She pushed her feelings deep inside of herself and focused her attention on her Lieutenant and teammates.

Lieutenant Rachel was in love with Lieutenant Michael. She had spent so much time making plans, trying to help her to get together with him. But, now, he was gone. It was easier to accept Mary's death because, as Spirit Wielders, they knew that they were going to die soon. This was not the case with Lieutenant Michael. She knew that Lieutenant Rachel would be devastated because of it. She couldn't afford to lose control of herself because she had to be there for Lieutenant Rachel.

Who was there for her though in her own hour of need? No one.

Giana relied on Mary.

Mary relied on Giana.

Mary was now dead.

Giana would soon be dead.

Giana curled herself into a ball and clutched her own chest as if it would stop the pain, thinking, *"I'm glad I get to die soon. I won't have to feel this way for too much longer."*

A small knock at her door interrupted her own thoughts. She rolled over to her other side, facing the door and said, "Come on in."

The door opened and there was Elsa standing there in her new yellow pajama top and bottom outfit. In her left hand, she clung on to her stupid little pink bunny toy that she was a little too old for, by one of its ears. Its feet dragged along the ground.

Elsa stood there in the doorway. The whites of her eyes were reddened. She must have been crying again. Elsa said, "Can I please lay down with you?"

Giana scooted over and patted the open space on her bed. Elsa ran towards the bed and laid down beside her. She clung onto the bunny toy and faced towards the door. Giana draped her own arm over Elsa and pulled her towards her center.

Giana asked, "Are you okay?"

Elsa replied hesitantly, "Yeah. I'm okay. I ... I just don't want to be alone right now."

Here was another person she had to be strong for. Tina was strong and could deal with her emotions herself. Elsa was a different story. In a way, Giana felt lucky to have people who relied on her for emotional support. It helped to make sure that she didn't lose control of her own emotions.

Elsa closed her eyes and didn't say anything.

Giana just held her. They would probably sleep together again.

Just then, another knock came to the door.

Elsa opened her eyes and looked to the door. Giana sighed and shouted, "Come in."

The door opened and Tina stood there in her black long shirt, holding onto the door knob with her right hand. Her face seemed emotionless. Giana knew her well enough to know that she wasn't emotionless. At times like this, her seeming lack of emotion was a big red flag that she was feeling really bad. She knew this from experience.

Tina spoke in her melancholy tone, "Can I lay with you too?"

Giana took her arm off of Elsa and slapped on the bed behind herself.

Tina walked around and crawled into the bed behind Giana. Tina leaned her back against Giana's back.

Altogether, they laid there silently. After about five minutes of silence, Tina suddenly spoke, saying, "I'm sorry if I made you feel bad earlier. I didn't mean too."

Elsa answered her, saying, "I know. That's just how you deal with it."

Giana began to feel Tina quivering against her back. Was she crying?

Tina spoke again. Her voice was just as shaky as her back, saying, "I-I-I'm s-s-sorry." She started to cry out loud.

It was extremely rare for Tina to show so much emotion. In fact, she couldn't think of a time when she had cried as much as she was crying right now.

Giana let go of Elsa and rolled over so that she could embrace Tina now. She draped her arm over Tina. Tina kept alternating her hands as she wiped the tears that kept falling from her eyes.

Elsa was just as surprised as Giana was. She dropped her toy bunny and rolled over and lifted herself up with her arm to see Tina quivering beside Giana. Elsa hopped over them and got in front of Tina. She draped her arm over Tina too and began to rub her back, saying, "It's going to be okay, Tina."

Tina blurted out, "They're all gone. Sarah's gone. Valerie's gone. Even that idjit Jennifer is gone."

Giana replied, "Yeah. They're gone from us, but a part of them is left behind inside our hearts. As long as we hold onto them in our hearts they're never fully gone."

Tina didn't say anything. Slowly she gained her composure and passed out in sleep. Elsa passed out next. Giana got up and turned off the light. She then got back into bed and closed her eyes. In the darkness, Mary's face came back to her. A tear rolled down from her eye, staining her pillow. She clenched her eyes and forced the emotion back inside of herself. She soon passed out too.

TEARS OF DARKNESS

CHAPTER 08

THE AWAKENING

- 1 -

Valerie sat leaning against the corner of the cockpit. She still seemed a bit giddy. Her eyes continued to glow with their yellow light. Her eyes seemed to roll back and forth as she looked around herself.

Michael sat next to her on the floor of the cockpit. He watched her. He felt anxiety over her current condition. But, Justice had assured him that it was normal.

Valerie's head slowly turned until her gaze seemed to focus in on him. She seemed to exert energy just to smile at him. Her eyes darted as if she were trying to find his face, even though he was sitting right next to her.

Valerie's eyes finally stopped at Michael's face. Her gaze seemed to stare right through him. She leaned towards him a little and said, "I can feel you inside me."

Michael replied, "Huh?"

Valerie began to tap over her heart with her fingers, saying, "I can feel you in my heart. It's like a little candle flame. I can hold your life in my hand. It's so warm."

Valerie leaned closer to him until her head was leaning against his arm. She placed her palm on the metal floor and began to tap it, saying, "This doesn't have any life in it. I can't feel it. But I can feel you and Sarah and Jennifer. I can feel everyone here inside me."

Michael put his arm around her back. She snuggled up alongside Michael and gently rubbed her cheek against his chest. He patted her on the back and she stopped moving. She said, "You're warm, Lieutenant."

Michael said, "I wish I could understand what you are going through."

Michael looked down at Valerie and she was already asleep. Sarah looked over at Valerie too. She said, "Is that going to happen to me too?"

Michelle said, "It's different for everybody. It's not something that we can describe."

Jennifer said, "How long will she be like this?"

Raphael said, "She'll probably be back to normal after a few hours."

Sarah said, "What if she isn't?"

Gabrielle said, "Well then, she'll just need a little bit more time. I know you're worried about your little sister. But, I promise you that she'll be just fine. You'll be fine too."

Michael looked down at Valerie. He then looked toward Raphael and said, "Raphael, may I ask you a question?"

Raphael began to blush. She brought her hands up to cover the look of embarrassment on her face. She squirmed in her seat and said, "Mr. Snyder, I ... I think I'm too young to be with you. I'm only sixteen and you already have my big sister."

Michael shook his face in shock. He exclaimed, "What? No ... no, that's ... that's not even remotely close to what I was going to say."

Michelle pointed at Raphael with a stern look on her face, saying, "Stop hitting on my man!"

Raphael clutched her own chest with her arms and said, "I'm sorry, big sister. He's just so warm that I couldn't help myself."

Michael took that as his que and said, "That's what I want to know about. What do you and Valerie mean when you talk about that warmth you can feel?"

Raphael looked disappointed. She dropped her arms and said, "Oh. Is that all you wanted to know?"

Michael nodded and said flatly, "Yeah. Nothing else." He moved his hand as if he were indicating a line he wouldn't cross.

Raphael tilted her head and began to rock slightly side to side. She said, "All living things have a spark of life. Valerie interpreted this spark as a little fire. When yellow-eyed Spirit Wielders can harness their full power, they can feel this spark of life. A yellow-eyed Spirit Wielder has the power to give energy to that spark of life. This is reflected by our ability to heal others and ourselves. We add energy to that spark and the whole body goes back to normal. We can also take energy away from that spark. If I smother that little flame inside you, you'll die."

Michael nodded and said, "I see. I know you said she'll be fine. But, I've never seen her like this before. It's like she's drunk or something like it."

Raphael tilted her head and stared blankly at him like he had said something crazy. She replied, "Like she's drunk? But she is drunk."

Raphael lifted the skirt of her frilly dress and pulled out a little silver colored metal flask. She held it up and said, "I gave her some of my liquor to help keep her calm."

Michael's expression changed to shock as he exclaimed, "What? You gave her alcohol!" He slammed both of the palms of his hands onto his face and rubbed them over his forehead.

Michael angrily said, "She's only nine years old! You can't give alcohol to a nine year old girl!"

Valerie began to stir against his torso. She said in her sleep, "Turn down the radio, Lieutenant. I can't hear Magical Girl Squad."

Raphael shrugged her shoulders and said, "She needed something to help her calm down and I didn't have anything else."

Raphael held up the flask and shook it gently in her hand, saying, "Did you need some too, Mr. Snyder?"

Michael dropped his hands from his face and said, "No, I ... damn it!" He grabbed the flask out of her hand, screwed off the cap, and took a quick swig. His face scrunched as he swallowed the strong drink. He exhaled loudly and screwed the cap back on. He handed it back to Raphael, saying, "Is that moonshine?"

Valerie talked in her sleep again, saying, "Mary wants a drink too."

Sarah began to chuckle. She said, "Yeah, she's drunk alright."

Michael turned his face to Raphael. He said, "Please don't give my team any more moonshine without asking me first. I know you did it because you thought it was the right thing to do. But, they're under my responsibility so ask me next time. Okay?"

Raphael squirmed in her seat and said, "Okay. I'm sorry, Mr. Snyder."

Sarah giggled and said, "Hey, Lieutenant. Can I get a taste of that drink too? It looks like fun."

Michael shook his head and said, "No, I have one too many drunk girls to deal with already."

Valerie spoke out again in her sleep, saying, "I love you."

Michael shook his head and said, "Geez, I can't believe you carry a flask of moonshine underneath your dress."

Raphael shrugged her shoulders and said, "What's wrong with that? I only use for emergencies."

Michael threw up his free hand in frustration, exclaiming, "But you're too young?"

Raphael tilted her head in confusion, saying, "Who says I'm too young?"

Michael chuckled and said, "The government, it's ..." He paused and realized what he was about to say."

Raphael, still tilting her head, smiled and replied, "I don't think anyone of us here really cares about what the government says anymore."

Michael waved her off and said, "Ah, forget it! Hey, Justice. Where're we headed next?"

Without turning from the controls, Justice replied, "We're going to our hide out on a small island known as Kaua'i. It is part of the Hawaiian Islands. We should be there in a couple of hours."

Michael tilted his head in confusion and said, "Aren't all those islands abandoned?"

Justice nodded his head and said, "Yes, Mr. Snyder. That's why it makes such a great hide out. There is nobody left there after the evacuation."

The last thing that Justice said caught Sarah's attention. She said, "Evacuation?"

Michael nodded his head and said, "Yeah. All the little island populations were forcefully evacuated to the great sector cities."

Sarah seemed confused. She said, "The Harvesters can't really swim so wouldn't it be better to leave people alone on the islands so that the Harvesters can't get them."

Michael shrugged his shoulders and said, "Well, normally I'd agree with you. But, knowing what we know now about the World Government, they probably didn't want to have any groups of people that weren't dependent on them."

Justice added his own voice on the matter, saying, "That's right, Mr. Snyder. When you're trying to control the population, you have to make sure that they are dependent on you. What you probably don't know is that any group of people who tried to resist the forced migration were slaughtered by nuclear missiles."

Sarah looked downcast. She lowered her gaze to the floor and said, "That's horrible. I could use a drink to get over my depression."

Raphael pulled the flask out from under her dress again with a huge grin. Michael looked at her sternly and pointed at her. She pouted, looking sad, and stuck the flask back under her dress.

Jennifer crossed her arms over her chest and said, "Why am I not surprised? They make me so angry, I ... I ... I don't even know what to do!"

Michelle held her hands up in front of her. She caused them to burn with her red fire. She smiled psychotically and said, "You kill them. That is what you do, little sister."

It was around evening time when the Spear of Destiny left for the region that was once known as China. It was early in the morning when the Spear of Destiny arrived in Kaua'i. The reason being that the speed of the Spear of Destiny rushed through the time zones quickly. The sky was still black and the sun wouldn't rise for a couple of more hours.

The Spear of Destiny touched down on an abandoned runway. The runway was a remnant of the old Lihue airport that was used before the island was forcibly evacuated by the World Government.

When the Spear of Destiny touched down, Jennifer excitedly said, "We're here! I want breakfast."

Valerie was still asleep as she leaned against Michael. A line of drool had dripped down the side of her cheek.

Justice got out of the pilots seat and said, "Welcome, my friends, to our home! Feel free to think of it as your home too."

Justice hit the control panel next to the door and it began to open. The cool morning air rushed in to replace the stale air of the cockpit. Sarah and Jennifer both inhaled deeply and exhaled joyfully.

Sarah excitedly said, "I can smell the sea!"

Jennifer said, "Yeah, I can smell the salt too. It's like I'm back home in Los Angeles Sector."

Sarah said, "I've always wanted to go to the beach."

Jennifer said, "To bad we don't have our swimsuits."

Michelle said, "I'm sure we could find you swimsuits if you wanted to go to the beach." Michelle paused and looked towards Michael. She continued, saying, "Unless, Mr. Snyder, you don't mind going skinny dipping with us." She brought her right hand thumb to her lips and began nibbling on the edge of her thumbnail. In exaggeration, her eyes darted up and down along his body line."

Michael held up the palm of his hand and said, "No thanks. I'll pass."

Michelle shrugged her shoulders, looking disappointed. She replied, "As you wish."

Michael stood up and stretched. He then bent over and picked up the sleeping Valerie. She lay motionless as dead weight in his arms. Sarah and Jennifer followed behind him as they stepped out of the Spear of Destiny into the morning air of Kaua'i. Jennifer and Sarah stretched.

Sarah said, "Is it too early for breakfast?"

Justice jumped out of the doorway of the Spear of Destiny. He threw his arms open wide and breathed deeply, exclaiming, "Ah, this is paradise, my friends!"

Gabrielle carefully stepped down the steps of the Spear of Destiny onto the pavement, saying, "I'll make us some breakfast."

Michelle followed behind her, saying, "And I'll make some tea."

Raphael came down the steps next and said, "Did you know we grow our own tea here?"

Michelle nodded and said, "Yes, little sisters, get ready to taste the best tea in the world. Even better than that old Darjeeling that we had yesterday."

Jennifer said, "Wow, you grow your own tea?"

Raphael nodded excitedly, saying, "Yes! We make lots of our own stuff here. It's the only way to be truly independent of the World Government. When the sun comes up, I'll show you our garden."

Jennifer nodded and said, "Okay."

Justice spun around in a circle and then stopped suddenly, pointing at a darkened building in the distance. He chuckled and said, "There is our home. It was an abandoned hotel. It is the perfect place to rest up before we take our next step in the war against the path of the future."

Justice raised his hand, stretching it out towards the sky. He exclaimed, "And Justice said, Let there be light." His hand began to burn with his white fire and the area around him lit up as if his hand was a torch in the darkness. Justice walked towards the abandoned hotel building in the distance. They all followed behind him as he led the way.

The hotel was dark. The silhouette towered above them. Michael guessed that it was about twenty floors. Justice corrected him by stating that it was twenty five floors. At its heyday, it was the most expensive hotel on the island. Now, it was a makeshift mansion to a group of rebels.

The doors were glass panes that could be easily pulled open by a gold colored bar along the side. Even in the darkness you could tell that the foyer was gilded with expensive items. The only apparent corruption was a phrase that appeared to be spray painted in red along the length of the doors. The phrase was 'Maison de Pax' or, in English, 'House of Peace'.

Justice held his palms up to tell them to stop. He said, "Wait here while I turn on the lights."

Michael said, "You still have power here?"

Justice stretched his arms open wide with a chuckle, saying, "Of course. I have set up a Tesla reactor. We will have all the power we need here."

Justice opened the door and stepped inside. His light slowly dimmed till it vanished behind something. After a couple of minutes, lights began to turn on in sections of the hotel until it was completely lit up. Justice then reappeared and beckoned them to enter into the foyer.

Josh opened the door and waved for them all to enter first. Michael, still carrying Valerie, entered in followed by Sarah and Jennifer. Their eyes wandered all around them as they admired the beauty of the hotel.

Michael noticed that there were paintings of people and landscapes hanging on the wall. Someone had painted over all the faces so that it looked like they were wearing white masks with happy, sad, angry, or indifferent expressions.

Justice spun around again, exclaiming, "Isn't it magnificent?"

Michael nodded and said, "Yeah. We don't have things like this anymore because of the war."

Justice stopped spinning and said, "Let's find a place for Valerie to rest and then you, Mr. O'Brian, and I can have a talk."

Justice held his hand out towards his girls and said, "My darling angels, can you please get things ready for Mr. Snyder and his girls?"

Michelle raised her hand up high and shouted, "Yes, Papa!" Her feet glowed with red fire and she sped off down a hallway.

Gabrielle held her hand out to Sarah and said, "Want to help me make breakfast?"

Sarah nodded her head and said, "Sure. I like cooking." She took Gabrielle's hand and she led her down the same hallway that Michelle had sped down just a moment ago.

Raphael held her hand out to Jennifer and said, "Want to go help too?"

Jennifer shrugged her shoulders and replied, "Okay, I guess." She took Jennifer by the hand and they followed behind Gabrielle and Sarah.

Justice waved Michael over, saying, "Come, let's get her into bed. Follow me upstairs. We've already prepared some rooms for you."

Michael nodded and followed Justice up the stairs in the lobby to the second floor. Justice opened a door and flipped the light switch. The room was just a standard guest room. The more expensive rooms were higher up in the hotel.

Justice led Michael into the back where the bed was. He pulled the covers back and Michael laid her on the mattress. He pulled the covers back over her and gently caressed her hair with a smile.

Justice said, "Let's go into the sitting room where we can talk about what is next."

Michael nodded and said, "Okay. Lead the way."

Together, they made their way back downstairs where Josh was waiting for them to come back. Josh called out as they walked down the stairs, "Is she okay?"

Michael nodded and said, "Yeah. She just needs to sleep it off." He chuckled and said, "I never thought I would have to deal with little girls getting drunk. Not even Mary actually took a drink." His smile faded as he thought of Mary again. He remembered her complaining about not being old enough to drink alcohol. She would never get that chance because he helped to poison her.

Josh sensed the change in Michael's mood. He tried to lighten the mood with a laugh, saying, "Well, as long they do not drive it should be okay."

Michael chuckled but quickly returned to his gloomy composure. Justice motioned for them to follow him. Justice led them down the hallway to what looked like some type of waiting room. The room was filled with recliner type chairs that were modeled after antiques from the Victorian era.

Justice sat down in a chair and motioned for them to sit down as well. Josh and Michael pulled their chairs and formed a triangle with Justice.

Justice tapped his fingers on the armrests of his chair. His emotionless mask portrayed nothing of what he might be thinking. Josh and Michael sat there patiently waiting for Justice to speak.

Justice leaned back and said, "So, do you still want to get your lady-friend out of Sacramento?"

Michael nodded and said, "Yeah. I do. I think she'll be a valuable asset to our cause. Plus, Giana, her red Wielder is in danger of dying from structural collapse. I don't want another girl I know dying from that poison cocktail."

Josh nodded and said, "Yeah. I saw the report that she had had her first period. I do not want to wait either. I want to get them out of there now too."

Justice leaned forward. He brought his hands together in front of his mask and said, "It won't be easy, like it was with you. We might have to invade your old complex and fight people you might know. Are you willing to do that, Mr. Snyder?"

Michael leaned back in his chair and nodded. He said, "I don't want to fight them but I will if I have to."

Justice dropped his hands and said, "If we head there, Mr. Schilds may have your friends killed just to spite you."

Josh shrugged his shoulders and waved his right hand, saying, "They may have them killed out of spite, even if we do not try to make contact."

Justice laughed out loud and exclaimed, "True! True!" He calmed down and calmly said, "Very well then, my friends. We'll go and rescue your friend and her squad tonight. We'll leave here at eight at night so that it will be one in the morning there. That will help give us the cover of darkness in our infiltration into Sacramento Sector."

Michael and Josh both nodded at Justice. Then they both turned to face each other and gave each other a look of mutual understanding.

Michelle suddenly came running into the room. She held something white in her hands that she embraced against her chest. There was a huge grin on her face. She ran up to Michael and gazed at him with hopeful expectation. She said, "We were so sure that you'd join us that I went ahead and made you a new outfit. I used the information that Mr. O'Brian gave Papa in the file so it should fit you. If not, I can fix it up."

Michelle held out the clothing towards him. It was folded nicely and had a new crisp feeling to it. Michael reached out and took it with a nod. He said, "Thanks. I appreciate it. May I try it on now?"

Michelle nodded and said, "Yeah. I made each stitch with love. I'll help you put it on if you want."

Michael waved his hand and said, "That's okay. I think I can manage on my own." He turned to Justice and said, "Guess, I'll go up to my room and try it on." He got up from his chair and left to go upstairs.

Michelle clapped her hands together once and said, "Oh, I'll go put on some tea now." She ran away and disappeared down the hall.

Michael walked up the stairs to the second floor again. He walked by Valerie's door and placed his ear against it. He didn't hear anything. He kept walking past the doors with other people's names on them. He came to a door with his own name on it written in what looked like red crayon. There were a couple of hearts sketched on the door as well. Michael shook his head and thought to himself that the drawings were probably Michelle's doing.

Michael opened the door and walked into the back room. He tossed Michelle's handmade clothing on what was now his bed. He looked around and saw a drawer. Out of curiosity, he approached it and opened the top drawer. It was filled with underwear and socks.

Michael picked up a pair of underwear and held it up. It looked like it was his size. He sighed in relief and said to himself, "Thank goodness. I missed wearing underwear."

Michael tossed the underwear on the bed as well as a pair of socks. He closed the drawer and began to look around the room. He saw another door by the door he entered and decided to see what it was. He opened the door and saw that it was a full sized bathroom like he thought it would be. He looked at the shower and then took a quick sniff of himself. He decided to take a quick shower before getting into his new clothing.

The water ran hot and quickly steamed up the room. He was happy to be able to have running water again. He didn't think that he would get to have running water, let alone hot water. He quickly jumped in and rinsed himself off. He shut off the water and dried himself with the towel that hung nearby.

Michael left the bathroom and changed into his new underwear. They felt stiff but they fit just fine. The socks fit too. He unfolded the bundle of clothing that Michelle had given to him. There was a lot more clothing than he expected. There was a long sleeved shirt, with a vest and a twin tail coat. There were pants too. All of these articles of clothing were white. The pants had a black stripe down each leg on the outside part. This new outfit was modeled after his old uniform, except that it was more tuxedo like.

Michael picked up the shirt and noticed that a black silk scarf fell out of it. He picked it up and put it on the bed. He put the shirt on and buttoned it up. It was a little loose but he was surprised at how well it managed to fit him without having measured him at all. It was well made.

Next, Michael put on the pants. These were slightly loose too but not enough that they would hang. In fact, he decided he liked the looseness since he felt that it would be easier to fight in if he had to fight. He decided the scarf was supposed to be some sort of tie like Justice wore. So, he wrapped it around the collar of his neck and tied it like a bow.

Next he put on the vest. The vest didn't have any black striping on it. The vest ended in two points along his legs. He put on the twin tail coat. The twin tails were long and ended in points just below his knees. The coat had black piping along the edges. Near the wrists there was a black ring around the cuff.

There was a black stripe in the middle of each front panel of the coat. The stripe ran from his shoulders to the base of the coat.

Michael went back into the bathroom and admired himself in the mirror. He felt a little awkward wearing a tuxedo style outfit, but he felt happy to be wearing his old white and black colors again. It was familiar to him and brought back fond memories; even if those memories were based on lies.

Michael stepped out of the bathroom and entered into the main room again. He noticed another door and opened it. It was a closet. Much to his surprise, instead of being filled with clothing it was filled with tools and weapons.

Michael saw a pair of combat boots on the floor of the closet and put those on first. They felt sturdy and fit him nicely. Next, he strapped a holster belt around his waist, underneath his vest and coat. He saw an older style matchlock pistol hanging on the wall. He picked it up and smiled, saying, "Is this what I think it is?"

Michael walked over to the window and opened it. He pointed the pistol in the air and pulled the trigger. There was a small pop and a black sphere of energy shot out of the barrel. It was based on the S.E.Re.F device, just like Michelle's pistol was. He put the safety on the pistol and stuck it into the holster on his belt.

Michael examined the other tools. He picked up a combat knife in a sheath and attached it to his holster belt. He looked over the other tools but decided that what he had was good enough. He shut the closet door and headed back downstairs.

As he was leaving his room, Valerie came stumbling out of her room. He saw her and said, "Hey, Val. How you feeling?"

She slowly turned towards him. She was clutching her forehead with her left hand. She said, "Not so loud, Lieutenant. My head hurts. I've never felt this way before."

Michael smiled and said, "Sounds like you got what is called a hangover. You yellow Wielders can't get sick normally with your power but since you drank alcohol ..."

Valerie leaned against the wall and said, "Was that what that drink was? Who would ever drink that for fun?"

Michael said, "Have you tried fixing it with your powers yet?"

Valerie tried to shake her head but then stopped and her face grimaced in pain. She said, "No, I didn't think of that." Her eyes glowed brighter for a moment and then went back down to their normal glow when she had her powers activated. She stood up and smiled, exclaiming, "Wow! It worked, Lieutenant!"

Michael put his hand on top of her head, saying, "You don't know how lucky you are to be able to get rid of a hangover with a mere thought."

With her headache dealt with, Valerie noticed the new outfit that Michael was wearing. She looked over his new suit and said, "Wow, Lieutenant! That's a fancy looking uniform."

Michael stretched out his arms and spun in a circle, saying, "Yeah, you like it? I thought Michelle said she was going to make me one. But, apparently, she did it before we joined up."

Valerie nodded her head and said, "Yeah. It's handsome."

Michael stopped spinning and dropped his arms back down to his side. He said, "I like the colors but I'm not used to wearing something fancy like this."

Valerie nodded her head with a smile and said, "We got a new life now so we need a new style."

Michael nodded in understanding and said, "Yeah, I guess you are right. Since, you've been asleep. I'll let you know now that we are planning on rescuing Squad Four tonight."

Valerie smiled and nodded again. She replied, "Oh, that's good. We can save Giana now from self-destructing too."

Michael put his hands on her shoulders and said, "It might be dangerous. We might have to fight people we know."

Valerie's face changed. She smiled even bigger. It reminded him of the smile he saw on Raphael's face when she murdered all those people with her power. Valerie looked up at him with her pure yellow eyes. With that same creepy smile, she said, "That's okay. If anybody tries to hurt my sisters, I'll just kill them. Where is everybody else right now?"

Michael dropped his hands from her shoulders. He stared at her with concern on his face. He said, "They're downstairs and down the hall waiting for breakfast."

Valerie nodded her head and said, "Oh, okay." She turned around and saw the stairs. She began to skip toward the stairs. As she skipped, she began to hum the tune to the theme song of Magical Girl Squad.

Valerie stopped at the top of the stairs and looked back to Michael, who was still standing there, watching her with concern. She said, "Wow, Lieutenant. This place looks huge!" She then took off down the stairs as she continued to hum the Magical Girl Squad theme song.

Michael could feel a change in Valerie. It was probably the influence of those three girls. He wondered if he should talk to her or just let it go. They were in a war after all. Was it better that they prepare themselves to fight people now, not just Harvesters? He decided to let it go and wait and see what would happen. He followed Valerie down the stairs.

- 2 -

Sarah stood next to Gabrielle in the large kitchen that was once used for fulfilling room service orders. Raphael and Jennifer stood side by side on the other side of the counter. Gabrielle ignored them and stood there crossing her arms over her chest. She stared at Sarah intently. Sarah stared back at her awkwardly. She felt uncomfortable being stared at so intently. She held her hands in front of the skirt of her dress and twiddled her thumbs.

Gabrielle finally spoke, saying, "What should we make for breakfast?"

Sarah looked away from her awkwardly and continued to twiddle her thumbs. She said, "Would ... would we be able to make pancakes?"

Jennifer excitedly tapped the palm of her hands on the counter, exclaiming, "Please, please! I'd love to have some pancakes and syrup!"

Gabrielle looked upward and said, "We can make pancakes but we don't have any maple syrup here. We got our own honey though. Would you still want pancakes, even though we don't have any syrup?"

Jennifer's face plummeted to the counter top as she let out an extra loud sigh exclaiming, "No syrup!"

Jennifer lifted her head up and disappointedly said, "I still want pancakes even though we don't have any maple syrup. Honey is almost as good." She slumped over on the counter.

In imitation of her, Raphael slumped over the countertop too, saying, "I still want pancakes even though we don't have any maple syrup."

Gabrielle said, "Great! We'll have pancakes and eggs." She pointed at Raphael and Jennifer saying, "You two work on the eggs. Sarah and I will work on the pancakes together."

Raphael and Jennifer saluted her together. Raphael said, "Sure thing, big sister!"

Jennifer said, "Yes, big sister!"

Raphael tapped Jennifer on the shoulder, saying, "Come with me, little sister. I'll show you where we keep the eggs."

Raphael headed towards a large stainless steel fridge in the back of the kitchen. Jennifer followed her. Gabrielle opened a cupboard door and pulled a large metal bowl out of it. She handed it to Sarah, saying, "Come, little sister. We'll get the things we'll need to make our pancakes."

Gabrielle headed towards a door marked pantry. Sarah followed her. Inside the pantry was loaded with different types of food. There was a large bucket marked flour on the floor. Sarah held the bowl and Gabrielle measured out the flour they would need. She then opened a container marked salt and threw in a couple pinches of salt. She took a scoop of baking powder and tossed it in as well.

They left the pantry and went to the countertop next to one of the stove sets. Gabrielle handed Sarah a large spoon and told her to mix it. Sarah started to mix the dry ingredients. Gabrielle then measured out some water and poured it into the bowl. Sarah stirred it up until the batter was completely mixed.

Sarah turned her head to see what Jennifer was doing. She was busy cracking eggs in to a bowl. Raphael was slowly spinning in a circle and singing some type of old rhyme about eggs. The words didn't make sense to Sarah.

Sarah focused her attention on Gabrielle again. Gabrielle was at the stove fussing with a large skillet. Sarah watched her and felt a little amazed. She said, "Big sister, I'm impressed at how much of your own stuff you make. It must be really hard. I don't think I could ever do that."

Without losing her focus, Gabrielle replied, "You are correct, little sister. Making our own stuff is hard. You don't think you can do it because you've been taught that you can't. Once you get used to it, you'll come to not only realize that you can do it, but you will prefer to make your own things."

Sarah looked down at the bowl of batter and said, "You think so?"

Gabrielle nodded and said, "I know so, because that is what happened to me. You see, little sister. I came to realize that the bad men gained power over the world because people stopped making their own things and relied on others to make things for them. The only way to be truly free is to make your own things. Freedom isn't easy but it is worth it. The bad men enslaved everybody because they ensnared them with the promise of making their lives easier. Remember this, little sister: Those who seek to set your life at ease, secretly see you as slaves on your knees."

Michelle suddenly burst into the kitchen. She started spinning around so that the hem of her dress lifted up like an umbrella. She exclaimed, "Mr. Snyder accepted my gift. That means that he loves me!"

Sarah handed the bowl of batter to Gabrielle and said to Michelle, "Lieutenant Michael is just a really nice person. If he accepted your gift it was because he was trying to be nice."

Michelle stopped spinning and clutched her chest, saying, "But my gift was his new uniform. He's going to wear it over his manly body. It'll be like I'm hugging him each time he puts it on."

Sarah shook her head and rolled her eyes. She replied, "I'm telling you the truth, big sister. Lieutenant Michael is in love with Lieutenant Rachel. I don't want you to be heart broken when we rescue Lieutenant Rachel."

Michelle's eyes looked like they were about to sparkle. She clasped her hands together and brought them underneath her chin. A look of pure hope shone from her face. She said, "No matter what, I won't lose hope. After all, I have an advantage over that Ray-chel. She's old and I'm still young."

Sarah said, "They're like the same age."

Michelle grasped her own arms across her chest and said, "I know that. Men like younger women so I got that advantage."

Sarah said, "If it's a race, Lieutenant Rachel has known him for years. I think they were friends since they were like eighteen or something."

Michelle suddenly, without warning, got really angry. She yelled out, "I can't help that!" and slammed her right fist on the countertop in front of Sarah. The metal of the countertop buckled and bent underneath the force of her fist. Out of fear, Sarah suddenly jumped back and was shaken. She nervously grasped her hands in front of her chest as she looked on in horror.

Gabrielle thrust the spatula she was holding in Michelle's direction and shouted, "Bad sister! You broke another countertop!"

Michelle's hands trembled. She grasped her hands together and looked at Sarah who was staring at her with wide eyes in horrific shock. She said, "I ... I'm so sorry. I ... I didn't mean to scare you like that."

Sarah nodded and hesitantly said, "Yeah. I know."

Michelle looked at the countertop and said, "Looks like I broke another countertop."

Gabrielle nodded and said, "Yes, sister. I just told you that!"

Michelle stepped backwards as if she were falling. Her back hit against the wall behind her. She slid down against the wall until she was sitting down on the floor. She brought her knees up and rested her arms on her knees. She buried her face in her arms and started to cry.

Sarah overcame her fear and looked at her with compassion as she watched her crying on the floor. She walked around the broken countertop and stepped up to the crying Michelle. She dropped to her knees and wrapped her arms around her and said, "There's no need to cry. I forgive you. It's not the first time a red Wielder has broken a table in front of me."

Michelle leaned into her embrace and said, "I'm...I'm a ba...bad girl. I did a ba...bad thing."

Sarah said, "It's okay. We all make mistakes. You're not a bad girl just because you made a mistake."

Michelle lifted her head and said, "I'm sorry. I'm really sorry I did that in front of you. I'll try to control myself better."

Sarah replied, "That's enough. Why don't you get up and make us some tea like you promised us you would."

Michelle's face lighted up and she said, "Oh, yes. I came here to make tea."

Sarah stood up and offered her a hand. Michelle took her hand and Sarah lifted her up off the ground. After she jumped up, Michelle grabbed onto Sarah in a big embrace. She said, "I love you so much, little sister."

Sarah replied in kind, saying, "I love you too, big sister."

Valerie heard talking in the distance. She ran towards the voices and came to a big door that could be easily swung open. She pushed on the door and it opened before her into a big kitchen. She saw Sarah with Gabrielle and Jennifer with Raphael. Michelle was by herself, in front of a stove, working with a tea kettle.

Valerie waved her hand high in the air and said, "I'm awake! This place is huge! I've never seen a kitchen this big. It's like this house kept growing on its own."

Sarah waved back at her and said, "Hey, Valerie. You're finally awake."

Jennifer called out to Valerie, saying, "It's about time you woke up. We've been doing all the work without you."

Valerie became embarrassed and said, "I didn't mean to sleep. I couldn't help it."

Sarah replied, "Yeah, we know. It's really big sister Raphael's fault for giving you alcohol."

A loud humph, came from Raphael's direction.

Valerie clasped her hands in front of her skirt and began to twist herself from side to side. She said, "I want to help. Is there anything I can do?"

Sarah said, "Not right now. We're almost done here. After breakfast you can do the dishes."

Valerie spoke out annoyed, "All by myself?"

Raphael said, "I'll help you, little sister."

Valerie nodded with a smile and replied, "Oh, thank you so much, big sister!"

Michelle poured hot water into a teapot and set the teapot on a tray. She picked it up and said, "Little sister Valerie, come with me and I'll show you where the dining room is. Then you can help me set up the place for breakfast."

Valerie nodded with a smile and excitedly ran up to Michelle. Michelle led the way out of the kitchen through the swinging door and down the hall to what looked like a restaurant. There were many tables with chairs scattered throughout the room.

Michelle walked up to the biggest rectangle table in front and set the tea tray on it. She said, "Help me get five more chairs to put around this table." Valerie nodded and began to grab some chairs. Together, they put the extra chairs around the table. Valerie counted them out and said, "Nine chairs. Oh, there's nine of us now."

Michelle nodded and said, "That's right. Let's go back and get the dishes now."

Valerie nodded and said, "Okay."

Together they set the table. Raphael and Gabrielle began to bring out the food. Valerie sniffed the air and said, "Oh! I love pancakes!"

Michelle ran out of the room and soon returned with Justice, Josh and Michael. As Michael entered the dining room, Sarah was surprised at his new uniform and said, "Wow! That is an awesome uniform, Lieutenant."

Michael ran his hands over the black stripes on his jacket. He said, "You think so? It felt a little awkward at first but I'm getting used to it."

Jennifer turned around to see his new uniform. She said, "Is that the clothing that Michelle made for you?"

Michael nodded and said, "Yeah. That's right."

Michelle, who was following behind Justice, slipped behind Michael and slid her arms around his chest from the back. She hugged him gently and said, "Every time you wear my clothing, Mr. Snyder, it's like my arms are hugging you all over your body."

With an annoyed and defeated look on his face, he let her embrace him from behind but let his arms droop along his sides. He said, "Yeah, yeah. I hear you."

As if Michelle was expecting a different response, her face became downcast. She slid her arms out from around his body and walked around him to the table. Michael watched her attitude and hoped that she was finally getting the message that he wasn't going to have a relationship with her.

They all sat down together and Valerie picked up her fork and knife. She started tapping the ends of her utensils on the table and chanted, "Pancakes!" over and over again. Suddenly she stopped and looked confused. She looked left and then right, and then looked left again and then back to the right. She said, "Where's the maple syrup?"

Justice chuckled and said, "Silly girl, we don't have maple trees here, so that means we can't get maple syrup."

A look of horror fell on Valerie's face. She slammed the ends of the utensils on the table and exclaimed, "What! No maple syrup?"

Justice nodded in his emotionless mask and replied, "That's right, little Valerie. But, we got honey and jam. You can put those on your pancakes instead."

Valerie dropped her utensils and covered her face with her hands. Sarah watched her and said, "You going to be okay, Valerie?"

Valerie held up a hand as if she were telling her to wait. After another moment, Valerie put her hands down on the table and replied, "I'll be o...o...okay." She took a couple of pancakes off of the platter and tossed them onto her plate mournfully. She took the jar of honey and spilled some on her pancakes. She then placed her palms together and said a silent prayer.

As Valerie was praying, Jennifer laughed at her and said, "You're so melo...melodramatic."

Sarah looked towards Jennifer and said, "Are you sure you can handle that big of a word?"

Jennifer seemed to ignore her instead of retorting back. Her eyes went wide. She suddenly slid her chair back and placed her palms over her heart. Her eyes became full of panic and she leaned forward. Her breathing became labored.

Sarah said, "You okay, Jennifer?"

Michael looked at Jennifer and saw that she was now hunching over and was having trouble breathing. He said, "Jennifer, what's wrong? Are you choking?"

Jennifer slid out of her chair and fell onto the floor.

Michael jumped up from his chair and ran over to her. Sarah and Valerie pushed their own chairs out and got down beside Jennifer.

Justice, as if nothing was happening, calmly said, "It appears it is her time."

Jennifer clutched her chest again and exclaimed, "It feels like something is beating in my heart that's not my heart."

Michelle sat in her chair and put a piece of pancake into her mouth, saying, "Oh, that's normal."

Jennifer's eyes began to burn with a red fire like never before. Her hands on their own began to burn with the same red fire. Michael, Sarah and Valerie realized that Jennifer was awakening to her full power.

Jennifer's feet started to glow with red flames too. She rolled over on her back and looked up at the ceiling. The look of terror on her face was replaced with a look of warm comfort.

Michael slid his hands underneath Jennifer's body and picked her up off of the floor. He sat down on the floor and cradled her in his arms, saying, "Are you okay now? Do you feel any pain? It looks like you got your full power now."

Jennifer looked up into the ceiling with a relaxed smile. She seemed a little out of it. She said, "I...I feel so light now. I didn't realize that I felt so heavy before. But, now I understand. I feel so light."

Jennifer looked into Michael' face. She smiled at him and placed the palm of her right hand onto his cheek and gently caressed it. Her hand continued to burn with red fire that seemed to spread over his entire face. The red flames felt warm against his skin.

Jennifer let go of his face and closed her eyes. She leaned the side of her face against his chest. She said, "Lieutenant, I remember when you held me like this after I cut myself in the shower and also when you stopped me from killing myself in the field. Do you remember?"

Michael nodded and said, "Yeah, I remember."

Jennifer continued, saying, "I understand now what I'm feeling in my heart. I can feel your heart beating inside my heart. I can also feel Sarah and Valerie beating inside my heart. I can feel everyone here. I feel your love for me. I love you too."

Michael didn't know what to do or say. He hadn't experienced this before. He wished he could understand fully what she was going through. Out of the corner of his eye he saw something shiny waving. He looked up towards the glimmer and saw that it was Raphael waving the small metal flask of moonshine. She smiled at him and pointed towards it with her other hand. Michael shook his head and glared at her. Raphael shrugged her shoulders and stuck the metal flask back under the skirt of her dress.

Michael focused his attention on Jennifer, who had her red, glowing eyes back open. She gazed lovingly up at him. He said, "Do you want to lie down? Or, do you want to keep eating?"

Jennifer said, "I want to keep eating. I'm hungry." She dangled her legs and Michael set her feet back down on the ground. Jennifer withdrew the red flames back inside of her body. Her hands and feet no longer burned with red flames. Her eyes continued to glow, just like Valerie's eyes; just like the eyes of the three angels.

Jennifer got back in her chair and put another piece of pancake in her mouth. She then shoveled some scrambled eggs into her mouth and chewed them together.

Michael, Valerie and Sarah sat back down and started to eat again. It seemed like Jennifer was staring at Michael but it was hard for him to tell since when their eyes glowed with light, it was impossible to tell where they were looking. He recalled the difficulty and trouble he had to deal with when he first met her.

Justice said, "Congratulations, Valerie and Jennifer! Now you have your full power and you are experiencing the full abilities that you can possess."

Justice paused. He lifted his mask slightly and shoved a small piece of pancake underneath it. He then continued, saying, "Now, about tonight everybody. We have decided to go and rescue Lieutenant Rachel Harris and her squad. Then, we'll continue to destroy the Harvester factories."

The girls all nodded their heads in excitement.

Michelle seemed annoyed and said, "Do we really need to go rescue that woman?" Everybody ignored her comment.

Sarah smiled, saying, "Oh good. I'll be happy to see Squad four again."

Jennifer said, "Yeah, even that idjit Gianna and Tina."

Valerie shoved another piece of pancake into her mouth and said, "I can't wait to show Elsa what I can do with my powers now."

Jennifer nodded and said, "Yeah, maybe I should challenge Gianna to a fight and show her how much stronger I am now."

Sarah glanced at her plate and poked at it with her fork, saying, "I hope I get my full powers soon too."

Gabrielle took a sip of tea, saying, "Don't worry, little sister. Your time is soon to come."

After breakfast was over, Sarah said, "Would it be alright if I took a bath now? I feel pretty dirty."

Michael nodded and said, "Sure. The rest of the day is yours to do what you want."

Michelle said, "We have a large bath in the spa area. We can all take a bath together if you want."

Sarah nodded and said, "Yeah. That sounds like fun."

Jennifer pushed her dirty plate towards Valerie and said, "While we're taking a bath, you can do the dishes."

Valerie glared at her and replied, "Yeah, yeah. I know. I'll go do them fast and then join you. So, you all better not be quick about it."

Raphael put her hand on Valerie's shoulder and said, "Don't worry, little sister. I said I'll help you so we'll do it twice as fast."

Valerie smiled and gave Raphael a firm nod. She jumped up and began to grab the dirty dishes off the table. Raphael joined her and the two of them managed to take all the dishes in one go.

Gabrielle scooted her chair back and stood up. She folded her arms across her chest and said, "Come, sisters. Let us retire to the bath."

Michelle, Sarah and Jennifer got up from the table.

Gabrielle glared at Michael and said, "Mr. Snyder, I know you are prone to indulging your animal urges but please refrain from peeping in on us while we bathe."

Michael leaned forward and rested his head on the palm of his hand. In annoyance he sighed and said, "I hope you don't actually believe that I would go that far."

Michelle clasped her hands in front of her dress. She fidgeted side to side and said, "If ... if you really felt the need, Mr. Snyder. I ... I wouldn't be opposed to it."

Michael, still resting his head on his hand, replied, "Don't worry. I have no interest in doing so."

Michelle, still fidgeting, said, "Really? Not ... not even a little bit?"

Michael bluntly said, "Nope."

Michelle's expression went gloomy and she said, "Oh, okay."

The girls headed towards the spa room. Jennifer said, "I'd be embarrassed if a boy saw me naked."

Sarah giggled and said, "But the Lieutenant already saw you naked."

Jennifer crossed her arms over her chest and exclaimed, "Don't bring that up! That's how I know it's embarrassing!"

As the girls left for the spa, Michael rubbed his hands over his face and sighed in frustration. He said, "I'm so tired of all these things they say. I can't tell if they are joking or being serious."

Josh leaned back in his chair at the table and said, "Michelle is being serious. She does not joke around. Gabrielle is the one joking around. Take it as a compliment. She feels safe enough to make jokes like that. Remember at the beginning when she would barely say anything and just stare at you, calling you 'bad man'. No, she is joking. If she seriously believed that, she would not talk to you."

Michael leaned back in his chair and said, "Well, that makes me feel a bit better. Though, it still annoys me."

Justice suddenly burst into laughter. After a moment he calmed himself down and patted the mask on his face, saying, "Don't mind me, Mr. Snyder. Just laughing at your seriousness. Please be patient with my angels, they don't know how to act around men very well. The only men they know are the bad men and me. Then, they got to know Mr. O'Brian and now you."

Michael nodded and said, "Yeah. I get it."

Gabrielle opened the door to the spa. There were several large tubs that looked like hot tubs. Gabrielle went to the closest one and turned it on. She then stepped away from it and began to undress herself. Michelle went to a shelf and pulled off a bunch of towels. She brought them to the bench near the hot tub. She then started to undress herself too.

Sarah and Jennifer watched as Gabrielle and Michelle began to take off the layers they were wearing. Underneath their dress they wore an undergarment and a petticoat. They took off their petticoat and dropped them on top of their dresses. The petticoat is what made their dress so puffy. They unbuttoned their undergarment which was a one-piece sleeveless suit that had straps on their shoulders. The one-piece suit ended just below their knees in ruffled leggings.

Sarah said, "You two sure wear a lot of clothing."

Gabrielle tossed her undergarment on top of her petticoat and said, "Helps keep the hungry animals at bay."

Jennifer tilted her head and looked confused. She said, "How does wearing lots of clothing stop hungry animals."

Michelle chuckled. She placed her hand on Jennifer's head and walked around her towards the hot tub. As she walked away she said, "So cute ... so innocent. My dear sister used a euphemism on you."

Jennifer turned around and said, "What's a you-fu-mi-zum?"

Sarah replied, "It means you use a nicer word to represent something else."

Jennifer nodded and said, "Oh."

Michelle lowered herself into the hot tub and said, "The hungry animals are men who want your body."

Jennifer felt stupid and said, "Oh, yeah. I get it."

Gabrielle joined Michelle in the bath. She rested her chin along the edge and said, "Come on, little sisters. Take off your cloths and get in."

Sarah and Jennifer glanced at each other and then started to take off their clothes. They put them on the bench and ran up to the hot tube. They climbed in.

Sarah couldn't help but notice Michelle's and Gabrielle's breasts in the water. She cupped her hands over her own breasts and wondered how much bigger they were going to get. It was harder having a male Lieutenant because she felt too embarrassed to ask him questions about her growing body. She was glad that Lieutenant Rachel was next door so that she could ask her those types of questions. At least that is how she thought when they still lived in the Wielder complex in Sacramento.

Sarah dropped her hands back in the water. She looked down into the water and watched the water ripple over the surface. She wanted to ask them a question but felt embarrassed about it.

Jennifer noticed Sarah's expression and said, "What's wrong Sarah? You got a problem?"

Sarah looked up at Jennifer and said, "Sorry, I was thinking about asking a question."

Michelle said, "What's wrong, little sister? You can ask us anything. We won't mind. Promise." She held up her arm to the square.

Sarah looked back into the water and said, "Oh, I was just wondering if you thought breasts got in the way of fighting too."

Michelle said, "Do you not like having breasts?"

Sarah moved her hand in the water and stared at the ripples she made. She said, "A little. They seem like if they get bigger then it will be harder to fight. I know there's nothing I can do about it but sometimes I wish I didn't have any."

Gabrielle crossed her arms over her chest and gently pushed her breasts together. She said, "It's true that they can get in the way of fighting but they have such an important purpose. They're for nurturing babies."

Jennifer said, "Now-a-days we don't even need them for that because we have baby formula."

Gabrielle's face changed to disgust and said, "Baby formula! That stuff is trash! God designed my body to give my babies all they need. Baby formula has things in it that can hurt your baby and it costs a lot of money. What God gave me is free and is designed to be best for my babies."

Jennifer looked down to the water, embarrassed. She said, "I was just sayin' what people do now."

Michelle waved her hand towards Jennifer and said, "Oh, don't mind her." She turned her attention to Sarah and said, "Are you afraid of getting older?"

Sarah said, "It's not that I'm afraid. All my life I've known that I would die before I could have children. I never really cared about that before. But, now that I know that I'm not going to die, I can do things like have children and grow up to be old like you."

Michelle interrupted her, saying, "We're not that old."

Sarah said, "Yeah, I know that. But, before I met you, I believed that I was going to die in just a year or two. Now I get to grow up and be a woman. I wonder just how much I'm going to grow."

Jennifer said, "I haven't really thought about that yet. But you're right. We do get to grow up and be adults now. One day I'm going to grow up and be a full grown woman. Wow. That's amazing."

Valerie and Raphael suddenly burst into the room. Valerie shouted, "Time for a bath!" She quickly stripped off her dress and slipped into the hot tub with a splash. Raphael took a little more time to undress but she soon joined them.

Valerie laughed and said, "One time, Sarah was in a hurry out of the bath and she fell and slipped on her butt."

Sarah rolled her eyes and said, "Yeah, yeah. You know we were having a serious discussion here before you rudely interrupted us."

Valerie tilted her head and said, "Oh, really? What about?"

Jennifer replied, "We were talking about breasts and how we get to grow up now that we aren't going to die."

Valerie waved her hand in the water and said, "Oh, really?"

Jennifer mildly splashed towards her and said, "Yeah. Thanks for spoiling the mood."

Valerie looked embarrassed and her face went downcast. She said, "I'm sorry. I was just trying to be funny."

Sarah put her hand on top of Valerie's head and said, "Don't worry about it, little sis."

- 3 -

After the girls had finished with their bath, they all took a nap in their new beds. The beds were soft and comfy; even more so since they had been sleeping in the field or on a hard cockpit floor.

Sarah laid down in her bed and threw the covers over herself. She rolled over and looked out of the window. The orange glow of the sun was just beginning to peak on the horizon of the sea. She closed her eyes and quickly went to sleep.

Unfortunately, it was as if she had just blinked her eyes. She opened her eyes and the sun was already in the sky and its yellow light brightened the landscape.

Sarah felt restless. She started to think about her long dead mom and dad. She was only eight when they died. Her memory of them, their faces, their voices, had already started to fade away. Instead, when she thought of a caretaker, Lieutenant Michael was the face she saw. She thought about her new big sisters and how they called Justice, Papa; even though he wasn't really their Papa.

Sarah got out of bed and left her room. She quickly walked down the open hallway to Lieutenant Michael's room. She opened his door, shut it behind herself and crept into his room.

Lieutenant Michael was lying face up on top of the covers, with his arm over his eyes. He was in a deep sleep and still wearing his new uniform, except that his boots were beside his bed.

Sarah approached him and carefully extended her hand to his shoulder. She shook him strongly enough to wake him up.

Lieutenant Michael began to stir. He lifted his arm and groggily looked up at Sarah. He said, "Huh? Sarah, is something wrong?" He quickly sat up and swung his legs around so that he was now sitting on the edge on his bed.

Sarah stood beside him. She took hold of his jacket and gently held onto it. It reminded him of the time Mary clung onto his jacket as he sat at the dinner table before he learned that she got her first period. He quickly brushed the thought aside to focus on Sarah. He said again, "What's wrong, Sarah? Is something bothering you?"

Sarah began to look embarrassed. Her cheeks became rosy and she fought to conceal a smile. Sarah paused and he waited for her to gain courage to talk.

Sarah opened her mouth and said, "Lieutenant, you said I could call you whatever I wanted too, right?"

Michael nodded and said, "Yeah. I remember."

Sarah said, "I ... I ... I was thinking, Lieutenant. I was wondering if it would be alright if ... maybe I called you ... dad?" She looked down to the floor and her rosy cheeks became even redder.

Michael was shocked. This was the last thing that he was expecting. He put a hand on her shoulder and said, "Really? You want to call me dad?"

Sarah nodded. She dropped her hand from his jacket and grasped her hands together in front of her chest. She started to slightly twist her body side to side. She replied, "Yeah. You're the only family I got: you, Valerie and Jennifer are all that I got left of my family. I want you to be my dad."

Michael smiled warmly. He reached his arms around her and hugged her tightly. He said, "If that is what you want, that is fine with me."

Sarah embraced him back. She said, "I ... I ... love you ... dad."

Sarah gently laid her head against Michael's chest. She said, "After Susan died, I wished I could grow wings and fly away from all of this war. When we would go out into the Harvester Zone, I would sometimes see a bird. It would chirp and fly away and I wished I could be like that bird."

Michael, still holding her, said, "Yeah, I understand. All of us want to get away from the war from time to time."

Sarah held onto him tighter and said, "But now that we are here and fighting against the people that made this war, I want to grow wings so that I can fly and save the people I love when they are in danger."

Suddenly the door to Michael's apartment was thrust open and then slammed shut. Valerie stormed in pointing at them and exclaimed, "I thought ... oh, it's ... it's just Sarah. That's okay then."

Michael released his hold on Sarah. Sarah turned around to see what Valerie was doing. They both looked confused as Valerie stood there in the small yellow dress that she had been wearing.

Michael said, "Valerie, what are you talking about?"

Valerie placed her hands behind her back and began to twist side to side. She gave a feigning innocence smile, saying, "Oh, I just felt that big sister Michelle would try to sneak in here tonight."

Michael, in understanding nodded and said, "I see. So you were worried about me?"

Valerie nodded and said, "Yeah. You've been away from Lieutenant Rachel for too long so I thought that you might be getting weak. You're only allowed to sleep with us girls or with Lieutenant Rachel."

The door opened again and Michelle entered into the room. Valerie turned and went wide-eyed. She thrust her arm out and pointed angrily at Michelle, saying, "I knew it. You were planning to sneak into Lieutenant Michael's bed and tempt him to do something bad!"

Feigning ignorance, Michelle looked shocked. She put her hands over her heart and gasped, saying, "Do something bad? No, I would never do that. I believe in having a wholesome relationship till we get married. I ... I only wanted to come in here so that I could memorize his scent. He smells very nice."

Valerie shooed at Michelle with her hand. She said, "As you can see, Lieutenant Michael is already busy. So, you can just go back to your own room!"

Michelle looked dejected. Her shoulders drooped and her arms hung by her side. She sighed and turned around, leaving the room.

Michael stood up and said, "Well, all the sleep has gone out of me by now so I think I'll go down stairs. You two want to come with me?"

Michael felt another presence. He tilted his head and noticed that Jennifer was somewhat hiding around the corner. He said, "Jennifer is here too? Why don't the three of us go downstairs and see what we can do."

As they left Michael's room, Michelle, Gabrielle and Raphael were in the middle of the hall, standing in a circle. They seemed to be discussing something.

Gabrielle noticed them first and said, "Little sisters, we don't have much time. We need you three to come with us. It's time we get you a real uniform."

Valerie's face lit up. She said, "Are you going to make me a pretty dress now?"

Raphael nodded and replied, "Yep, you can come with me and I'll show you how it's done." She held out her hand to her. Valerie ran up to her and took her by the hand. They walked together to the stairs, holding hands, and went down the stairs together.

Gabrielle extended her hand to Sarah. Sarah looked at it and then walked up to her, taking her by the hand. They casually followed behind Raphael and Valerie.

Michelle put a huge, somewhat menacing grin on her face. She held her hand out to Jennifer. Jennifer glared at her and said, "I'll race you." She then activated her power in her feet and skated down towards the stairs at amazing speeds.

Michelle turned around as Jennifer sped past her. She shook her fists and said, "No fair! That's cheating!" She activated her power and her hands and feet burned with red fire. Instead of skating towards the stairs after her, Michelle jumped over the railing of the second floor.

Michael stood there in shock as Michelle leapt over the railing. He ran over to the railing and watched as Michelle landed on the floor safely. Michelle flipped Jennifer off and skated down the hallway.

Jennifer trailed behind her and shouted, "You cheating cow!"

Michael shrugged his shoulders and yawned. He said out loud to himself, "Well, if they're busy, I guess I'll go back to bed." He turned around and went back into his room, shutting the door behind himself.

Michelle sped past Gabrielle and Raphael. Sarah and Valerie jumped out of the way. Jennifer soon sped past them a second later.

Michelle made it to the door first. The words 'sewing room' were scribble on the top portion of it in crayon. She lifted her arms in victory and jumped up and down, exclaiming, "I won! I won! You slow poke."

Jennifer reached her a moment later. The red flames on her feet withdrew back inside of her. Jennifer conceded her defeat, saying, "Yeah, yeah. You won. I would have won if I jumped over the balcony too."

Michelle opened the door and Jennifer stepped inside. The room was small. It was filled with rolls of fabric and had three small tables in the middle arranged in a triangle pattern. Each table had a sewing machine on it.

Michelle sat down at one of the tables. As she sat down, the rest of the girls came into the room. Gabrielle and Raphael sat down at their own tables.

Michelle said, "Alright, sisters. What kind of dress do you want?"

Sarah, Jennifer and Valerie paused to think. They looked at each other waiting for someone to speak first.

Sarah took the initiative as the oldest. She said, "I don't know what Jennifer and Valerie want. But, I really liked what you did with Lieutenant ... my ... dad's uniform."

Valerie turned to her quickly and said, "Are you calling the Lieutenant dad now?"

Sarah became submissive and blushed. She said, "Yeah, he is more like a dad to me so I am going to call him dad. He said it was okay."

Valerie tilted her head and looked upward in thought. She said, "I see. Was that why you were talking to the Lieutenant a while ago?"

Sarah nodded her head.

Jennifer said, "That's nice. I only lost my parents a few months ago so I don't think of the Lieutenant as a dad. He's more like a big brother to me. I always wanted a big brother."

Michelle butted in, saying, "So, what do you mean about the uniform?"

Sarah turned back to Michelle and said, "I like how you based it on his original uniform. I like your dresses but they are too frilly for me. I feel it would be too hard to fight in. But, if it was a little less frilly, I'd feel better about it."

Gabrielle pulled out a pad of paper, saying, "I think I have an idea that fits your description."

Gabrielle started to sketch. After a couple of minutes she said, "Ta-dah!" And revealed her idea. The dress would be all white and laced up in the front on the bodice. On each side of the front of the bodice, was a blue stripe like her old uniform. The skirt had three short layers that ascended, leaving a gap that revealed the next layer. The last layer would end at her knees. Around the hem of each layer was a ring of blue. On the two sides of each layer of the skirt was a vertical stripe that went from the top of the skirt to the blue ring below. The color bar was equally placed on each layer so that it looked like one stripe. The triple-layered skirt was not overly frilly and draped in a small A-frame.

Sarah took the picture and carefully looked it over. She held it up for Valerie and Jennifer and said, "What do you think?"

Valerie nodded and said, "I like it."

Jennifer said, "Yeah. Me too."

Sarah handed Gabrielle the picture and said, "Okay. What do we do next?"

Gabrielle put the picture down and said, "We were planning on showing you how to make your own dresses. But, it looks like we don't have that much time so we'll do it for you this time. We just need to measure you and you can watch and see how we do it. This way you'll get an idea for next time.

The angels pulled open a drawer on their tables and pulled out their own tape measures. Michelle measured Jennifer. Gabrielle measured Sarah. Raphael measured Valerie. The three angels then quickly went to work at cutting fabric into patterns and began to sew them together. After a couple of hours they were finished.

Valerie quickly stripped out of her temporary yellow dress. Raphael had finished her dress first because Valerie was the smallest of the three of them. She pulled the new dress over her head and let it drape down over her body. She tightened the lace on her bodice and tied it into a bow.

Without a mirror, Valerie looked down at herself. She twirled around and watched the skirt of her dress lift up as centrifugal force lifted the hem of her skirt. She stopped twirling and felt a little dizzy. She smiled with glee and said, "I absolutely love it!"

Raphael clasped her hands together in front of her chest. She smiled and her yellow glowing eyes seemed to sparkle. She said, "You really love it?"

Valerie twirled around again, stopping suddenly so that the skirt of her dress swayed back and forth. She said, "Yeah! I love it. I want to go show Lieutenant Michael."

Valerie took off running out of the room. She stopped and looked left and right, wondering where the Lieutenant was. She heard male voices coming from the lounge room. She took off running towards the voices.

Valerie opened the door and stepped inside. Justice and Josh were sitting there enjoying some tea. Valerie looked left and right.

Josh and Justice stopped talking and turned to look at her. Josh said, "Is everything okay, Valerie?"

Valerie nodded and replied, "Yeah. I just was looking for Lieutenant Michael. I wanted to show him my new dress."

Josh nodded and said, "That is a very nice dress. I do not think your Lieutenant has woken up yet."

Valerie's eyes went wide. She exclaimed, "What! He went back to sleep? That slacker." Without another word, she ran out of the lounge room and ran back down the hall. She ran into the foyer and up the stairs to Michael's room.

It was true. Lieutenant Michael was passed out on the bed. Valerie squared her arms on her hips and shook her head. She spoke softly, saying, "That slacker."

Valerie walked up to the bed and softly crawled on top of it. She then stood up and began jumping up and down. She shouted, "Wake up, Lieutenant!"

Michael was quickly forced awake. Out of surprise, he fell out of bed and looked around with a confused look. He saw Valerie standing on the bed with a goofy grin on her face.

Valerie flicked her hair back over her shoulder and pointed at Michael, saying, "You've been sleeping while everyone else is working!"

Michael stood up and brushed his uniform off with his hand. He scratched his head, saying, "Sorry. I was just really tired after all. Oh, look. Is that your new dress?"

Valerie nodded and said, "Yeah, do you like it?"

Michael reached up and slid his hands under her armpits. He lifted her up off of the bed and set her down on the floor. He rubbed her on top of the head and said, "Yeah. I really like it. It reminds me of your old uniform and the dress the other girls wear."

Valerie spun around and then stopped. She said, "Yeah. Sarah and Gabrielle designed it together. Jennifer and Sarah are going to have the same design. But Raphael finished mine first."

Michael held out his hand to her and said, "I can't wait to see all of them. Why don't we go downstairs and have a snack. I'm getting hungry."

Valerie nodded and accepted his hand. Together they went downstairs and headed towards the kitchen. As they entered the hallway. Sarah and Jennifer came out of the sewing room.

Jennifer stopped in her tracks and blushed in embarrassment. She wasn't mentally prepared for Michael to see her yet. She crossed her arms over her chest. Her gaze lowered and she seemed more subdued.

Sarah stepped in front of Jennifer. She lifted the hem of her dress and spread it out as if she were about to do a curtsy. She looked to Michael and said, "What do you think of my new dress, dad?"

Michael was taken back. He remembered the conversation that he had just had with Sarah. He wasn't used to it. He nodded and replied, "Yeah, I love your new dress."

Sarah dropped the skirt of her dress and then twirled around once. She stopped and then struck a pose. She placed her left hand on her hip and raised her right hand to the back of her head. She held that position for a moment.

Michael knew that position. It was the same one that Mary liked to do when she was teasing him. The thought brought a twinge of pain in the pit of his stomach. She'd never get to try on any more outfits. It was because he had helped to poison her. She was dead because of his ignorance. He quickly pushed the pain of his emotions deep inside him. He put a smile on his face and placed his hand on top of Sarah's head. Sarah smiled back at him.

Jennifer stepped around Sarah. She seemed more relaxed but a little bit nervous still. Her upper lip protruded over her bottom lip into a childish pout. She looked up nervously at Michael while still crossing her arms over her chest.

Michael reached out and put his hand on her head, saying, "Don't worry, Jennifer. Your new dress is cute on you too."

Jennifer quickly suppressed a smile. Her cheeks became rosy as she blushed in embarrassment.

Michael squared his arms on his hips and said, "Alright, who's hungry? I know I am."

Valerie raised her hand in excitement, saying, "I am! I am!"

Sarah raised her arm high in the air and said, "Me too!"

Jennifer, still acting a little embarrassed nodded her head, but didn't say anything.

Michael said, "Come on then. I'll make us a snack."

A woman's voice behind them exclaimed, "I don't think so!" It was Michelle.

Michael turned around and said, "What? I can't have a snack?"

Michelle squared her arms on her hips, and replied, "No, you can have a snack but I don't want you messing up my kitchen. I'll make you and the little sisters a snack."

Michael's arms dropped to his side. He said, "But I know how to cook. I don't want to be a bother to you."

Michelle pointed at him and said, "It will be more bothersome if you mess up my kitchen. That's my room. You stay out of it. Go wait in the dining room. Oh, but the little sisters can help me if they want."

Sarah said, "Sure. I'll help."

Jennifer and Valerie nodded together and said in unison, "Okay."

The three girls followed Michelle into the kitchen, leaving a confused Michael standing in the hallway. He scratched his head, sighed and then headed into the dining room to wait.

Valerie skipped beside Jennifer as they headed into the kitchen. Once inside, Valerie asked her, saying, "How come you we're acting so embarrassed when you showed your dress to the Lieutenant?"

Jennifer shrugged her shoulders and replied, "Oh, I was thinking about something Michelle said."

Sarah chuckled.

Jennifer blushed again.

Valerie, becoming even more curious said, "Well, come on. What did she say?"

Jennifer glanced at Michelle, who was heading towards the fridge. She said, "Oh, when I was putting on my new dress, she said that my new dress would make all the men fall in love with me. She said that the Lieutenant might fall in love with me."

Sarah laughed again.

Valerie rolled her eyes and said, "Geez ... you shouldn't listen to a word that woman says. The Lieutenant loves Lieutenant Rachel so he's not going to fall in love with you."

Michelle pulled out a large box out of the fridge and brought it in front of them. She smiled slyly as she placed the box gently down on the metal counter top. She said, "Valerie, are you sure that is the problem? What if the real problem is that Jennifer wants Mr. Snyder to fall in love with her?"

Jennifer shook her head vigorously, exclaiming, "No! No! That's not true! I'm too young to think about stuff like that."

Sarah held up her pointer finger, saying, "Well, that's not exactly true. If you remember, we caught her trying to see Elric's butt on that one episode of the Lost Sword Saga."

Valerie's eyes widened in remembrance. She said, "Oh yeah, that's right. I remember that."

Jennifer became subdued and said, "Why'd you have to bring that up?"

Sarah said, "Come on, Jennifer, it's okay to admit that you like boys now."

Michelle waved at them and said, "Come on, stop teasing your sister. There's nothing wrong with having those feelings." She pointed at Jennifer and continued, saying, "But, understand this, little sister, I won't give my man to you no matter what so you should just give up on him."

Jennifer shook her head and rolled her eyes. She crossed her arms over her chest and stood there silently in annoyance.

Michelle opened the box and revealed a half-eaten carrot cake. She said, "We should finish this cake today. I'm sure it'll go bad soon. I'll make some tea to go with it. That will be our snack."

Michelle put some water in a kettle and set it on the stove top to boil. She grabbed nine small plates and put a slice of cake on each of them. She took a large tea pot and put a few scoops of black tea into it. She took a few trays and set all the things they needed on them.

The girls each took a tray and headed into the dining room. Michael, Josh and Justice were already there. Gabrielle and Raphael were sitting with them.

Michelle and the other girls set the table with the cakes and tea and everybody enjoyed it together.

- 4 -

Hours passed. The three angels took Sarah, Jennifer and Valerie around to complete their chores. Justice, Josh and Michael worked alongside them. Michelle helped Jennifer practice with her new powers. Raphael helped Valerie to explore her new powers too. Gabrielle trained with Sarah, even though she hadn't gotten her full powers yet. Gabrielle told Sarah that "You can manipulate your light any way you want over your body as long as you can visualize it properly. When you get your full powers, you won't need to carry any sticks. Your body will be your weapon."

As the time reached eight O'clock at night in Hawaii, they made their way back towards the Spear of Destiny. They entered the craft and Justice took it up into the air.

Michelle, sitting on the floor, crossed her arms across her chest. She spoke and couldn't hide the annoyance in her voice. She said, "It's already crowded in here. With these new people, it'll be even more crowded."

Gabrielle said, "I guess some of us will have to sit on somebody's lap."

A mischievous smile formed on Michelle's face. She tilted her head and looked upwards with her eyes. She said, "That's true. I can sit on Mr. Snyder's lap then."

Valerie shooed at her with her hand and said, "You're too big. I'll sit on his lap to make room for more people."

Michael ignored the argument and said, "Let's talk about the plan again."

Justice chuckled and said, "Good idea, Mr. Snyder."

Michael said, "You're going to land the Spear of Destiny on the roof of the Phoenix Guard Complex."

Justice replied, "Yes. We'll all stay here and then you and your girls will go retrieve them down below."

Michael said, "Do you really think that is best? Don't you think you should come with us?"

Justice shook his head and said, "Oh, no. There is so much surveillance equipment there that the moment that I step out of the Spear of Destiny, they'll recognize me. You'll have more time if you four go by yourselves. The moment they notice me, they'll send units to apprehend me. Then, it'll get bloody and I'm sure you don't want me to kill people that you might know. No, no. You four should be good enough. If things go bad, I can always come to your aid."

Michael put his hand on Sarah's head and said, "When we get inside Squad four's apartment, I want you to stand in the hallway entrance and act as a look out. Okay?"

Sarah nodded her head and said, "Aye, Lieutenant."

Michael put a hand on both Jennifer's and Valerie's head, saying, "You two, I want you to work together to wake up Tina and Elsa. Okay?"

Jennifer nodded her head and said, "Aye, Lieutenant!"

Valerie smiled and said, "Aye, Lieutenant! No problem."

Michael put his hands down and said, "I'll get Lieutenant Rachel and Giana up. When you wake them up, take them into the hallway and wait for me. Okay?"

Sarah, Jennifer and Valerie nodded. There was a little tension in the air. They were both excited and nervous to be doing this mission.

The Spear of Destiny arrived above the sector of Sacramento. It hovered over the Phoenix Guard complex. It gently landed on the roof top with a light thud. None of the roof top lights were on yet, which means that nobody noticed their landing.

Michael stood up. Sarah, Jennifer and Valerie jumped up with him. Theirs eyes glowed with the light of their colors. Michael put his hand on the control panel and the door began to open.

Justice suddenly reached out and grabbed his arm. He said, "If you go out there, they'll know that you are trying to rescue Lieutenant Rachel. She could be on a mission. If she is not there then they will most certainly kill her."

Michael nodded in understanding. His face was stern as he stared back at Justice. He said, "I understand the risks."

Michael jumped out of the Spear of Destiny. Sarah, Jennifer and Valerie followed behind him. They walked up to the door and Michael put his hand on the door knob. As soon as he gripped the handle, all of the roof top lights lit up at once. Michael said, "Looks like they know we're here now."

Michael opened the door and said, "Let's run back to our floor. Don't forget, it was the fifth floor."

Jennifer said, "It hasn't been that long, Lieutenant. We haven't forgotten where we live."

They took off running down the stairs together. They ran down to the fifth floor and entered the hallway. It felt like a dream to be back in their home but there wasn't any time to reminisce.

They ran to Squad four's door. Michael put his hand on the doorknob. He turned the handle and it opened. Most teams didn't lock their doors since the building was already secure. They entered into the apartment. Sarah stood in the mouth of the hallway while the others went back towards the individual bedrooms.

Michael entered Giana's room first. She was fast asleep in her bed and didn't notice anything going on around her. He turned on the light and quickly moved to her bed. He put his hand on her arm and shook her, saying, "Giana, it's Lieutenant Michael. Wake up!"

Giana started to stir. She opened her eyes and looked up at Lieutenant Michael. She blinked her eyes a couple of times and stared blankly up at him. She rubbed her eyes and said, "Oh, am I going to have one of those dreams where we are going to kiss and do perverted things?"

Lieutenant Michael bopped her on top of the head, saying, "Nope, this isn't a dream."

Giana sat up and rubbed her head, saying, "Owe, Lieutenant. That hurt. Wait! You're alive!"

Lieutenant Michael said, "Yeah. I'm alive. No time to explain though. We got to get you girls out of here."

Lieutenant Michael grabbed Giana by her arm and dragged her out of bed. After tripping over herself, she gained her balance and followed him into the hallway. He then ran to Lieutenant Rachel's room.

Sarah stood there in the mouth of the hallway. Giana walked up to her and said, "Am I really awake?"

Sarah nodded, without taking her eyes off of the apartment door. She said, "Yeah. It's good to see you're okay."

Giana replied, "I don't know what's going on but I want an explanation as soon as possible."

Jennifer ran into Tina's room. She flipped on the light and ran to her bed. She shook her and shouted, "Wake up!"

Tina woke up and looked at her in confusion. She said, "Ah, I'm just dreaming again." She rolled over and pulled the covers back over herself.

Jennifer shouted, "Nope! Time to get up. No time to explain."

Jennifer pulled the blankets off of her bed and picked her up. She ran out of the room with Tina in her arms. She ran up to Giana and dropped Tina on the floor with a loud thud.

Tina sat up on the floor, rubbing her backside, saying, "Ow, you idjit! What'd you do that for?" She stood up and seemed more awake now.

Jennifer squared her arms on her hips and said, "`Cause you wouldn't get up! That's why."

Tina woke up even more as she realized who she was talking too. She exclaimed, "What! You're alive!"

Jennifer nodded with a smile, saying, "Of course I'm alive. What? You think a few Harvesters could stop me?"

Tina reached out and grabbed Jennifer's dress across her chest. She exclaimed, "You made me worry! Give me back my tears!"

Jennifer smirked at her, saying, "What? You cried for me?"

Tina let go of her dress and quickly turned around. She crossed her arms over her chest, saying, "No ... no, I didn't. You're not worth crying over. Who cares about you?"

Valerie flipped the light switch on in Elsa's room. As she ran up to Elsa's bed, Elsa opened her eyes and drowsily looked towards her. She sat up and said, "Valerie? Is that really you? What's going on?"

Valerie nodded and replied, "Yeah. It's me. I got to wake you up and get you out of here. There are bad people coming to kill you."

Elsa swung her feet over the edge of her bed and said, "Huh? Why? I don't get it."

Valerie pulled on Elsa's arm, saying, "Just come on. I don't have time to explain now. I promise to tell you everything later."

Elsa stood up and said, "Okay. I trust you, or, I'm dreaming, so it doesn't really matter."

Valerie pulled Elsa toward the door. Elsa suddenly stopped and said, "Wait a sec. I got to get something." She ran to her desk and grabbed something small off of the top. She then ran back to Valerie and followed her out of the door.

Lieutenant Michael opened Rachel's door. He flipped on the light. She was laying peacefully on the bed, hugging on to a pillow. He recognized the pillow. It was his own pillow. He recognized the mark on the edge of it. He walked towards her and said, "Rachel. Get up." He took her arm and shook her.

Rachel began to stir. She opened her eyes and looked towards him in confusion. Her eyes then went wide and she sat up quickly, saying, "Huh? Michael? You're alive. I thought you were dead! What the hell happened to you?"

Michael smiled at her and said, "I went on a little detour. I don't have time to explain it all. I need you to come with me right now."

Rachel swung her feet over the side of her bed and stood up, saying, "Okay. I trust you."

Suddenly there was a loud crash. Sarah's voice echoed down the hall as she yelled, "Dad! They're here!" There was the rat-tat-tat sound of a gun on auto-fire, followed by the pinging of bullets ricocheting off of Sarah's shield.

Michael grabbed Rachel's hand. He pulled her towards the door.

In the hallway entrance, Sarah stood with her blue shield barrier around the other girls. Michael and Rachel ducked down so that they could hide behind the barrier.

In the doorway and kitchen was a squad of about a dozen men with assault rifles pointed in their direction. One of the men shouted at them, saying, "Surrender you traitors! We got barrier busters!"

On the barrel of their guns was a small tube. The leader of the men, pointed his riffle at Sarah's barrier and pushed a button on the tube underneath his barrel. There was a slight thunk-noise and a sudden explosion on Sarah's barrier. There was a shower of sparks as an explosive device exploded on her shield.

The man called out again, saying, "These charges are designed to bust open your shield. You won't be able to stop us."

Sarah turned her head towards Michael, saying, "I don't know what that was but it was really powerful. I think it really can bust my barrier eventually."

There was another explosion next to Sarah. Another one followed that followed by another. Sarah could feel the energy draining from her. She started to panic and began to say in her head over and over, "I got to hold it and protect everyone!" She focused on pouring all her energy into her barrier.

Sarah felt a pulse in her heart. She felt time start to slow down around her. She felt something new inside herself. She could begin to feel all her friends around her. It was a feeling that she never felt before. She thought she heard the fluttering of wings inside of her head. She started to feel faint. She shouted, "Tina! Put up your barrier! I'm going to pass out!"

Without hesitation, Tina erected her own barrier around them all. Sarah's barrier disappeared and she collapsed on the floor. She looked towards Michael, saying, "I ... I feel ..."

Sarah's eyes began to burn with blue fire. The blue light of her hands began to burn with blue fire. She got onto her hands and knees and stared at the floor. She hung her head and said, 'Yes, I can feel it now."

Lieutenant Rachel watched without understanding. She said, "What's going on with Sarah?" There wasn't any time to answer her.

Sarah sat up on her knees. She looked towards the men who were firing their barrier busters at Tina now. Explosions continued to rock the apartment around Tina, who was starting to feel the drain of her own energy.

Sarah smiled blissfully at them. She chuckled and said, "Yes, I feel where you are now." She stood up and crossed her arms over her chest, placing the palms of her hands on to her own shoulders. A blue light began to cover her body. She began to step towards the men slowly. She stepped outside Tina's barrier and continued to walk towards them slowly.

The soldiers started to fire their barrier busters at her directly, but they had no effect upon her. Sarah suddenly stopped walking and spread her arms out wide to her sides. Blue light began to pour out of her back and formed what looked like two giant bird wings made of blue light.

Sarah crossed her arms over her chest again, forming an X. The blue wings of light folded themselves over her body. She then thrust her arms outward and the two giant wings swept across the doorway and the kitchen. All the soldiers were picked up by her wings and thrust into the wall. The kitchen was utterly demolished by the blue wings of light. All the soldiers were flattened against the wall. Some were unconscious and bleeding. Others were writhing in pain and groaning.

Tina looked on in horror at the sight. She exclaimed, "How the hell did you do that?" Sarah ignored her question. There wasn't any time to answer it. Instead, she focused on the soldiers who were writhing in pain and groaning. Tina dropped the barrier and Valerie stepped out.

Valerie stepped up beside Sarah and looked at all the men. Valerie shook her head and said, "You bad men tried to hurt my sisters!" She stretched her right arm out, with the palm of her hand facing upward. Her fingers clawed into the air and her hands began to burn with yellow fire. Small streams of yellow light left the bodies of the men and flowed into Valerie's hands. After about ten seconds, the yellow light stopped flowing out of the men. They had stopped moving and their now vacant eyes were void of life.

Valerie dropped her hand and said, "I killed the ones who tried to hurt my sisters."

Michael took Rachel's hand again and said, "Okay, we got to get to the roof. Our transport is waiting for us."

They headed for the door. Sarah stepped out first. More men were coming out of the stairwell, down the outer hallway. They pointed their riffles at Sarah and fired.

Sarah, held her arm up as if to block their bullets. As she moved, the blue wings of light moved to protect her.

Jennifer said, "It's my turn!" Her feet began to burn with red fire and she sped off down the hallway towards the men.

The men pointed their riffles at her and fired. A blue sphere of energy suddenly appeared around Jennifer as she continued to speed down the hallway. The bullets ricocheted off of the blue barrier around Jennifer.

Red fire burned around Jennifer's hands. The fire formed itself into the shape of a blade over each hand. The blades then seemed to morph into giant claw shapes that seemed to be an extension of her fingers.

Jennifer crashed into the men, knocking them off of their feet. The blue sphere vanished around Jennifer and she began to strike out at the men as they scrambled to get back up. Limbs and heads were severed as they moved. When Jennifer was done, all the soldiers were killed. There was a bloody mess underneath her feet.

Jennifer waved towards Michael and shouted, saying, "It's all clear, Lieutenant!"

They all ran up to Jennifer. They saw all the slaughtered men in pieces in the stairwell. Rachel covered her mouth and said, "What the hell is going on? Why are they attacking us? How did your girls get so much power?"

Michael shook his head and said, "I promise I'll explain after we get out of here. Please, you just got to trust me right now. I need you to trust me."

Rachel nodded and said, "Okay, I trust you."

They stepped over the shredded bodies. Giana looked back at the mess and grimaced. She said, "This is disgusting!"

They ran up to the top of the stairs and opened the door. Michael said, "Look, there's our ..." He stopped suddenly, causing the others to crash into him.

In between them and the Spear of Destiny was a man. The man stood with his back to them. He grasped his hands behind his back. He wore a black twin tail tuxedo jacket and black pants.

The man slowly turned around. His eyes were glowing bright white. He was also wearing a black button up vest and a silk bow tie.

Giana, Tina and Elsa stared at him in shock. Tina said, "It looks like that man is a Wielder."

Giana said, "But I never heard of a white Wielder or even a man being a Wielder at all."

The man pulled a pocket watch out of his pants and looked at the time. He put the watch back into his pocket.

The man stretched his arms out wide and said, "Greetings, Mr. Snyder! IT told me that you would come here. I've been waiting for you for the past two days. I was beginning to think that IT might have been mistaken. But, you have proven to me that IT is never wrong."

Michael placed his hand over his new pistol. He replied, "Pardon me, sir. I don't know who you are. But, I know you are with the Path of the Future. I don't care about what that Lucifer program says. But, I'm not going to allow you to keep doing what you are doing."

The man dropped his arms and said, "My name, Mr. Snyder, is Jesse Roc."

Michael said, "It is nice to meet you, Mr. Roc. But, we are going now so we won't be getting to know each other."

Mr. Roc, still standing there with his hands behind his back, said, "I wanted to have a little chat with Adam. But, he wouldn't come out. Perhaps, if I beat you to a bloody pulp, Adam will feel like talking. I am not amused like Mr. Schilds is. I have no conviction against killing you right here and now."

Sarah shouted at him, "I won't let you touch my dad!"

Mr. Roc glared at her. He said, "Oh, really? Stop me then, if you can!"

Mr. Roc's hands and feet began to burn with white fire. He suddenly shot across the roof, heading straight for Michael. He pulled his right fist back as far as he could and shouted a battle cry.

Michael stood there without flinching. As Mr. Roc shot across the roof, the wings of blue light shot out of Sarah's back again. One of the wings thrust itself in front of Michael's body.

Mr. Roc's right fist smashed into Sarah's wing of blue light. There was an explosion of sparks. The air began to fill with the smell of ozone. Sarah then used one of her wings to throw Mr. Roc in the opposite direction. He flew through the air and landed on his feet on the other side of the roof. His feet skidded back several feet leaving skid marks on the roof.

Mr. Roc stood up straight and laughed. He stretched his arms out wide and shout, "Yes! Now that is what I call power! I think I won't even have to hold myself back. Let's see how long you can last against my true power!"

Mr. Roc stretched his arm out toward Sarah with his palm facing her. His hands still burned with white fire. Instinctively, Sarah recognized the move.

He was going to use a spear of light. Sarah crossed her arms across her face in an X shape. Her wings moved according to her will and folded around her body.

Just as Sarah's blue wings of light surrounded her body, a beam of white light poured out of Mr. Roc's hand and hit Sarah on her blue wings of light over the area of her chest. Sarah felt the pressure of the beam and braced against it with her feet. The beam began to push her back, causing her feet to rip trails on the roof top.

Mr. Roc shouted, "I'll burn you to ashes, bitch!"

Valerie shouted out, "You bad man! Stop trying to hurt my big sister!"

Valerie took a step forward and thrust her arm towards Mr. Roc. Her hands began to burn with yellow fire. She clawed her fingers into the air and tried to pull energy out of Mr. Roc. She could feel the flow of energy from him. A stream of yellow light left his body and went into Valerie's hand.

Mr. Roc stopped firing his spear of light at Sarah. He twisted his body towards Valerie and glared at her with as much hatred as he could muster. He thrust his hand towards her and shouted, "You little bitch! You think you can hurt me that way?"

Valerie began to feel energy leaving her body. It was a strange sensation. As energy left her body, it was replaced by energy from his body. A stream of white light left her body and flowed into his hand.

Sarah held up her own hand towards Mr. Roc. She began to fire pulses of blue light at him. Mr. Roc held up his hand and created a barrier wall. Sarah's spear of light smashed into his shield and caused an explosion of sparks. The smell of ozone thickened in the air.

Jennifer dashed out towards Mr. Roc. Her hands burned with red fire and formed into the shape of claws. As she got closer to Mr. Roc, Sarah stopped firing her spear of light ability to avoid hitting her.

Jennifer leapt towards him and began to slash at his body with all her might. With each slash of her fiery claws, she grunted in exertion.

Mr. Roc blocked each one of Jennifer's attacks with his white burning hands. Each time, Jennifer struck him, there was an explosion of sparks.

Mr. Roc pulled his left arm back and lashed out at Jennifer with all his strength. As his arm hurled towards Jennifer, Sarah erected a barrier around her. His fist smashed into the barrier and caused another explosion of sparks.

Jennifer went flying backwards inside the barrier and crashed into the wall where the door to the stairs were. The barrier cushioned the impact but Jennifer began to gasp for air, having the wind knocked out of her. A cut on the back of her head began to spit blood.

Valerie shouted, "Jennifer!" She pointed her other hand towards Jennifer. Jennifer began to be surrounded by yellow light. The wound on the back of her head closed up. Jennifer felt a renewed energy flowing into herself.

Mr. Roc waved his hand violently once through the air, shouting, "Enough! I grow weary of this game." He reached into his left pocket and pulled out a little black box. He pushed a little button on the device.

All at once, Sarah, Jennifer, Valerie, Giana, Tina and Elsa collapsed on the floor. It was another suppressor field.

Giana said, "What the hell is this? Why can't I move?"

Tina said, "It hurts! I think all my power is gone."

Elsa said, "Please! Make it stop!"

Sarah shouted at them, saying, "Don't try to fight it. You'll only get hurt. He's using a suppressor field to stop our powers."

Mr. Roc stuck the device back into his left pocket and said, "Ah, yes! That's better. You all look much better prostrated on the floor like that. Now, I can have a little fun with you, Mr. Snyder. When I'm through with you, then you can watch me have a little fun with each one of your little girls. Then you'll beg for me to kill you. And, I will. I am a merciful being after all."

The white fire on Mr. Roc's right hand, formed into the shape of a blade. He smiled at Michael and stepped slowly towards him. Michael put his hand on his pistol and gripped the handle.

A flash of blue suddenly sped towards Mr. Roc and crashed into him, causing an explosion of sparks. It was Justice.

Mr. Roc skidded across the floor and twisted himself to face Justice. He said, "Ah, Adam, the fallen one. So, you have finally decided to join us."

Justice held his fighting stance and said, "I'm here Roc, so what do you want?"

Mr. Roc threw his arms wide open and said, "What do I want? I want your head on a silver platter!"

Mr. Roc skated towards Justice. Justice skated towards Mr. Roc. They collided together in the middle of the roof and began punching at each other while also trying to block the other's attack. Sparks exploded from in between them.

Mr. Roc ignored his own defense and managed to evade Justice's block to hit him square in the chest. Justice took this advantage and struck Mr. Roc in the face.

Justice skidded backwards, causing rips to form in the floor of the roof. He hunched over and started coughing as he gripped his chest with his left hand.

Blood began to trickle from underneath his mask. His eyes glowed even brighter and the blood stopped flowing. He had healed himself.

Mr. Roc also skidded backwards, causing rips to form in the floor of the roof. His lower jaw hung in place. It was completely smashed. Blood poured out of his mouth. He began to laugh at the sight of all the blood pooling down by his feet. His eyes glowed brighter and his jaw went back to being normal and the blood stopped flowing out of his mouth.

Mr. Roc threw his arms out wide and shouted, "Yes! This is what we were born for! To dominate and destroy those who are weak! You are weak now, Adam. I will destroy you!"

Justice straightened his mask. He threw his arms wide open too and began to laugh, saying, "I haven't had this much fun in ages, Roc!"

The two of them skated to each other again and began to lash out at each other even more violently. Sparks continued to explode around them. Justice focused his attacks on Mr. Roc's lower body. Mr. Roc kept aiming at Justice's head.

Justice grazed Mr. Roc's left thigh. Mr. Roc smashed down on Justices head, causing him to be thrown down to the floor. Justice rolled away from him and leapt across the roof. Blood began to pour from underneath his black, tricorn hat. The blood shortly stopped as he healed himself.

At the exact same time, the girls, who were still lying face down on the floor, felt all their strength return to them. They all started to stand up.

Mr. Roc noticed them and reached into his left pocket. He pulled out the suppressor field device and it fell apart in his hand. He laughed and said, "I see what you did there, Adam. That was a gutsy move."

Justice replied, "I'm glad I could impress you, Roc."

Mr. Roc put the broken device back into his pocket and said, "Now, if I continue this fight, I'll have to fight a bunch of people at once. That's not very fair."

Michelle suddenly appeared out of the Spear of Destiny. She skated straight for Mr. Roc who had just erected a white light barrier sphere around his entire body. Michelle slashed at the barrier, causing sparks to fly in all directions.

Mr. Roc ignored her attacks and lifted himself up into the air so that he hovered about ten feet in the air above them. He looked down at them and glared with anger at them.

Gabrielle jumped out of the Spear of Destiny and stretched her arm out towards Mr. Roc. A blue beam of energy poured out of her hand and pulsed against the barrier shield, causing sparks to shower down below over them.

As he hovered over them safely in his barrier shield, he laughed and said, "I'm sorry, Adam. It looks like I will have to cut short our time today. Next time though, I will have your head on a silver platter."

Mr. Roc pointed at Michael and said, "Next time, Mr. Snyder. Next time, I will have my way with you." He then sped away in the distance.

Michelle waved her fist at Mr. Roc as he sped away. She yelled, "Get back here, you coward! I'm not done with you yet! I've got to pay you back for what you did to my sister!"

Michael turned to Rachel and said, "Are you okay?"

Rachel stood there watching the sky with her mouth agape.

Michael spoke again, saying, "Hey, Rachel. You okay?"

Rachel's head slowly lowered. Her eyes followed till they were focused on Michael. She said, "What the hell did I just see?"

As she stared at Michael, the vision of the Spear of Destiny came into focus. Her face twisted in confusion and she tilted her head, saying, "Huh? That looks just like the alien space ships that attacked earth in the Hour of Despair."

Michael nodded and replied, "It is."

Rachel turned her head and saw Justice in the distance, brushing off his clothing. He was surrounded by his angels, who were fussing over him and making sure that he was alright after that fight. She said, "And he looks just like that crazy terrorist."

Michael nodded and replied, "Well, sort of. But he's not really such a bad guy once you get to know him."

Justice grabbed on to the collar of his frock coat and called out to them, saying, "I prefer the term mad, not crazy. Thank you very much."

Rachel focused her attention back on Michael, saying, "And ... you're alive? How are you alive? I was so worried."

Justice called out again, saying, "I hate to be pushy. But, we really need to get out of here."

Michael grabbed Rachel's hand and pulled her towards the Spear of Destiny. Their girls followed behind them.

Raphael jumped out of the Spear of Destiny holding four folded white robes in her hand. She handed them to Michael. Michael took the robes and said to Squad four, "You all need to take off all of your clothing."

Confusion fell on all of their faces. Giana tilted her head and said, "I'm surprised how bold you're acting, Lieutenant Michael. I never thought you'd be so forward with all of us at once."

Michael rolled his eyes and said, "There are tracking devices in all your clothing. You have to take off your clothing and change into this robe or those men who attacked us will be able to find us again."

Rachel nodded and took the robe. Giana, Tina and Elsa followed her example. Justice got back in the craft and Michael turned around to give them some semblance of privacy.

They started to get out of their clothes. Giana said, "Lieutenant Michael, I bet you're just burning with desire to turn around so you can watch Lieutenant Rachel get naked."

Lieutenant Rachel reached over and smacked Giana in the back of the head.

Giana caressed the back of her head, saying, "Ow, Lieutenant. Why'd you hit me this time?"

Lieutenant Rachel said, "Stop being so crude!"

Lieutenant Michael, keeping his back towards them, said, "Well, I'd be lying if I said I didn't want to see that."

Lieutenant Rachel looked downward and blushed.

After Squad four changed into their robes, Michael, Sarah, Jennifer and Valerie stepped into the Spear of Destiny. Rachel and her team followed behind them.

As Rachel entered, Josh held his hand up in greeting and said, "Hey, Rachel."

Rachel stopped and looked at him. She said, "Hey, Josh. I knew you'd be lurking somewhere in the shadows behind all this."

Josh shrugged his shoulders and said, "You do not know the half of it, sister."

- 5 -

Michael dropped down to the floor of the cockpit inside the Spear of Destiny. He leaned up against the wall and tilted his head upward with a sigh. He said, "Ah man, that was intense. I'm glad we made it out of there in one piece."

Michelle began to gaze at Michael's lap. Valerie and Jennifer noticed her and quickly jumped into Michael's lap before anyone else could sit down. Michelle glared at them but didn't say anything. Sarah sat down on Michael's left side.

Rachel and the other girls followed their example and sat down. Rachel sat down on Michael's right side. Giana sat down beside her, followed by Tina.

To save room, Elsa sat down in Rachel's lap. She kept her right fist tightly closed as if she were holding onto something.

Michelle, Gabrielle and Raphael sat down in front of them, facing them. They stared at the new girls with somewhat menacing grins, except for Michelle, who was looking at Rachel up and down and glaring at her as she sat next to Michael.

Rachel still seemed to be in a daze. She looked around the cockpit and then looked towards Michael. He stared back at her. She said, "You're still alive?"

Michael nodded and said, "Yeah. I'm still alive."

Rachel leaned over and rested her head on his shoulder. She said, "Losing you hurt me so much. I ... I thought I lost you forever. I thought I'd never get to see you again." Tears started to roll down her cheeks.

Michelle sat there as still as she could, except for her fingers which danced in place on her thighs as she sat there agitated.

Michael said, "Sorry about that. It was necessary."

Rachel, still resting her head on his shoulders, replied, "Why? What's going on? Who was that crazy guy back there? Who are these people here?" She pointed towards Michelle, Gabrielle and Raphael.

Michael held his hand towards the three angels, saying, "This is Michelle, Gabrielle and Raphael."

Rachel nodded her head towards them and said, "You three are Wielders, right? But, you three are far too old."

Michelle crossed her arms over her chest. With as much hostility as she could muster, she said, "I'm still younger than you."

Gabrielle started to act really shy again.

Raphael nodded and said, "Yes, we are Papa's Wielders. I'm sixteen."

Gabrielle muttered shyly, "I'm seventeen."

Michelle said, "I'm eighteen."

Giana looked back and forth intently. She said, "Does this mean there's a way to stop our powers from destroying our bodies?"

Michael said, "Not quite. I discovered that the reason your bodies self-destruct is not because of your powers, but because of the weekly injection we give you girls. If you don't get the shot, then you don't self-destruct."

Rachel became more alert. What he said shocked her more than what just happened to them. She exclaimed, "What? But those shots are designed to strengthen their bodies, not kill them!"

Michael shook his head. He said, "Yeah, that's what we were told but it's a lie." He pointed at Justice and said, "That man over there, he invented that shot.

He also created an antidote to undo the effects of it. None of the girls have to die now from their power."

Justice said, "It's true. My three daughters are proof of it."

Giana ran her hands through her hair and clung on to it. Her voice started to sound shaky. She began to tremble, saying, "I ... I don't have to die from my power?"

Michael nodded and said, "Yeah. That's right. The shot also suppresses your power. That's why Sarah, Jennifer and Valerie are much stronger now."

Giana covered her face with her hands. Michael could tell that she was trembling. Tina sat there even more emotionless than usual, which meant that she was trying really hard to suppress her emotions. Elsa looked around at everybody and seemed really confused still.

Michael proceeded to tell them everything that they found out together. As they learned the truth of what was going on, they sat and absorbed it in. There were points at which they started to cry together off and on. Sarah, Jennifer and Valerie couldn't stop themselves from crying with them.

After Michael had finished explaining everything that he had learned, he said, "That's why I've done all this. Will you four help us fight against the Path of the Future?"

Rachel nodded, saying, "Yeah. It might be pointless but it is the right thing to do."

Giana smashed her fist into the palm of her hand and exclaimed, "Of course! Let's take those sons of bitches down!" She than flinched and waited for Rachel to hit her in the back of the head. But, fortunately, Rachel was too distracted by what was going on to notice. Giana breathed a sigh of relief.

Tina nodded and said, in her melancholy tone, "I guess so. Not like I got anything else to do."

Elsa looked downward and shyly said, "Okay."

Justice pulled a small case out of his coat pocket and tossed it at Michael. Michael caught it and opened it. There were three old-style syringes inside filled with a silver colored serum.

Michael picked up a syringe and held it up for them to see. He said, "This is the serum that will get rid of the toxin and nano-machines that have built up in your body. Do you girls want to take this?"

Giana thrust her arm out and said, "Yeah, doc! Stick me with your needle. I can't let Jennifer get stronger than me."

Jennifer stuck her tongue out at Giana and said, "You wish you could keep up with me."

Michael tied the rubber band around Giana's arm injected the needle into a large vain. He used a cotton ball to stop the bleeding.

Giana said, "Wow, I can feel something warm spreading through my body."

Valerie excitedly said, "That means it's working!"

Michael than injected Tina and Elsa. The three of them held cotton balls over their injection point.

Elsa looked downward again. She still seemed embarrassed. She shyly said, "Valerie."

Valerie turned to look at her and said, "Yeah, Elsa?"

Elsa held up her right fist. She stretched her arm out to Valerie and opened her fist. Sitting in the palm of her hand, was a small monarch butterfly hair clip.

Valerie's eyes went wide and her jaw dropped. She recognized the thing that Elsa was holding. It was the hair clip that she got from her parents.

Elsa said, "When I thought you were dead, I took it to remember you. But, since you're still live, I want to give it back."

Valerie smiled and picked it up. She threw herself at Elsa and wrapped her arms around her, saying, "Oh my gosh! Thank you so much! I thought I'd never get to see that again."

Elsa held her back tightly and said, "I'm so glad that you are all still alive." She started to cry again.

Valerie started to get teary-eyed and said, "Oh, no. If you cry again, I'm going to cry again." Valerie stated to cry too. She pulled the hair on her right side back and clipped her hair up.

Rachel said, "What are we going to do now?"

Michael said, "We are in the middle of destroying the Harvester factories. We're probably going to go back to doing that."

Justice said, "We'll go back to our base first so that your friends can get on some real clothes. Then we'll head to the Harvester factory that is in the area formerly known as Mexico."

Michael nodded. He looked to Rachel. Rachel looked towards him. She rested her head on his shoulder and fell asleep.

The Spear of Destiny landed back on the air strip in Kaua'i. When the door opened, Michelle, Gabrielle and Raphael quickly rushed out. The inside of the cockpit was stuffier than normal.

Michael shook Rachel by the shoulder to wake her up. As she awoke, the others woke up and started to stretch. Michael stood up and extended his hand to Rachel. She took it and he pulled her up on her feet. They left the Spear of Destiny together.

Finally, Justice came out of the Spear of Destiny and approached Rachel and her girls. He took of his hat and extended his hand to Rachel. Rachel took his hand. Instead of shaking it, Justice lifted it up and then bowed, bringing her hand up to his mask. He pressed his mask on her hand as if he were kissing it. He let her hand go, replaced his hat on his head, and stood up straight, saying, "Charmed to meet you, Miss Harris."

Rachel looked questioningly at Michael. He shrugged his shoulders as if to say, "Yeah, he's weird."

Rachel replied to Justice, "It is good to meet you too, Mr. Justice."

Michelle apparently couldn't bear holding herself in any longer. She walked over to Michael and wrapped her arm around his. In response, Michael lifted his arm out of her grasp. Michelle wrapped her arm around his arm again. Michael again pulled his arm out of her grasp. Michelle wrapped her arm around his arm a third time. In defeat, Michael let his arm hang and he sighed, tilting his head away from her.

Michelle giggled and sneered at Rachel. She looked her up and down in disgust, saying, "Just so you know, Ray-chel. Michael and I have declared our eternal love for each other. We're going to get married. You're not needed anymore, you old hag!"

Rachel turned to face her. She looked at her in surprise, saying, "Excuse me?" She looked to Michael and saw the look of annoyance and defeat on his face.

Rachel then turned back to Michelle and looked her up and down. She gave a smug smile and a slight chuckle, saying, "I'm sure."

Justice butted in, saying, "Angel, we don't have time to play right now. Let's go back to the house."

They headed back to the old hotel. Rachel and her girls admired its beauty. They headed towards the sitting lounge and sat down together.

Justice said, "My darling angels, before we get back to work, I need you to make clothing for our new team members. Okay?"

Gabrielle nodded her head.

Raphael smiled at the new girls and said, "Okay, Papa."

Michelle jumped up and said, "I already made a dress, for Rachel."

Justice said, "Really?"

Michelle replied, "Yeah. Hold on."

Michelle skated away using her power. She shortly returned holding a clump of brownish fabric in her hand. She held it up for all to see as it unrolled in front of everybody. It was a large burlap sack with an image of a potato printed on the front. Above the picture was the phrase 'Idaho Potatoes'. A hole was cut in the top for the head and two slits were made for the arms.

Michelle held up the potato sack with a huge grin. She said, "I thought this would be good for Rachel because she's all lumpy like a sack of potatoes."

Giana started to laugh. She said in between burst of laughter, "Lumpy ... like a sack of potatoes ... I ... I got to remember that one!"

Rachel glared at Giana.

Sarah brought her hand to her lips and held her lips tight to prevent laughter from escaping. It was only moderately successful.

Justice waved for Michelle to come over to him and then patted his knee. Michelle put her hands down and walked over to Justice. The look of playful guiltiness fell on her face. She smiled and sat on his lap sideways.

Justice said, "Now, my darling red angel, I know you don't like Ms. Harris but we're on the same team so I need you to play nice. Can you try to play nice for me and get along with her?"

Michelle fidgeted on his lap and said, "Yeah, I can try to play nice."

Michelle stood up and walked over to Rachel. She extended her hand to Rachel and said, "I'm sorry I said you looked like a lumpy sack of potatoes."

Rachel stared at her hand for a moment and then took it, saying, "Okay, I forgive you. Let's be friends."

Justice said, "See, you can all be friends. Angels, why don't you take our new friends to the sewing room and make them new dresses now."

Michelle turned to Justice and bowed slightly, saying, "Yes, Papa."

Gabrielle and Raphael stood up to join Michelle and, together, they led Rachel and her girls back to the sewing room.

After several hours, they came back wearing the same type of dresses that Sarah, Jennifer and Valerie were wearing.

Rachel's dress had black stripes in place of the colored stripes. Rachel modeled it for everyone and said, "I feel a little awkward wearing a dress like this. But, it is cute. It makes me feel like a doll."

Michael watched Rachel intently as she modeled her new dress. He said, "It looks really good on you."

Rachel smiled and said, "Thanks! Those three are very skilled at sewing."

Giana showed off her dress. She spun around and said, "Don't I look cute too, Lieutenant Michael?"

Michael nodded and said, "Yes, yes. You look cute in your new dress too."

Tina looked annoyed and stood there with her arms crossed over her chest. She spoke in her melancholy tone, saying, "It doesn't make me feel like I'm dead inside."

Elsa put her hands on Tina's shoulders and said, "That's just her way of saying that she likes it. Can't you just say that you like it?"

Tina shrugged her shoulders and replied in her melancholy tone, "It's fine."

Elsa took hold of the hem of her own dress and flared it saying, "Well, I like it a lot. Thank you for making it for me." She curtsied to Raphael, who was the one who made her dress.

Justice stood up from his seat and said, "Excellent, ladies! Now we are ready to get back to work!"

Michelle, Gabrielle and Raphael prepared some provisions and placed them in baskets. They returned to the Spear of Destiny and left for the next Harvester factory that was placed in the area that was once known as Mexico.

Justice took Rachel and her girls into the Harvester factory instead of Michael and his girls so that they could see the Harvesters being raised for themselves. The Harvester factory was left empty of personal like with the others. They were prepared for the shock of seeing Harvesters being raised, but it was still horrifying to see it for themselves. They placed the S.E.Re.F device in the middle of the facility and returned quickly to the Spear of Destiny. They watched the black sphere of energy consume the facility and then disappear into a giant crater in the ground.

Justice quickly sped the Spear of Destiny northward. The next Harvester factories were in the areas formerly known as Alaska and Canada. Michael asked, saying, "Justice, where are we going next?"

Justice cleared his throat and said, "I want to make a quick stop in Denver Sector, Mr. Snyder."

Michael didn't know if there was anything else left in Denver Sector after the nuclear strike demolished everything. He replied, "Why are we going there? That whole area is just scorched lands now."

Justice chuckled and said, "Call it a faint hope, Mr. Snyder. It will either be nothing or everything."

Michael looked to Rachel and shrugged his shoulders, saying, "Great, whenever he keeps it a mystery it usually turns out to be pretty big."

Rachel said, "Really?"

Michael smiled as he remembered the adventures he experienced since Josh came back to him. He dropped his hands so that they were resting on the floor of the cockpit. He said, "They wouldn't tell me a thing like I told you about it. They made me wait and see it for myself."

Rachel put her hand on top of Michael's hand. Michael turned his hand over and they interlocked their fingers together. Rachel said, "I can understand that. If anyone else had told me all of that, I wouldn't have believed a word of it. But, I believe in you."

A couple hours later, the sun was fully in the sky. The Spear of Destiny hovered over the area that was once the sector of Denver. It was the site where they first saw Justice when he destroyed the wall using explosives. The Spear of Destiny landed on the outskirts of Denver. The door opened and they exited the craft, except for Josh who stayed with the Spear of Destiny.

The whole sector had become a ruinous heap. Fragments of the wall were scattered all over the place. The ground was scorched black from nuclear bombing. The buildings in the region were nothing more than piles of chard wood, blackened bricks and twisted metal. Scattered among them were bones of people and armored shells from dead Harvesters.

Valerie looked around at the scorched lands and said, "I can feel the land crying out to me. It wants to be healed."

Raphael said, "Remember what I told you, it will take all your life if you listen to it."

Valerie nodded and replied, "Yeah. I remember. But, still, it is very sad to hear."

Justice said, "Everyone, stay on your toes. This is now a Harvester Zone."

Michelle said, "Don't worry, Papa. We'll make short work of any Harvester that comes our way."

Justice said, "Alright, everybody. There is supposedly a secret facility under here. Hopefully it is still accessible and not cleared out."

Justice began to walk in seemingly erratic paths. No one else knew what to look for so they kept quiet and followed him. From time to time, they ran into groups of Harvesters. They were quickly killed by the three teams with little effort. Giana, Tina and Elsa got to see first-hand the increased power of those who did not have their power suppressed by the weekly injections.

After what felt like several hours, Justice started to clap his hands together in applause. He stretched his arms out wide and exclaimed, "Me thinks I've found the location."

In front of them was the framework of what used to be a brick structure. Michael looked around and said, "I don't see anything special here."

Justice spun in place once and then pointed at the doorway that was left standing. He said, "See that triangle symbol?"

Michael began to look intently at the doorframe. He noticed a small green painted triangle on the side of the doorframe. He said, "Yeah, I see a green triangle, but, so what? Does it mean something special?"

Justice nodded and said, "Yes! That is a symbol relating to the Path of the Future. This building on top was cover for another facility."

Justice walked up to the doorframe. He stepped through it and into the open framework of the ruined building. He waved for them to stop and said, "Stand back while I clear away the rubble."

Justice lifted his hands to the sky and they began to burn with white fire. He pointed his palms at the ground and white spears of light poured out of his hands. He spun around as all the rubble began to burn away all around him. When he was done, there was a large hole in the ground that revealed a secret entrance. Justice said, "See, what did I tell you."

The secret entrance was a story below the ground. They had to jump to get down to it. Sarah picked up Valerie. Her blue wings of light poured out of her back. She gently hovered down and set Valerie down on her feet. Her blue wings of light returned back inside of her.

Jennifer's hands and feet began to burn with red fire. She picked up Michael in her arms and jumped down to the floor below. She set him down.

Giana picked up Elsa and followed after them. Tina used her shield to cushion her fall. Justice picked up Rachel and jumped down. Gabrielle helped Raphael down and Michelle jumped using her own power.

The door was well secured. It seemed even more stable than the doors to the Harvester factories. Justice walked up to the door and knocked on it. He stroked the bottom of his mask in thought.

Michael said, "Can you get through that door too, like before?"

Justice replied, "Oh, yes. Not a problem." His hands glowed with white fire again and he began pounding on the door. After ten strikes the door began to buckle. On the eleventh strike the door collapsed right in front of them with a heavy metal clang revealing an extended hallway.

Air began to rush out of the entrance way. The air smelled old and stale. The hallway was dark. The sun shone into the entranceway revealing a thick layer of dust all over the floor.

Justice held up his shining hand and stepped forward. The others followed him. The white fire of his hand helped to chase the darkness away as they ventured forward. Their feet kicked up the thick dust that covered the floor.

Valerie said, "What is this place?"

Justice, continuing to move forward, replied, "This, little Valerie, is Adam's old laboratory. This is the place where Adam created that horrible injection that suppressed your powers."

Valerie looked around and said, "Oh."

Justice came to a metal panel on the wall. He opened it up and began to flip on switches. There was a very loud click and lights suddenly filled the hallway. The lights gave them a full view of the abandoned laboratory.

They followed Justice down the hall till they came to a large metal door on the left side. Justice said, "This is the room where Adam developed the vile injection. He spent day after day here until it drove him mad. This is the place where Adam died and Justice was born!"

Justice lifted his hand to a numbered control panel. He typed in a string of numbers and a green light lit up on the panel. The door then slid open revealing an old laboratory. Justice bowed to his teammates and motioned them to move forward, saying, "Please, step inside."

Michael took a step inside first, followed by Rachel. The girls entered after them. Michael looked around the room. The inside of this room was not as dusty as the hallway. It must have been sealed to prevent dust from getting in. There were two examination tables up front. They both had harnesses on them. Michael bent over and looked at the harnesses. There were streaks of dried blood on them. The harnesses were kept at length where it would be easy to keep a nine year old child tied down.

There was a desk that was cluttered with old yellowed paper. Michael couldn't make sense of the formulas hand written on them.

There was a sink with rusted surgical tools tossed inside of it. Empty glass beakers lined the countertop.

On the other side of the sink, there was a dulled stainless steel mirror. Beneath the mirror was shattered glass.

Justice slowly walked to the back of the room. There was a locked cabinet in the back. Justice walked up to the cabinet and placed his hands on the edges. He leaned forward and rested his mask against the door of the cabinet and sighed.

Michael said, "Are you okay, Justice?"

Justice stood back up straight and said, "You wanted power to protect the ones you love, Mr. Snyder? Is that correct?"

Michael nodded and replied, "Yeah. You know it."

Justice looked towards him as he held onto the cabinet door. He said, "Unless this place was cleaned out, there is one vial of transcendence serum here. They gave it to Adam so he could do work on the injections. This one vial can give you the same powers that I have, that they have."

Michael's eyes went wide. He said, "I ... I can have that power too?"

Justice nodded and said, "Yes, Mr. Snyder. If that one vial is in here, it can give you that power."

Justice ripped the door off of the cabinet. The room light lit up the darkness inside the cabinet. There was one glass tube with a silver colored top. Inside the glass there was some type of blue gel that seemed to be used for suspension. In the center of the gel, there was a small vial.

Justice unscrewed the silver colored top. He poured the blue gel into his hand and the small vial slipped into his palm. He held the vial with his thumb and index finger. He lifted it up for everyone to see. The vial was clear and revealed an off-white looking liquid.

Justice said, "This, my friends, is the Transcendence serum." He walked over to a drawer and pulled out a syringe. He held the vial in his right hand and the syringe in his left.

Justice walked over to Michael and said, "This serum is a poison and will kill you if you are not strong enough to endure the trial. Nine out of ten people are killed by it. If you take it and survive, it will be one of the most painful experiences that you will ever endure. But, it will give you the power you seek. Do you still want to go through with it? Are you strong enough?"

Michael slowly nodded and said, "I don't know if I'm strong enough. But, if I can get this power so I can protect my girls, then I'll take that chance. How soon can you inject me?"

Justice shook his head, saying, "Oh, no, Mr. Snyder, if you want to be injected you will have to do it yourself. I swore to God that I would never ever inject another person with this poison."

Michael took the vial and the syringe.

Sarah reached out and grabbed his arm, saying, "Don't you think we should all talk about this?"

Michael shook his head and said, "I'm sorry, this isn't up for discussion. If this serum can give me power to fight, then I'll try it. That way you don't have to fight anymore."

Valerie took hold of his other arm and said, "We don't mind fighting, Lieutenant. We're used to it."

Michael shook his head again and said, "No, you girls have done enough fighting. It's my turn to shoulder that burden."

Jennifer started to cry. She kept wiping her eyes as the tears streamed out. She said, "We don't want you to die, we love you."

Michael pulled Sarah, Jennifer and Valerie into an embrace together and said, "I love you too. I don't want to lose any of you either. But, I wouldn't be able to live with myself if I didn't try. I've helped to cause you girls so much pain. It's my turn."

As Michael held them, Sarah and Valerie started to cry too. After about a minute, he let them go. They continued to cry silently and tried to use their begging faces to change his mind. It didn't work.

Sarah said, "Please, dad. Don't risk it!"

Michael smiled at her. He put his hand on her head and said, "Don't worry. It'll be alright."

Justice said, "Sit on the table and inject yourself. After doing so, lie down and I will harness you so that you don't hurt yourself or others."

Michael nodded and sat down on the examination table. Justice moved to the head of the table and waited.

Rachel walked up to him and took hold of his arm. She said, "Can I talk you out of this?"

Michael shook his head and said, "No, I need to do this."

Rachel lowered her head and started to tear up, saying, "I know. But, I already lost you once. I don't think I can take losing you again."

Michael put his hand on her cheek and wrapped it around the side of her neck. He looked into her eyes and said, "I love you, Rachel." He pulled her face close to his and kissed her on the lips. She accepted it and held onto him, kissing him back. After a few moments, their lips broke away from each other. He gently pushed her back away from him.

Giana, Tina and Elsa were too shocked to say anything. This is what they had been waiting for. But, they were too surprised by the suddenness of it and distracted by the fact that Michael was going to do something that could kill him.

Michael took the cap off of the needle and stuck it into the vial. The off-white liquid slowly filled the syringe.

Justice turned to the girls and said, "This can be really horrible, I think you girls might want to stand in the hallway and wait."

Sarah shook her head and said, "No, I'm going to stay by him to the end."

Jennifer nodded and said, "Yeah, if being here will help him be stronger than I'm going to stay here."

Valerie shook her head vigorously and said, "I'm not leaving either."

Giana, Tina and Elsa agreed together that they would stay too.

Michelle, Gabrielle and Raphael stood back at the foot of the table. They didn't seem worried at all.

Michael held the needle to his arm. He looked to the crying faces of Sarah, Jennifer and Valerie who were standing on the left side of the table. He gave them a smile and said, "Don't worry, girls. It'll be alright."

Michael looked towards Rachel and her girls, who were standing on the right side of the table. He gave them a smile and repeated, saying, "It'll be alright."

Michael drew the needle closer to his skin. Justice suddenly shot his hand out and grabbed Michael's wrist on the hand that held the needle. He said, "The Path of the Future thinks that hate is what gives them power. It's not hate that gives you power, Mr. Snyder, it's love. Remember that."

Justice let go of Michael's wrist. Michael nodded and turned his attention to the needle again. He stuck the needle into his blood vessel and pressed the plunger. The off-white fluid left the barrel of the needle and flowed into his blood stream.

Michael handed the syringe to Rachel and laid down. Justice quickly adjusted the straps and put his arms and legs in them. He secured the final harness around his waist.

The Transcendence serum felt cold and slimy as it entered his vein. The coldness began to spread throughout his entire body. The coldness began to change to a tingling sensation. The tingling began to change into prickling. His breathing became labored. He began to feel pain. It started to feel like his body was on fire.

Tears started to stream down Michael's face. He cried from the increasing pain. His body lost control of itself. He would have started to flail his arms and legs if they were not tied down. Everyone backed away from him to avoid getting hit from his jerking limbs. Michael started to scream in agony. He screamed for help but there was nothing they could do.

Sarah, Jennifer and Valerie covered their ears and turned around so they didn't have to watch it. They squatted down to the floor.

Tina ran out of the room and collapsed into tears on the floor. Elsa and Giana ran out to help her. Giana picked her up and sat Tina on her lap. They held each other as Michael screamed in agony. His cries echoed through the abandoned hall.

Michael suddenly blacked out and went still. A small trickle of blood slipped out of his nostrils and tear ducts, running down to the table top. The skin on his wrists and around his ankles were red and scrapped so that patches of blood seeped out of his skin.

Rachel looked at him and said, "Is ... is he dead?"

Sarah, Jennifer and Valerie uncovered their ears and turned back around to look at him.

Justice checked Michael's breathing and said, "No, he's still alive."

Sarah said, "What's going on now?"

Justice replied, "The serum is infecting every cell in his body with its poison. The serum is judging him to see if he is worthy of receiving its power."

Valerie said, "How long does that take?"

Justice replied, "There is no set time. He will either wake up when it is done or he will die."

Rachel took his right hand into her own and held it.

Sarah took his left hand into her own hand and held it.

Valerie put her hands over his heart and closed her eyes.

Jennifer said, "What are you doing?"

Valerie replied, "I don't know what else to do. So, I'm going to pray." She closed her eyes and bowed her head and prayed silently in her heart. She could feel the slow beat of his heart through her hands.

Jennifer put her hands on Michael's left arm. She didn't know anything about prayer but she focused her mind on giving him strength.

Michael continued to lay there motionless and unconscious as the poisonous serum infected every cell of his body. Now began the trial to see if he was strong enough to endure the poison.

TEARS
OF
DARKNESS
CHAPTER
09
SPEAR OF DESTINY

- 1 -

Michael's awareness suddenly woke up. There was nothing but darkness around him. Or, was his eyes just closed? He heard a faint noise in the distance. It was like a voice. It was familiar to him. He focused in on the voice, "...ake ... jit"

Michael felt something heavy on his chest. He tried to sit up but the force that pressed against his chest prevented it. The familiar voice started to sound closer, it became more clear, "...ant ... ake up ... jit."

Michael began to focus on the voice. He started to remember that he was supposed to be doing something. But, he couldn't remember exactly what it was he was supposed to do. The voice repeated itself, "... tenant ... wake up ... ou ...jit."

The familiar voice suddenly came really close to him. It was the voice of a girl. The voice repeated herself, "Lieutenant! Lieutenant, how long are you going to sleep? Wake up, you idjit!"

Michael said to himself, "Oh, am I asleep?" He focused on waking up. His eyes started to open and bright light filled his sight, causing him to squint. Slowly, the light began to fade and the shadowy figure of a girl, sitting on his chest, began to take shape.

The girl's figure started to become clearer as he focused on it. The shadowy form gained color. The girl was wearing a white dress with red stripes. It was the uniform of a red Wielder. Her black hair was pulled up into long twin tails on each side of her head. She had red eyes. Her form became clear and he recognized her voice and face; it was Mary.

Mary was sitting on his stomach. Her hands rested on his chest, over his heart. She was smiling down at him.

Michael looked up at her with surprise. He realized that he was laying on the floor. He sat up and Mary slid down onto his lap. She wrapped her legs around his waist and slid her arms around his back. She turned her head to the side and rested her face against his chest. She said, "I've been calling out to you like forever! You've been asleep for too long. I never thought you'd wake up."

Michael looked around himself to see where he was at. The only thing he could see all around him was whiteness. It was too confusing so instead he focused on Mary. Some memories began to return to him. He wrapped his arms around her and said, "I thought you were dead? Am I dead? Where are we?"

Mary lifted herself off of his chest. She put her hands on his cheeks and looked into his face with a smile, saying, "I'm not dead. I live right here in your heart. I kept trying to speak to you but you wouldn't listen. I thought you'd never wake up again. I was really worried."

Michael looked down at her and said, "Oh, really? I'm sorry."

Mary said, "That's okay. I can't stay mad at you because I love you."

More memories began to return to him. He remembered her sacrifice. Mary was dead, yet she was right here with him. He said, "Am I dead?"

Mary dropped her hands from his face and shook her head. She said, "No, you're not dead, silly. But, you did something really stupid didn't you?"

Michael didn't know what she was talking about. He looked at her with confusion and said, "What did I do that was stupid?"

Mary giggled and said, "You don't remember? You injected yourself with poison because you thought it would make you stronger."

That memory suddenly flooded back into Michael's mind. He said, "Oh, yeah. I remember now."

Mary said, "Why'd you do that?"

Michael said, "I wanted to get stronger so that I could protect you girls."

Mary replied, "Really? Are you sure you didn't do it because you feel guilty and wanted to punish yourself? You think that risking your life is an equal trade for losing my life?"

Michael looked away from her and said, "Maybe ... I don't know."

Mary took hold of his face and forced him to look at her. He shifted his eyes to look away from her. She said, "You feel responsible for my death, don't you? You remember every single time you injected me with that big, dumb grin of yours. Every single time you injected me I grew closer to self-destructing."

A tear rolled down Michael's cheek.

Mary stood up. She walked around behind him, got on her knees, and wrapped her arms around his neck. She leaned over against his back and brought her lips to his ear. She whispered into his ear, saying, "I don't blame you, idjit. You don't have to keep hurting yourself, you know."

Mary pointed off in the distance. She said, "Do you see that over there?" His eyes followed where her finger was pointing. All he saw was whiteness. He said, "I don't see anything."

Mary, still pointing, her voice full of anxiety, replied, "Look again! Don't you see it?"

Michael looked again. This time he saw brownish lines that seemed to be twisting around on the floor. Michael stood up to get a better look. He squinted his eyes. The brown lines seemed to be moving towards him.

Mary stood up and wrapped her arms around his left arm. She said, "They're coming to kill me, you have to stop them!"

Michael said, "What are they?"

Mary shuddered and said, "Snakes! They're trying to kill us. They're poisonous. You have to protect me."

Michael nodded.

The snakes came closer. There were eight of them. He could see a darkened diamond pattern along the length of their bodies. They had rattles on their tails. The first snake coiled itself and shook its rattle. It leapt at Michael. He caught it in midair. He placed the head of the snake on the ground, underneath his boot and stepped on it. The head of the snake was crushed underneath his boot. Red blood flowed out from underneath his boot, staining the whiteness of the floor underneath him.

Mary took a few steps back. She brought her hands together underneath her chin. She looked worried as she watched Michael kill the snake.

The other snakes became agitated. Two snakes leapt at Michael at once. He caught one of them. The other snake sunk its fangs into his thigh and wrapped its body around his leg.

Michael swung the rattlesnake that he caught in the air. He slammed its head on the ground over and over again till blood started to fling around him. Specks of blood spotted his pants.

Michael dropped the dead snake and began to pound his fist on the head of the snake that was biting his thigh. The spot where he was bit began to feel like fire. He slammed his fist repeatedly on the snakes head. Blood began to gush out from the snake, staining his right fist with blood. Specks of blood spotted his jacket now.

The five snakes that were left, jumped at him at once. Being overwhelmed, he couldn't catch any of them. One snake bit into his right wrist. Another snake bit into his left wrist. The third snake bit onto the spot above his right ankle. The fourth snake bit into his left thigh. The fifth snake bit into his neck. Where ever a snake bit him, he felt their venom like fire spreading through his muscles. He felt fire all over his body now.

Michael grabbed the snake that was biting on his neck. He tossed it on the ground and stomped on its head until blood spilled under his boot. He grabbed the snake on his right wrist and tore it off of his arm. He dropped it on the ground and smashed its head with his foot. The snake twisted and writhed on the floor as he stomped on it in anger. Finally, the snake died and blood oozed out from underneath his boot.

Michael grabbed at the third snake that had bit into his left wrist. He tossed it on the ground and smashed it with his boot again. More and more blood started to stain his uniform.

Michael smashed his fist over the fourth snake that was biting his left thigh. After several strikes the snake let go of his thigh and dropped to the ground. He crushed its head with his boot. Blood spilled out from underneath his boot.

Michael grabbed the last snake. He tore it off of his right leg and swung it around, slamming its head on the ground. As he swung it, blood sprayed on his uniform covering it with small specks of blood.

With the last snake dead, Michael dropped to his knees. His whole body felt like it was on fire from the venom that had spread into his body. He looked up into the whiteness of the ceiling and groaned in pain.

Mary started to clap her hands. She approached him and said, "Good job, Lieutenant. You killed them all."

Michael looked downward to see all the carcasses of the eight dead snakes he had viciously killed to protect himself and Mary. To his surprise, all the snakes were gone. Instead of seeing eight dead snakes, there were eight dead bodies of little girls. He recognized all of them immediately: Carol, Alice, Cheryl, Susan, Mary, Sarah, Valerie and Jennifer. Their faces were black and blue from bruises. Blood had spilled from their mouths, noses, ears and other wounds that were on their heads. Their little bodies were twisted and contorted from being brutally beaten to death. Their eyes looked filled with terror and all the light was gone out of them.

Michael looked down in shock at all their dead bodies that he was kneeling over. He looked down at his hands. He was covered in their blood. His pants were soaked in their blood. His jacket was spotted with their blood.

Mary spoke to him again, saying, "Yep, you killed them all, Lieutenant. They're all dead now."

Michael's hands began to tremble as he stared at all the dead bodies. He started to cry as he looked into all of their fearful faces. He said, "I ... I killed them. I ... I didn't mean to ... to kill them."

Mary said, "But you did kill them. Look, more snakes are coming. You have to kill them."

Michael looked up. In the distance he saw eight more snakes slithering towards him. He watched them and said, "I ... I can't kill them again."

Mary replied, "If you don't kill them, they'll kill both you and me. I thought you wanted to protect me?"

The snakes slithered closer and closer. Michael still knelt on the ground surrounded by the dead bodies of all his girls. When the snakes were close enough, they leapt onto him and sunk their fangs into his flesh. He felt the fire of their venom spreading throughout his body. Michael knelt there and let them bite into him.

Mary called out to him, saying, "If you don't kill them, they'll kill you."

The pain that spread throughout his body became unbearable. He started to grab at the snakes and crush them to death like before. As soon as all the snakes were dead, their bodies morphed into the dead bodies of his eight girls. Their twisted and beaten carcasses rested over the previous eight dead bodies around him.

Mary clapped her hands again and said, "Good job, Lieutenant. You killed all the snakes."

Michael looked down at the sixteen dead bodies of his girls. His hands were covered in even more blood. His white uniform was stained even more with their blood.

Michael heard Mary's voice again. She said, "Look, Lieutenant! There are snakes coming to kill you and me. You have to stop them!"

Michael looked up and saw eight more snakes slithering towards him. He started to cry again. He shook his head and said, "I ... I can't do it again. I know that if I kill them they'll turn into you girls."

Mary said, "If you don't kill them, you'll die and then I'll die. Is that what you want? I thought you wanted me to keep living?"

Michael shook his head. Tears streamed down his cheeks and said, "Of course I want you to live, but I don't want to kill them either."

Mary replied, "If you don't, we'll die."

The snakes leapt on him again. He tried to ignore them but the pain from their venom became unbearable as fire spread throughout his body again. He began to rip the snakes off of his body and crush them with his fists. This time, as soon as he killed a snake it transformed into one of his girls. Their dead bodies were added to the sixteen others all around him.

Michael stared at the twenty-four twisted and broken bodies of little girls all around him. He looked up into the whiteness above him and covered his eyes with his bloody hands. He screamed at the top of his lungs out of frustration and pain.

Mary clapped her hands again and said, "Good job, Lieutenant. You killed all the snakes."

Michael ignored her and looked into the distance. Eight more snakes were slithering towards him. He shook his head and cried. He shouted at Mary, "How many times do I have to kill the snakes!"

Mary replied to him, "What are you talking about, idjit? Once you kill the snakes, they're dead. You can't kill them again once they're already dead."

Michael sat down on his butt and crossed his legs. He said, "This isn't real. These snakes aren't real. They're a reflection of my guilt. I kill them and they turn into you girls because I feel responsible for killing you because I gave you a shot. I don't need to kill the snakes."

Mary replied, "But if you don't kill the snakes, you'll die."

The snakes slithered up to him again. They rattled their tails and hissed aggressively at him as he sat there watching them.

Michael spoke to them, saying, "I'm sorry that I had a hand in killing you. I didn't realize what I was doing then, but despite that, you all suffered because of it. I'm sorry. I'm so sorry. There's nothing I can do about that now except to accept it. That pain will be a part of me forever. You are all a part of me forever."

The first snake leapt at him. He grabbed it in midair. He stared at the snake's face and said, "I know you, you are Carol. One of my first team members. You are a part of me." He took the snakes head and stuck it into his mouth and swallowed it down his throat. Without seeing their human form he began to recognize each one of his girls in each snake. He named them and then swallowed each one of them until there were no more snakes left. The fire of their venom seemed to disappear from his body as he swallowed them one by one.

Mary clapped her hands and said, "Good job, Lieutenant. You got rid of all the snakes. But, there is one snake left."

Michael looked in the distance but didn't see any snakes coming to him. He stood up and turned around to look at Mary. Mary smiled at him and then her body began to morph into the body of an extremely big snake. It grew larger and larger. The diameter of its body grew till it was as tall as Michael. It could eat him in one bite. It hissed and flicked its tongue at him.

The snake lunged towards Michael. He tried to dodge out of the way. He hit the side of the snake's body and Michael was thrown about five feet.

The snake turned around and tried to run over him again. He dodged out of the way and managed to avoid getting hit. As the snake's body passed him, he punched it. It did nothing. He might as well have hit a brick wall.

He shook his head and said to himself, "I'm not strong enough to beat this thing on my own."

Michael suddenly felt something tugging on his jacket. In surprise, he looked down and saw little Alice standing beside him. She looked up at him and gave him a big grin with her freckled cheeks. Her curly red hair was all matted like it normally was. She said, "You're not alone, Lieutenant. I'm with you."

Michael put his hand on her head and said, "Alice, is that really you?"

Alice nodded and said, "I'll give you some of my power." She put her hands on top of his and picked his hand off of her head. She held his hand and closed her eyes. Her face showed her deep concentration. After a moment, her body began to fade away like a mist. As she faded away, his hands started to glow with red light like her hands did when she was alive. Alice faded away completely but her power was now inside his own hands.

The snake lunged at Michael again. Michael dodged it and punched at its side. The massive snake rolled over and shrieked like a Harvester. The snake became more aggressive and tried to bite him as it lunged at him. Michael dodged it. He still wasn't powerful enough.

Michael felt another small tug on his jacket. He looked down and saw Cheryl. She smiled at him and said, "You can't fight without me, Lieutenant!"

Michael nodded and said, "You're right, we're a team so we have to work together."

Cheryl took his hand and said, "I can't fight beside you anymore but I can fight inside of you." She closed her eyes and focused her energy on him. Her body started to fade away like mist until it was completely gone.

Michael looked at his hands. His right hand was glowing with red light and his left hand was glowing with blue light. The snake lunged at him. A blue shield barrier went up around him. The snake bit onto the barrier so that Michael was completely in its mouth. The snake shook its head and then spat out the barrier, causing Michael to be tossed across the way. When he hit the ground, the barrier disappeared. His feet skidded along the ground a few feet backwards.

As the snake circled around him, it smacked him with its tail, causing him to be thrown about thirty feet away from the snake. He landed on his back with a loud thud. His whole body was in pain, both from being struck and from hitting the floor.

Michael opened his eyes. He saw two pairs of yellow eyes looking down at him. It was Carol and Susan. They smiled at him.

Carol giggled and said, "Long time no see, Lieutenant!"

Susan said, "You look hurt pretty bad. Do you need some help?"

Michael nodded. His body was still in pain. He said, "I need you to help me stop the snake."

Carol nodded and said, "Of course, Lieutenant!"

Susan replied, "We're a team so we got to help each other!"

Together, Carol and Susan put their hands on his chest. They both glowed with yellow light. The yellow light moved over his chest and covered his whole body. He felt the pain go away. Carol and Susan's bodies began to fade away like a mist. He felt their power move inside of him.

With his new power, Michael braced his feet and held up his fists in a fighting stance. He prepared himself to fight the snake directly.

The snake stared directly at Michael. Its tongue flicked towards him. The snake began to charge at him.

Michael erected a shield barrier around himself. The snake crashed into the barrier and shrieked in pain. Michael lowered the barrier and grabbed onto the snakes head. With all his strength he lifted the snakes head up and tossed it away from himself. The snake flew through the air and landed about thirty feet from him.

Michael felt the surge of power and strength flowing through him. He felt his hatred for his enemy begin to grow.

Justice's voice echoed into his memory, saying, "It's not hate that gives you power, it's love." He felt that something was wrong. He said, "This isn't right." He remembered all the other snakes that he had fought before. Each one of those snakes ended up being one the girls. He knew what he had to do to beat this snake.

The snake trembled and uncoiled itself. It stared at Michael and flicked its tongue. It charged at him at full speed.

Instead of getting into a fighting stance, Michael stood up straight and opened his arms wide. He smiled at the snake and shouted, saying, "I know who you are! You are the regret I feel over Mary! I'm not going to fight you. You're a part of me that I need to accept."

The snake grew closer and closer to Michael. He didn't move or brace himself for its charging strike. The snake ran up right to him and suddenly changed its shape into that of a thirteen year old girl with red eyes and black hair pulled back into twin tails. She jumped up and threw her arms around his neck.

Michael threw his arms around her back. The force of her crashing into him, caused him to spin around in a circle with her hanging around his neck. She laughed as she was spun around in a circle.

Michael slowed his spinning and then came to a stop. Mary hung around his neck. He held her against himself. He bent over forward so that Mary's feet were firmly set on the ground. Mary let go of his neck. He stood up straight.

Mary reached up and put her hands on his shoulders. Michael put his hands on her shoulders.

Mary asked, "I was really worried, Lieutenant. I tried to talk to you, but you kept pushing me down into the pit of your stomach. I belong in your heart, not your stomach, idjit."

Michael nodded and said, "I know. I'm sorry. The pain of losing you was worse than losing all the others. So, I pushed my feelings for you away so that I didn't have to feel that pain anymore."

Mary grabbed him by the collar and forced him down onto his knees. She ran her hands through his hair and brought her hands on to his cheeks. She looked down at him with a smile and said, "Is it okay if I keep fighting alongside you, Michael?"

Michael nodded and said, "Of course, Mary. I need all your strength too."

A tear came to Mary's eye. She smiled at him and said, "I can't fight beside you anymore. But, I can fight inside of you. I'll give you all my power so that you can protect Sarah and Valerie for me. Okay?"

Michael nodded.

Mary, still holding onto his cheeks, lowered her face till her nose was touching his. She said, "I love you, Michael." She kissed him on the lips. He felt the warm sensation on his mouth. Mary started to fade away like mist. He felt her being absorbed into his body until she was completely gone. But, she wasn't gone. He could feel her inside of him now.

Michael felt an even greater surge of power flowing through his body. He looked down at his hands. They began to glow white. The blood that was staining his hands began to crack like a shell. The cracked spots of blood began to fall off of his hands and uniform until his body was completely free of blood.

Michael's hands glowed brighter and brighter until they burned with fire. The white fire spread up his arms and all over his body. It wasn't a burning sensation. Where the fire spread there was warmth. His body began to feel light.

The world around him seemed to tremble. Black cracks seemed to form in the unending whiteness around him. Chunks of whiteness began to fall away revealing the laboratory that he was actually in. He heard Mary's voice like an echo in his head, saying, "Get up, Michael! It's time to wake up!"

Michelle, Gabrielle and Raphael sat on the countertop nearest to Michael as he laid there, tied down, on the examination table. They were drinking tea. It had been almost an hour since Michael had taken the Transcendence serum.

Sarah, Jennifer and Valerie were still standing beside him. Sarah was holding his hand. Jennifer and Valerie laid their hands on his arm. They watched him to see if he would wake up.

Rachel held on to his other hand. Giana, Tina and Elsa had come back into the room. They stood beside him and waited.

Justice paced back and forth along the length of his room. His fingers fidgeted in worry. He had seen this process several times and was worried about what would happen if Michael failed, like most of the others who had taken the serum.

Michael, who had been motionless for an hour, suddenly gasped for air. In surprise, everyone jumped back from the examination table. Michael started to convulse on the table. He opened his eyes and white light poured out of them.

Rachel exclaimed, "What's going on?"

Justice threw his hands up high into the air and shouted, "Praise the Lord, he won! He is transcending now!"

Michael stopped convulsing on the table. White fire began to spread throughout his body. The white fire began to concentrate in his hands and feet. They burned with the white flames.

Everyone gathered around Michael as he lay on the table. Michael slowly turned his head to look around. He felt dizzy. His head pounded and he felt like he could throw up. The white fire in his hands and feet withdrew back into his body. His eyes were now pure white like Justice's eyes.

Rachel said, "Are you okay, Michael?" Her voice seemed to echo in his ears.

Sarah said, "Dad, can you hear us?"

Michael slowly spoke up and said, "I ... I can ... hear you. I'm alive?"

Michelle jumped up from off the counter top and said, "See. I told you he'd be just fine. I knew he was strong inside."

Justice unstrapped Michael's arms, legs, and waist from the examination table. He said, "You've transcended, Mr. Snyder! How do you feel?"

Michael, still laying down, replied, "Honestly, I feel like I got hit by a truck. Is it okay if I just lay here for a little bit?

Justice nodded and said, "Of course! You've been through quite the ordeal." Justice raised the back of the examination table so that Michael's head was raised up higher than the rest of his body.

Michael felt Rachel's hand in his own. He looked towards her and smiled. He tightened his grip a little on her hand. She gazed back at him. The tension in her heart fell away and was replaced by relief. A tear rolled down the side of her cheek.

Michael turned his head to look at Sarah, Jennifer and Valerie. He smiled at them and said, "See. I told you everything would be alright."

A rush of emotions fell upon Sarah, Jennifer and Valerie as all their pent up tension fell away like a dam opening up and spilling water into a river. They suddenly burst into tears and dropped their faces onto his body as they cried. Michael lifted his arm and patted each one of their heads as they continued to cry into his uniform.

Michael remembered his experiences from his inner struggle. He remembered their broken faces when he crushed their snakes. He put his arm back down and said, "Now, I'm like you girls. Now I can fight beside you, like I should have been doing before. We're a team and I need all of you with me to help me fight. You're a part of me forever."

The girls reached out and clung onto his uniform as they buried their faces into his clothing. They continued to sob until they were out of tears.

- 2 -

Michael laid there and rested on the examination table. His eyes were now pure white as the eyes of the transcended were. The dizziness faded away.

Sarah, Jennifer and Valerie glared at him. Sarah spoke harshly, saying, "You made us worry too much!"

Michael nodded and said, "I know. I'm sorry."

Valerie said, "So, how do you feel now that you've transcended?"

Michael thought for a moment. He replied, "Well, my body feels lighter than I remember." He didn't want to discuss it but he also felt that a heavy weight on his heart had been lifted. He didn't recognize it before, but, now that it was gone, he realized that he felt even more guilt than he realized. By accepting all of those things, he felt better inside. He felt closer to the girls that he had lost and the three that were still alive.

Jennifer crossed her arms over her chest and scowled at him, saying, "Don't ever do something like that again, okay?"

Michael nodded and said, "Yeah. Okay. I promise I won't do that again."

Jennifer said, "Now that you have our power, I expect a lot more out of you, okay?"

Michael nodded and said, "Yeah. That was the point of all of this. But, I still need you to fight beside me. I can't do it all by myself."

The girls' countenances softened up and they lightly smiled.

Giana started to smile mischievously. She eyed Rachel from the side and then eyed Michael from the other side. She slid over to stand next to Rachel and said, "So, Lieutenant Michael. We all saw you kiss Lieutenant Rachel. Does this mean that you two are going to be together now?"

Michael wrapped his arm around Rachel's waist and pulled her closer to himself. He nodded, saying, "That's my plan."

Rachel tilted her head forward and looked towards the floor. Her cheeks started to turn red as she blushed brightly.

Michelle, still sitting on the countertop, took another sip of her tea. Her face showed signs of her annoyance. She put her teacup on the saucer and set it down next to herself on the counter. She said, "I don't get what you see in that woman, Mr. Snyder. I don't think you two go together very well."

Rachel started to open her mouth. Before she could say anything, Giana inserted herself between Rachel and Michelle. She put her left hand on her hip and pointed at Michelle with her right hand. She glared at Michelle, saying, I don't know who the hell you think you are. But, I've been trying to get these two together for months!"

Giana brought her hands up below her chin and balled her fists tightly. She said, "I tried plan after plan and this guy was just too dense to notice." She pointed at Michael who sat there looking confused at what she was saying.

Michael said, "Huh? Plans?"

Tina said, "She means Operation Cupid, but it turned out to be Operation Stupid."

Elsa chuckled at the memory.

Giana pointed at Michelle again, saying, "Now, finally, finally it works out! There's no way in hell that I'm going to allow a cow like you to get in my way!"

Valerie raised her right fist and exclaimed, "Yeah! You tell her Giana!"

Giana crossed her arms over her chest and gave Valerie a silent nod of approval.

Michelle's frustrated face turned into a huge grin. She smiled psychotically at Giana. Sarah recognized that face and ran around the table to stand behind Giana.

Michelle tilted her head to the side and placed both of her hands on the edge of the countertop. She crossed her feet and said, "So, you think you're strong enough to stop me?" Her hands and feet began to glow with red fire as she sat there staring at Giana.

Giana's hands and feet began to glow red. She held up her arms in a fighting stance and said, "Yeah! Bring it on, cow!"

Michelle suddenly darted at Giana faster than ever before. Giana became surprised and fell over backward into Sarah's waiting arms. Sarah immediately put up a barrier around the two of them. Michelle's fist slammed into Sarah's barrier, causing an explosion of sparks to fly in all directions.

Giana, still leaning back in Sarah's embrace, exclaimed, "Woah! Holy crap!"

Michelle chuckled at Giana and turned around. She went back to the counter and sat down. She picked up her saucer and teacup and took another sip of her tea as if nothing had happened.

Sarah let her barrier down. Giana stood up straight and brushed herself off out of nervous habit. She turned around and said to Sarah, "Geez! She be crazy!"

Justice cleared his throat and said, "Angel, what did I tell you before?"

Michelle shrugged her shoulders and said, "I wasn't really going to fight her. I only wanted to intimidate her a little."

Giana exclaimed, "A little? You're psycho!"

Michelle shook her head and said, "I'm not really the psychotic one here." She pointed to Raphael and continued, saying, "She's the one who has psychotic episodes from time to time."

Raphael was in the middle of taking a sip of tea. She lowered her teacup and looked around at everyone nervously. She raised her hand and waved her fingers at Giana, saying, "Sometimes I lose control of myself." She raised her teacup again and took another sip.

Giana looked at Raphael in confusion. Giana turned her head to look at Gabrielle, who sat there stoically, sipping on her own cup of tea. Giana shook her head.

Michael slowly twisted his body and let his legs hang over the table. He said, "I think I feel good enough to walk now."

Michael slid down off of the edge of the table and stood up straight. Rachel put her hand on his shoulder and said, "Are you sure you can walk, Mr. Snyder?"

Michael nodded and said, "Yeah. I feel much better now." He wrapped his arm around Rachel's shoulder. Rachel wrapped her own arm around his torso to help keep him steady.

Justice nodded and said, "If you are feeling up to it, we'll head back to the Spear of Destiny."

Michael nodded and said, "Yeah. It's probably a good idea to get out of here. We've been here for several hours after all. Not good to stay in one place for too long."

Justice nodded and said, "Quite right, Mr. Snyder. Quite right."

Justice opened the door and everyone followed behind him. Michael let go of Rachel and was able to walk without any difficulties.

They stepped out into the hole that Justice created in the ground. Justice jumped up an entire floor level in one leap. Michelle followed behind him. Gabrielle grabbed onto Raphael and erected a barrier around herself. They hovered up out of the hole.

Michael looked at his hands and said, "Wait a sec. How am I supposed to turn this power on?"

Sarah said, "It's hard to explain. You just feel it in your heart and it turns on."

Jennifer nodded and said, "Yeah. It's hard to explain. But, for me, I just think it and I feel power flowing."

Valerie added in her own experience, saying, "For me, it's like I want it and it comes."

Giana took hold of Tina and Elsa in each one of her arms. She leapt up and set them safely on edge of the hole. She jumped back down and picked Rachel up. She jumped back up the side of the hole and landed on top with the others.

Giana called out to them, saying, "Come on slow pokes! You're making everybody wait!"

Jennifer jumped up out of the hole and landed beside Giana.

Michael stared at his hands and tried to will them into turning on. Nothing happened. After a minute of trying to turn on his powers, he dropped his hand down and sighed, saying, "I'm sorry, Sarah. I can't seem to do it. Can you please lift me out of here?"

Sarah nodded with a grin. She said, "Don't worry, dad. You just need time to feel it out. If you were born with it, it would be second nature to you now." She put her arm around Michael's waist and her other arm around Valerie. She erected a barrier around herself and hovered into the air. She gently landed on the edge of the hole and released the barrier.

Michael looked at his hands and tried to activate his power again. It didn't work. Justice approached him and put his hand on Michael's shoulder. His emotionless mask portrayed nothing of what Justice was thinking. Justice said, "Don't worry, my friend. It takes us all some time to get used to it."

Michael couldn't hide the dismay on his face but he nodded and said, "Yeah. Thanks. I just thought it would be easier. That's all."

Justice nodded and said, "It would have been far easier to die. But, you endured the suffering of your whole being. Now, you just need time to master your own soul."

They headed back to where the Spear of Destiny was. Along the way, they ran into a very large pack of Harvesters.

Michelle clapped for joy, saying, "Oh, goody! I finally get time to play." Her feet and hand burst into red flames. The red fire of her hands took the shape of two swords. She skated towards the closest Harvester and sliced off its head in one strike.

Jennifer activated her own power in her hands and feet, which burst into red flames. She manipulated the flames on her hands into the shape of a blade. She skated towards Michelle and the two of them worked together to cut down the Harvesters.

Giana crossed her arms over her chest and looked annoyed.

Rachel noticed her and said, "Don't you want to go out there too?"

Giana shrugged her shoulders and said, "Yeah, but my power isn't strong like that yet. There's not much that I can do on my own right now."

Valerie put her hand on Giana's shoulder and said, "Don't worry, in a few days you'll get your full power too. That's what happened to us."

Sarah extended her arm and faced her palm towards a large group of Harvesters. She said, "The older you are the longer it takes. I was the last one to get my full powers because of that."

Sarah's hands began to burn with blue flames. She targeted a line of Harvesters and let loose her spear of light ability. A beam of blue light shot out of her palm and pierced through the first Harvester. It pierced through the second, third and a fourth Harvester. It then hit the ruins of a building and caused a large explosion. Sarah put her hand down and smiled at Giana, Tina and Elsa.

Tina, in her melancholy voice, said, "Cool."

Elsa turned to Valerie and said, "What will I be able to do with my full power?"

Valerie said, "You'll be able to steal life and give it back. So, just like normal but it is super strong. Watch!"

Valerie ran out towards the Harvesters that Jennifer and Michelle were keeping occupied. Michael yelled out, "Valerie, what are you doing!"

Valerie, still running out, shouted, "Don't worry, Lieutenant! I'll be alright!"

As Valerie ran, her hands began to burn with yellow light. She got close enough to the Harvesters that they noticed her and started running towards her. She stopped running and held up the palms of her flaming hands. Yellow streams of light started to flow from the remaining Harvesters.

There were about forty Harvesters left that the others had not killed yet. They became sluggish as their energy left their bodies and flowed into Valerie's hands. The Harvesters started rocking and then just sat down and died. Valerie ran back to Elsa and squatted down on the ground. She put her glowing hands on the ground and released all the energy she collected. Yellow light flowed through the cracks on the ground. Tiny green sprouts burst through the soil in a radius of twenty feet around them. This small section of desolation began to return to life.

Valerie said, "See? That's just normal."

Michelle, who appeared behind her, suddenly bopped Valerie on the back of the head, saying, "No fair! It's no fun, little sister, if you just kill all the Harvesters at once. I wanted to play with them some more. And, no that was not normal."

Valerie turned around and said, "What's not normal?"

Michelle replied, "I mean it's not normal for you to be able to selectively take life from all those Harvesters in the region like you just did. Raphael can't do that. She can only take life from something if it is up to twenty feet from her. And, she can't control it. She pulls the life out of everything around her. It appears to me that only you have that ability. So you shouldn't be saying that Elsa will be like that too."

Valerie turned to Raphael and said, "Is that really true?"

Raphael nodded shyly and said, "Yeah. You have a different power than I do. That is why I tell everyone to stand back when I take energy."

Valerie brought her finger to her lips and tilted her head in deep thought. She said, "Really?"

Michelle said, "Yeah. So try not to show off, okay? You'll make her feel bad."

Valerie looked at Raphael and said, "I'm sorry if I made you feel bad. I didn't mean too."

Raphael shook her head and said, "Oh, no. I don't feel bad. I'm happy for you because if you're stronger, then we're all stronger together and that is a good thing. So, please, use all your power when you want to and don't worry about me."

Valerie said, "Oh, okay. That makes me feel better."

Raphael walked up to Valerie and hugged her. She rested her head on top of Valerie's head. Valerie hugged her back.

With all the Harvesters dead that were in the area. They went to the Spear of Destiny unhindered. Josh opened the door. Justice stepped in first and took his place in the cockpit. Josh moved back down to the floor in the corner of the cockpit. Gabrielle sat down next to him, followed by Michelle and Raphael.

Giana, Tina and Elsa went in next sitting down next to them. Rachel followed them and sat in the other corner.

Michael stepped inside. Josh looked up at him and said, "Your eyes! What the hell happened to you?"

Michael sat down on the floor in front of Rachel. Sarah, Jennifer and Valerie sat down next to him, in front of the others. Michael smiled and looked at Josh with an air of pride. He said, "I took the Transcendence serum."

Josh quickly looked at Rachel. Rachel nodded in confirmation. Josh turned back to Michael and said, "I'm glad. To be honest, Justice offered it to me first. But, I did not feel I would survive the ordeal. I knew though, deep down inside, I knew that if anyone was strong enough, it would be you."

Michael said, "All three of us are together now, as it should be. Together, we'll end this war and make a future for ourselves." He took Rachel's hand. He leaned forward and reached out towards Josh. Josh took his hand and nodded with a smile.

Michael let go of their hands and held up his hands for Josh to see. He said, "I got the power in me but I can't seem to turn it on."

Josh said, "Try not to think about it, brother. It will come to you when you are ready for it."

The door of the Spear of Destiny closed and Justice lifted it up into the air. He said, "We got three more Harvester factories to destroy. We'll take care of those today. We'll head to the Harvester factory that is in the area formerly known as Alaska."

Jennifer raised her fist and said, "Yeah, let's go and kick some more butt!"

As they moved towards the next Harvester factory. Michael tried to focus on his power. He sat there motionlessly and tried to find that little place in his heart that his girls talked about where he could flip the switch of his power. He still couldn't find it.

A few hours later, they reached the next Harvester factory. It was abandoned like the other ones, as Mr. Schilds promised. Justice planted the S.E.Re.F device and they watched the black sphere consume the area.

The next Harvester factory was in an isolated region in the north eastern shore of what used to be known as Canada. As they traveled there, again Michael tried to focus on finding the source of his power. By the time they got to the next Harvester factory, Michael still couldn't find it. He began to feel hopelessness inside of himself.

Justice planted the S.E.Re.F device inside the abandoned Harvester factory. They watched the black sphere of energy consume the area, leaving nothing but a large crater in the ground where the facility used to be. They headed towards the final Harvester factory in the area that was once known as Egypt.

Michael stopped focusing on trying to activate his power. Instead, he thought about his experience when he was dreaming, or hallucinating, due to the poison of the Transcendence serum. He thought about Mary. He wondered what Mary would really say right now about what he did. Deep inside his heart, he felt a very tiny voice that was barely audible. He recognized it. It was Mary's voice inside of him. It whispered, "Believe in yourself, Michael. I believe in you!"

Michael focused on the voice. Instead of pushing his thoughts of Mary into the pit of his stomach, he left it there in his heart. He didn't want to push it away anymore. He let it grow inside his heart. Instead of the pain that would normally come when he thought about Mary, he felt a calm tranquility. He felt a tiny spark burn inside his heart. That was it.

Michael focused on the little spark. That spark came from his love for all the girls that had been under his command. It came from Mary deep inside of his heart. Her barely audible voice spoke to him again, "I believe in you!" The little spark began to grow. It grew brighter and hotter.

Michael, who had been sitting on the floor of the cockpit inside the Spear of Destiny, opened his eyes. His eyes began to flicker on and off with white light. Suddenly they turned on completely and glowed a bright white.

Michael held up his hands for everyone to see. His hands began to glow with a white light. The white light grew brighter and brighter till it burst into white flames. Michael smiled and laughed in delight as he stared at his flaming hands.

Everyone congratulated him. He turned the little spark off and his hands and eyes stopped glowing. The fire withdrew inside of himself. He focused on the little spark and it grew again. His hands and eyes glowed brightly.

Justice said, "See, Mr. Snyder. I knew you could find a way to do it."

Michael gleefully nodded and said, "Yeah. Now I really feel it. I feel you all inside of me now and it gives me strength. I know what you were talking about for myself now."

Michael reached over and rubbed the top of Sarah's, Jennifer's and Valerie's heads. They smiled. Jennifer lowered her gaze and started to blush a little.

After several hours, they reached the final Harvester factory. Justice and his angels went into the facility, while Michael and his girls stayed above and practiced. Michael tried out his new powers. He used the flames in his feet to skate like Jennifer could do. He erected a barrier around himself like Sarah could do. He pulled out his knife and sliced a cut on his arm. He healed it like Valerie could do. He punched an abandoned stone wall and it shattered into bits.

After about twenty minutes, Justice and his angels came running to the Spear of Destiny. Michael and his girls joined them and they quickly entered the Spear of Destiny and launched it into the air. They watched as the S.E.Re.F device consumed the facility, leaving a giant hole in the ground.

With the destruction of the last Harvester factory, they had dealt a serious blow to the Path of the Future. There were only three things left that needed to be dealt with and then humanity could become free of the Path of the Future.

- 3 -

Justice's group rested in a hidden location in the area that was formerly known as India. They discussed the next phase of the rebellion as they sat in the dark of the night around a campfire with the soft hum of the Anti-Harvester device.

Justice, Michael and the three angels would be dropped off at the foot of the mountain Nanda Devi. They would hike up the mountain to the fortress created by the Path of the Future. Josh would lead the other group in the destruction of Lucifer's Throne, also known as the International Space Station, and then capture the Global Media Center.

Sarah exclaimed, "No, dad, you're not leaving me behind. I want to go with you!"

Valerie nodded her head and said, "Yeah, you can't leave us behind to worry about you. I'm going to go with you and help!"

Jennifer said, "You said that we were a team and that you needed us to fight with you. Now you want to go out there by yourself?"

Michael said, "But it's going to be really dangerous ..."

Sarah interrupted him and said, "So what? When have we fought together and it hasn't been dangerous?"

Michael replied, "We could be going there to die."

Sarah said, "Yeah, even more reason we should go with you. Don't get all cocky because you've transcended now!"

Michael relented. He ran his hands through his hair with a heavy sigh and said, "Okay, fine. You three can come with me. But, I don't want you three taking unnecessary risks."

Sarah saluted him with a smile, saying, "Got it, Lieutenant!"

Valerie nodded enthusiastically with a big grin on her face.

Jennifer nodded and said, "Okay."

The next morning, they woke up as the sun was climbing over the horizon. The fire pit was still smoldering. The light revealed the devastation of the area. Harvesters, being attracted to human life, had started to gather around them to the extent that the Anti-Harvester device would allow them too.

After breakfast, they entered the Spear of Destiny probably for the last time. There was a nervous tension in the air and everybody stayed quiet as Josh piloted the Spear of Destiny to the location where they would be dropped off.

Justice opened his backpack and said, "I got presents for all you girls." He pulled what looked like a black neck choker out of his bag and held it up for them to see. Justice said, "I made this device to prevent the Suppressor Field from working on your bodies. If you wear this, they won't be able to drain your powers and stop you from fighting."

Michelle said, "Papa, you had that the whole time?"

Justice nodded his head and replied, "I did but I couldn't use it before this moment because I didn't want them to know that I had something like this. They might have come up with a counter to it."

Michelle shrugged her shoulders and said, "Oh, okay. I see."

Justice handed each one of the Wielders a choker and they put it around their necks. When they pressed the ends together they felt it warm up around their necks and felt a slight vibration.

Shortly thereafter, the Spear of Destiny reached the foot of the Nanda Devi Mountain. Below them it looked like thousands of Harvesters were swarming around the base of the mountain. The door to the Spear of Destiny slowly opened allowing the chilled morning air to spill into the cockpit.

Josh said, "I can't get any closer or their anti-air defenses will kick in. There's also no place to land safely so you'll have to jump."

Sarah said, "Valerie and I will clear an area for you to jump into."

Michael nodded his head and said, "Okay."

Justice and the three angels stood up. Justice put his hands on Michelle's cheeks and said, "This is it my angels. This is the moment we've been waiting for."

Michelle said, "Yes, Papa. We'll make those bad men pay for what they did to us."

Justice put his hands on Gabrielle's cheeks and said, "Don't forget, we got to do everything we can to put a stop to them."

Gabrielle nodded and said, "Yes, Papa." She tugged at the straps of her backpack.

Justice put his hands on Raphael's cheeks and said, "If we don't win then everybody loses."

Raphael's hands started to tremble. She grasped them together and said, "Yes, Papa. I'll make sure that they don't win no matter what."

As Justice gave his little pep talk to his angels, Michael hugged Rachel goodbye. They held onto each other for about a minute without saying anything.

Giana, Tina and Elsa each gave Sarah, Jennifer and Valerie a hug goodbye. Giana said, "Kick them in the butt for me!"

Jennifer gave her a thumbs up and said, "You got it!"

Josh turned around in his chair and said, "Good luck, brother. Tell me all about it when you get back."

Michael nodded and said, "Yeah. Count on it."

Sarah picked Valerie up in her arms and walked over to the door. Her hands burned with blue fire. Sarah looked at Valerie and said, "You ready?"

Valerie gave her a thumbs up. Her hands burned with yellow fire. Sarah nodded and jumped out of the Spear of Destiny. Two blue wings of light shot out of her back and she began to slowly descend to the surface.

When Sarah's feet touched the ground, her wings swept around her, throwing Harvesters across the way. She put up a large barrier around herself and extended it to about ten feet in radius, pushing the Harvesters back.

Sarah put Valerie down and said, "Okay, sister, do your thing."

Valerie nodded and lifted her hands up. They began to glow brighter. Streams of yellow light began to flow from the Harvesters around them and flowed into Valerie's hands. The Harvesters became sluggish. They sat down and died. There seemed to be several hundred dead Harvesters in the area. Valerie knelt down and placed her palms on the ground and released the energy she collected. Tiny sprouts began to grow in the charred dirt around them.

Justice looked down from the Spear of Destiny and said, "It's clear." He jumped out of the doorway and landed beside Valerie and Sarah. Jennifer jumped out next, followed by Michelle, Gabrielle and Raphael. Gabrielle held onto Raphael and the two descended down gently in her blue barrier shield.

Michael stood in the door of the Spear of Destiny. He looked down at the people below him. Sarah, Jennifer and Valerie waved up at him. He turned his head and looked at Rachel. He smiled at her one last time and then jumped out of the Spear of Destiny. The door slowly closed.

The eight of them watched the Spear of Destiny slowly turn and then speed away from the area. They would have to hike up the mountain and deal with the people in the fortress above.

Valerie climbed up on top of a dead Harvester and looked up the mountain. She could see the tiny outline of something that looked like a castle. She pointed up at it and said, "I think I see the castle. You know what, this reminds me of that one episode of Magical Girl Squad where they had to fight the evil king that lived in the castle on the mountain."

Sarah nodded and said, "Yeah, I remember that episode. It was a really good one."

Jennifer jumped up besides Valerie and said, "Remember, the Path of the Future put clues in Magical Girl Squad. That episode was probably trying to tell us where we had to go to stop them."

Sarah surrounded herself with a barrier and lifted herself onto the dead Harvester next to Valerie and Jennifer. She put her barrier down and held her hand out with the palm facing down. Valerie put her hand on top of Sarah's hand. Jennifer put her hand on top of Valerie's hand.

Sarah said, "Let's keep each other safe and put an end to this war."

Valerie nodded and said, "Yeah, let' put an end to the evil king on the mountain, like the Magical Girls did!"

Jennifer said, "We'll put an end to the people who stole our lives from us and then go back home ... home, they stole that from me too."

Michael called out to them, saying, "Come on girls, we got some hiking to do!"

The girls collectively shouted, "Okay!" They jumped down from the Harvester and followed after him.

Rachel sat in the back of the cockpit. She seemed somewhat depressed. Giana sat on her right side. Elsa sat on Rachel's left side. Tina sat beside Elsa. Josh sat in the cockpit chair and continued to pilot the Spear of Destiny.

They were silent for a while. Giana became frustrated at the silence and said, "Okay, if nobody's going to talk about it, I will."

Rachel, in a subdued tone, said, "What do you want to talk about, Giana?"

Giana replied in annoyance, "What do I want to talk about? Geez, you be dense, Lieutenant. We can have some girl talk now and talk about your next move with Lieutenant Michael."

Tina leaned forward and glared at Giana. A look of annoyed confusion fell on her face. She said, "Girl talk? How can we have girl talk if Mr. O'Brian is sitting up there?"

Josh said, "Oh, do not worry about me, girls. Just talk about whatever you want. I will not mind at all."

Giana pointed at Josh and said, "Yeah, don't worry about that pompous ass over there!"

Rachel, without energy, said, "Giana, language."

Giana said, "But, Lieutenant. You said I can swear when I'm out in the field. We're out in the field now. Besides, it's not like you're really a Lieutenant anymore."

Rachel, in her tired tone, said, "Whatever, Giana. I don't really care anymore."

Josh said, "So, Rachel. How long have you had a crush on Michael?"

Rachel paused for a moment before answering. She replied, "For too long."

Josh said, "And now you have to separate so soon. Must be troublesome for you."

Rachel said, "You have no idea."

Giana said, "So, Lieutenant. Where do you want to get married?"

Rachel turned her head away from her and looked at Elsa. Elsa looked up at her with a smile. Rachel put her hand on Elsa's head and said, "Not going to think about it till all this is over. Right now, all I want to think about is the mission."

Giana replied, "Oh, you don't think Lieutenant Michael can handle himself? Don't worry, Sarah, Valerie and Jennifer are there with him so he'll be alright."

Sarah held her palm up at a line of Harvesters that were running towards her. She unleashed her spear of light ability, burning a hole through seven of them that stood in a line. Sarah said, "Wow, I can't believe they charged at me in a line."

Jennifer's feet burned in red flames. She skated from one Harvester to the next, crushing their heads in one blow. Sparks flew as she smashed her burning fist into each Harvester. Jennifer called out, saying, "Valerie, there's too many on this side. Take 'em out, okay?"

Valerie stood next to Michael. She nodded and said, "I got it, sister." She held her hands up and her eyes began to glow even brighter. Many small streams of yellow light began to flow into Valerie's hands. The Harvesters became sluggish and then sat down dead. Valerie pointed her hands toward both Sarah and Jennifer. The energy that she collected from the Harvesters flowed into them, restoring their tired muscles from constantly fighting.

Jennifer jumped from her position and landed next to Sarah and Valerie, who stood in front of Michael. Michael rubbed the top of each of their heads, saying, "Good job, girls."

Valerie shouted at the three angels, saying, "Aren't you three done yet?"

Michelle shouted back at her saying, "Don't worry about us, little sis. We got this!" She skated from Harvester to Harvester slicing off their heads as if they were paper dolls.

Gabrielle said, "Nevertheless, this constant stream of Harvesters is annoying. Perhaps, sisters, we should be more aggressive and stop playing around with them." She held her palms up and two streams of light poured out of her hands, burning the area wherever they touched. She swept her power over the land and burned huge numbers of the Harvesters in the wake.

Raphael stood in the midst of a huge pack of Harvesters and unleashed her absorbing power, causing all that approached her to fall over dead. She laughed and said, "I don't think we've ever killed this many Harvesters at once before. I think I broke my own personal record."

Michelle slaughtered the last of the Harvesters that remained and the three angels joined the rest of them. Jennifer crossed her arms over her chest and looked up arrogantly at Michelle. She gloated, saying, "Looks like I beat you, big sister."

Michelle crossed her arms over her chest and sneered at Jennifer, saying, "Yeah, no doubt. If you keep making Valerie do all the work for you, then no wonder you finish first."

Jennifer sneered back at her and said, "That sounds more like an ex..." Jennifer suddenly went silent as the sound of a hundred smashing jars crashed all around them.

Sarah recognized the sound. They looked around and saw dozens of purplish-black thorns sticking in the ground. Michael shouted, "Take cover! Archer class bombardment!"

Everyone ran and hid behind a large rock that was fallen down on its side. There was a slight buzz in the air and then another dozen purplish-black thorns crashed into the ground right where they were standing before. A few seconds later, there was another barrage from the Archer-class Harvesters, and another barrage after that. The barrages got closer and closer to where they were hiding.

Michael stuck his head out over the rock and tried to find the Archers. He counted them. There were about forty of them.

Valerie said, "Oh no, these are the same guys that tried to kill Sarah."

Michael said, "We've got to be careful. Those thorns have pierced through blue Wielder shields before. We shouldn't trust that your new powers will be able to stop the thorns."

Gabrielle nodded and said, "I hate to admit it, but I don't think my own shields can stand up to those thorn-things."

Sarah shook her head and said, "But we can't stay here forever. Their barrages are getting closer and closer to our position."

Michael said, "Just give me a minute to think of something."

Sarah shook her head again and said, "There's no time. I'm not going to allow anybody else to die because of those things!"

Wings of blue light sprouted out of Sarah's back. She levitated off of the ground and rose into the air.

Michael shouted at her, saying, "Don't be stupid! Come back here!"

Sarah shook her head and said, "Sorry, dad! I'm not going to let the things that got Mary killed, kill anybody else I love." She sped off in the direction of the distant Archers.

Sarah heard a slight buzz in the air and dodged upward. A barrage of thorns flew past her feet. Instead of targeting her friends, the Archers were now targeting her as she flew towards them.

In the past, these things were what led to Mary's death. If only she hadn't been struck in the stomach by one of their thorns, she could have stood beside Mary and protected her. "Never again!" She told herself.

As she flew closer, she could see the Archers aiming for her. She preemptively dodged their attack. Another barrage was aimed at her and she altered her position to dodge it too. She was close now.

Sarah saw the next attack coming. They were starting to predict her own movements and work together. Just like last time, these Harvesters were smarter than the normal kind. She dodged their next attack, but a thorn grazed her arm, leaving a small scratch that began to moisten with blood.

Sarah became angry. She dodged the next attack, but it grazed her left thigh. The Archers increased in their skill some more.

Sarah felt their next barrage coming. They were shooting in all directions around her and straight through her current position. There was no time to escape. She wrapped her wings of blue light around her body. She felt the push of thorns against her wings of light. There was an explosion of sparks in front of her as the thorns clanged against her wings of light. She had managed to survive the first barrage.

Sarah said, "I don't have much time!" She sped closer to the Archers before their next barrage could be launched. Time was up. She quickly wrapped her wings of light around her body again and the thorns ripped at her wings. More sparks exploded around her. Cracks began to form in her wings of light where they struck her. She probably wouldn't survive another barrage.

Sarah sped towards the Archers as fast as she could. If only she could get right up to them and hit them with her spear of light, she would make it. She got closer and closer, but it was too late. Another group of Archers seemed to come out of nowhere. They fired their barrage of thorns at her. There was a buzz in the wind as the thorns were propelled out of their backs.

Sarah stopped in her tracks. Instinctively, she wrapped her wings of light around her body. She waited for the explosion of sparks and the inevitable collapse of her shield.

Suddenly, she felt arms grab her from behind. There was an explosion of sparks but the explosions were not against her wings of light. She looked up to see Gabrielle holding her from behind. Gabrielle had erected her own barrier around her just as the Archers had fired their own barrage of thorns.

Gabrielle smiled down at her and said, "Did you really think you could do it on your own?"

Sarah shook her head and said, "No, but I didn't have much of a choice."

Gabrielle said, "Let's go!"

The two of them finished the distance before the Archers could fire their next barrage. The two of them landed in the middle of the Archers' pack and stood back to back. They both lifted up their palms and pointed them towards the Archers.

Gabrielle shouted, "Burn in hell!" Two spears of light poured out of her hands and began to tear through the Archers in a wake of destruction.

Sarah did the same. Her spears of light poured out of her hands. She shouted, "This is for Mary, you stupid bugs!" The Archers started to scatter but it was too late. Sarah and Gabrielle, working together, slaughtered all the Archers around them till they were all dead.

Sarah felt a sense of relief inside of her heart. She had finally defeated the Harvesters that had prevented her from helping Mary in the past.

Sarah and Gabrielle flew back to where the others were waiting for them. Valerie healed Sarah's scares. The energy transfer from Valerie replenished her spent energy.

Michael put his hand on Sarah's head and said, "Good job."

Sarah smiled up at him and said, "Thanks, dad. I ... I ..." Sarah started tearing up. She covered her face with her hands and wiped her tears.

Michael hugged her and said, "What's wrong? Are you hurt?"

Sarah shook her head. She said, "I ... I stopped the things that got Mary killed. I was able to do it. I did it for Mary."

Michael held her and stroked the back of her head. Valerie put her hand on Sarah's back. A tear rolled down her own cheek as she remembered what happened to Sarah. Mary stayed behind to keep Sarah and her alive so they could escape. She understood Sarah's feelings.

Giana rocked side to side, bumping into Rachel. She sighed heavily and said, "I'm getting bored! Are we almost at that stupid space station thingy?"

Josh said, "Yes, Giana. We are almost there."

Giana dropped her fists onto the floor and said, "Geez! I'm so bored. I want to crack a few shells. You know I'm a soldier right?"

Josh said, "Yes, Giana. I know. You know that we are doing a mission that is really important so try to contain yourself."

Giana crossed her arms across her chest and rolled her eyes. She said, "Yeah, yeah. I know. We got to destroy that throne thing or else it won't mean anything down there. Geez, I'd rather be down there with Jennifer cracking shells like I crack nuts!"

Rachel said, "You don't have your full power yet. You wouldn't survive."

Giana slammed her fist into the palm of her hand, saying, "Yeah, I know that. When the hell am I supposed to get my full powers? Like, I took a piss last night and I looked down and was like, 'holy crap, it's silver just like they said.' That means it's workin' right?"

Josh replied, "Yes, Giana. That means it is working. Give yourself a few days. Just to warn you though, since you are the oldest, it will take you longer to get your powers than the others."

Giana crossed her arms over her chest and said, "Yeah, yeah. I remember. It's not my fault though. I blame my Lieutenant. She's the one who forced me to take those shots."

Rachel said, "Sorry about that. I feel horrible."

Giana said, "Don't worry, I forgive you."

Tina suddenly thrust her hands over her ears and then slammed the palms of her hands on her thighs. She yelled, "Oh my gosh, Giana! Can't you shut up for one damn second! You've been talking nonstop for the past hour!"

Giana said, "I'm bored! I can't help it, O Great Queen of Darkness! O, have mercy on me!" Giana put her fists together and covered her mouth with her fists. She twisted side to side as she pretended to be in fear of Tina.

Josh interrupted them and pointed out in the distance. He said, "Look, girls. You can see Lucifer's Throne now."

Giana jumped up and looked over Josh's shoulder. She saw a tiny grayish speck begin to grow bigger in the cockpit window.

Giana said, "Oh, cool. How're we going to destroy it?"

Josh said, "Oh, it will be easy. We will just use the S.E.Re.F device and vaporize it."

Giana rolled her eyes and said, "That's so boring!"

As Lucifer's Throne got larger, they could make out the giant golden panels that drifted on the magnetic field of the earth. The panels looked like giant wings that menacingly threatened the people on the earth below.

The Spear of Destiny reached the required distance from the station for the S.E.Re.F device to reach it. Josh matched the speed of the Spear of Destiny to the speed that Lucifer's Throne traveled around the earth so that it neither got closer or farther away from them.

Josh began to press some buttons on the control panel. He took a key and inserted it into a key hole on the control panel. He turned the key and a small door opened up on the control panel. A red button rose up from the opening and started to flash.

Josh put his finger on the button and said, "How art thou fallen from heaven, O Lucifer, son of the morning! How art thou cut down to the ground, which did weaken the nations!"

Josh pressed the button. There was a loud clank and the tip of the nose on the Spear of Destiny began to open up. In the opening of the nose, there was a distortion of light. Light from the sun began to be absorbed into a pitch black sphere. The sphere of blackness suddenly shot out toward the space station. It hit the center of the space station. The black sphere of energy began to grow larger and larger until it consumed the entire station. The black sphere of energy disappeared and the space station was completely gone. Not even a small trace of it was left. Lucifer's Throne was destroyed.

Justice suddenly put his left hand to his left ear. He stopped walking. Everyone around him stopped. Justice threw his hands up into the air and started laughing hysterically. He gained some composure and exclaimed, "They did it! Lucifer's Throne is no more! The last remnant of that damnable program is inside that fortress!"

Michelle, Gabrielle and Raphael began to clap their hands and jump for joy. Michael and his girls were happy but didn't feel the need to express it in the same way as Justice and his angels were doing.

Michael said, "Well, I'm happy about it. But, it's not like it was an actual fight. They basically just pointed a gun at something defenseless and shot it."

Justice thrust his fist outward and shook it, saying, "But, Mr. Snyder. Now that the global network is down, the internet is shut off all around the world. This will get every ones attention. When they switch to the backup system in an hour or so, everyone will have their eyes glued to their little screens. Then, when the message is shown to the entire world, everyone will be paying attention."

Michael nodded and said, "Yeah, I get it. I'm happy too, but we still have our own part to play before we can call it a victory."

Justice put his hands behind his back and leaned towards him, saying, "Boo, you're no fun, Mr. Snyder. You need to savor every victory you get."

The Global Media Center was located in the New York Sector. From it, all news and information that was approved by the World Government was made available to the citizens of the world. Anyone who gained control of the facility would have the ability to spread information to people all over the earth.

Several hours after destroying Lucifer's Throne, Josh landed the Spear of Destiny outside the Global Media Center Complex. As the Spear of Destiny descended from the sky, people noticed it and started to panic as they recognized the shape of the Spear of Destiny.

Josh opened a case and revealed some older looking weapons. He handed Rachel a pistol in the shape of an old matchlock. Rachel looked at it confused and said, "Do you really expect me to fight with this old thing?"

Josh held up his own pistol that looked like a matchlock and said, "Do not worry. These pistols use the same technology as the S.E.Re.F device."

Rachel examined the pistol more closely and said, "Oh, really?"

Josh handed a pistol to Giana, Tina and Elsa.

Elsa took the pistol but stared at it with a look of worry on her face. She said, "I don't think I can shoot a person."

Tina held her pistol up in a pose and said, "Why? They're no different from animals. We kill animals all the time. These people are worse than animals because animals only follow their instincts. These people are trying to kill off everybody in the world."

Giana looked over her pistol and said, "I'm not used to fighting with weapons."

Josh said, "You all need to get used to it because we are going to be fighting against people. People who have guns and will not hesitate to kill you to keep their power."

Giana dropped her pistol to her side and said, "Yeah, I get it, Josh. But, none of us have ever done anything like this before so give us a break."

Josh opened the door and stuck his head out. There was a small crowd of people frozen in terror as they stared at the Spear of Destiny.

Josh jumped out onto the pavement. Rachel followed behind him. Giana, Elsa and then Tina followed after. Josh typed a code into the small control panel on the Spear of Destiny next to the door. The door shut and locked itself.

Tina stopped and cupped her hands over her ears. She said, "I hear a rumbling sound."

Rachel nodded and said, "Yeah, I hear it too. Sounds like a tank."

Altogether, they looked in the direction that the sound was coming from. In the distance, an armored tank circled around the corner and began to roll towards their location. The tank stopped and its turret began to rotate towards them.

Josh shouted, "Tina! Barrier!"

Tina's hands glowed with blue light. She put her hands together and a small sphere of blue light came out of her chest and grew till it surrounded them all in a blue sphere of light.

The tank fired a blast. There was a loud explosion. An armor piercing shell hit the side of the Spear of Destiny. There was a loud ping and the shell ricocheted off of the side of the Spear of Destiny. The shell hit a small building and exploded, causing the building to burst into flames.

The people who were frozen in fear from the sight of the Spear of Destiny, fled at the sound of the explosion. There were screams of terror as they fled. Some people shouted that the aliens were invading.

Josh shouted out, "Tina, drop barrier!"

Tina dropped her barrier, exposing them to the outside world. Josh aimed his pistol at the tank and fired. There was a small pop. A small sphere of black energy rushed out of the barrel of the pistol and slammed into the body of the tank. The tank rocked at the impact. A hole appeared in the place where it was struck. There was a loud explosion and the tank burst into flames.

The girls watched it in shock. Giana said, "Whoa, that's one powerful gun." She held up the gun and pointed it towards the burning tank and shot at it. There was another small pop and a small sphere of black energy rushed towards the tank, hitting it in the track. The sphere expanded and vaporized a fourth of the tank in that area. Giana brought the pistol barrel to her lips and blew on it. She said, "I think I could get used to this!"

Josh said, "Come on, let us go before we get more company."

They ran up the street toward the Global Media Center. It was not a wide building but it was tall. It towered over the wall of the New York Sector. There was a small concrete barrier around it to keep people out.

Josh ran up to the gate and tugged on it. It was locked. He expected that. He turned to Giana and said, "Giana, can you bust the gate down?"

Giana interlocked her fingers together and stretched out her arms, saying, "Can I bust down this gate?" She brought her red glowing fist back and then slammed it on the gate. The gate buckled and blew wide open.

Giana pretended to dust her hands off and said, "Yeah, I can bust this gate down."

Tina suddenly put her barrier shield up. The force of the barrier pushed everyone to the side of the open gate. There was suddenly the ringing of automatic gun fire. Bullets pinged off of her shield and ricocheted in random directions.

Tina charged at the soldiers without being told to.

Rachel yelled at her, saying, "What the hell are you doing?"

Tina yelled back, "Distracting them."

The soldiers ignored the others and fired at Tina who ran towards them. Josh and Rachel aimed their pistols at the soldiers and began firing. Spheres of black energy shot through the air and expanded over their location killing many of the soldiers. Other soldiers had limbs severed. They flopped around on the ground in pain.

Josh and the others ran up to Tina. Josh counted all the soldiers that were still moving. He pulled out a different pistol that used regular bullets. He walked up to the soldiers that were only maimed and shot each one of them in the head to finish them off.

Josh motioned for them to follow him. He opened the door to the lobby of the Global Media Center and found it abandoned. They stepped inside. Josh said, "Remember, this is a military facility so expect heavy resistance."

Justice and his group continued their hike up the mountain. The fortress in the distance got bigger and bigger as they approached it. They had reached a height where there were no more Harvesters coming after them. Justice said that it was because there was an Anti-Harvester device keeping them away. Unlike most other parts of the world, this area around them was relatively unharmed from the scars of war.

An hour later, they saw a large dirt road. They followed the dirt road upward and it led to a wall with a large solid gate. Justice stretched his arms out wide and said, "This is the outer wall to the fortress inside. On the other side, our destiny awaits. Everyone should activate their powers now."

Everyone's hands began to burn with the flame of their color. Justice and Michael's hands burned with white flames. Michelle and Jennifer's hands burned with red flames. Gabrielle and Sarah's hands burned with blue flames. Raphael and Valerie's hands burned with yellow flames.

Justice approached the gate and pulled his fist back. Michael called out and said, "Wait a sec. Would you mind if I do it?"

Justice chuckled and bowed to Michael as he waved his hand towards the gate, saying, "By all means, Mr. Snyder."

Michael approached the gate. He pulled his fist back and slammed it into the gate. The gate buckled and burst open. He chuckled and said, "I always wanted to do something like that."

Justice stepped forward through the gate. Michelle followed behind him. She curtsied to Michael and said, "Mr. Snyder, thank you for opening the door for me. You have such good manners."

Michael waved her through, saying, "You're welcome.

Justice suddenly stopped dead in his tracks. There was a man in a gray business suit approaching them. The man's eyes glowed with white light, which was proof that he was also transcended. He held his hands behind his back and walked with an air of arrogant pride.

Michelle saw him and said, "Papa, can I kill him now?"

Justice held up his hand and said, "Not yet, my angel. Let's see what he has to say first."

They continued forward towards the man walking towards them. As the man got closer, Justice recognized the man's face. He said, "Ah, it is Mr. Carns, the tenth chair."

Mr. Carns held up his hands to show that they were empty and said, "Hello Adam the fallen one, it is a pleasure to meet you again. I will say that you have certainly impressed us."

Justice bowed and said, "Likewise. Mr. Carns, I didn't expect that the number ten chair would be used as a messenger boy for us."

Mr. Carns ignored him and turned to Michael, saying, "And you, Mr. Snyder. I see that you have transcended. This is certainly most unexpected. I welcome you to the headquarters of the Path of the Future."

Michelle pointed her hand to Mr. Carns and said, "Come on, Papa. Just let me kill him so we can move on."

Mr. Carns held up his finger and waved it at her, saying, "Now, now, darling. Don't be too hasty. You see, there are about forty S.E.Re.F devices pointed at you right now. If we wanted too, we could simply end your existence right now. But, Mr. Schilds has asked me to escort you all into our sanctuary so that you can talk. If you kill me here, all those S.E.Re.F devices will fire."

Justice approached Mr. Carns and said, "I see. Lead the way then. We will take Mr. Schilds up on his generous offer."

They walked through two more gates, following Mr. Carns. They approached the front entrance of the main fortress. It was a massive structure. The path leading to the front of the fortress was decorated with statues of important men from the past, with names that Michael and the girls didn't know. Men of old who had contributed to science, which science had brought the Path of the Future to where they are now. There was a massive monolithic monument to the side. The large stones were set up like Stonehenge and there were writings on the face of the stones in many different languages.

The front door was massive and gilded in gold. There were scenes of men doing things that Michael and the girls couldn't recognize etched into the doors. Along the bottom of the doors were the images of stacks of books, each book containing the name of a science. In the middle of the doors was an image of a globe being stuck on both sides by men with giant hammers. In the left corner, there was the image of a wolf wearing a sheep's skin. Coming out of its mouth was a phrase in what Michael thought was Latin, but he couldn't read it.

Another panel contained a tree with two men below it grasping at fruit. There was another scene of children being led away from adults, probably their parents, by a man with a flute. There was another scene of three people laying in coffins. One person held onto a book with a cross, star and crescent moon on it. The second person held onto a stalk of corn. The third person held onto a large metal chain. There were many other scenes that Michael and the girls couldn't recognize, but must have held some special type of meaning.

The doors suddenly opened and revealed the foyer of the building. The inside of the building appeared to be based on baroque designs. Lots of things were gilded in gold. There were many paintings of men on the walls, again people they didn't recognize.

There was a large staircase in the back that was carpeted in red. Their eyes traced up the staircase. At the top of the staircase stood two familiar men, both wearing black twin tail suits and matching vests: it was Mr. Schilds and Mr. Roc.

- 4 -

Giana pulled her fist back and punched the locked door open to the stairwell. They would have to walk up the stairs to the media center room. Tina, with her barrier activated, took the point and everybody followed her up the stairs with their pistols drawn.

There was a light clanging sound that seemed to roll down the stairs like a rock. Tina saw an olive green ball the size of a baseball rolling down towards her. She shouted, "Grenade!"

The grenade dropped down by the base of Tina's shield and exploded. Scraps of metal bounced off of her shield and were deflected back up the stairs. Josh pointed his pistol upward and began firing at the upper levels of the stairs. Soldiers used automatic rifles to shoot back at them. Their guns were silenced as the spheres of dark energy ripped through the stairs to kill the soldiers. Blood flowed down the stairs.

Elsa dropped her pistol and squatted down on the floor. She covered her ears with her hands and started to cry.

Rachel dropped down beside her and said, "Come on, Elsa. You've got to be strong for us."

Elsa shook her head and said, "I can't do this! I can't kill people!"

Giana squatted down and took Elsa's pistol from off the floor. She said, "Don't worry Elsa, you don't have to fight. But, we need you to come with us and be our healer. Okay?"

Between sniffles, Elsa replied, "O-okay. I-I'll try." She stood up and clung onto Rachael's dress.

With the current soldiers defeated, they continued their ascent up the stairs to the tenth floor.

Mr. Schilds stood beside Mr. Roc. He opened his arms wide and took two steps down the stairs. He said, "Welcome to my humble home Adam, Mr. Snyder, girls. You've done well to make it here."

Justice slightly bowed toward Mr. Schilds and said, "We are grateful for your kind invitation."

Mr. Schilds took two more steps down the stairs. He clapped his hands together and said, "Come, come on up and I will personally give you the grand tour." He held a hand out towards them.

Justice nodded and said, "That would be very kind of you, Mr. Schilds."

They walked up the stairs toward Mr. Schilds. As they approached, Mr. Schilds turned around and walked back up the stairs. As they followed him, Mr. Roc glared at Michael and said, "You're lucky. I wanted to kill you right at the gate."

Mr. Schilds stopped walking and turned to Mr. Roc, saying, "Now, now, Mr. Roc, where are your manners for our guests?"

Mr. Roc sneered at Michael but kept silent. As Justice's group passed him, he followed behind them with Mr. Carns.

As they followed Mr. Schilds, he began to lecture on all the décor as they passed by. He described various rooms they passed and even some of the long history of his family as they operated in Europe before the creation of the World Government.

Jennifer sighed and whispered, saying, "This is so boring."

Michael put his finger to his lips and glared at Jennifer. Jennifer stopped talking.

Mr. Schilds brought them to the end of a hallway where there were two large wooden doors. Mr. Schilds pointed his hand toward the doors and said, "This is what you are looking for Adam. This is the Throne Room of Lucifer."

Raphael's hands began to tremble. She took a step back and said, "I've been here before."

Mr. Schilds looked at her with a creepy grin, saying, "Yes, my little cupcake. This is where I brought you to perform the glorious sacraments upon the altar of Lucifer. Do you remember? You always were my favorite little girl."

Raphael took a step back and bumped into Gabrielle. Gabrielle hugged her from behind and said, "Don't worry, sister. We're not here to perform their sacraments. We're here for the plan."

Raphael closed her eyes and said, "Yeah, I know. I'm okay. I can do it."

Mr. Schilds opened the Throne Room door. The room inside was very large. In the back, there was a large black box about four feet wide and three feet tall. To the left and right of the black box was a large marble pillar. The floor of the room was tiled with alternating black and white tiles in a checker-board pattern. Standing around behind the black box were seven men in various colored and styled suits.

Justice stepped forward. He counted the men. He said, "Mr. Schilds, I was expecting to find all twelve chairs here. Where are number eleven and twelve?"

Mr. Schilds walked around to the front of the black box. Mr. Roc and Mr. Carns joined the seven men behind the black box.

Mr. Schilds said, "Oh, Lucifer told me to dispatch them to the Global Media Center, so I did. From what I hear, your friends are already invading the center. When they reach their destination, they will be slaughtered by chair number eleven and twelve."

Mr. Schilds put his hand on the top of the black box and said, "You know, Adam. It really annoyed me when you destroyed my space station. But, it was merely an annoyance as I was able to restore all the networks back to the older ground based system."

Justice and the others stepped fully into the room. Justice closed the doors behind them. He put his hand on Gabrielle's cheek and said, "My darling blue angel, don't let anyone get past these doors."

Gabrielle nodded and said, "Yes, Papa." She stood in front of the doors and waited with her hands crossed over her chest.

Mr. Schilds stretched his arms out wide and said, "Come now, Mr. Snyder. The only reason I allowed you all to come was so that I could talk with you."

Michael stepped forward. He stood about ten feet away from Mr. Schilds. Mr. Schilds glared at him and observed the marks of transcendence in his eyes, hands and feet.

Mr. Schilds said, "It appears I was wrong about you, Mr. Snyder. I can see that you have transcended. There is much strength in you. But, don't be conceited in thinking that you can overcome the ten of us. I brought you here to make you an offer."

Mr. Schilds walked towards Michael. He stood in front of him and put his hands on Michael's shoulders, feeling his muscles. He said, "You are strong, Mr. Snyder. I want you to stand at my side. I can give you anything you want in return. If you want money, I can give you more money than you'll know what to do with. If you want women, I can give you all the women you want, of any age or type; boys, if you prefer. If you want power, I can give you all the power you want under me. You can be a ruler over many sectors. Did you know that I have the blood of all your lost girls in my files? If you want, I even have the power to clone any or all the girls that you lost. I can even bring Mary back to life. The only thing I ask is that you kneel at my feet and pledge your loyalty to Lucifer and his Path of the Future."

Michael brushed Mr. Schilds hands off of his shoulders and turned around. He looked back at his girls with a smile. They looked back at him and waited for his response. Sarah slowly shook her head.

Michael started to laugh. He turned back around to face Mr. Schilds. He said, "You can give me Mary back?"

Mr. Schilds nodded his head and said, "Yes, I can bring her back to life if that is what you want me to do for you."

Michael laughed again. He said, "You might be able to bring her body back. But, can you bring who she is back? The Mary that you would give me, would she remember all the time we spent together? Would she remember all the times I comforted her when she was scared or sad? Would she be able to laugh with me at all the fun times we shared? Would she still love me? I don't think so. All you can give me is an imitation. Mary's gone because of you, and for that reason I've come here to kick your ass and put a stop to your insanity so that no one else has to suffer this way!"

Jennifer raised her fist and said, "Yeah, you tell him, Lieutenant!"

Mr. Schilds sighed and walked back towards the black box. He faced Michael and said, "I am sad to hear that because I don't like wasting useful things. I had hoped that you would come to your senses. But, it appears that I will have to kill you and the others. You could have been so great, Mr. Snyder. But, you are a fool to the end."

Michael said, "I might be stupid. But, even if I die, I'll be able to stand before whatever being created me with my honor and integrity intact."

Mr. Schilds said, "Mr. Snyder there is no such thing as a creator, there is no such thing as good or evil. We are what we make ourselves to be. The way of this world is power and dominance and I am the most powerful man in the world. You won't be able to stand against my power."

Justice stepped forward and stood next to Michael's side. Justice said, "We are already standing against you. Whether we win or not is not yet determined. But, when good men stand by and do nothing, then they have already lost. We will fight with our very lives to overcome your evil. And, God willing, we will overcome your false system!"

Mr. Schilds grinned at Justice and Michael. He said, "Very well then. We shall see who is in the right by who survives."

Mr. Schilds turned to Mr. Roc, saying, "I have been waiting for the Wielder Suppressors to kick in. Either they are not working, or they have something that can nullify it."

Mr. Roc stepped forward and said, "They are on and working. It must be the latter."

Mr. Schilds tilted his head to the side and looked upward. He said, "I see. So they must have some new technology that counteracts it. Well, no matter. I would rather preserve the lives of the Wielders for our sacraments later. Why don't we do this then, Mr. Roc. Why don't you and I fight these two heretics ourselves? After we kill them, we can take the girls for our own use."

Mr. Roc stepped beside Mr. Schilds. He nodded and said, "That's fine with me. But, I want to be the one who kills Adam."

Mr. Schilds nodded and said, "Very well. I shall take great pleasure in breaking Mr. Snyder."

Mr. Schilds and Mr. Roc's hands began to burn with white fire. Mr. Schilds smashed his fists together, causing an explosion of sparks. He laughed and said, "Just so you know all know, we have also created some new technology. There is a field in this room that prevents the use of all of our healing abilities. That will make this fight so much more interesting. If anybody gets hurt, there will be no way to fix them."

Justice said, "I see. So, if it will just be the two of us and the two of you, may I have your word that you won't hurt the others?"

Mr. Schilds nodded and said, "Yes, you have my word that as long as they stay out of it, we won't touch them, till you are dead first of course."

Sarah opened her mouth and was about to speak. Michelle suddenly grabbed her from behind and covered her mouth with her hand. She whispered into Sarah's ear, "Wait, don't get involved. We can stand back and watch their movements so that if we need to fight we can be better prepared."

Sarah nodded and Michelle dropped her hand from her mouth.

Valerie looked at her hands and said to herself, "If anybody gets hurt I won't be able to help them?"

Jennifer said, "Guess we'll just have to avoid getting hurt."

Mr. Schilds and Mr. Roc took off their jackets and vest, dropping them on the floor. They then took off their scarves and unbuttoned their shirts. They also let them drop to the floor. Michael and Justice watched them undress. There was tension in the air as they watched them. Mr. Schilds smashed his white, burning fists together again, causing sparks to explode between his hands.

Mr. Schilds said, "So, you ready?"

Josh, Rachel, and the girls stood around the door that would lead them into the tenth floor. There was no way to tell what was on the other side of the door. They expected that there would be a large contingent of soldiers ready to meet them.

Josh put his hand on the door knob and looked at Rachel. Rachel looked back at him and nodded. Josh twisted the knob and pushed opened the door. Rachel raised her pistol and entered the room and looked around. There was no one there. She said, "This is weird, nobody's here."

Josh entered beside her and looked around the room too. He didn't see anyone either. They lowered their pistols and took a deep breath. Josh said, "Either they gave up or there is some sort of trap here. I would plan on the latter."

The room was filled with giant computers and control systems. It was from this central location that the World Government controlled the flow of information to the public. There were a few desks in the front and offices in the back.

Giana, Tina and Elsa stepped in behind Rachel. Giana said, "Maybe we already got all the soldiers?"

Josh shook his head and said, "Do not count on it. They would not abandon such an important post so easily."

A door to an office opened in the very back of the room. Two men wearing the long black trench coat of an intelligence officer stepped out of the open door.

Giana stared at them and noticed their eyes. Their eyes were glowing with white light. Giana pointed at them and said, "Hey, those guys are transcended."

Josh nodded and said, "Yes, I can see that. They are also the heads of the Intelligence Division."

Elsa said, "Do you know them, Josh?"

Josh nodded and said, "Yes, I do."

One of the men stepped forward and said, "Hello, Josh. I'm so glad that IT sent me here today. I wanted to be the one to personally kill you."

Josh said, "Hello, Zack. I will admit that I am rather surprised to see you here."

The man that Josh called Zack chuckled and said, "IT is far smarter than any of us. That is why I always obey IT. IT never leads me on the wrong path. You betrayed IT. And for what? Absolutely nothing. The others are killing your friends right now and we are going to kill you." Their hands and feet suddenly burst into white flames.

Josh chuckled and said, "Well, you are welcome to try." Josh lifted his pistol and began to fire at them. The two of them, using their skating ability, dodged the black spheres of energy that raced towards them.

Rachel, Tina and Giana joined Josh in shooting at the men as they skated around the room, dodging their fire.

Giana became frustrated. She exclaimed, "Ah, screw this!"

Tina nodded and said, "We're not good at fighting like this. Let's do it our way, Giana."

Giana nodded. She dropped the two pistols on the ground and grabbed a metal chair that was nearby. Using her strength she tore off two of the legs and handed them to Tina. Tina took them and covered them in her blue energy.

Rachel said, "Do you two think you can actually fight them like that?"

Giana put her left hand on her hip and pointed at herself with her right thumb, saying, "Of course we can fight them! Those two ain't worth a bug!"

Giana and Tina stepped out towards the two men. Josh and Rachel stopped shooting. The two transcended men stopped skating around.

Zack laughed. He said, "Do you two bitches think that you can really fight us?"

Giana held up her fists and said, "Uh, yeah. That's why we're here."

The other man reached into his pocket and pulled out a small black device. He laughed and said, "Sorry to break it to you but I brought this special gift just for you."

The man pressed the button. Nothing seemed to happen. He quickly examined the device and pressed the button a second time. Again, nothing happened.

Giana squared her arms on her hips and said, "Uh, what's that? Is that one of those Suppressor Devices?" Giana tapped the black choker around her neck and said, "You see this here? It stops those things from working. Sorry 'bout that."

Suddenly, there was a small pop. The man holding the device looked downward and saw a large whole in his stomach from where the S.E.Re.F device had hit him. Josh had fired his pistol at the man as he was playing with the Suppressor Device. The man dropped the device and felt around the hole in his gut. He said, "You, you've killed me?"

Josh lowered his arm and said, "Yeah, now it is more fair."

The man fell over and quickly died as his blood pooled on the floor.

Zack focused his attention on Josh. He skated towards him. Giana jumped in front of the man and swung her fist at the man. Zack blocked her punch with his hand, causing an explosion of sparks.

Giana recoiled from pain. She said, "Ouch, I actually felt that."

Zack and Giana began to punch at each other and block the other's fist from hitting. Tina jumped in from behind and swung the two chair legs she was using at him. Zack blocked them with his foot and then tried to kick Tina in the chest. Tina crossed her chair legs over her chest. The man's foot struck them, causing sparks to explode. Tina was pushed backwards and skidded across the floor. Tina ran back to help Giana. The two of them began to work together,

Giana would strike at him and then Tina would use the two chair legs to block his own attack.

The man swung his leg around and hit Giana along the side of her body. She felt her ribs break from the blow. Giana crashed into Tina and the two of them together flew across the room, crashing into the wall. Giana clutched her chest and gasped for air.

The man held his palm up at them and said, "I'll burn you bitches to ashes!"

Tina, recognizing his posture, jumped up to her feet and erected a barrier around herself and Giana. A stream of white light poured out of the man's hand and smashed into Tina's barrier. She felt the intense energy drain from the man's spear of light.

The man grinned in excitement and started to walk towards Tina and Giana. The shield barrier around the girls began to crack. The man laughed and said, "Get ready to die!"

There was a small pop. The man stopped firing his spear of light ability at the girls. He looked downward and saw a giant hole in his chest where a black sphere of energy had devoured the area of his heart. Tina looked through the hole in his chest and saw Rachel holding up her pistol at him.

The man turned around and clutched the hole in his chest. He said, "You'd shoot a man in the back?"

Rachel, still holding up her pistol at him, said, "Best place to shoot a man trying to kill little girls."

Rachel aimed her pistol again and shot the man in the face. The man's head disappeared as it was absorbed by the black sphere of energy. He dropped to his knees and fell over on his side dead.

With the man dead, Tina lowered her barrier and dropped to her knees. She was panting heavily as she struggled for breath. She laid down on the ground next to Giana.

Giana said, "You alive, Queen?"

Tina chuckled, saying, "Yeah. Really tired. You alive, cow?"

Giana said, "Yeah. Ribs broken though."

Elsa and Rachel ran over to Giana and Tina. Elsa knelt by Giana. Her hands were glowing with yellow light. She put her hands on Giana's chest. Yellow light began to cover Giana's chest. Her bones began to mend and the pain left her body.

Rachel picked Tina up and helped her to her feet, saying, "You two were really brave. I'm proud of you."

Tina looked at the man that Rachel had killed. In her melancholy tone, Tina said, "So much power and so much pride, but death still comes to all like the daily ocean's tide."

Elsa, who was helping Giana to sit up, said, "Tina, that was deep."

Tina, still exhausted, ignored Elsa's comment and pointed at Josh, saying, "You owe us a pizza party for all of this."

Josh nodded his head and said, "You got it."

Josh pulled a small external hard drive out of his pocket. He said, "Now we can expose the truth to everybody in the world."

Rachel said, "Do you think they'll believe it?"

Josh shrugged his shoulders and said, "Maybe not at first. But, they will not have a choice as the truth is proven before their very eyes."

Mr. Schilds lunged at Michael. Their white flaming fists clashed with each other causing an explosion of sparks between them. The smell of ozone grew. Mr. Schilds brought his face up close to Michael's face. He grinned and said, "I'm going to tear you limb from limb!"

Michael pushed Mr. Schilds back. Their fists clashed wildly. Sparks continued to explode between them. The smell of ozone filled the room. Mr. Schilds laughed as he swung wildly at Michael.

Michael was a trained soldier and kept his calm as he engaged Mr. Schilds. He knew that if he took a serious blow, he would not be able to heal himself, nor would Valerie or Raphael be able to heal him. As he blocked Mr. Schilds' attacks, he watched for patterns in his opponent's movements. He noticed a pattern in Mr. Schild's stance, who wasn't trained for combat. Michael swept his foot out and caught him off balance. Mr. Schilds fell to the floor.

Mr. Schilds jumped up and sneered at Michael. He raised his palm at Michael. Michael recognized the move from watching Sarah and other blue Wielders. Michael raised his own palm and the two of them shot a white spear of light at each other. The two beams struck each other, causing an explosion of sparks in the middle. They continuously fired at each other with their beams meeting in between them. There was a large explosion and both Mr. Schilds and Michael were thrown in opposite directions across the room. They landed on the floor on opposite sides of the room.

Mr. Roc leapt at Justice. Justice grabbed onto Mr. Roc's arms and held them. Mr. Roc smiled and said, "Yes, I finally get to kill you. I've been waiting for this moment a very long time."

Justice replied, "Even if you kill me, I'll still win. The justice of God will always prevail over the wicked!"

Mr. Roc freed his arms from Justice's grasp. The two of them clashed with their arms, causing sparks to explode between them. The two of them wildly struck at each other. Their movements were so fast that it looked like streams of light dancing around. After about five minutes of their clashing, Mr. Roc ignored Justice's own attack and landed a powerful blow on Justice's mask. At the same time, Justice used that opportunity to strike Mr. Roc in the face.

Justice was knocked backward from the blow. His body twisted in the air and landed on the floor. His mask cracked in half and fell off of his face, revealing the scares on his face. Blood dripped from his mouth onto the floor. He couldn't heal the injury.

Mr. Roc was also knocked backward. His body twisted in the air and landed with a thump on the floor. Blood poured out of his mouth. He stood and grinned as blood dripped from his lips. He said, "Yes, Adam, doesn't it feel good? Dominating another being! Forcing your will on them. Yes. You are a broken man and I will finish you off!"

Justice jumped up and kicked the remnants of his shattered mask away from him. He took his hat off of his head and dropped it on the floor. He jumped at Mr. Roc, who in turn jumped at him and the two of them began to clash again.

Josh took the external hard drive and inserted the USB into the main computer. He uploaded a file and then began to broadcast it to the world using the official emergency system of the World Government. Devices all over the world would immediately cease their normal operation and display the World Government logo with the words 'Official Emergency Broadcast' under it.

After the emergency broadcast signal, devices all over the world began to automatically play a video in a loop. The video began with Josh explaining who he was. He described the rebellion against the World Government. The video then began to present all the evidence of the crimes of the Path of the Future. They revealed the Spear of Destiny and how the S.E.Re.F device was used to slaughter the people of the world. They revealed the lie of the Harvester origins and how they were created. They revealed the truth about the creation of the Spirit Wielders and the injections used that led to their deaths. They showed how the rebellion destroyed the Harvester factories and other Path of the Future installations.

Justice and Michael continued their struggle against Mr. Schilds and Mr. Roc. They had been fighting for about ten minutes now and the girls watched with nervous apprehension as the fight continued.

Justice and Mr. Roc clashed and kept striking each other. In a moment of weakness, Mr. Roc struck Justice on his upper right arm. Justice screamed in pain as his right arm bone was shattered from the blow. With Justice being disoriented, Mr. Roc used the opportunity to smash his fist into Justice's face.

Justice flew across the room. His body twisted from the blow he received. He landed on the floor and remained motionless. His jaw was shattered. His right arm was shattered. The angels cried out, "Papa!"

Mr. Roc laughed and shuffled over to Justice as he laid sprawled on the floor. He stood over his broken body and said, "You see, Adam. You are not strong enough to oppose us. You should have just stayed in your place and everything would have been fine."

Despite the pain in his face Justice managed to give a slight laugh. He struggled to speak, saying, "I ... I've already ... won. You ... won't be able ... to undue ... the damage ... I've done."

As Justice finished speaking, small alarms started going off. Mr. Roc pulled his smart phone out of his pants pocket and looked at the screen. The World Government logo appeared on the screen with the words 'Official Emergency Broadcast' displayed under it. The video Josh had uploaded began to play exposing the Path of the Future.

Mr. Roc broke his phone in half and said, "No matter, Adam. The people of the world are so stupid that if we have the World Government say that it was a hoax perpetrated by anti-government rebels, they will believe it. The people will believe anything as long as we put an official stamp on it."

Justice, still struggling to speak said, "D-d-don't underestimate them."

Mr. Roc kicked Justice in the ribs causing them to break. He said, "You are as good as dead, now watch as we kill your friend."

Mr. Roc leapt at Michael. Michael now began to fight both Mr. Schilds and Mr. Roc. Jennifer pointed at them and said, "Hey, you said one on one, that's cheating!"

Michelle jumped over to Justice and picked him up off of the floor. She jumped back to where she was and held him in her arms. Blood still dripped from his mouth. Raphael and Gabrielle knelt beside him. All three of them were crying as they looked over his broken body. He looked up at them and said, "Don't worry, my angels. Remember the plan and remember that I love you."

Michelle kissed him on the forehead and said, "We love you too, Papa."

Gabrielle held his left hand and said, "Thank you, Papa for freeing us. I love you."

Raphael put her hands on his chest and said, "I love you too, Papa." Her hands burned with yellow flames over his chest.

Valerie said, "What are you doing? Are you trying to heal him even though the field prevents healing?"

Raphael shook her head with a smile. She said, "No, Papa's giving me all his energy. It's part of the plan."

Valerie looked confused. She said, "Plan? What plan?"

Gabrielle said, "You will see."

The light faded from Justice's eyes as Raphael drained him of his life energy. Justice's body drooped and he finally was dead. Michelle closed his eyelids and then clung onto him in a tight embrace. The three angels wept over his dead body.

Michael was growing tired as he was fighting both Mr. Schilds and Mr. Roc now. Michael knew that he had to even things out now or he wouldn't last much longer. Mr. Roc was already tired from receiving several wounds from Justice. It would be easier to deal with Mr. Roc first.

Michael pushed Mr. Roc, causing him to stumble backwards. He leaned over, kicked Mr. Schilds in the chest, pushing him backwards and then smashed his fist, with all his strength, into Mr. Roc's face.

Mr. Roc was thrown backwards. His face started to fall apart from the crushing blow. He landed on the floor on his back. His arms and legs wide apart. His face was an open hole and his brains and eyes spilled out on the floor in a pool of blood. He was dead.

Mr. Schilds quickly jumped back up and struck Michael in the shoulder, crushing his left shoulder. Michael turned around and punched Mr. Schilds in the right arm, crushing the bone in his arm. They both stood there staring at each other, panting, while blood dripped from their lips.

Michael and Mr. Schilds leapt at each other, despite the pain and began to clash again. To the surprise of all, they each landed a blow to the face of the other at the same time. They both flew backwards in the air and landed on the ground. They were both motionless.

Sarah, Valerie and Jennifer shouted at the same time, "Lieutenant Michael!" They ran over to him. He was still breathing but seemed to be unconscious.

The seven remaining members of the Path of the Future walked over to Mr. Schilds. He was still breathing but was also unconscious. The third chairman of the Path of the Future stood over Mr. Schilds and said, "You are as good as dead. I am now the first chair of the Path of the Future." The man caused his feet to burn in white flames. He lifted his foot in the air above Mr. Schilds' head and smashed his foot down, causing Mr. Schilds' head to be smashed under his foot. His brains spilled onto the floor and blood pooled around him.

The man laughed and said, "Now we will destroy the rest of you!"

Michelle let go of Justice's dead body and skated towards the eight men.

Raphael sat down on Justice's broken body and pulled a small device out of her backpack. She pushed a button and the number ten appeared on a small screen. It started counting down by the minute.

Gabrielle erected a small barrier around herself and Raphael. Raphael laughed and said, "This is Papa's vengeance, his tears of darkness will engulf this whole building!" The small device in her lap was a S.E.Re.F device weapon. She was going to kill everyone in the building along with herself, Gabrielle, and Michelle.

Jennifer and Sarah began fighting with the other men too, like Michelle was. They were all outnumbered but they fought with great intensity causing sparks to fly all over the place.

Valerie stood next to Michael. Three men ran up to her. Two of the men grabbed Valerie and held her up by the arms. The third man stood over Michael and put his burning foot on his face.

Valerie screamed, "Don't you touch him!"

The two men that were holding Valerie's arms began to pull on her arms. They laughed as Valerie realized the horror that she was about to experience. She started to scream in pain and cried.

Jennifer saw what was going on. She watched as everybody was fighting around her. Time seemed to slow down in her mind. She remembered watching her old team mates get torn apart by the Harvesters. She yelled out, "Not again!"

Jennifer hurled herself at the man that was pressing down on Michael's face. Her foot hit the man in the face and he stumbled backwards. Jennifer used her other foot to kick the man in the face again and to propel herself in the other direction. The man's face split open and he fell backwards onto the floor and died.

Jennifer repositioned her feet as she flew towards the man on Valerie's right side. Her foot hit the man in the face. He let go of Valerie's arm as he stumbled backwards. Jennifer kicked the man in the face with her other foot, causing it to split open too. The man fell over backwards and died on the floor.

Jennifer twisted her body in the air and swung her leg around, kicking the other man who held onto Valerie along the side of his face. The force of the blow caused the man to be thrown sideways. He let go of Valerie's arm as he was pushed over onto his side.

Jennifer landed on her feet next to Valerie. Valerie hugged her and said, "Thanks for saving me."

Tears started to roll down Jennifer's cheeks. She hugged her back and said, "I'm glad I was able to make it this time. I won't let anymore friends get killed!"

The man that Jennifer didn't kill jumped up and leapt away from them. He saw Raphael holding onto the S.E.Re.F device and smiling psychotically. The man pointed at Raphael and Gabrielle, shouting, "They are trying to detonate a S.E.Re.F device!"

The men who were fighting Sarah and Michelle, jumped away from them and landed next to Gabrielle. They began punching at her barrier. There were seven minutes left on the countdown timer.

Michelle jumped next to Sarah and said, "My sisters and I got to hold out long enough for the S.E.Re.F device to explode. We also got to make sure that nobody escapes from this room. There's no reason for you and your sisters to die with us. You can take, Mr. Snyder and get out of here if you want. This is our chance to avenge Papa and carry out his justice. If Mr. Snyder wakes up, tell him that I still love him."

Sarah nodded and said, "Good luck!" She ran over to Jennifer and Valerie, who stood next to Michael. He was still unconscious on the floor.

Sarah put a hand on Jennifer and Valerie's shoulder. She said, "Our big sisters are going to detonate a S.E.Re.F device and kill the rest of the chair members of the Path of the Future. They said we can leave with Michael and get out of here before it detonates. Jennifer, I need you to carry Michael."

Jennifer nodded and picked up Michael in her arms. He was much bigger than her and hung lifelessly in her arms.

Sarah, Valerie and Jennifer ran to the door behind Gabrielle and opened it. Michelle made sure that nobody followed them. Sarah shut the door behind herself. Michelle stood in front of it to make sure no one else could leave.

Sarah stood in between Valerie and Jennifer. She erected a barrier around herself and the others. She lifted them up into the air and quickly flew down the corridor. She flew towards a large window and smashed through it into the open air of the sky. She flew down the mountain path and landed them at the outside gate that they first entered into.

The time on the clock continued to count down. The men continued to smash their fists against Gabrielle's shield to no avail. Sparks kept flying around them. Michelle stood by the door and laughed at their pointless struggle.

The new number one chairman shouted, saying, "We've got to save the Lucifer program or else it will be all over!" He ran over to the black box between the pillars with another man and began to fidget with it and unscrew it from the floor.

Michelle shouted, "No you don't! This is Papa's vengeance!" She jumped over to them and began to fight with the two men to stop them from saving the Lucifer program.

There was one minute left on the timer. Four of the men continued to smash their fists against Gabrielle's barrier to crack it while the last two fought with Michelle to save the Lucifer program. Cracks started to form in Gabrielle's barrier.

Gabrielle said to Raphael, "Sister, looks like my energy is starting to deplete."

Raphael nodded and said, "Yes, sister. I can see."

Raphael put her yellow flaming hand on Gabrielle's foot and said, "I'll give you all of my life and Papa's life."

Yellow light poured into Gabrielle. All the energy that Raphael had, including the energy she took from Justice poured into Gabrielle. The cracks in Gabrielle's barrier disappeared and the barrier was now twice as strong as before. Raphael dropped down dead at Gabrielle's feet. Her body slumped over and collapsed on top of Justice's dead body.

The clock continued to count down ... thirty seconds ... twenty seconds ... The men who were trying to smash Gabrielle's barrier began to smash it with even more intensity.

There were ten seconds left. Gabrielle smiled psychotically at them. She laughed and said, "Burn in the fires of hell with your Lucifer program!"

Five seconds ... four seconds ... three seconds ...

Gabrielle said, "We'll be with you soon, Papa."

Two seconds ... one second ...

A black sphere expanded from the S.E.Re.F device. The black sphere of energy engulfed the room and expanded till the entire fortress was consumed by the sphere. The sphere disappeared and all that was left of the fortress was a giant crater in the ground.

Sarah, Jennifer and Valerie sat around Michael as he lay unconscious on the ground. There was a loud cracking sound and they looked over toward the fortress in the distance. A black sphere of energy engulfed the fortress and then disappeared leaving a giant crater in the ground.

Valerie started to cry again. She said, "Our big sisters are dead too."

Tears started to fall from Sarah as she cried.

Jennifer joined with them as tears rolled down her face too. She said, "At least they took the bad men with them."

Valerie said, "Is Lieutenant Michael going to die too?"

Sarah said, "I don't know. You tried healing him and it didn't work. That field thing made it so he can't be healed by your power even out here."

Valerie put her hands on his chest again and began to pour energy into Michael.

Sarah said, "What are you doing? It won't work. All you'll do is give up your own energy."

Valerie shook her head and said, "I don't care! I'm going to heal him no matter what! I'm not going to lose another team member because I'm not strong enough! I am stronger than ever before so I can make it happen!"

The grass around them started to wither and die. Valerie drained the energy out of the plants around her. It still wasn't enough energy. Valerie reached out even more. Trees and bushes in the distance started to die as they gave up their energy, but it still wasn't enough.

Valerie searched even deeper, she started to feel a small beat of energy below her. It was coming from the earth itself. She reached out to that small beat of life beneath her and grabbed a hold of it. The small beat of life became a raging fire as the earth itself began to pour energy into Valerie.

The fire in Valerie's hands began to spread over her entire body. Sarah and Jennifer became startled as Valerie's entire body burst into yellow flames. They jumped away from her in case it would affect them too.

Valerie focused all her energy into healing. As the life force of the earth flowed into Valerie, she heard a tiny voice inside of her heart, saying, "Live, my children." The fire around her body became hot and burned even brighter. The fire moved onto Michael's chest and began to spread outward from where her hands were placed. The fire spread over his entire body.

Valerie could feel his bones being repaired underneath her hands. She said, "It's working!"

Michael suddenly gasped for air and opened his eyes. Valerie began to pull the yellow flames back into her body. The flames left Michael and still surrounded Valerie. She stood up and tried to shut off her power. She let go of the life force of the earth that she had tapped into. Slowly the flames began to disappear back into her hands. Then, her hands stopped burning too.

Valerie smiled and collapsed onto the ground. Sarah and Jennifer ran back over to her. Sarah picked her up off of the ground and held her. She said, "Are you okay, Valerie?"

Valerie smiled as tears rolled down the sides of her cheeks. She said, "I did it. I was able to heal him. I found the power I couldn't find when you were about to die and Mary had to sacrifice herself. I was strong enough this time."

Jennifer sat next to Michael. He laid there staring at the sky. He said, "I feel like crap. What happened? Why are we outside?"

Jennifer helped him to sit up. He saw the giant crater where the fortress was. He said again, "What the hell happened?"

Sarah explained everything to him. He accepted it. He stood up and helped Jennifer to her feet. He turned to Valerie. Sarah was still holding her in her arms. He said, "Thanks for saving me, Valerie. Are you okay?"

Valerie nodded and said, "Yeah, I'm just really tired."

Michael said, "We should head down to the place where we're supposed to meet up with Josh and the others. Can you walk?"

Valerie shook her head and said, "I don't think I can walk yet. I feel very weak."

Michael bent over and picked Valerie up out of Sarah's arms. He said, "That's okay, I'll carry you till you feel better."

Valerie blushed a little bit and embarrassingly said, "Okay, Lieutenant."

Michael held out one of his hands to Sarah and helped her to stand up. He said, "Come on, girls. Let's get away from this evil place."

Together they walked down the side of the mountain. When Valerie felt rested, Michael put her down and the four of them walked to the place where they were to meet the others. As they reached that place, the Spear of Destiny flew overhead and landed near them. The door opened and the people inside of it jumped out to meet them.

Michael and Rachel embraced and kissed each other first. Sarah, Jennifer and Valerie took turns hugging Giana, Tina and Elsa.

Tina pointed at Josh and said, "Okay, where can we go to get pizza now?"

Giana said, "Let's go to Italy on the way back. I bet they have some good pizza."

Josh nodded and said, "Okay, okay. We can go to Italy for some pizza if you want."

Michael put his arm around Rachel and Josh's shoulders and said, "On the way, we got some stories to share."

Josh nodded and said, "Yeah, so do we."

They went into the Spear of Destiny and Josh sat back down in the pilot's seat. The Spear of Destiny lifted back into the air and sped off towards their next destination.

Epilogue

Michael stood on the grass in the back of his yard. He held the hands of a little girl who was a year old. She had soft brown hair that was tied into two tiny twin tails. The little girl had brown eyes that were full of life. She wore a red and white dress with a checker pattern on the skirt, a red bodice and white short sleeves. The little girl clung on to his fingers as she tried to walk across the way.

Rachel stood about six feet away from her. She squatted on the grass and held her hands out to the little girl and smiled at her. She said, "Come on, little Mary. Come to mama."

Michael helped lead little Mary by the hands towards Rachel. When they were half way to Rachel, Michael let go of her hands and little Mary ran towards her mother. As she ran, she tripped and fell into her mother's waiting arms. Rachel scooped her up and held her against her chest, praising her.

Since the destruction of the Path of the Future, no more girls were born into the world with the odd red, blue or yellow eye color. No more Spirit Wielders were given the injections that led to their self-destruction. No more girls had to die from structural collapse.

Valerie was returned to her surprised family in the Reno sector. She was both excited and apprehensive about leaving her team to return to her family. But, in the end she was glad to be back at her home with her mom and dad. Michael, Sarah and Jennifer kept in contact with her so there was no time to miss each other.

Giana, Tina and Elsa were also returned to their respective families. They also kept in contact with each other and their friends in Squad three.

Sarah and Jennifer no longer had families to go home to, so Michael adopted them. And, when Michael and Rachel got married, she became their mother too. Six months later, Rachel was pregnant with little Mary.

Since there were no more Harvester factories, the number of Harvesters started to quickly decline. Former Spirit Wielders voluntarily hunted the Harvesters that remained until they were extinct from the world. The lands scorched by the war slowly started to regrow life.

Since there was no more Path of the Future to support the World Government, the World Government quickly fell apart. Most sectors began to reunite into their old national alliances. New nations were also created by sectors that didn't reunite. The new governments hunted down all the people who knowingly supported the goals of the Path of the Future. The supporters were judged and punished according to the will of the people that had captured them. There were many executions for crimes against humanity.

With the Harvesters gone, people began to move themselves out of the walled sectors. Humanity began to reclaim the land that the Path of the Future had robbed from them. People began to be more self-sufficient as they worked the land, making their own things instead of relying on large corporations to provide for them.

The people of the world were now free to guide their own destinies without the interference of the Path of the Future. Whether that peace would last would depend upon the diligence of the people that remained in the world. As long as people are imperfect, there will always remain the danger that wicked men and women would use their power to enslave and destroy the world. But, if the people are diligent in safe guarding their families and liberties from the corruption of the wicked, then no force will have the power to enslave or destroy them as they had done in the past.

THE END

Afterword

This is the last volume of Tears of Darkness (unless lots of people request side stories). To all of you who read the complete series, you have my personal thanks and gratitude. If I could, I would give all of you a big hug! But, I can't so you will have to pretend to feel my arms around your back and my warm body pressing up against you.

I hope that you enjoyed this series as much as I enjoyed writing it. It was a dream of mine to write this story and I am so happy that I was able to finally finish it. There are more stories that I have in mind to write but I need to see if it would be worth writing them.

Big thanks to my niece who kept drawing pictures for my book. Big thanks to everyone who helped me to edit. And most of all, big thanks to everyone who read my story. To me, you are the super hero!

Big hug and kisses to you!
- Sophia Liddell

If you want to stay updated on my projects please visit my blog @:
sophialiddellbooks.webs.com

You can also find me on Crunchyroll:
www.crunchyroll.com/user/SophiaLiddell

You can also join the TEARS OF DARKNESS Group on Crunchyroll:
www.crunchyroll.com/group/Tears_of_Darkness

www.ingramcontent.com/pod-product-compliance
Lightning Source LLC
Chambersburg PA
CBHW031319170626
46807CB00002B/484

* 9 7 8 1 7 3 2 3 0 4 9 4 9 *